The Finish Line

Grace Newman lives in Los Angeles with her husband and their dog, Daisy. Originally from Gloucester, Grace grew up as an avid Formula 1 fan and has had the pleasure of watching Jensen Button and Lewis Hamilton win the World Driver's Championship, which is where her love of the sport was born.

Also by Grace Newman

Racing Hearts
The Finish Line

THE FINISH LINE

GRACE NEWMAN

canelo

HERA

First published in the United Kingdom in 2026 by

Hera Books, an imprint of
Canelo Digital Publishing Limited,
20 Vauxhall Bridge Road,
London SW1V 2SA
United Kingdom

A Penguin Random House Company
The authorised representative in the EEA is Dorling Kindersley Verlag GmbH.
Arnulfstr. 124, 80636 Munich, Germany

A CIP catalogue record for this book is available from the British Library.

ISBN 978 1 83598 384 3

Printed and bound in Great Britain by Clays Ltd, Elcograf S.p.A.

Look for more great books at
www.herabooks.com | www.dk.com

I

For the people that have been told that asking for help is a weakness, and for those that smile when you just want to scream. You're not alone.

This one's for you.

Prologue

Lily

The club's pounding bass echoed in my ears as we pushed through the revolving doors into our hotel lobby. My body was still buzzing with adrenaline from my Las Vegas Grand Prix win. Considering it was a casino, the lobby of the Venetian Hotel was relatively calm at this hour, just a few scattered guests and staff. Music from the casino floor hummed in the distance, but here in the marble-floored expanse, surrounded by elegant Greek statues, it felt almost peaceful.

"I'll walk you to your room," Henri said, his hand finding the small of my back as we headed toward the elevator.

I looked up at him, smiling widely. "Such a gentleman."

His lips quirked into that lazy grin that drove me crazy. "Always."

My feet ached in my heels, the cost of spending the past three hours dancing. As my third victory of the season, this Las Vegas win had been special, with Henri coming second in his Hermes F1 car, and Georgia, my teammate, coming in third.

We made it to the elevators, and Henri pressed the call button. The doors slid open almost immediately, and we stepped inside. The sudden quiet, the enclosed space, it felt intimate after the chaos of celebrating.

I caught my reflection in the mirrored wall. Flushed cheeks, smudged eyeliner, hair wild from dancing. My black dress was slightly askew at the shoulder.

Henri stood beside me, top button undone, looking unfairly handsome for someone who'd matched me drink for drink. He'd been watching me all night with those devastating hazel eyes of his, and he was watching me now.

"Thirty-one?" he asked, his finger hovering over the button panel.

"Yup," I confirmed, my voice coming out breathier than intended.

He pressed the button. The doors slid shut, muffling the casino floor, and finally it was just the two of us. Henri leaned against the wall, that slow smile again playing at his lips.

"That overtake on Georgia in Turn 14," he said. "Absolutely mad."

"Mad brilliant or mad stupid?"

"Both." He pushed off the wall, moving closer.

The elevator jolted into motion, and I swayed slightly—whether from the movement or the champagne, I wasn't entirely sure. Henri's hand came to my waist, steadying me, and suddenly we were standing much closer than we were a moment ago.

Three years. Three years of stolen glances in the paddock, of text messages that had started professional before becoming good-night texts that were anything but. Three years of finding excuses to stand just a little too close in press conferences, of "it's too complicated" and "maybe someday."

And tonight, I'd conquered Las Vegas, and I was done ignoring the tension between us. His thumb stroked slowly against my waist, through the thin fabric of my dress.

"Henri…" I said softly.

"*Oui, ma belle?*" His voice had gone rough, and his other hand came up to cup my jaw, tilting my face toward his. "Lily, you're—"

"If you say drunk, I swear—"

"—incredible," he finished. "You were incredible today. You *are* incredible."

My heart stuttered. "Henri."

But there was no response from him, just deep longing in his eyes. He leaned forward, his lips just barely touching mine.

And then he kissed me.

Finally, *finally* kissed me, and it was everything I'd imagined during all those long nights on the road, alone in hotel rooms, trying not to think about him. His lips were soft at first, then gentleness gave way to hunger. I pressed closer, three years of want pouring into it, my fingers curling into his shirt as his hands slid into my hair, tilting my head back. My back hit the elevator wall, but I didn't care about anything except the way we moved together, the way his thumb traced along my jaw, the small sound he made against my mouth when I pulled him impossibly closer.

When we broke apart, we were both breathing hard, his forehead resting on mine.

The elevator chimed. Thirty-first floor.

Henri caught my hand, lacing our fingers together as the doors opened. We made it maybe three steps down the hallway before I pulled him back, kissing him again, pushing his back against someone's door, not caring if anyone saw.

"Room," he managed against my lips. "We should… your room."

"Right. Yes." I fumbled for my key card, nearly dropping it twice as Henri's hands stayed at my waist, his mouth finding my neck. "You're not helping."

"Don't want to help," he murmured softly into my ear. "I want to do the opposite of help."

Finally, the door swung open, and we stumbled inside, a tangle of limbs and laughter and three years of pent-up tension. Henri turned me to face him, and suddenly the laughter faded into something more serious, more intense. He was looking at me like I was something precious and completely irresistible all at once.

Henri caught my wrists gently, bringing them to his lips. "Are you sure, *ma chérie*? Once we do this—"

"Henri." I freed one hand to cup his face. "I just won Las Vegas. I've never been surer of anything in my life. Now stop being a gentleman and kiss me again."

The laugh that escaped him was warm and rough and perfect. "As you wish."

—

I woke to the sound of my phone vibrating against the nightstand. Sunlight streamed through the gap in the hotel curtains, and for a disorienting moment, I couldn't remember where I was. Then I felt the warmth of Henri's body beside me, his arm draped across my waist, and last night came rushing back in vivid detail.

My phone rang again.

I carefully extracted myself from his embrace, grabbing a T-shirt from the floor and pulling it on before padding barefoot into the suite's living room, closing the bedroom door softly behind me.

The phone screen showed an unknown number with a German country code.

My heart stopped. I stared at the buzzing phone, my thumb hovering over the answer button. A German number could only mean one thing.

I swiped to answer, my voice rough with sleep. "Hello?"

"Lily, good morning. This is Felix Hoffmann, Team Principal of Rennen F1."

The world tilted. Felix Hoffmann. The man who'd built Rennen into one of the most dominant forces in Formula 1. The man whose junior team I'd left when I signed with Valkyrie three years ago. The man who could give me what I'd been chasing during my contract at Valkyrie: a real shot at the World Championship. Even this year, Georgia had already won the championship by sixty-three points in last week's Grand Prix.

I sank onto the couch, gripping the phone tighter. "Felix," I managed, my voice steadier than I felt. "Good to hear from you."

"Likewise." His tone carried that same measured authority I remembered from my academy days, the thick German accent unchanged. "I hope I'm not interrupting your celebrations. Congratulations on Las Vegas, by the way. Excellent drive."

"Thank you."

"Do you have a moment to talk?"

"Of course," I said. "What's this about?"

"I think you know, Lily," he said, and he almost sounded amused. "With Eric moving to another team, we have a seat open at Rennen. And after considerable discussion with our board, we'd like to offer it to you."

The phone nearly slipped from my hand. The Vegas strip visible through the window suddenly seemed too bright, too surreal, for this moment to be real.

The open Rennen F1 seat was going to be *the* seat everyone wanted. With the car specs changing next year, Rennen F1 was rumored to have the best engine. No one knew for certain, but they had a history of dominating new regulations.

And they *definitely* had the money.

"You want me," I said slowly, testing the words, "to drive for Rennen F1."

"We want you to *win* for Rennen F1," Felix corrected. "We've watched what you've done at Valkyrie over the past three years. You helped contribute to three Constructors' Championships and had consistent podiums—proof that you can handle the pressure and perform at the highest level. You've been instrumental in making Valkyrie one of the top teams on the grid."

It had been three years of fighting for respect in a male-dominated sport, of proving that a female-run team could compete with—*and beat*—the established F1 giants. Three years of standing on podiums, of battling wheel-to-wheel with the best drivers in the world, of showing everyone who doubted us that we belonged.

"But we also know you haven't been given a fair shot at the Driver's Championship," Felix continued, as if reading my thoughts. "Georgia is Valkyrie's priority, as she should be. She's a three-time World Champion, and Isabelle has built the team's strategy around her. That's not going to change."

He wasn't wrong. I'd spent my entire time at Valkyrie F1 as the second driver, and I was growing tired of it. Tired of hearing "hold position" over the radio. Tired of watching Georgia spray champagne from the top step while I stood below.

Georgia may be my best friend, but she was also my teammate, and Valkyrie would always choose her. It wasn't personal; it was *practical*. Georgia had proven herself.

"At Rennen," Felix said, "there's no predetermined number-one driver. The best driver wins. We think that can be you, Lily. The question is whether you believe it too."

Did I? After three years of smiling through post-race interviews while swallowing my frustration, of watching my teammate win while I played support, did I believe I could be a champion too?

The answer came swift and certain, burning through the doubt like fire. *Yes.*

I hadn't spent three years in Formula 1 to remain in Georgia's shadow. I'd fought too hard, sacrificed too much, proven myself too many times to accept second place as my ceiling. I wanted to win a championship, not just the odd race.

I wanted *the* Championship. And I couldn't win it at Valkyrie.

"I want this," I said, the words tumbling out breathless and certain. "Felix, this is an incredible opportunity. I'm thrilled to accept."

"Excellent." I could hear the smile in his voice. "We'll have team and sponsorship contracts drawn up this week. Your manager will receive everything within forty-eight hours. There are the standard clauses, of course. Performance requirements, media obligations, that sort of stuff."

He paused, as if he were flipping through some pages in front of him. "We'll also be adding a morality clause."

The suite suddenly felt too warm. "A morality clause?"

"Yes. No illegal activities, no behavior that could bring Rennen into disrepute, a couple of limitations on relationships. Your manager will go over the specifics." He paused again, as if waiting for my reaction.

Did I hear that right?

"Limitations on relationships?" I tried to keep my voice casual, confused, but my mind was already racing. What did that even mean?

"Nothing too restrictive," Felix said smoothly. "This particular clause was actually requested by one of the sponsors you're bringing over, which was a bit surprising to us. It may not be a terrible idea. We all want to ensure that certain standards are maintained."

"My sponsors requested it?" Sponsors were part of the package in Formula 1. I'd be bringing major brands with me to Rennen—funding that made me valuable to the team beyond just my driving. It was standard practice: sign the driver, get some of their backers too. The backers often signed on directly with the team, and they had a lot of sway on contract negotiations. My current Valkyrie contract was filled with requirements, from specific PR appearances to limits on dangerous activities such as skydiving.

I felt a flicker of annoyance. "Assurances about what, exactly? I'm a professional driver. I don't see how my personal life would hurt anyone's brand."

"I'm sure it won't be an issue," Felix reassured me. "As I said, it's quite straightforward. The specifics will be in the contract, and your mother will walk you through everything."

My mind flicked back to last night. Behind that bedroom door was Henri. Henri, who drove for Hermes Racing, Rennen's biggest rival. Henri, who I'd finally allowed myself to have just hours ago. Henri and I hadn't had a chance to discuss last night, but something pricked at the back of my neck.

Did limited relationships mean no dating other drivers?

"I'd like to discuss the specifics with my manager before I agree to anything," I said, trying to keep my voice level.

"Of course, of course. Take your time, review everything thoroughly. Have her reach out once you've gone through it all." His voice warmed again. "But Lily? Welcome to Rennen F1. I think this is the beginning of something really special."

The call ended, and I sat there on the couch, staring at my phone. My dream job. The seat I'd been working toward my entire career.

So why did my chest feel tight?

Before I could second-guess myself, I pulled up my manager's contact and hit call.

She answered on the second ring. "Lily! Darling!" Her voice was bright with excitement. "Rennen F1! Oh, sweetheart, this is incredible. This is everything we've been working toward."

I blinked. "Hi Mum—"

"Felix called me right before he called you. I've been working on this all week with them but didn't want to get your hopes up until it was official." She laughed, delighted. "You're going to be racing for one of the most established teams in Formula 1!"

"Yeah, it's amazing," I said, trying to match her enthusiasm. "So, Mum, about the contract, Felix mentioned a morality clause?"

"Oh, yes. Good. I think that's excellent, actually. Your sponsors will feel much better having that in your contract with Rennen."

I blinked. "But what does it mean? I don't have this in my contract with Valkyrie."

"Yes, well, Rennen is different. You're going to a proper team now." The insult on Valkyrie wasn't lost on me. My mother had never liked the team principal, Isabelle. Papers rustled in the background. "Just basics about maintaining a professional image, not utilizing certain rival brands, the same additions about dangerous activities—"

I cut her off. "Felix mentioned something about relationships?"

Another pause. "Ah, yes. There are personal conduct provisions. You cannot engage in romantic relationships with other competing Formula 1 drivers during the term of your contract."

The words hit me like cold water. "So, I can't date other drivers."

"Well, that's not a problem, right?" My mother asked it so casually, like she was confirming a dinner reservation.

I couldn't bring myself to answer that question—not with who was lying in the other room. "And you think this is fine?"

"Of course, darling. It shows you're serious and professional. That you're there to race, not to… well." She paused delicately. "Not to get *distracted.*"

Something cold settled in my stomach. "Distracted by what?"

"Lily, let's be realistic. You can be seen as a little overly friendly in the paddock."

The words landed with careful precision. "Overly friendly? Mum, I'm just being myself—"

"Oh, come on, Lily. You bat your eyelashes, you laugh a little too loudly at people's terrible jokes, and you touch their arms when you talk to them. It simply gives the wrong impression. The cameras catch it all the time, and your sponsors have noticed. They've invested large sums of money in you, and they want to know you're focused on racing, not on flirting with half the grid."

Heat flooded my face. "That's just how I am! If I were a man, no one would—"

"But you're not a man," my mother said, her voice sharpening. "And whether it's fair or not, this is how you're perceived. They want reassurance that you're focused on racing, not on your social life… which shouldn't be a problem, seeing as how you aren't dating any of the other drivers anyway."

"And if I don't agree to the clause?" I asked, trying to keep my voice down so as not to disturb Henri with the chaos whirling in my head.

"Well, we could go back and negotiate, but…" My mother's pause was heavy with implication. "Some of the major sponsors you bring with you to Rennen may get nervous. They've invested significant money in you, Lily, and securing those contracts wasn't easy."

She paused, her voice taking on that practical tone she used when discussing business. "The personal sponsors you bring to Rennen are part of *your* value to them or to any team on the grid. Plus, we don't want that media circus Georgia and Luca had to go through—it was almost a PR disaster for them."

"I need to think about it," I said quietly.

"Lily—"

"I said I need to think about it." My hands fisted so tightly I could feel my nails digging into the skin. "I'll call you back."

I hung up before she could respond. The Vegas strip was visible through the window, glittering in the morning sun, but all I could see was the choice laid out before me.

My dream. Or whatever last night with Henri had been.

I heard movement from the bedroom. When I pushed the door open, Henri was already getting dressed, pulling on his jeans from last night. His back was to me, but I could see tension in his shoulders.

He turned, and the look on his face, closed off and distant, was nothing like the warmth from last night. "Hey."

"Hey," I said back, reaching for him. "You okay?"

"Fine." He reached for his shirt, not quite meeting my eye. "Congratulations. I heard some of your call with Felix."

"You heard?"

"Hard not to." He focused intently on buttoning his shirt. "Eric's seat. That's huge, Lily."

"I can't believe he offered it to me." I crossed to him, trying to recapture some of the excitement I'd felt earlier. "I mean, me? Driving for Rennen next year?"

He turned then, and pure, genuine joy lit up his face for just a moment. "I can believe it, Lily! I knew they'd be mad not to sign you." He pulled me into a brief hug. "You're going to be brilliant there." But when he stepped back, the warmth was already fading, replaced by something more guarded. "When do you sign?"

"They're sending contracts this week. There's just something I need to think on…" I hesitated. "There's a clause. Felix said my sponsors requested it. It feels… odd. It doesn't feel right."

He eyed me cautiously, like he was trying to find some words to say but just couldn't get them out. "Lily, don't let anything stand in the way of this contract. This is your best shot to be World Champion. Sign whatever they put in front of you."

The certainty in his voice caught me off-guard. "But—"

"I should get going." He was already moving toward his shoes by the door, his jacket draped over a chair. "Need to prepare for next week's Grand Prix."

Confusion twisted in my chest. "Wait, what? No, come on. Stay. Have breakfast with me. We can celebrate!"

"I can't." He wouldn't look at me as he pulled on his shoes.

"What do you mean? Stay and have breakfast with me. I want to celebrate with you, and maybe we can talk about last night?"

He finally turned to me then, and the worry in his eyes made my heart clench. They held something gentle but resolute, with a small tint of grief.

"Look, Lily, last night was great," he said softly. Not unkindly, but with a finality that made my stomach drop. "*Really* great, but there's nothing to discuss."

"Henri—" He didn't mean this. Three years of stolen glances and small touches could not amount to a one-night stand.

Why is he running?

"I'm not looking for a relationship," he said, the words careful and deliberate. "I thought you knew that. We both need to focus on racing now. You especially." He gave me a small, sad smile. "My priority is winning next year, and starting a new relationship now? It's just too much."

"That's bullshit," I said, my voice small. "One night, and you're just… done? You got your fill?" There was no ignoring the deepening hurt ringing in my chest. "We finally give in to three years of wanting each other, and now you're *good*?"

"It's not like that." He ran a hand through his wavy, chestnut-colored hair.

"It certainly sounds like that," I protested.

"I need to focus on the championship next year. On winning." He shook his head. "There can't be any distractions."

"Henri, are you scared? Because we can—"

"I'm not scared, Lily." His voice was firm. "This is just what's best for both of us."

I wanted to argue, to tell him he was being a coward, that last night clearly meant something and he knew it, that three years of desire didn't just evaporate because things got difficult. But what was the point? He'd already made up his mind.

"Fine." I wrapped my arms around myself.

He moved toward the door, still not meeting my eye. He cupped my face gently and pressed a kiss to my forehead. Then my cheek. It was soft and achingly tender, and somehow that made it worse.

"I'm glad I got to celebrate with you last night. I'm so proud of everything you've accomplished," he said quietly. "You're going to be World Champion, Lily. I know it."

And then he was gone.

I stood in the middle of the suite, listening to the door click shut.

My phone sat on the coffee table where I'd left it after hanging up on my mother. I stared at it for a long moment, then I picked it up and opened my messages.

I'll sign it, I typed to my mother. I hit send before I could change my mind.

My phone buzzed with my mother's response.

Mum:
Good girl. This is the right choice. I'm so proud of you.

Only time would tell if this would come back to haunt me.

Chapter One

Lily

Leaving Valkyrie F1 might have been the biggest mistake of my career.

Or so everyone liked to tell me.

Sitting in the cockpit of your car during a race probably isn't the time to be having this debate, I argued internally.

"Lily, we're seeing more rain in sector two," my engineer's voice crackled through the headset, sounding almost bored, which pretty much described Mark to a tee. He had beautiful blond curly hair that sort of radiated sunshine, but his demeanor rivaled that of a stern primary-school teacher ready to lecture at a moment's notice. "It's getting heavier. Box this lap for new tires."

I clicked the radio. "Are you sure? Feels too early." Changing tires to inters when the track was only a little damp could be disastrous for my race.

"Box, box," was all Mark said back.

Heavier drops hit my visor as I backed off the throttle, approaching the pit entry. The pit crew swarmed the car the instant I stopped in the box, and two and a half seconds later, I was released back onto the track, tires ready to deal with the rain beneath me. I just needed to survive another twenty laps.

Fortunately for us, the tire change had worked perfectly. Within three laps, I was picking off cars and going up the positions. The rain intensified, exactly as predicted, and suddenly the order reshuffled in my favor. By lap thirty-two, I was P6, which was great considering I'd started P12. Since I had qualified so poorly, scoring points would feel like a victory. And with the way I was driving, there was even a possibility for a podium.

Rain truly was the great equalizer.

"This is good, Lil. Keep pushing. We think the rain should stop in ten minutes." Mark only called me Lil when he was pleased, Lily when he felt neutral about my performance, and then the worst, *Lillian Blackwood*, when he felt as though he'd ended up with the short end of the stick by becoming my racing engineer.

After last week's Grand Prix, there'd been a bit too much *Lillian Blackwood*. I grinned inside the helmet. "Good" was an understatement. These were laps meant to win the race.

Another near-perfect lap went by. Considering it was raining, this was the pace we wanted—the pace we *needed* if we were going to get a podium in Miami. The car felt alive beneath me. The rain, and that earlier tire change, was working, allowing me to easily pass the cars in front.

"Take that!" I screamed into the air, the words swallowed by the loud roar of my engine. With a win in Miami, we would—

Without warning, the wheel twitched in my hands. Just a shudder, which I chose to ignore, as my hands tightened around the wheel grip.

Probably nothing.

Then it happened again, harder this time.

"Something's wrong." I wasn't sure if I'd remembered to press the radio button. The wheel felt different, like there was a disconnect between my inputs and the car's response. The car snapped right, then left, fighting me like she had decided we weren't on the same team anymore. The sensation was immediate and horrifying, like the wheel had suddenly become a decoration, disconnected from the car entirely.

"Shit!" I hauled left on the wheel, overcorrecting, and the car whipped in the other direction.

No, no, no! But the car had no desire to listen to my protests. It lurched forward, momentum carrying me toward the racing line, where—

A flash of bright purple filled my vision. A Hermes car was right beside me, trying to overtake me.

Not the time! my brain screamed, but there was no way to avoid what came next.

My car's nose slammed into the Hermes's sidepod with a terrifying squeal. The purple car lurched sideways from the force, the right wheels breaking contact with the tarmac. Time stretched impossibly thin as I watched the Hermes car tilt, tip, then flip with horrifying slowness, rotating through the air.

It arced toward the barrier, tumbling, carbon fiber pieces shedding across the tarmac.

My own car bounced from the impact, the steering wheel wrenching from my hands as I spun. The world became a blur of gravel and grass.

This is bad, this is bad, this is bad.

The screech of metal on gravel filled my ears, drowning out everything else. Every muscle in my body tensed against the spin, useless, just along for the ride. The car shuddered violently one final time, then went still.

Then came the silence, thick and suffocating. Or maybe it wasn't silence at all. Maybe my ears were just ringing too loud to hear anything else. Smoke rose up from somewhere to my left as my eyes watered behind the visor.

"Lily? Lily? Are you okay?" The sound of my radio startled me.

"Yup," I whispered, my voice coming out shaky, vowels stretching in my thick Liverpudlian accent the way they always did when adrenaline hit. "*Stilllll* here. Allllll gooood."

Silence echoed on the other end, and I could picture the team in the garage, exchanging glances, trying to assess whether that slurred drawl meant I was actually fine or concussed and lying.

When I thumbed the visor up, cool air rushed over my face. For just a second, it felt refreshing, and I welcomed the small breeze, even if it was filled with smoke. Behind me, my own car sat stuck in the gravel, wafts of smoke escaping it. It would need a tow, but surprisingly, the chassis looked more intact than I'd expected.

Some luck at least.

I scanned my surroundings, and my stomach felt sick at the sight in front of me. The Hermes car was strung up between the barrier and the fencing, with its debris littering the gravel.

"Shit, shit, shit." The words tumbled out as I broke into a run. Marshals shouted from behind, their voices ordering me back, but I ignored them.

I have to know. I have to see if he's okay.

My legs felt disconnected from my body, racing boots slipping on the loose gravel with every stride. The distance between my car and the Hermes felt infinite, and the air felt stickier as I got closer.

Please be okay, I begged the universe. The marshals were shouting louder now, words I couldn't process over the squeal in my ears and the horrible thoughts running through my head: *I hit him. I caused this. This is my fault.*

For one horrible, endless moment, the driver inside was slumped forward against his seat belt. I went to reach down, but before I could touch him, his arm twitched, and he jerked himself backward.

He was moving.

The relief was so intense it nearly knocked me back, but it only lasted a split second before a new wave of horror washed over me. I'd just destroyed someone's race. And possibly their car. I'd hit them, sent them barrel-rolling into the barriers. What if they needed a new engine—

Stop spiraling. Help first, Lily. Guilt later.

I leaned back into the cockpit, where I finally caught the glint of the driver's helmet through my haze. Bright gold, scratched and smeared, but unmistakable. The number 72 glared up at me.

Of all the drivers on the grid, of course I fucking hit Henri.

The press was going to have a field day with this one. The chaos of hitting F1's golden boy, and my number-one rival for the championship, would undoubtedly last until summer break. But there was no point in contemplating that now.

Henri fumbled with the harness, his gloves slipping against the latch.

"Hold on, I've got you." My voice cracked as I reached down into the cockpit, fingers finding the stubborn buckle. I yanked hard until the latch snapped open with a click. Henri jerked his head toward me. His visor was streaked with dirt.

"I've got it." His voice was strangely calm, but the steel in his eyes when he looked up at me was pure Henri.

"Shut up and let me help." I yanked harder, ignoring his protest. His weight was solid, dragging against me as I hauled him upward. The rain was starting to let up, but his race suit felt slippery and hard to hold. "Good grief, you weigh a million pounds."

Together we staggered out of the wreckage. My boots slipped in the gravel, but I clung to him stubbornly. The second we cleared the car, he shoved me away, falling slightly backward. He swayed for a second, legs shaky, as he ripped his helmet off in an effort to steady himself.

His dark hair was plastered to his forehead with sweat, his face flushed. But his eyes… His eyes were blazing with something that looked an awful lot like hatred.

"I said I don't need your help."

I wondered if his words tasted as bitter as they sounded.

"I got that," I mumbled, the sarcasm in my voice my only defense. His eyes narrowed at me as he took a step forward, then stumbled. His hand shot out, grabbing the twisted barrier for support. Henri's fingers were trembling, and not the subtle kind you could hide, but a visible, full-body shake that rattled through his shoulders and down into his knees.

He blinked hard, twice, like the world around him refused to stay in focus. Finally, he looked up again. "Let's hope this isn't a sign for how the rest of this season is going to go for you, Blackwood." He paused, letting his words hit. "Or how you intend to race."

He thinks I did this on purpose. My blood boiled—half-guilt, half-indignation at his insinuation—but still I reached out to help steady him again. And again, he tried to shove me back.

"Oh, come on," I scoffed. "Do you really think I'd stoop that low?"

His look told me he absolutely did, and the certainty written all over his face felt like a knife in the back. Henri Dubois and I may not be friends anymore, but for him to think that low of me made my chest burn with anger.

Everything tumbled out in a rush. "Something went wrong with my steering, Henri. Why on earth would I risk not finishing this weekend?"

Unbelievable.

"Oh, I don't know, maybe because you knew I had that pass and that you couldn't catch me in the rain." I could feel his glare, cold and furious.

He's serious. He actually believes I would throw away my race weekend and risk both our safety, just to take him out because I couldn't beat him fairly.

But why was I even surprised?

This year our team principals had turned what should have been a clean championship fight into something toxic. They had been bitter rivals for years, and as Henri and I had climbed to the top of the standings, their feud had infected everything. All of a sudden, every racing incident got twisted into a deliberate attack.

The Hermes's principal, Verhoeven, seemed to think I had a personal vendetta against Henri, that every overtake was reckless, every defensive move unsportsmanlike. It didn't matter what the stewards ruled or what the data showed—in Hermes's narrative, I was always at fault. Always out to get him, always the villain in his story.

Something raw and bitter had formed where our friendship used to be, leaving my once-friend unrecognizable.

Not that there was much of our friendship left to save anyway.

After that night in Las Vegas, everything changed. I'd drifted off to sleep thinking we'd figure out how to make a relationship work as drivers between two different teams. Instead, he'd come up with some pitiful excuse and fled.

There were no more late-night calls, no funny memes or silly texts making fun of overly serious journalists. That casual easiness between us had disappeared.

But it was pre-season testing that had truly cemented the end of our friendship. When Hermes posted suspiciously fast lap times, Felix accused them of running illegal parts. Hermes fired back, claiming Rennen's car design violated regulations. The FIA had to step in with inspections, and suddenly Henri and I were caught in the middle of a technical war neither of us had started. By the time the first Grand Prix started, Henri had transformed into this cold stranger who looked at me like I was the enemy.

Don't. Don't think about that now, Lily.

A marshal's hand on my arm caught me off-guard, and he slowly led me into the emergency car. I watched Henri get into a separate one, the marshals fawning over him as he crawled into the back.

The drive to the paddock felt like a lifetime. My knee ached, my ribs throbbed, and the smell of smoke clung to the back of my throat. Owning the first major crash of the season wasn't exactly how I'd planned to start out my three-year Rennen contract.

The moment I walked into the garage, the atmosphere shifted. Conversations hushed and mechanics stared as I walked through. Every pair of eyes seemed to carry the same question.

Did Lily Blackwood crash into Henri Dubois on purpose?

Honestly, the suspicion on their faces felt almost worse than Henri's accusation.

Andy, my physio, burst through the crowd, crashing into me. His arms locked around my shoulders, solid and steady. For a moment I let myself sink into him—into the comforting hold that had followed me to countless different circuits every season. Into the one person who'd unpack my favorite tea in every unfamiliar hotel room, who'd remember which side of the treatment table I preferred, who'd learned exactly how long to let silence sit before cracking a joke.

When we separated, I yanked off my helmet, wiping a tear that had formed in my eyes.

"You all right?" His green eyes bore into me with an intense, searching look. His hands hovered near my shoulders, ready to steady me.

Was I? Now that was a loaded question.

"Well," I said finally, "at least we know the safety features work." My lips stretched into what felt more like a grimace than a smile. Andy's face twitched with something between sympathy and discomfort.

Just as well. The joke had fallen flat, another casualty in what was quickly becoming the worst day of my racing career thus far.

Over Andy's shoulder I spotted Felix, tall and composed, with a dark suit pressed to perfection. The man who'd taken a chance on me, convinced the Rennen board that I was worth the investment, and promised me opportunity.

The man who now had to explain to sponsors and the board why his new driver had just caused the biggest crash of the season.

He wasn't glaring or frowning. Instead, he just watched me with that steady, measured gaze of his. The kind of look that could peel back excuses without a single word.

Somehow, I'd managed to get myself a team principal who smiled less than my last one at Valkyrie F1.

Mark, my engineer, hovered just behind Felix, headset still crooked over one ear, curls frizzed like he'd been dragging his hands through them since the crash. The bags under his eyes had deepened since this morning, and the tight lines on his face told me I'd just made his already impossible day significantly worse.

"Lily." Felix's voice was calm, low, *almost* kind. "Are you hurt?"

"Ego's more bruised than I am," I said, forcing a small smile.

Felix didn't reciprocate, but he let out a quick exhale that might have been relaxation. "Good. That's what matters first."

Mark, my engineer, stepped in, tablet already in his hands. "Telemetry showed a throttle spike and a steering imbalance right before impact. Can you walk me through what you felt?"

I hadn't been out of the car more than ten minutes, and Mark was already into it. But that was his job, wasn't it? That was what made him one of the best race engineers in the paddock. And considering I'd made a mess of things today, I didn't have the heart to tell him to piss off and give me five minutes to breathe.

Andy put up his hands to protest, but I shook my head, a silent plea to stand down. Mark and I had to work together all season, and I didn't need my physio starting a war with my engineer.

I shifted on sore legs, reliving the crash in flashes. "The wheel twitched twice. Then it went light, like the car wasn't listening to me anymore."

Mark tapped something into his tablet, brow furrowing. "So, you're saying mechanical failure, not driver error?" The question landed like an accusation, even though his tone was neutral. It took everything within me not to scoff.

He's just doing his job, Lily, I reminded myself.

"I'm saying I don't normally like to play bumper cars in the middle of a race." I tried to keep my voice light and easy.

Felix pinched the bridge of his nose, the only crack in his otherwise perfect composure. "We'll have the car analyzed. Let's get you evaluated by a doctor. Andy will walk you to your driver's room. The doctor will be in shortly."

Nodding, I gave my team one last round of thanks. I'd barely taken a step when Felix's hand touched my shoulder.

"One more thing." His voice was measured, but there was something uncomfortable under it, a tightness that didn't match his normal composure. "I'll make sure Bertha has answers ready for you. Media will be all over this. Hermes will probably turn this into a circus and demand the FIA investigate."

Of course Hermes would.

They'd been demanding FIA investigations all season, turning every minor incident into a major scandal, filing complaints over the smallest infractions, playing the victim for the cameras while Verhoeven, Hermes Team Principal, made dramatic speeches about safety and integrity. All while doing the exact same things they accused us of.

Felix added, "Don't worry, we have your back. I'll see to the FIA personally."

"Thank you," I said, meaning it completely.

Felix's expression smoothed back into neutral territory, and he gave me a single nod before turning back to the engineers. The one thing I knew about Felix more than anything: he would always support his drivers.

Andy walked me down the narrow corridor toward the medical office, hovering like a nervous shadow. He kept glancing at me as though he wasn't sure if I'd shatter.

"You're really okay?" he asked quietly.

"Yeah, yeah. I'll live." When we reached the door, he opened it for me, motioning for me to head inside.

"All right, I'll go see where that doctor is. Be back in a few."

"Thanks, Andy."

Once the medical checks had been completed, I was able to get back to my driver's room. I peeled off my gloves and tossed them onto the chair, flexing my aching fingers. I was about to fling myself on the couch, until a bouquet of flowers caught my eye.

On the coffee table sat a neat flower arrangement in a clear glass vase, bright and cheerful and completely out of place compared to how I felt. The bouquet was full of lilies, naturally, because someone in PR had probably thought that was clever, mixed with sunny yellow daisies and a few white roses. A silver ribbon had fallen off the vase, probably dropped by some sponsor's assistant rushing through the delivery.

For a moment, I let myself breathe in their scent. Sweet and fresh, their smell cut through the lingering smoke that clung to my race suit.

Then I noticed the small white envelope tucked among the stems. My name was scrawled across it in black ink, the handwriting unfamiliar. My fingers tore open the envelope, and I peered inside.

Inside was a small card with decorative gold edges.

I turned the card over in my hands, and my breath caught in my throat.

> *MESS UP HENRI AGAIN AND NEXT TIME YOU WON'T WALK AWAY. YOU DON'T WANT TO OWE ME, LILLIAN.*

Well, shit.

Chapter Two

Henri

Helmet on, gloves tugged tight, I sat in the cockpit and tried not to focus on the thud of my own heartbeat. It'd been two weeks since Miami. Two weeks since Lily's mistake had flipped me upside down, costing me the race. The racing stewards had called it "an incident," which made it sound like a casual coincidence rather than a car forcing me to flip and hit the wall hard enough that I could hear my bones rattle.

Rennen's official apology had been pathetic. Lily's worse. She'd smiled that infuriatingly media-trained sunshine smile and blamed "unexpected behavior" and "a systems fault," as if a gremlin had yanked the wheel right out of her hands. Or that the car had decided to run itself across the track for fun.

According to my PR team, I was supposed to nod and say, "These things happen."

Lily and I had spent all of pre-season testing trading fastest laps back and forth. The press had already anointed us the rivalry to watch this year. Him versus her, Hermes versus Rennen. Formula 1's two oldest and most decorated teams were back at it again. And the fact that Felix and Verhoeven had been bitter rivals back in their racing days? That only added fuel to the fire.

Not that I'd helped matters when I lost my temper in the post-race Miami press conference. Since then, I'd given the journalists two weeks' worth of material, each day bringing a fresh headline about our "toxic feud."

I missed what Lily and I used to be, but I'd killed that possibility the morning I walked out of Lily's hotel room last year.

I could still hear her voice on the phone with her mother.

"I need to think about it."

Just that inkling of doubt had made my stomach turn sour. I couldn't be the reason Lily put her dreams at risk, so I'd made the decision for both of us—told her I wasn't interested in a relationship, made it about focus and competition, and given her an easy out. I'd made it my choice so she wouldn't have to. Then I did the only thing I could do. I walked away to remove any pressure.

Looking at the mess between us now—the hostility, the headlines, the passive-aggressive press conferences—I was right. How could we maintain a relationship while fighting for the same championship? While her contract explicitly forbade it? While our teams could barely exist in the same paddock?

How could two rivals possibly date each other while fiercely vying for the world's most famous racing title?

My only focus needed to be this championship. For the first time in five years, my Hermes car was the fastest car on the track. New engineering regulations had been introduced this year, and Valkyrie F1— the team that had crushed everyone for the past several seasons—was struggling to adapt. My sister, Georgia, was no longer dominating races or the World Driver's Championship.

This was finally my year to win the championship of my dreams; to earn the top spot. As long as I could keep Lily behind me.

I had hoped the Rennen car wouldn't be as powerful as everyone expected, but the moment it hit the tarmac in Barcelona's pre-season testing session, I knew this year's fight was going to be between the two of us.

The media may have underestimated Lily, but I didn't. She was ferocious and hungry to win, and now she had a new team and engine behind her. And as each race went on, the aggressive driving between the two of us only grew.

The fact was, only one of us could be crowned the driver's champion, and I was hell-bent on it being me.

I forced a breath, feeling it catch in my chest. Miami's race was behind me, and I needed to leave it there. There was no changing the past, and I had to focus on the Canadian Grand Prix.

Montreal was going to be *my* race.

In the simulator runs, our lap times had been promising—quick enough to put a cautious smile on my engineer's face. That fragile optimism was exactly what I needed to hold onto, along with the promise that Hermes wouldn't botch the race strategy.

"Okay, Henri. Free practice 1." Michael's voice slid into my headset. "Remember, this track really wears down those tires."

My fingers drummed on the wheel impatiently—once, twice, three times—a nervous tick I'd never broken. Michael kept going on about brake migration and delta targets, but the words blurred into white noise. All I could hear was the thrumming of my pulse as I watched small droplets of rain tumble down outside the garage.

"Henri, did you copy the—"

"Yes," I cut him off, sharper than I meant. My throat was as dry as sand, my tongue stuck to the roof of my mouth. "I got it."

He sighed but didn't push. Michael had been my race engineer for almost eight years—long enough to know when I was being difficult; long enough to recognize when pushing would help and when it would just make things worse. Michael knew how to read me better than I could probably read myself.

The car dropped off the jacks with a thud. Gray sky flashed beyond the grandstands as the rain picked up.

Great, more rain. After the Miami incident, I felt like I'd had enough rain for a lifetime. Rain meant less control, more variables, more opportunities for things to go catastrophically wrong.

Or for your rival to send you crashing into the barrier.

Turn 1 arrived fast—faster than I expected, even though I'd driven this track a hundred times. I hit the brake a touch too early, feeling the car's weight shift forward, the rear getting light. My intermediate tires, still cold, protested with a small slide.

"Nice and smooth," Michael reminded me gently.

I ignored him. The next corners felt twitchy, and I was late and then early through the turns. Not bad enough to warrant a radio call, but not the kind of lap that got you P1. It was the sort of thing a rookie would call fine.

But I wasn't supposed to be fine. I had to be perfect.

What the hell is wrong with you? I chastised myself for my lack of focus.

Somewhere between Turns 5 and 6, I realized I had stopped breathing again. I exhaled slowly, dragging air back through gritted teeth, into my burning lungs, just the way a sports psychologist had told me to years ago.

The sort of breathing I'd watched my sister do to quell her anxiety.

Breathe. One. Two. Three. Four. Out.

Except the breathing wasn't doing shit. My hands continued to shake against the wheel, and I missed another key corner.

"More push this lap," Michael said in my ear. "Find your marks. No heroics."

I grumbled something unintelligible back into the radio. Michael, to his credit, ignored me. I started the lap, forcing the throttle earlier, trying to be brave in Turn 1, but I overdid it. Too much commitment on entry, too hesitant on exit. It all felt wrong.

Again, I forced myself to inhale deeply, to focus on the windy, wet road ahead instead of the chaos rolling around in my head. The next turn approached. My right foot hovered over the brake pedal, judging the moment.

Wait.

Wait.

Now!

And then, at the last second, something inside me hesitated. Some primal part of my brain that, heading into the barrier, remembered the sound of my tires straining on the gravel.

And that hesitation cost me.

I clipped the inside curb too aggressively, trying to make up for the late entry. The car jolted sideways, and pure instinct made me overcorrect. My hands yanked the wheel right.

The rear spun out, and suddenly I was half a lane wide, cutting across the racing line at completely the wrong angle.

No, no, no…

For a heartbeat that stretched into eternity, I froze. My hands locked on the wheel, my brain screaming commands my body couldn't process.

In the mirror, a flash of black and silver appeared.

Lily. Her Rennen livery caught me completely off-guard. She was right there, closing fast on a flying lap of her own.

"I'm going to hit her. Oh god, I'm going to—" The words tore out of me.

She reacted instantly, her reflexes sharper than mine in that critical moment. Her foot came off the throttle, lifting just enough to slow. The black-and-silver Rennen darted to the outside, taking the long way around, giving us both room even though I'd left her none.

Controlled and composed. Exactly as we'd all been trained to be since our first days in karting.

The whole sequence had lasted maybe two heart-beats. Two heartbeats where I'd almost repeated Miami's incident, except this time it would have been my fault. Unquestionably, undeniably mine.

But she'd saved us both.

Her sleek, black car disappeared around the next corner, carrying away with it whatever remained of my pride.

"Henri!" Michael's voice sliced through the static, filled with worry. "You okay?"

The concern in his tone made something twist in my gut; made the heat of embarrassment crawl up my neck.

Say something. Answer him.

My pulse pounded behind my eyes, and I couldn't seem to press the radio button. Couldn't make my fingers move to that small switch on the steering wheel.

Frozen. You're frozen again, just like—

"Henri," Michael said again, softer this time. Not angry, just worried. That worry was somehow worse than anger would have been.

"I'm fine." The words came out flat, mechanical, utterly unconvincing.

Liar.

The rest of my lap was an echo of the first. Slow, chaotic, untidy. Michael didn't comment until the next lap went just as badly.

"Box this lap."

Three simple words. I hated how much relief overtook me as soon as the pit entry appeared, hated myself for being grateful for the escape. This wasn't me. I didn't run from bad sessions. I fought through them, pushed harder, and found the speed through sheer determination.

Except today, I just couldn't.

Back in the garage, I killed the engine and sat for a moment in the bleak silence, the cockpit feeling too small, too hot, despite the cool Canadian air. Finally, I unlatched the helmet, lifting it free.

Dampness hit my face, and my eyes stung from sweat, wind, and something else I refused to acknowledge. I blinked quickly, desperately hoping no cameras had caught the moment of weakness. The garage had gone quiet around me. As an F1 driver, you wanted to maximize your free practice sessions, and here I was, squandering mine. We had three hours this weekend to get the car set up correctly for qualifying, and I was panicking, wasting away valuable minutes.

They all saw me flounder out there.

Michael appeared beside the cockpit, crouching down to my eye level with the ease of someone who'd done this a thousand times. His expression was as steady as ever, his weathered face creased with lines earned from years of racing—not unkind, because that wasn't in his nature.

But his eyes held questions I didn't want to answer.

"Tell me," he said simply.

Not "what happened?" or "what's wrong?" Just "tell me." Like he already knew there was something beyond the lap times—something deeper than setup issues or tire troubles.

"Front felt… bad," I said automatically, reaching for the easy technical explanation. My voice came out hoarse, raw. "Understeer in the high-speed stuff. Rear hopped over the curbs in the chicane. Brake migration might be off, or maybe the—"

"Not the car," he interrupted quietly, firmly. "You."

The words hit like a physical blow.

"Don't do that." I tried to keep my voice level, but the edge still slipped through. "If the front's washing out—"

"Henri, you froze." His hand gripped the edge of the cockpit. "Right in the middle of the track, you just seemed to *freeze*." He paused for a moment.

I'd never heard Michael's voice shake before. Not in eight years. Not through crashes, mechanical failures, or championship losses.

"You're bracing before the corner even starts. Your heart rate is all over the place. And you almost collided with Lily before sending yourself into another wall. If she hadn't avoided—" He stopped himself, dragging a hand over his face. "If she hadn't reacted, we'd be having a very different conversation right now."

Each observation landed with a blow, precise and devastating. But it was the tremor in his voice that really got me, the barely controlled fear of an engineer who'd just watched his driver nearly cause a catastrophic accident.

My fingers tapped against the edge of my wheel. Once, twice, three times. That nervous tic again. The words hung between us.

"She was too close." Even as I said it, I knew how weak it sounded. How desperate.

"She was exactly where she was supposed to be. It's free practice."

I didn't have an answer for that. My throat locked up around the thousand excuses clawing to get out. Michael just looked at me for a long moment, giving me space to say whatever I needed to say.

"Let's try this again. Tell me what happened."

But I couldn't. The words wouldn't come.

"She had room," I insisted, because pride always moved faster than common sense.

"She had room because *she* made it," Michael said, and now there was an edge creeping into his voice. "Not because you gave it."

I tipped my head toward the timing screen, desperate to redirect this conversation anywhere else. My name sat at the very bottom, a pale white embarrassment. Lily's was perched neatly at the top, bold and smug. My shoulders ached from the tension I couldn't seem to let go.

Michael studied me quietly, like he was running data through his head, checking for what was fixable and what wasn't.

"Hey." He put a hand on my shoulder, grounding me. "This track suits you. You don't have to fight it to go fast."

I wanted to believe him. To feel the confidence that used to come naturally; the certainty that I belonged here. That I could win.

But all I felt was exhaustion.

He tapped the halo twice—that small, rhythmic sound he always made when he was trying to steady me. "All right, listen. Here's what we do." My eyes met his as he continued. "One safe lap through the fast section. Show your body what calm feels like. Next lap, we'll let it flow. Hands lighter. Breathe down the straights. Neat first, quick second. That's it."

"But—" I started, ready to argue for something I couldn't identify.

Michael raised his hands, a quiet warning. "Give me something solid," he said, voice even. "Then build. And if we're not the fastest, that's okay. There are two more sessions."

He stood before I could answer, and I reached for my helmet, sliding it back over my head. The garage blurred into flashes of purple and gold as I drove out of it and back onto the track.

"All clear." Michael's voice was calm over the radio. "Keep it simple."

"Copy," I whispered back, though it was mostly to myself.

The out lap was quiet. I focused on warming the tires, letting the circuit unfold without expectation. The curbs, the braking points, the familiar hum of Montreal's track.

Then came the first proper lap. The quick S-turn approached, that same section that had bitten me earlier. My pulse spiked instinctively, almost like panicked muscle memory was trying to take over.

No, not this time.

In. Across. Out. I gave myself just enough room for error, not too much, not too little. The car didn't fight me this time. For the first time that day, I felt my lungs actually work.

That's it. That's how it's supposed to feel.

I logged the sensation somewhere deep, where it couldn't slip away when I needed it most. The lap connected cleanly, one corner folding into the next. And then the second. Each turn was deliberate, mechanical at first, then instinctual. By the time I reached the S-turn again, something inside me had steadied.

We repeated this over and over again, with each lap feeling better than the last.

"Great middle section, Henri. Exactly what I wanted to see. Box this lap."

"But we're not top—"

"Box," he repeated, gentle but firm. Reluctantly, I complied, swinging the car into the pit entry.

Michael was waiting when I rolled to a stop, that near-grin he never quite committed to tugging at his mouth.

"That's the template," he said simply.

I nodded in appreciation, though it felt half-hearted. Fourth fastest. Which wasn't bad, considering how I'd started the session. But it wasn't good either. Not for what Hermes expected of me.

Michael looked quietly pleased, but I couldn't bring myself to match his optimism. Someone handed me a towel, and I wiped the rain from the back of my neck before following Michael toward the debriefing room.

I collapsed into my seat while Michael set a bottle of water in front of me, his tablet glowing beside him. The walls of the briefing room seemed to inch closer with each passing second.

His eyes met mine, searching. "What happened out there?"

This was one of the reasons I'd always liked Michael. No bullshit. No empty praise or hollow reassurances designed to protect fragile egos. Just direct, honest communication. But right now, that directness felt like standing naked under a bright light, every flaw and weakness exposed.

"Nothing." I reached for the water, taking a sip to buy myself time. "Just a bad run."

"That's not an answer." His tone stayed even, but I suspected the patience underneath it was wearing thin. "Where did the anxiety start? First corner? The S-turn? The rain?"

"There was no *anxiety*."

Michael's eyebrows lifted a fraction.

"The car just wasn't working with me today." I stared at the water bottle, unable to meet his eye. He was watching me, waiting for me to say something that wasn't a deflection, but I didn't have anything to give him.

Miami flashed through my mind. The car flipping, spinning through the air for just a few seconds before slamming into the barrier. It'd only lasted a moment, but it'd felt like an eternity. I could still feel it, that sickening helplessness from the lack of control. In the moment, all you can do is wait and hope. Hope the car holds itself together. Hope the barriers absorb the impact. Hope you walk away with nothing more than bruises and wounded pride.

This wasn't new territory for me. That paralyzing fear had found me once before, back in my junior F2 days. But I didn't want to think back to that.

"Look, I recovered," I said finally. "The rest of the session was fine."

"Fine isn't the standard." Michael set the tablet down, folding his hands on the table. "This isn't about one bad corner. It's about how you've driven this whole weekend, and on the sim, since the crash."

"I'm driving the same way I always have."

Michael gave me a disbelieving snort. "You're second-guessing yourself. Braking early. Overcorrecting. That's not you, Henri."

I wanted to argue, to tell him he was wrong, but the words stuck in my throat. I took a long drink of water, buying myself whatever time I could find. But this was Michael. He'd seen me in every condition: rain, dry, tired, injured, angry, happy. He knew my driving as well as I did, probably better.

There would be no lying to Michael.

"What do you want me to say?" The question was loaded with defensiveness, but Michael's expression only softened. "That I'm scared? That I flinched? That driving through that turn felt like—"

I stopped myself, turning my eyes back toward the empty TV screen. Michael studied me for a long moment, the only sound between us the frantic tapping of my fingers.

He thinks I'm broken. He thinks I can't do this anymore. He's going to tell Verhoeven, and they're going to bench me, or worse. I tried to shove back all the self-doubt that was crowding my mind.

"Let's take a break. This afternoon is FP2," Michael continued, as if sensing he was about to hit the mental wall I'd put up. "It's a fresh start. But Henri, I just have to say, if you're dealing with any lingering effects from Miami, there's help we can get you."

"I said I'm fine!" The words exploded out of me. My neck burned hot—the kind of heat that wasn't from effort but embarrassment.

Michael's offer was genuine, well-meaning. I could see that in his expression; hear it in his voice. But all I felt was a surge of hot, defensive anger mixed with shame.

No. I'd been down this road before. No one wanted a weak driver. Formula 1 had come a long way in discussing anxiety and mental health, but were they ready for a driver who couldn't do something as simple as drive in the rain?

What did Michael want me to admit? That something in me had gone hollow at the worst moment? That I'd felt something I hadn't in years?

There wasn't a clean sentence for any of that. And even if there were, I wasn't about to hand it to him.

Chapter Three

Lily

The weekend's free practice sessions and qualifying were finally over, and now all that stood between me and a quiet Saturday evening was the press pen, which would no doubt continue to spend half its time dissecting Henri's driving choices during Friday morning's free practice.

What the hell had gotten into him?

After the crash in Miami, I'd tried to extend an olive branch. I'd called him repeatedly, apologizing and trying to explain the incident, but he never answered. So instead, I'd poured my apologies into voicemails that he probably ignored.

I exhaled slowly, pushing the thought aside as I climbed out of my car's cockpit. It didn't matter what Henri thought. This week was a new race, and I had qualified second today. I had a real chance to win tomorrow, and if I did, I'd be on top in the championship standings.

Focus on that, not Henri.

"Great work!" Mark's voice crackled through the headset. Then he appeared in person, jogging around the car to meet me as I pulled off my helmet. "Impeccable driving this weekend. Unfortunate that Henri got P1 after he had such an abysmal Friday. Let's just hope he can keep his car to himself…"

The comment landed with more weight than Mark probably intended.

The sun had broken through today after Friday's rain, and Henri had somehow clawed his way to pole position in Qualifying. Something petty and raw inside me wanted to join Mark's dig, but considering my car had actually caused a crash, I decided I couldn't face the hypocrisy.

"I can practically smell the podium champagne!" I said brightly, forcing enthusiasm into my voice.

"Well, just remember, we don't collect trophies until Sunday."

Thanks, Mark, I thought sarcastically. *I had no idea how this worked.* Mark's ability to puncture a good mood was unmatched. I huffed a quiet laugh, trying to shake off the irritation, when movement at the back of the garage caught my eye.

"Oh God," I groaned.

Mark looked up, giving me an apologetic smile.

Bertha Higham, Rennen F1's Head of Communications and Media, weaved her way through the garage crowd with unmatched determination. She was wearing *that* expression. The one that said she was not to be trifled with.

Here we go.

"Mark!" she called out, waving him down with one perfectly manicured hand. "I told you I needed her immediately after qualifying."

He rolled his eyes with barely concealed disdain. "Yes, because media management is obviously much more important than actual engineering work..." His mumbling dripped with so much sarcasm you could practically see it pooling on the garage floor.

Bertha approached, arms crossed. "What was that?"

Mark smiled, one of those shit-eating grins, before motioning elaborately in my direction. "Nothing. She's all yours, Bertha."

Traitor.

Bertha turned to me, her expression softening by about one degree, before thrusting a sleek black folder into my hands. "Media in ten." Her tone was professional, but her expression carried the faintest trace of apology. Rare for her, which meant she knew exactly how rough this session would be.

"The English pool wants you and Henri together," she continued. "Then solo for the locals. These are your approved answers, and no ad-libbing this time, please."

"I'll stay on script," I promised lightly.

Bertha's eyes narrowed, unconvinced. "You said that after Miami."

Well, to be fair, I hadn't exactly meant it in Miami.

I'd known precisely what the press were going to ask— could have written the questions myself: *Was it intentional? Do you think you belong in F1? Should women be allowed in the sport if they can't control their cars?*

No part of me had been willing to sit back politely while they wrote me off after one mechanical failure. Or let them paint me as the reckless female driver who'd taken out poor, innocent Henri through sheer incompetence. Hermes had enjoyed throwing around comments about Rennen's inability to design quality cars.

The interviews after the crash were an exercise in endurance. I'd made it through the first two interviews on script, nodding at appropriate moments, giving measured responses.

And then *Sports Daily* had asked if I thought I owed Henri an apology for "dangerous driving," and something in me snapped.

I'd told them, rather politely, exactly where they could shove their double standards. Pointed out that when male drivers had mechanical failures, no one questioned their right to be in the sport. Mentioned that perhaps they should wait for the stewards' investigation before pronouncing judgment.

The headlines were merciless: *Blackwood Defensive After Crash. Rennen Driver Refuses to Take Responsibility.*

I shifted my weight from one side to the other. "I remember."

"Good. So, this time, let's be measured. Oh, and"—Bertha's fingers drummed against her tablet, her mouth opening and closing twice before she found her words—"try not to sound so flippant."

Flippant.

Smiling had always been my armor, the thing that kept me from showing how rattled I really was underneath. It was easier to be the cheerful one, the woman who laughed off the whispers and met every loaded question with sunshine.

The strategy had worked at Valkyrie, when the team had started with me and Georgia as the first female driver pairing in F1 history. We'd been explicitly told to win people over.

"Smile more. Be approachable. Be likeable. Make the sport fall in love with you."

If I had learned anything during my motorsports career, it was that nothing placated a crowd like a disarming smile, even if it *was* fake.

The media room was cramped, the kind of space that always felt too small for the number of journalistic egos crammed into it. Bright lights shone overhead, casting an unflattering glow that made everyone look slightly ill. Sponsor logos covered most of the wall behind us.

Bertha pointed me toward my seat, second from the left. The one designated for P2.

Henri arrived a moment later with his PR team, like bodyguards protecting something valuable. His expression was fairly neutral, but I could see a small smile hiding behind his eyes. He was pleased with himself, as he should be.

After his disastrous free practice yesterday, today he'd managed to beat me by thousandths of a second for pole, which I was a bit peeved about. Two seats down, Éliott Simon, another driver, was already holding court, charming the front row like it was second nature.

Press conferences had always felt oddly comfortable to me, which I knew was weird given how many drivers dreaded them. But there was something predictable about the format, something manageable. Questions you could anticipate, and answers you could prepare for, especially with a good PR team.

My mother had always claimed I had a gift for "smoothing edges"—for taking pointed questions loaded with subtext and turning them into something softer, more palatable. For defusing tension with a well-timed smile or a self-deprecating joke. That skill had served me well when I wasn't the main story or the one in the hot seat; when I could sit in the supporting role and watch other drivers, like Georgia, squirm under scrutiny.

But now, sitting at P2 in the championship, just a few points behind Henri, I was undeniably in the hot seat. And my answers to their questions definitely carried real consequences.

Being next to Henri again felt strange in a way I couldn't quite articulate. The last time I'd seen him this close was Miami, right after the crash, when I'd helped him out of his car. He looked exhausted, like sleep had evaded him over the past few days.

But even tired, Henri had this captivating, quiet command that drew attention without effort. When he spoke, his voice carried that low, deliberate confidence that made interviewers lean in closer. Something about his hazel eyes, the way they watched you with complete focus, made you feel like you were the only person in the world worth paying attention to.

No wonder I caved and gave in to my feelings for him last year. But the Henri sitting next to me wasn't the same man from last season. The suave, nuanced answers might sound familiar, but the voice behind them had changed—sharper now, more focused, tinged with frustration. He was desperate to win this championship, and that desperation had transformed him.

It had probably transformed both of us. Eight races in, and it had all but consumed the two of us.

Henri finally glanced in my direction, his eyes meeting mine for the briefest moment before he gave a curt nod. "Blackwood."

So, it's like that, is it?

"Dubois," I answered, matching his tone, though I added a small smile meant to bridge the gap. He didn't return it, but his posture loosened. A subtle tell, like he'd almost considered further acknowledging me.

Fine. I didn't like him much either right now anyway.

A British voice cut through the loud chatter, a signal the conference was about to start. "Lily! A solid P2 today. How does it feel?"

"Obviously would have liked P1," I said with a grin. "But all things considered, I'll take finishing without hitting anyone as a win."

A few journalists chuckled. I knew they were going to ask about the almost collision this week, so I figured getting out ahead of it would be easiest. Although that probably wasn't what Bertha had hoped for.

"In all seriousness, the team worked hard this week, and we're seeing the success from that work."

"Tell us," an American journalist piped up. "That moment with Henri during free practice yesterday—any thoughts on that near-miss? It looked a little tense." He leaned forward eagerly, his press badge swinging against his lanyard.

This was why I loved the American journalists: they got to the gossip right away. No need for chitchat. And as a British driver, I appreciated that.

"We both went for the same line," I said lightly. "It happens. That section's tight. Anyone who's driven it knows there's not much margin."

"Henri," the journalist followed up, like a shark sensing blood in the water, "do you feel like you left her enough room?"

"We made no contact," Henri replied.

There was no stopping the snort that left my mouth, and I could practically feel Bertha's invisible hand squeezing her stress ball somewhere in the back.

"Right. But it was close?"

His voice was level, but I noticed the small finger taps on his knee—his age-old tell that he was nervous. "As Lily said, we both wanted the same piece of track."

An understatement. But I bit back what I really wanted to say. He'd nearly put me into the wall—a topic that Felix had been allowed to mention during his team principal interview, but which I'd been told to ignore. I suspected Bertha couldn't control Felix's frustrated outbursts toward Hermes like she could mine.

I leaned toward the mic, giving them the answer Bertha had prepared. "Honestly, the camera angles can be deceiving. There was more space than it appeared on the broadcast."

"It looked tighter on TV than it felt in the car," Henri added, and I had to give him credit—his voice carried just enough casual confidence to make it sound believable.

"Well," a different voice cut in, female this time, "I assume he apologized to you after this weekend's incident? Given what happened in Miami?"

The question hung in the air. Henri's fingers tightened on the microphone, a small but visible tell that he was already done with this line of questioning. I suspected he was probably as sick of hearing about yesterday's free practice as I was hearing about Miami.

This ought to be good.

"Look, my car had a little steering issue," Henri said slowly, deliberately. Then he turned to me, and a knowing grin curved on his lips. "Lily knows what that's like."

He paused, and I watched danger dance in his hazel eyes. Henri Dubois was many things, but gracious in defeat wasn't one of them. "But of course," he continued, voice dripping with false sweetness, "I'm always happy to offer an apology to her. One similar to the apology she gave me in Miami."

Prick!

Henri punctuated the jab with a subtle wink, brief enough that the cameras might miss it, but obvious enough that I definitely didn't.

"Well, Henri," I began, forcing sincerity into my voice even as fury burned in my chest, "I'm sure you'll give me a detailed tutorial on proper apologies once you've mastered that particular art yourself."

Two can play at passive-aggressive, golden boy.

The next question came fast, cutting through whatever retort Henri might have been formulating. "Henri, let's talk more about Friday's free practice sessions. Your lap times were slower than your expected pace. Was there a specific issue with the car or setup? It almost looked like you froze out there. Was there a malfunction?"

The word "froze" seemed to hang in the air, and Henri's shoulders stiffened beside me. He leaned toward the mic, but nothing came out at first. His mouth opened then closed again. The silence stretched just long enough to make everyone in the room lean forward.

Well, that's new.

The Hermes media darling, fluent in charm and control, suddenly looked like he'd forgotten how to speak.

"We had, um,"—he swallowed visibly—"some setup challenges we were working through."

He tried for a smile, his trademark effortless grin, but it faltered halfway, giving more grimace than charm. As he stumbled through the rest, something about "finding the right balance," I watched him out of the corner of my eye. The set of his jaw, the tight pull at the corner of his mouth, the crease between his brows. His rambling was so unlike him that I found myself unable to look away from the train wreck unfolding beside me.

His rambling finally trailed off. A few journalists exchanged glances, but most just nodded mechanically. One bad weekend for Hermes wasn't exactly headline news.

My eyes drifted over to Éliott. He was Henri's best friend on the grid, the two of them having raced together their entire lives. The French driver wasn't smiling anymore. His easy charm had flickered off, replaced by something akin to concern.

He was watching Henri the same way I was.

"Right, so setup challenges," another journalist pressed, clearly unsatisfied with the vague response. "What exactly were the issues you—"

"I said there was nothing wrong!"

The room froze like someone had hit pause on a video. Even the moderator's hand stilled on his tablet. Henri never raised his voice. Not in interviews, not in the paddock, not even after crashes. This person next to me definitely sounded like Henri, but they felt like a stranger.

He immediately realized his mistake, and I watched the change happen in real time. The widening of his eyes, the color draining from his face, the way his hand flew up to rake through his hair before rubbing down his face in a gesture that looked more like desperation than frustration.

"I meant…" He took a breath, trying to reset. "We're reviewing the data. That's all. Standard procedure after any session where the lap times aren't quite where you expect."

Éliott leaned forward, offering him the smallest lifeline. "I think what Henri means is that we're all still finding our rhythm this early in the season. Setup tweaks, getting a feel for the car. It's an ongoing process. You have to remember, our cars are brand-new to us. These new engineering specs, they're difficult to learn."

Fortunately, the moderator seized the moment. "All right, that's all the time we have. Thank you, everyone."

As chairs scraped and journalists began gathering equipment, I risked a glance at Henri.

He was already standing, moving to leave with mechanical precision, his PR team closing around him like a protective detail. His face had gone carefully blank again, that professional mask firmly back in place.

But his hands were shaking.

Just slightly, barely noticeable unless you were looking for it, but I saw the tremor in his fingers as he straightened his team polo, the way he shoved them quickly into his pockets to hide it. I watched him disappear through the media-room door without a backward glance, Éliott close on his heels.

Bertha appeared at my side, tablet hugged to her chest like a shield. "Not bad," she said. In Bertha-speak, that was practically a standing ovation. "Though next time…" She paused, sighing. "Well, it could've been worse."

I'd take it.

Chapter Four

Lily

By the time I reached the Rennen garage, all I could think about was sleep. I was halfway to my driver's room when a smooth, unmistakably English voice cut through the air.

"Lillian."

Oh, brilliant. Just what I need right now.

My mother stood framed in the doorway like she'd been posed there by a photographer, pearl-colored blazer gleaming under the room's lighting. One manicured hand rested on her handbag as if she was worried someone might steal it from under her nose.

No team gear, of course. Victoria Blackwood didn't wear anything that hadn't hit the runway.

"Mum," I greeted with a casual smile.

"There's someone here who wanted to say hello." Based on the unusual giddiness of her voice, I knew whoever it was must have been important.

Marcus Freeman appeared behind my mother, his six-foot-something frame making her look almost childlike by comparison. The CEO of BetHere Gaming had his silver hair combed back so severely it looked painted on, and his smile reminded me of every used car salesman I'd ever met. His tanned hand was already extended toward me.

"Lily! The car looks excellent this weekend. Really fantastic work from you this season."

I took his hand, trying to force down the exhaustion. "Thanks, Mr. Freeman. Appreciate you coming by."

"Please, call me Marcus." He grinned wider. "I was just telling your mother how impressed we've been with your performance. You're doing wonderful things for both Rennen and F1."

"She's always been driven," my mother bragged. "Even as a young girl. She won her first karting championship at eight, you know."

"Mum—" I had no doubt Marcus knew all of this, but he just beamed at my mother. "That kind of dedication is exactly what BetHere looks for in our partnerships. We're not here to just back drivers; we want to back champions."

Champions who make you money.

"Well, I should let you rest." Marcus stepped back, his gold cufflinks catching the light as he checked his Patek Philippe watch. "Big week ahead. But I wanted to pop in, see the talent up close."

"I appreciate it." I smiled.

"Let's arrange a dinner sometime. You, me, your mother. Discuss the future." He winked.

I nodded, jaw aching from the smile that now felt a bit too forced. Marcus shook my hand again, squeezed Mum's shoulder, then disappeared down the corridor.

The second he was gone, my mother turned to me.

"He's a very important sponsor, Lillian." Her tone shifted, sharpening. "So, if you see him again, be sure to say hello. His company has historically sponsored F1 teams, but there's interest in some individual deals too."

Finally, Victoria's eyes swept over me, assessing the rumpled sleeves of my team half-zip and the grease stain on my jeans.

"My goodness, you look dreadful." Her voice made me straighten up, a reflex so ingrained I couldn't override it even if I wanted to.

"Well, I did just finish qualifying?" Not that my mother had bothered to watch it. That I was sure of.

"Don't be flippant. It doesn't suit you." Well, at least now I knew where Bertha had gotten the word from.

She took a seat on my sofa, motioning for me to do the same. "I watched your press conference. Not too terrible. At least you skipped the jokes this time."

I folded my arms defensively, suddenly too aware of how small the driver's room felt with her in it. "Aren't you the one who told me to distract them with my 'sunshiny personality'?" I made air quotes around the phrase she'd used so often over the years.

"Smile, Lillian. A sunshiny *smile*." Her sigh was deliberate, in an over-the-top theatrical way. Something she'd perfected since my childhood. "No words needed. Just that lovely, disarming expression you do so well."

"Thanks for the advice," I said, holding up my phone with my lap-time data. "But as you can see, I'm doing fine."

"Fine isn't the goal," she said matter-of-factly. "Winning is."

Unless it was with her.

There was no *winning* when it came to dealing with Victoria Blackwood. Only surviving.

"You know I only want to help," she said softly. "We've come this far…"

I bit back a sigh. "I know you do, Mum. And I try to listen."

Her smile curved, faint and satisfied, like I'd just passed a test I didn't know I was taking. "Good. Then you'll appreciate what I've come to tell you."

Ah, the real reason she was here. It never seemed to be just to see me race.

"I ran into Oliver Johnson this afternoon. Remember him from school?"

I blinked. "Ollie?" Ollie and I had been classmates growing up, and then we'd raced together a bit as teens, before he joined F2. He was everywhere lately, his face plastered across F1 media. The rising podcaster and the charming face behind *The Home Stretch*, F1's largest podcast. His career had exploded over the past two seasons.

And apparently, so had my mother's interest.

"You know he's running *The Home Stretch* podcast," she continued airily. I went to tell her that yes, I obviously knew, but my mother had already launched herself into her next thought. "We ran into each other earlier today. He had nothing but lovely things to say about you."

"Yes, well, that's nice, Mu—"

"Anyway, we were talking, and he was telling me how he would love to catch up with you, so I told him that you would have dinner with him tonight."

"It's the night before a race!" This was crazy, even for my mother. "Mum, are you out of your mind?"

"Well, you have to eat, don't you?"

I couldn't believe what I was hearing.

"And why not do it with someone successful and charming? He's always been fond of you. And he also happens to be single."

I let out a quiet, disbelieving laugh. "You once told me his mother was the most pretentious person you'd ever met."

She flicked her wrist dismissively, gold bracelets catching the light. "You can't fault a person for their parents, Lillian."

And thank God for that, I thought.

"You know he once glued my math book shut, and right before finals too."

Her lips pursed into that familiar half-smile. "Oh, Lily, boys will be bo—"

"Dear God, Mum, please do not finish that sentence."

She waved me off, likely annoyed with my *melodramatics*. "He's grown into quite a young man. Exactly the sort of person you should be seen with."

There it was, that real agenda. Ollie's grandfather had been a famous driver back in the seventies and was now the chairman of several charities. Their name carried weight in the racing world.

"So," I said slowly, "is this PR, or matchmaking?"

"Dinner with Oliver will be mutually beneficial." She looked down at her nails, inspecting them for a moment. "He'll get some insider knowledge for his podcast, and you'll get valuable visibility. You're at a new team now. This sort of press will be good for you, and Ollie is a safe choice to do it."

Each word pricked more than it should have, finding soft spots I thought I'd armored against years ago.

"My results speak for themselves, Mum. I don't need a man to validate them. Plus, what about this morality clause? Wouldn't want the dinner looking like I'm on a date..." I added that last part with perhaps a bit too much sarcasm.

"Darling, you're missing the point." Mum waved her hand dismissively, as though brushing away my concerns like they were merely crumbs from a lap. "You're allowed to have romantic relationships, but with the right person. Oliver isn't a rival. Plus, he has a massive platform. Your sponsors will love it."

I wonder if Ollie knows about my mother's little matchmaking agenda.

Her lips curved into a small, satisfied smile. "Just remember, Lily. We're building something here. You're representing women in motorsport, and more importantly, representing Rennen's investment in you."

The guilt trip was expertly deployed, hitting exactly where she intended.

Before I could formulate any response, she stood, smoothing her blazer. "I'll have a dress sent to your hotel room within the hour." She paused at the door, delivering her final instruction. "And for heaven's sake, keep the jokes to a minimum."

Before I could reply, she leaned in, pressed a faint kiss to my cheek, and turned toward the door. But something stopped her. She took in the vase in the corner of the room, the one whose flowers had held the note from Miami. I'd meant to throw it away, but the team had packed up my driver's room before I'd gotten the chance. When it appeared again in Montreal, I couldn't bring myself to toss it. Instead I'd slipped out to a supermarket and bought fresh flowers.

Something bright to replace the bad memory.

My mother's nose wrinkled slightly. "Lily." Her tone carried that particular disappointment I'd become accustomed to. "They look like they're from a *grocery store*."

"They are, actually," I said carefully, trying to keep my voice neutral.

"Good God. They look terribly cheap." She moved closer, inspecting the arrangement with a critical eye, which was ironic, since my mother had a black thumb. "Lilies and daisies? Honestly, if you must keep flowers in your workspace, at least choose something with more sophistication. An orchid, perhaps. Or a proper arrangement from a florist."

I looked at the flowers one more time and opened my mouth, the confession hovering at the edge of my tongue. *Should I tell her?*

The words sat there, heavy and unspoken.

"Actually," I started, then I stopped. My mother's gaze felt heavy as she watched me. "Um, I sort of wanted to ask you something. I received a... note. It was a bit nasty, felt different than the usual 'women don't belong in racing' garbage I usually get..."

I stopped, waiting to see her reaction, but her expression didn't change. No concern creased her brow; no maternal instinct kicked in.

"Oh, darling. You're at a larger team now. It's going to come with more visibility. You're in the spotlight!" She adjusted her handbag on her shoulder. "You're not the first woman in a male-dominated space to receive attention from sad little people with too much time on their hands."

"Right, but this note was in my room... and seemed to maybe be from someone who lost some money—"

At that, my mother cut me off. "Just ignore them." The command was flat, shutting down any chance of an argument. "And for God's sake, don't make a fuss about it."

I blinked. "A fuss?"

"Lillian." She turned fully toward me now, and I recognized the look. The one that said I was being difficult again. "You're already under enough scrutiny. The last thing you need is to give anyone more reason to think you can't handle the pressure. That you need special protection or coddling. The team doesn't need a reason to question whether a female driver is worth the trouble," she continued, softer now, like she was doing me a favor. "And with BetHere being such a big sponsor, we don't want to bring them any negative attention, hm? You know, Marcus is very involved with a few different companies as a board member. This relationship could grow into something else!"

I swallowed down the rest of my words, letting them sink back down to where they belonged. She was right. One complaint, and I'd become the difficult woman who couldn't take the heat. A liability who needed protecting.

I'd seen what had happened to my friend Abby over in Indy Car. She'd complained, and the team had stopped prioritizing her at sponsorship events.

"Yeah, you're right. It's no big deal."

"Good girl." She smiled, genuine this time, and kissed my cheek again. She cast one last glance at the vase before exiting the room. Her heels clicked across the floor, crisp and even, echoing long after she'd disappeared.

My eyes drifted back to the flower arrangement. Innocent, cheerful, perfectly ordinary flowers bought from a perfectly ordinary shop. Nothing threatening. Nothing dangerous.

Nothing like the original bouquet that had come with a message promising violence. The threat lived in my mind now, playing on repeat during quiet moments, crowding in when I should have been sleeping or visualizing race strategy.

Someone with access to the paddock, to team hospitality areas, to my private driver's room, had gotten into my room and left flowers.

And I'd told no one.

But was my mother right?

Making a big deal about threatening fan mail would just prove to my critics that women in F1 were too fragile for the pressure, too emotional to handle the spotlight. That I needed special treatment, coddling, protection the male drivers didn't require.

I knew for a fact that Henri had never reported hate mail. Or my teammate Luca. They probably received worse as they'd been racing longer, but they didn't run crying to team principals about mean notes tucked into bouquets.

And they certainly didn't keep the vase and fill it with flowers like some sort of twisted memorial. I grabbed my water bottle, taking a long pull to wash down the bitter taste in my mouth.

I couldn't have Felix second-guessing his investment. Besides, what would reporting it actually accomplish?

An investigation into one note felt silly and would probably go nowhere. If it was someone who'd lost money on me, they probably just wanted to let off some steam. I didn't want to make a fuss over one of Rennen's biggest sponsors. The fact was, gambling was big business, and the sponsorship revenue was growing each year.

It was one note, I reminded myself. *Probably from some drunk fan who was angry about the crash and wanted to lash out.*

I'd deal with it if another showed up.

Chapter Five

Henri

I followed the bustling streets of Montreal to my sister's hotel: a sleek high-rise tucked between the glass towers of downtown. The elevator whisked me up to the fifteenth floor, and I found myself standing before room 1542, hand raised to knock, when the door swung open before my knuckles could make contact.

Typical Georgia, my twin sister was always one step ahead of me. After qualifying today, she'd invited me to hers and Luca's hotel room to celebrate my P1.

Hers and Luca's room.

That still felt surreal sometimes, my sister dating my former teammate. The guy I'd spent three years racing alongside at Hermes. It felt like a lifetime since then.

We weren't particularly close when he was at Hermes, and at the time, I wasn't exactly thrilled that my teammate was dating my sister. But Luca had won me over with that cocky Italian flair of his and his signature Cheshire cat grin that made it impossible to stay annoyed at him for long. He could charm the pants off a snake charmer given half the chance, and he was good to Georgia, which was what mattered.

She'd qualified P6 today for Valkyrie—not what she'd hoped. Valkyrie were having a rough start to the season.

As with most spec changes in Formula 1, the previous year's winning team didn't always get it right. But still, three seasons in Formula 1 had proved Georgia belonged here just as much as I did. Maybe more, considering she'd won the last three Driver's Championships.

"About time," she said, stepping aside to let me in. "I was afraid you couldn't find the place!"

I pushed past her, dropping my racing bag by the door as I entered the suite. The familiar scent of her favorite pine candle hit me immediately.

After securing P1 in qualifying, I should've been celebrating, but my mind kept drifting back to yesterday's free practice. To that moment when Lily's car nearly kissed the wall because of my error. She'd saved it, of course.

Stop thinking about it.

"Earth to Henri," Georgia said, waving a hand in front of my face. "You just grabbed pole position, and you look like someone stole your favorite watch."

"Sorry, Georgie, just trying to remember what qualifying P6 feels like. It's been so long since I've been back there."

She scoffed, giving me a playful shove that nearly knocked me off-balance. "That's rich coming from someone who's spent the past three years *watching* me win championships. A couple of pole positions this season, and suddenly you've got amnesia?"

I laughed, shaking my head as I followed her deeper into the suite, but when I turned the corner into the living room, my smile faltered. The sight before me didn't exactly match the quiet, celebratory evening I had in mind.

Lily sat comfortably on the couch next to Luca, her auburn hair loose and wavy around her shoulders, freckles visible across the bridge of her nose. She wore a cream sweater tucked into black trousers—simple and understated. Beautiful in that effortless way. She looked relaxed, completely at ease, like she belonged there. Given that Luca was her teammate, that wasn't too far off.

A year ago, the sight of her would have made me smile. I would've dropped onto the couch beside her, stolen one of her biscuits, let our easy banter fill the room. Now it just made my jaw clench. I hated how much changed between us. Hated more that I couldn't seem to stop noticing her.

"What the fuck are you doing here?" The words were out before I could stop them.

"Robbing the place," she said without missing a beat, waving a nearby candlestick in my direction with a quick grin. "Georgia and Luca always get the nicest suites."

I dropped onto the couch across from them, ignoring her. From behind, a comforting hand squeezed my shoulder. Georgia, steadying me like always. She'd always been there for me. Even when we competed for championships, we never stopped supporting each other.

Luca extended a packet of biscuits my way, but I shook my head. He offered them to Georgia and Lily instead, who each took one eagerly, like they hadn't eaten in days.

My stare stayed fixed on Lily, watching her dip her biscuit into her cup of tea. "Your dietician lets you eat sugar? Guess even he knows you won't be winning this year." Every inch of me knew how ridiculous that sounded, but nothing irked me more than seeing the person standing between me and the championship looking perfectly comfortable in *my* sister's room.

She only snorted, that infuriating smile never wavering as she made a show of slowly shoving the entire biscuit into her mouth. A crumb caught at the corner of her lips, and my eyes tracked it as she brushed it away with her thumb.

I tore my gaze away, the room suddenly ten degrees warmer. Once, I'd found that stubborn streak endearing. I would've matched it with a grin and a joke designed to coax out her laugh. Now, we goaded each other until something inside me threatened to crack.

"Well, hello to you too," Luca laughed. "I see getting pole hasn't improved your sparkling personality."

"Sorry, I wasn't expecting anyone else." The words came out as a sigh, my hand gesturing vaguely toward Lily, who kept smiling at me like she'd won something.

She always looked so happy, and it was infuriating.

Lily turned to my sister, not remotely attempting to hide her smug grin. "Well, as much fun as I'm sure this"— she motioned, dramatically, toward me—"will be, I need to go get ready for dinner."

Georgia rolled her eyes but said nothing. Over the past six months, my sister had often found herself stuck between a rock and a hard place when it came to Lily and me. Lily was her former teammate and close friend. They'd entered Formula 1 together, two women on the grid full of men. They'd battled sexist journalists and won three Constructor's Championships. That bond went deep.

Lily and I had always bickered when it came to driving, but after Las Vegas, the casualness of our friendship and *"oops, sorry, I didn't mean for it to come across that way"* had disappeared. It'd escalated from professional rivalry into something sharper, more personal, bleeding into every interaction. With each race, the discomfort between us seemed to grow into something neither of us knew how to control.

Or knew how to stop.

I looked up at Lily, who'd thrown on a maroon blazer over her outfit, the fabric settling perfectly across her shoulders. The color brought out the warmth in her auburn hair, making her green eyes seem brighter somehow.

"Dinner plans before a race?" I scoffed, raising a curious eyebrow. "Who's the poor bastard?"

"Wouldn't you like to know?" She cocked her head, auburn strands brushing her cheek as that bright, infuriating smile returned. My heart skipped, just for a second.

I couldn't look away—my gaze was drawn back in like a magnet. She looked at me like she knew exactly what effect she had; like she enjoyed watching me squirm.

"Lily has dinner with Ollie." Luca wiggled his eyebrows suggestively before propping his feet up on the coffee table.

Something sharp and ugly twisted in my gut—a feeling I had no right to feel when the choice to not be together had been mine.

Lily took my silence for confusion. "You know, devilishly handsome, blond hair, bright blue eyes."

"Oh, Henri knows who he is," Georgia interjected, shooting me a look. "They were teammates in F2."

Lily's eyebrows lifted, genuine interest sparking in those green eyes as she properly looked at me for the first time since I'd walked in. My pulse kicked up traitorously.

"Well, must be off," she said brightly, moving toward the door. She passed behind the couch where I sat, and for one brief moment, I felt the warmth of her presence at my back, caught a drift of her floral perfume. My entire body went rigid, like if I moved even slightly, I might do something stupid. Like reach for her and ask her to stay, just as she'd done in Las Vegas last year.

She paused—I felt rather than saw it—and I wondered if she was looking down at me; wondered what her expression would be if I turned around.

But I didn't.

Then she continued past, now finally in view, turning back to me from the safety of the doorway with a look of pure mischief. "And don't worry, Dubois, I'll be sure to stay out of your way tomorrow."

"See that you do." I turned to face her, narrowing my eyes, heat prickling at the back of my neck as I crossed my arms.

Still paused at the door, she looked at me with an expression far too smug for someone starting P2 in tomorrow's race. "Though if you drive like you did in free practice, I won't need to. I'll be too far ahead."

Her wink hit harder than any insult could have. Something hot and frustrated coiled in my chest, making it difficult to breathe properly. The door shut behind her, and the suite fell silent.

"Henri?" Georgia's voice cut through the fog. "You're gripping the armrest like you're trying to strangle it."

I released my death grip on the leather, relaxing my fingers.

"She's just messing with you," Luca offered. "You know how Lily is."

"Unfortunately." Glancing at the biscuits scattered across the coffee table, I grabbed one, shoving it into my mouth.

That was the problem. I did know what she was like. Knew exactly how she could unravel me with a single look, a throwaway gesture. The way she'd winked, casual and teasing, sent my thoughts spiraling to places they had no business going. Under no circumstances could I have Lily Blackwood. After all the bad blood this season, we weren't the same people who'd fallen into bed together last year.

I couldn't allow us to be. My only goal was to win this championship. Georgia had won the Driver's Championship three times, but I hadn't even won Monaco, my home race. This year had to be different, and with how fast my car was, I had to take advantage of this year.

There would be no distractions, especially not from the one person who wanted more than anything to take my dream away.

Luca shifted uncomfortably, sipping his tea as if it might save him from being caught in the crossfire of my anger. He made eyes at my sister, and I could see they were having one of those insufferable conversations couples had without speaking.

"I really wish one of you would tell me what exactly happened between the two of you last year. You went from genuine friends to…" Georgia stopped, catching my deliberately blank expression. The wall I'd thrown up so many times was now automatic. Her hands went up in surrender. "You know what? Never mind. Enough about Lily. How are *you* doing?"

"Fine." Not entirely true, but the word was habit these days.

Georgia's brows arched, unimpressed by the obvious lie.

I scrubbed a hand over my face as I stared at the burning candle in front of me. Its once comforting scent now felt suffocating. "Do you think Lily made the right choice when signing with Rennen?"

"What's wrong with Rennen?" Luca almost looked offended. Unfortunately for Luca, while the Rennen car had been brilliant for Lily, he'd struggled a bit in the first few races, although his P2 in Miami had set him up for better success. He was starting to get the hang of it, and I had to remember he was also a threat this year in the Rennen car.

"Why does it matter what I think?" Georgia prodded.

"It doesn't," I said quickly. "Just…"

My sister stopped me. "Lily's done something even I never could. She's managed to break into one of the oldest, most decorated F1 teams. Instead of sitting in comfort, being protected by a completely female-owned and run operation, Lily sank her toes into the deep end. Rennen F1 is as boy's club as they come."

She paused, holding my gaze. "And you know what? She just might prove that she made the right decision. She's second in the championship, Henri. *Second*. In her first season with them."

Luca cleared his throat. "It's true, Henri. I mean, in engineering meetings she's focused, full of good ideas. I've driven this car for two years, and she's just come in and usurped me. Honestly, it's so impressive I haven't had time to be angry that my new, younger teammate is beating me."

I took a long sip of the tea Luca set down earlier, using the moment to compose myself. Georgia sighed, long and heavy, and for the first time that night I properly looked at her. The exhaustion was there in the tightness around her eyes, the way her shoulders carried tension even sitting down. The forced brightness that meant she was pushing through fatigue to be here for me.

Guilt hit me hard. In all my stewing and whining about Lily and pole position and everything spinning out of control, I hadn't taken a single moment to ask my sister how *she* was doing.

"How are you feeling at Valkyrie?" I asked finally. "P6 is good considering the issues you told me about."

"Tough this season," she admitted, some of the brightness fading from her voice. "We knew we'd probably struggle with the regulation changes, but this feels brutal. Still, I believe the team can get us there. If not this year, then next."

The brutality of Formula 1. Every few years Formula 1 changed engineering specs, and this year had brought a design overhaul. While it was helpful in resetting the field, it felt crucifying to whoever had been in first place last year.

"You sound like you're already bracing for disappointment." Georgia had dominated the past three years, but now? Now she was fighting to get on the podium. "I'm sorry, Georgie."

"Well, not all bad, eh?" she laughed, bumping my knee with hers. "It'll finally give you an opportunity to beat me."

I returned the gesture, though with considerably less enthusiasm.

Truthfully, it was all I'd thought about since pre-season. From my first flying lap, I could taste the success. This year I refused to be Georgia's brother trailing behind, the driver who was always *almost* as good but never quite enough.

This year I was going to win the World Driver's Championship.

"Well, I'm sure you'll still make it hell for me."

Georgia laughed, shooting me an appreciative smile. "Someone has to keep you humble."

"Isn't that what the media is for?"

As soon as I said the word, Georgia and Luca locked eyes again. Another silent conversation passed between them.

"So," she said casually, but I heard the probing in her voice, "about that press conference earlier…"

My entire body went rigid. "What about it?"

"Henri." She leaned forward, elbows on her knees. "You practically froze when they asked about your pace. And that outburst? You should be thanking the other drivers for defusing whatever that was."

"Oh, please. They were just playing it up for the journalists."

Georgia's hand found my wrist, stilling the restless tapping I hadn't realized I was doing against the armrest. "I'm the one who gets flustered, who says the wrong thing, who needs media training refreshers. You're the one who makes it look effortless. What happened today?"

The concern in her voice threatened to crack something open inside me. Something I'd worked hard to keep sealed since Miami. Since the crash that played on repeat behind my eyelids every time I closed my eyes.

The sound of metal tearing. The smell of burning rubber. The moment when everything went wrong.

"I'm fine."

"So you keep saying." Georgia's grip tightened slightly, her thumb finding my pulse, which was now racing. "That moment in free practice yesterday—"

"Was nothing." I cut her off.

"Henri—"

"I said I'm *fine*, Georgia. *Arrêt!*" I pulled my hand away from Georgia's grip, standing abruptly enough that my knee hit the coffee table, making the teacups rattle.

My feet were already moving me toward the door, and I grabbed my bag in one swift motion.

"I need to prep for tomorrow's Grand Prix." I didn't look back, couldn't bear to see the worry etched across Georgia's face. "Thanks for the tea."

The door closed behind me with a soft click, cutting off whatever Georgia had started to say.

Chapter Six

Lily

I palmed the inside of my blazer to check for my room key and suddenly felt the stiff edge of the note instead. I'd forgotten I'd thrown the note inside this jacket.

It'd been almost two weeks since I got it. Two weeks of me blatantly ignoring that terrible gut feeling that nagged at me. I'd memorized every word by now.

Next time, you won't walk away.

The handwriting was neat, controlled, nothing like the chaos it promised. But I'd convinced myself my mother was right and had put it to rest.

This dinner with Ollie would be a good distraction. Or, at least, *a* distraction. His social media had taken off over the past year, and I was happy to hear that F1 wanted him to run their *Home Stretch* podcast, a show that focused on drivers' home races, or their chosen favorite race if they didn't have one. Between the podcast, his social media, and the published freelance articles, his name was all over motorsport.

Ollie had selected a place that had about half a dozen restaurant essays written about it from the sort of magazines you'd see in hotel lobbies. He was already seated at our table when I arrived, and I had to actively stop myself from gawking at him.

He sat with one leg crossed over the other, arm hooked casually over the back of his chair, blond hair catching the restaurant's ambient lighting in a way that seemed almost unfair. He looked like he'd walked off a magazine cover instead of just arriving for a casual dinner between old classmates.

When did he become this handsome? My mother had been right about one thing. He'd certainly grown up and filled out since school. The scrawny kid with braces had transformed into someone who belonged in a modeling career. Easily 6'1", he had a lean athletic build, a sharp jawline, and blond hair that fell in perfectly ruffled waves. But it was his eyes that really struck me: startlingly blue, almost unreal in the restaurant's lighting, framed by unfairly long lashes. No wonder his social media had exploded.

"Well, well, well, if it isn't Little Miss Sunshine!" he called out as soon as he noticed me, standing to kiss each cheek before pulling out my chair. "Even after a full day of qualifying, you still look magnificent."

My cheeks flushed as I took a seat. "Liar," I laughed. "I look like I could be auditioning for *The Walking Dead*."

"Rubbish!" His smile was warm and contagious. "If you were a zombie, I'd gladly let you take a chunk out of me." He winked, and I found myself smiling at his cheesy joke.

The server appeared with a wine list. I reached for it, but Ollie closed it with a decisive snap that felt more confident than rude.

"The Solvang Cabernet, please. A bottle." He placed the order with the easy confidence of someone who had thoughts on tannins and how assertive the taste of wine should be. I didn't usually drink before races, but I figured one glass wouldn't hurt.

"You like a cab, yes?" he asked, not bothering to wait for an answer before continuing. "Bold, structured, a little arrogant—"

"Ah, a bit like you," I teased. He cocked his head, and for just a moment uncertainty flickered across his face, before it vanished behind that classic smile that had captured audiences across social media.

"Guilty as charged," he laughed finally. "But this one has an excellent flavor profile, especially for the duck. Which you're absolutely getting."

"Oh, am I?" I raised a questioning eyebrow, amused by his presumption.

"Trust me." The way he said it, with that disarming smile and those impossibly blue eyes focused entirely on me, made it very easy to want to. "You know, I've been thinking about this dinner all day. When your mother mentioned you might be free, I immediately moved my other plans." He leaned forward. "I mean, dinner with *the* Lily Blackwood, future F1 champion. Dream of a lifetime!"

I felt my cheeks flush. "Ollie—"

"I mean it." His hand found mine across the table, thumb brushing my knuckles. "The way you drive? The way you handle the pressure? Most people would crumble, but you just shine brighter. It's remarkable. *You're* remarkable."

The sincerity in his voice caught me off-guard. Before he could finish, the wine came, which I appreciated. I took a sip, enjoying how much it didn't taste like cheap supermarket wine.

"Good?" Ollie asked, watching my reaction with obvious satisfaction.

"Annoyingly good," I admitted. "When did you become a wine snob?"

"We prefer to call ourselves *enthusiasts*," he corrected with mock offense. "And I'll have you know I've spent considerable time developing a sophisticated palate."

"You mean you Googled 'impressive wines' before dinner."

His laugh was genuine, unguarded. "You wound me, Blackwood. I can't show up to nice dinners like a complete philistine."

He'd planned this. He *wanted* to impress me. The realization sent butterflies through my chest—something I hadn't had since Las Vegas last year. It felt *good*.

For a while, conversation flowed effortlessly. Ollie told stories about advertisers demanding he wear branded socks on camera, about the chaos of managing his growing social media presence while trying to maintain journalistic integrity. I countered with tales of my neighbor's cat, who'd somehow learned to unlock windows back at my condo in London.

Somewhere in the corner, a table of tourists erupted into another round of laughter that bounced off the exposed brick walls. By the time the plates were cleared, I felt genuinely relaxed. The note tucked in my blazer pocket seemed less threatening, the championship pressure less suffocating, the world less complicated.

"So," Ollie said, leaning back in his chair, "was the duck as good as promised?"

I nodded, resting a hand on my stomach, glad that the race was in the afternoon tomorrow. "You win. The duck was incredible."

"Of course it was." His grin stretched wide, self-satisfied in a way that should've been obnoxious but somehow wasn't. "I have impeccable taste. You'll learn to trust me eventually."

Eventually. Like this was going to be a regular thing. The thought sent another pleasant flutter through my chest.

I rolled my eyes, laughing, reaching for my glass. From our little table outside, you could see the bustling walkway next to the restaurant. After a few more glances, movement on the sidewalk caught my attention.

An unmistakable figure emerged from the stream of pedestrians. Floppy brown hair caught the breeze and lifted slightly, framing features I'd come to know far too well. His purple jacket was draped effortlessly over one arm, his bag slung across his shoulders.

Henri.

He must have been on his way back from Georgia's. My eyes watched him, and just as I was about to excuse myself to the restroom in order to avoid the potential awkwardness of him seeing me, his gaze lifted. Our eyes met, and for a heartbeat, I didn't breathe.

I suspected Ollie noticed. His hand brushed mine where it rested on the tablecloth. To anyone passing, we must've looked like a couple leaning in for a private joke.

Henri slowed, just barely. His eyes flicked from Ollie's hand to my face, then back again, before his jaw tightened. He didn't stop, didn't say a word, just strode past, shoulders rigid.

"Hey, Henri!" Ollie called out cheerfully, voice carrying on the sidewalk.

Henri stopped, and for a moment I wondered if he might ignore us completely.

But he didn't. He turned, that same neutral expression from this afternoon's press conference strewn about his face.

"Ollie," Henri said finally. "Blackwood."

What is it with the last names?

Ollie beamed, leaning back with deliberate ease. "Henri Dubois, in the flesh. Been a while, mate! Come, pull up a chair." His hand brushed mine again on the table. Casual, but clearly intentional.

Henri's eyes lingered on that point of contact a second too long before lifting to mine. Something flickered in his expression—something I couldn't quite read.

"I don't want to interrupt," he said, the words polite but distinctly cold.

"Nonsense!" Ollie turned to me for approval, but I cast him a look that clearly said, *Stop while you're ahead.*

"How was your sister's?" I asked, injecting false cheerfulness into my voice.

"Fine." Henri's face remained studied, solemn, giving absolutely nothing away.

"We were just saying how Montreal has a way of surprising you. Fantastic food, great company." His eyes cut to me as he picked up his wine, toasting it in the air.

Henri gave the faintest nod, his eyes on Ollie's drink. "Enjoy your wine." With that, he adjusted the bag on his shoulder and continued on, disappearing into the crowd without a backward glance.

"Now, Henri is someone I cannot figure out. You know we used to race together in F3 and F2. Brilliant driver, but a mystery of a person. He was always so… closed off." Ollie chuckled as he shook his head. "That was a rough free practice he had on Friday… and an even rougher press conference." Ollie leaned in, eyes glinting. "If you ask me, he's circling the drain."

"Ollie!" I gave him a small rebuff. "He's just stressed because he finally has a chance to win this season. He spent so many years coming in second to his sister." Even though Henri had been a thorn in my side all season, hearing how others talked about him still irked me.

Maybe because I knew what it felt like to be talked about that way. Or because he used to be my friend, and there was a small part of me that still felt some loyalty to the friendship we once had.

"Well, that's very kind," Ollie said, studying me with those blue eyes, "considering he tried to ruin your free practice."

"That wasn't intentional," I sighed, surprising myself by defending him. "Henri's a lot of things, but he wouldn't deliberately block someone during a flying lap."

Ollie's eyebrows lifted, clearly amused. "Defending your rival now? Oh, sweet Lily. Will I ever be able to get you to say a mean thing about anyone?"

I half-laughed. "I'm not defending anyone." I took another sip of wine, feeling the warmth spread through my chest. "Just stating facts."

"Right." He dragged out the word, and I knew he was studying me. You can take the journalist out of the media pen, but never the insatiable curiosity out of the journalist.

The bill arrived, and Ollie slipped his card inside without hesitation, handing it back to the server without even looking at it.

"My treat," he said, waving me off before I could even find my wallet.

"Thank you. Dinner was lovely."

"And the company even better." He winked before sliding out of the table and pulling back my chair. He flagged down the waiter with an easy smile. "Would you mind taking a quick photo for us?"

The waiter obliged, taking Ollie's phone.

"Need at least one photo from tonight. Can't have dinner with the future World Driver's Championship winner and not document it."

The camera clicked.

"Cheers," Ollie said to the waiter, then he glanced at the photo. "Oh, that's a good one. We look properly fancy, don't we?" He pocketed his phone as we headed toward the door.

As we walked toward my hotel, Ollie offered his arm, but I shrugged him off, suddenly aware of how visible we were on the Montreal streets. When we reached the lobby of my hotel, I mumbled something about needing sleep before tomorrow's race. Ollie caught my hand briefly, his thumb brushing across my knuckles in a way that sent warmth spreading up my arm, before he leaned in for a kiss on each cheek.

"I had such a lovely time tonight, Lil," he said, genuine warmth in his voice. "Can't wait to see you on the podium tomorrow."

By the time I'd swiped my keycard and stepped into my room, exhaustion had hit all at once. The city noise outside faded to a muffled hum, and I let my blazer slide off, tossing it onto the chair with a contented sigh.

"Rough night?"

I jumped but couldn't suppress the smile that immediately spread across my face.

"Jesus, Andy. Don't sneak up on a woman."

My physio was sprawled in the armchair, legs crossed casually, studying me with knowing eyes.

"Team gave me an extra key. Someone's got to keep you alive." He looked me up and down, taking in my obvious good mood. "You look very nice for just a casual chat with Georgia. Where were you really?"

I kicked off my shoes and fell back onto the maroon sofa, unable to hide my grin. "None of your business."

"Darling, everything you do is my business." Perhaps a tad dramatic, although over the past three years, Andy had become more than my physio. He was coach, advisor, babysitter, and friend.

I held his stare before letting out a hesitated sigh. "Fine. With Ollie Johnson."

Andy groaned, dragging a hand down his face. "Oh, Lily, no. The podcaster?"

"He's not just a podcaster," I said defensively. "He writes articles too, and some good stuff."

"Uh-huh." Andy's tone was deeply skeptical. "Where did this *brilliant* writer take you?"

"This gorgeous little restaurant close to the hotel. We had a beautiful table outside with a nice view of the city."

Andy stared at me. "Outside? Where every reporter, sponsor, and half the bloody paddock could walk by? Lily—"

"It was *nice*, Andy," I interrupted, leaning forward enthusiastically. "Really nice. He ordered this great wine which he knew would pair excellently with the duck that he—"

"Um, did he order for you?" Andy's voice was flat with disbelief.

"He made a *recommendation*," I corrected, rolling my eyes. "No need to defend my honor. When did you become such a cynic? He was a complete gentleman."

"Lily…" Andy sat forward, elbows on his knees, his expression turning serious. "Just be careful with this one, yeah? I'm sure there's nothing he'd love more than dating an F1 driver to boost his career. The guy lives to turn stories into clicks and engagement."

"Why are you being like this?" I stood up, suddenly annoyed at having my good mood punctured. "I had a nice dinner with an old friend who turned out to be really interesting and charming. That's it. You're reading way too much into this."

Andy studied me for a long moment, and I watched something shift in his expression, realization hitting. "Oh my god. You like him, don't you?" He tsked, but a smile grew on his face. "Never thought blond hair and blue eyes was your type."

I crossed my arms, swaying a hip to the side. "I–I mean, he's nice. And yes, fine, I think he's attractive. Is that a crime?"

"Not a crime," Andy said carefully. "You're right. I'm sorry." He stood, grabbing his jacket. "Look, you're a grown woman, and I trust your judgment. Plus, since your mother threw him at you, I imagine he doesn't jeopardize this stupid morality clause that was shoved into your contract."

Right after I'd signed, I'd called Andy to complain about it. As my personal physio, he was well aware of all my contract stipulations. "Andy—"

"It's bullshit, Lily." His voice was sharp now, frustrated. "It's bullshit that you have one and your teammate doesn't. What century are we living in?"

"It's not exactly from Rennen," I said quietly, sinking back onto the sofa. "It's from a sponsor. They wanted… assurances."

"Assurances," Andy repeated flatly. "That you won't—what, date the wrong person?"

"That I won't create controversy that reflects poorly on their brand. And the team." The words came out like I'd rehearsed them. Because I had. To myself, to my mother, trying to make peace with it. "And my mother thought it was smart to add protections. Even after three years, it's still hard keeping sponsors as a woman, Andy. You know that. So, I agreed."

Andy's jaw worked, clearly biting back what he really wanted to say. "Right. Because God forbid you be seen with another driver in a way that might generate the wrong kind of headlines."

My mind flashed back to Las Vegas. To my hotel room, and the way Henri had looked at me that night—like he'd finally found something he'd been searching for. I would've tried. Would've found a way to navigate the complications, the clause, all of it. But he never gave me the chance to even suggest it. He just left after some pathetic excuse, and the rejection stung worse because I still didn't really understand why.

My throat bobbed as I pushed the memory down where it belonged, buried and forgotten. "Ollie's safe," I said, forcing brightness back into my voice. "He's media, not a competitor. No conflict of interest."

"Safe," Andy echoed, although his tone made it sound like an insult. He sighed, scrubbing a hand over his face. "Just keep your eyes open, yeah? Make sure he's interested in Lily the person, not Lily the driver."

"I'll be careful."

Andy grabbed my shoulder gently. "I'm heading out. Get some rest, all right?"

I nodded, watching as he grabbed his jacket and left. The door clicked shut behind him, leaving silence.

Safe.

The word clung to me as I pulled the covers up, my eyes tracing the hotel ceiling's texture in the dark. Ollie was safe, straightforward, and most importantly, interested in me. Not like Henri, who'd bolted the morning after our night together. He'd done all the things Henri hadn't.

The realization came unwanted but impossible to deny. Henri wanted a single night, then vanished. Told me racing took priority, that he lacked time for more. A relationship would've been too much of a distraction for him.

But not Ollie. And tonight had been *fun*. Devoid of any expectations or fighting or championship battles.

I found myself almost looking forward to the next time I'd see him.

Chapter Seven

Henri

I should've been over the moon today. Pole position at Montreal was exactly what I needed. It was a chance to silence the doubters who'd been whispering that Henri Dubois had lost his edge. This track suited me, and I'd won here two years ago.

But as the rain began to fall, a knot tightened in my stomach.

Everything around me faded as I prepared for the race. Michael's calm voice in my earpiece felt distant, like he was speaking from underwater.

"P1, Henri. Good grid position," Michael said through my earpiece, his voice maddeningly calm. "Rain's holding steady. Full wet tires to start, but we'll keep an eye on the weather. Hoping it dries up soon."

"Copy." My voice came out steadier than I felt.

I climbed into the car, rain drumming against my helmet as I settled into the cockpit. The familiar routine should've been comforting—harness clicks, wheel check, radio check—but my heart was already hammering too fast.

Behind me, Lily sat in P2. I could see her car in my mirrors, that distinctive Rennen livery that had haunted me all season. She'd be coming for me today. Whoever won this one would be the leader in the championship.

Just drive, I reminded myself. *Like you've done a thousand times before.*

Water pooled on the track, turning it into a minefield of standing water with limited visibility. My hands found their position on the wheel, muscle memory taking over even as my mind screamed warnings.

The lights began their sequence.

One red light. Then two lights. Rain hammered against my visor.

Three lights.

Breathe. Just breathe.

Four lights. Five lights.

Don't think about Miami. Don't think about the barriers. Just—

Lights out.

My start was perfect. Rear tires bit into the wet surface with just enough grip to not lose traction. Water sprayed around me, obscuring my vision as I maneuvered into the first turn, relying on instinct rather than clarity.

As lap after lap went by, I tried to ignore the ever-growing spiral of dread, but it was no use. Behind me, I heard the chaos, someone locked up, tires screeching, but I was already focused on Turn 1.

I pushed through the opening laps. There was a rhythm to my driving, a drive that should have felt like second nature. But today, the torrential rain transformed every corner into an uphill battle, and instead of exhilaration, I felt an overwhelming sense of fear.

"Lily's P2, three-tenths back," Michael confirmed.

Too close for my liking.

By lap ten, it became painfully clear that something was wrong. In the S-section, the momentum I usually embraced turned into a hesitation that nearly cost me.

Why couldn't I just let go of this feeling?

"Lily's pushing," Michael said on lap fifteen. "She's faster through the S-section."

Of course she was.

We settled into a rhythm over the next several laps, me defending, Lily attacking, both of us locked in a private war while the rest of the field tried to keep up. She tried moves I knew were coming because I'd studied her racing for three years. But with every lap, I could feel the car starting to struggle. The tires were giving up, losing grip incrementally. And my corrections were getting larger, more desperate.

At lap thirty-one, Michael's voice rang out, "Box, box." We switched to intermediates, tires for slightly drying but wet weather, and for a fleeting moment, hope sparked inside me. With fresh tires, I could feel the grip returning. For the first time all race, I felt a glimmer of hope.

Then Lily pitted.

"Slow pit stop at Rennen," Michael reported, satisfaction in his voice. "You've got some breathing room."

I pushed hard on the new tires, trying to build space between us, trying to create enough cushion that even my hesitation in certain corners wouldn't matter. For five precious laps, I let myself believe. The new tires gripped better, the car felt alive beneath me, and the gap between us held steady. I could win this. I could *actually* win this.

Then Lily passed P3, and then P2.

I felt it before Michael said anything—that creeping uneasiness that started in my gut and spread through my chest. When his voice finally came through, it only confirmed what I already knew.

"Lily right behind," Michael said, his tone shifting from confident to cautious. "One second faster than you that lap, Henri."

Then came the moment I'd been dreading, the part of the track that just hadn't worked for me all race. The part where I lost time to Lily.

The sharp hairpin stretched ahead of me, demanding everything—complete commitment and absolute trust. My brain knew exactly what to do. I'd taken this sequence a thousand times before.

But my body betrayed me.

My foot lifted without permission. A fraction of a second, nothing more. Just enough time for the panic to flood in: *You're going to crash, you're going to crash, you're going to—*

The rear end stepped out. My hands moved on instinct, catching the slide, wrestling the car back into line. I kept it off the barriers; kept it pointing forward.

For a split second, relief washed through me.

Then I realized what I'd done.

That moment of fear had cost me everything. In my mirrors, I saw Lily commit where I'd hesitated. She dove inside, fearless and precise, and suddenly we were side by side. So close I could see her helmet, could almost feel the heat of her engine.

We hung there together—two cars, two drivers, one clean racing line.

Then she was ahead.

"Fuck!" The word exploded out of me.

"Stay calm," Michael said, but I could hear the defeat in his voice. "Six laps left. You can still catch her."

But I couldn't, and we both knew it.

My tires were gone, shredded by my laps of desperation. Hers were newer, better, gripping where mine slid. And more than that, she wasn't fighting herself. She was just driving.

I pushed anyway, because that's what you do. You push until the checkered flag; until there's nothing left to give. But with every new lap, she pulled further ahead.

By the time we came around for the final lap, the gap between our cars was four seconds and growing. I crossed the line in second place, the word "P2" tasting like failure.

Through my visor, blurred slightly by rain, I watched Lily climb from her car. She stood on the chassis, fist punching skyward, screaming her triumph to the gray Canadian sky. The entire Rennen garage erupted around her, jumping and hugging and celebrating the kind of victory I'd let slip through my fingers.

I couldn't make myself move. The engine ticked as it cooled. Rain drummed against the car, and I just sat there, numb, trying to understand how I'd let this slip away.

When I finally forced myself out, my legs nearly gave out beneath me. I yanked off my helmet with shaking hands, rain immediately soaking through my hair, mixing with sweat and something that might have been tears. I kept my eyes down, looking anywhere except at her.

"Good drive," Michael said through my earpiece, but it felt obligatory. We both knew it hadn't been good enough.

The podium ceremony was torture. Standing one step down from Lily, watching her lift the trophy, listening to her anthem play while rain continued to fall. She sprayed champagne with the kind of abandon that came from genuine joy, soaking the crowd, soaking me, not caring about anything except her win.

When we finally escaped the podium, when the cameras had stopped rolling and the post-race interviews had ended, I couldn't get away fast enough. My team tried to follow, Michael calling my name, but I didn't stop until I'd reached my driver's room.

My phone buzzed; probably Michael checking in on me. Maybe to talk about what had gone wrong, but there was no point. No strategy could fix what had happened out there. No tweak to the setup could mend what felt broken inside me or erase the fear lodged in my chest.

I kept seeing it. That moment in the corners when my body refused to obey. When panic seized my foot and lifted it just enough. Just long enough for Lily to see the opening and take everything. The rain continued outside, steady and relentless, drumming against the windows. I sat in the dark, staring at nothing, feeling the weight of it all crushing down.

I was now second in the championship.

Fuck.

Chapter Eight

Henri

I lost the race an hour ago, but the real punishment was just beginning.

Bright lights buzzed overhead, casting a harsh glare across the cramped space packed with vultures who made their living picking apart every mistake you made on track. The weight of second place settled like lead in my chest, and now, an hour later, it had only gotten heavier.

Another second place. Another race where I'd done everything right except in the moment it mattered most.

My mind replayed that moment on a loop: that split second where I'd overcorrected, and Lily had slid past on the inside line. And I'd just watched her pull away.

Now I sat at a table, draped in sponsor logos and a fake smile, while Lily glowed beside me. We were only separated by a few points, but it felt like a mountain's worth.

I reached for my purple water bottle, if only to give my hands something to do besides tap my knee repetitively. The cold plastic against my palm gave me something else to focus on.

"Lily, congratulations on a brilliant drive today." The first journalist leaned forward. "That overtake on Henri was fearless. Can you walk us through it?"

"Honestly, I just saw the gap and went for it." Lily's genuine smile spread across her face—the one that had graced magazine covers and sponsorship ads for years. "Henri defended brilliantly, but in those conditions, you have to commit fully or not at all."

A small jab from Lily and a reminder of why I'd lost this race. I couldn't defend against her—not in those conditions. Not in the *rain*. The part of me that knew how to drive in wet weather had disappeared. My driving hadn't caused the accident in Miami, but my brain wouldn't let me keep going today. Fear and anxiety were funny like that.

"And Henri." The journalist turned to me. "That must have been frustrating, especially since you started on pole. You seemed to lose pace in the final stint. Were you finding it harder to push in today's conditions?"

Yes. "No. Today was about execution, and Lily executed better."

Another hand went up, and the moment I saw who it belonged to, I had to plant my feet on the floor just to stop myself from running.

Oliver Johnson. *I guess they're letting anyone into the post-race interviews now.*

That smug face stared at me from across the conference room, pencil poised above his notebook. The memory of him at dinner with Lily burned through my chest as Ollie smiled at me from his seat. He looked different from our F2 days—taller, more refined, carrying himself like he belonged in rooms he used to sneak into. Apparently, a hundred thousand followers had transformed him from paddock hanger-on to front-row journalist with a laminated press badge.

Judging by the fact he was at dinner with her last night, I knew Lily's mother at least approved of him. No way Lily would be allowed to attend a dinner like that without her mother's approval.

"Henri, after watching you struggle in wet conditions twice now, do you think there's a psychological component?" Ollie's voice carried that same easy confidence he'd displayed last night. "Some drivers develop mental blocks after crashes."

The blood drained from my face before rushing back twice as hot. My jaw clenched so hard I thought my teeth might crack.

"There's no mental block." The words snapped out of me. "I made a mistake. Drivers make mistakes. That's racing."

"But given your Miami crash—"

"I didn't crash in Miami." My voice rose before I could stop it. "Lily crashed into me. *Big* difference." Lily shifted beside me, her shoulder brushing mine for just a second before she pulled away.

"Of course," Ollie continued, scribbling something in his notebook with deliberate slowness. "Though some might argue that developing caution after such a violent incident is natural."

"I'm not cautious." My hands found the table edge, gripping hard enough that my knuckles went white. "I led the race for almost all of it. That's not cautious driving."

"Until the hairpin."

The room was dead silent, except for a few scribbles from various journalists, and the occasional cough. Every camera lens was pointed at me, waiting for me to break. My heart hammered against my ribs, and somewhere in the back of my mind, I knew I should smile and deflect like the media training taught us. But Ollie's smug expression, the same one he wore last night when he'd deliberately touched Lily's hand while looking straight at me, made something snap.

Something I couldn't explain.

"You want to talk about *that* corner?" I leaned forward. "Fine. I pushed the limits in conditions that would make most drivers back off. You know, Ollie, if you want to write about psychological problems, maybe focus on why you're asking questions designed to get a clickbait headline instead of doing actual journalism."

The F1 moderator stood, hands raised. "Let's keep this professional—"

But I was already up and moving toward the door, my vision tunneled, every sound magnified—the scrape of chairs, the rustle of notepads, the explosion of camera clicks that followed me like a swarm. The questions kept coming, voices overlapping into white noise, but I didn't stop.

The hallway air hit me like a slap, cooler than the press room, and I forced myself to walk instead of run. To maintain some shred of composure even as my heart felt like it was about to explode. People stared as I passed: mechanics, engineers, other team personnel. I could feel their eyes tracking me; could practically hear the whispers that would start the moment I turned the corner.

I shouldered through the garage, past my car, and finally reached my driver's room. The door had barely clicked shut before Ruth, Hermes's Head of PR & Communications, materialized, as if she'd been waiting in the wings for exactly this moment.

"What was that?" No preamble or sympathy. Just Ruth in full crisis-management mode.

I didn't answer. No part of me trusted any of the words that would come out.

"The FIA are probably drafting a reprimand as we speak." Her voice was tight.

I yanked my team polo over my head, the fabric catching on my chin before I wrestled it off and threw it toward the couch. It missed, crumpling on the floor. "Then send me the fine."

"It's not about the money, Henri."

"Then what?" I spun to face her. "I just spent thirty minutes being asked if I'm too traumatized to drive in the rain. If I've developed some psychological problem. Like one mistake erases everything I've done this season. Like I'm some fragile—"

"Stop." Ruth's voice cut through my rising anger. Her expression softened, but her tone stayed firm. The epitome of professionalism—everything I apparently couldn't be today. "It's about maintaining composure when they're trying to get a reaction. Which is exactly what that journalist wanted, and exactly what you gave him."

"Oliver." His name tasted bitter. "And he's *barely* a journalist."

"If he's in the press room, then he matters. You're a public figure. He has every right to ask difficult questions." She took a seat on the armrest of my couch, perching there as she watched me. "This is the job, Henri. Racing is only half of it. The rest is managing your image, handling these questions with grace."

"I'm not going to sit there and let people question my ability," I said, but even I could hear how hollow and defensive it sounded.

Ruth studied me for a long moment, and I wondered what she saw. A driver cracking under pressure? A liability? A PR disaster waiting to happen?

When my sister joined Valkyrie three years ago, she was the paddock's worst nightmare—impulsive, emotional, prone to exactly this kind of outburst. Now it was my turn to be the one who couldn't hold it together.

"I don't know what's gotten into you this season, Henri, but we need you to snap out of it. Racing is only part of your job. Don't forget that." She stood with a sigh, giving me one last glance before exiting the room, leaving me with my thoughts. The closed behind her with a finality that felt like judgment.

Silence crashed over the room like a tsunami. No more cameras or questions. No more eyes watching my every minute expression for signs of weakness. I stared at my reflection in the darkened television screen mounted on the wall. My hair stood in every direction where I'd run my hands through it, and my face looked almost unrecognizable with exhaustion.

Nothing this weekend had gone to plan. Absolutely nothing.

-

The hotel lobby was all polished marble and cold elegance, the kind of place designed to make you feel underdressed. Tonight's post-race team dinner had run three hours longer than it needed to, and I was tired. Tired of everyone's forced smiles over pasta, tired of awkward conversations about next weekend's race, all while they carefully avoided mentioning today's disaster.

I'd escaped as soon as was socially acceptable, citing my throbbing head as an excuse, which wasn't entirely a lie.

After practically sprinting to the elevator, I just caught the doors before they closed.

"Oh."

The sound caught me off-guard, and my head snapped up.

There, standing in the corner, was Lily.

She wore a black dress that hugged her curves perfectly, and her hair was loose around her shoulders instead of pulled back in its usual ponytail. With her champagne-flushed cheeks and slightly smudged eyeliner, she looked more relaxed than I'd seen her all season.

My throat went dry, and the elevator felt several sizes too small. That floral scent she wore filled the enclosed space, cutting through the lingering smell of the team's cigar smoke that clung to my jacket. It invaded my senses, making it impossible to think about anything except how close we were in this small space.

My finger found the button already illuminated. Thirty-first floor. Same as mine.

Merde.

I kept my gaze locked on the numbers climbing. Anywhere but at her. The walls seemed to press in with each passing second, the silence heavy enough to suffocate.

I made it exactly four floors before the quiet cracked me open. "You nearly took me out in Turn 9."

Her laugh was brittle. "Well, you nearly took me out in free practice."

My fingers started to tap against my thigh. "That was different."

"Why? Because it was *you* doing it?"

I glanced at her then; I couldn't help it. Those defiant green eyes met mine, challenging and fierce. Something hot and unwelcome twisted in my chest. Heat that had nothing to do with anger and everything to do with how that dress cut across her collarbone, how her lips were stained dark from whatever wine she drank at dinner.

"Because I wasn't myself," I snapped.

"Oh?" She seemed genuinely curious by my response, tilting her head in a way that made her hair slide over one bare shoulder. "Then what were you today?"

The answer stuck in my throat. *Trying not to think about what would happen if my car went into the wall again.* "Doesn't matter."

"It does if you're planning to wrap yourself around a barrier and take me with you."

"Like you did to me in Miami?" Heat flared in my chest, welcome this time, because anger I could handle. Anger made sense.

That got her. She spun, hands on her hips, and suddenly we were close enough that I could see her breathing had gone shallow and quick, making that gold necklace rise and fall against her skin. I could count the freckles scattered across her collarbone. "For the last—"

But before my brain could catch up with my body, before I could think through the consequences of stepping so close to Lily, I moved toward her, closing the distance between us in one step.

"You're insufferable," I whispered, my voice rough.

"And you're impossible." Her words came out breathless, and I watched her throat work as she swallowed.

My gaze dropped to her lips—I couldn't help it—and when I looked back up, I saw that she'd been watching my mouth too. My hand lifted, drawn toward that loose strand of hair falling across her cheek—

The distance between us evaporated.

Her mouth met mine halfway, fierce and demanding, and every coherent thought scattered. She tasted like red wine and something sweet, addictive, dangerous. My hand slid into her hair, angling her head back as she pressed closer, her fingers twisting into my jacket.

Wrong. After what I'd told her in Las Vegas, this was so wrong.

But her lips parted underneath mine, and suddenly wrong didn't matter. Nothing mattered except the soft sound she made in the back of her throat, the way her nails dug through my shirt, the heat of her body against mine in this too-small elevator climbing toward floors neither of us cared about anymore.

The elevator pinged.

We stumbled out still tangled together, her back hitting the hallway wall as my mouth found that spot just below her ear. She gasped, fingers tightening in my hair, pulling me closer.

"Which room?" The words came out rough against her throat.

"3117."

We made it maybe ten feet before I kissed her again—couldn't help it—spinning her around until she was pressed against the wallpaper. Her leg hooked around mine, the slit in her dress revealing smooth skin that my hand found without thinking.

She broke away, breathing hard. "Come on."

At her door, she fumbled with the key card, hands shaking as she swiped it once, twice. The light flashed red both times. I pressed against her back, kissing her shoulder, her neck, anywhere I could reach.

The lock finally clicked green. We practically fell through the doorway, my shin cracking against a small entryway table. Pain shot up my leg, but when I bent down to massage it, I saw a note with her name written across it on the floor. There was no signature, nothing to indicate who had sent it. I took it out of the envelope, read it twice, then looked up at Lily, who was now reaching for it.

"What is this?"

"Give it back." She grasped for it again, but I stepped back, the piece of paper clasped tightly in my hands.

"What is this?" I demanded again. "Someone threatened you. When?"

"It's just a note, Henri." She rolled her eyes, though something flickered in her expression—something that looked like fear but was quickly replaced with indifference. "Can you not make this into a whole thing?"

"A whole thing?" I stared at her. "Someone is *threatening* you."

"Someone sent me hate mail. It happens." She snatched at the card again, and this time I let her take it, watching her fingers close around it like it meant nothing. Like it hadn't made my blood run cold. Like it wasn't making me want to track down whoever wrote it and—

"This isn't a tweet or an Instagram comment, Lily." I fought to keep my voice level. "This was *given* to you. When?"

"After Miami." She tossed the card back onto the coffee table like it was junk mail. "And nothing's happened since, so clearly it was just some idiot blowing off steam."

"You don't know that's all this is."

"And you don't know it isn't." She moved past me toward the minibar, and I caught another wave of that floral scent. It didn't distract me this time; I was too busy trying to reconcile how casually she was treating all this, like we were discussing the weather. "Look, Henri, I appreciate the concern or whatever this is, but I'm fine. It's one note from one crazy person. I'm not going to run to security over every piece of hate mail I get."

"This isn't…" I grabbed the card again, holding it up. "This specifically mentions me. 'Mess up Henri again.' What does that even mean?"

She took a long drink of water, her expression unreadable. "Probably referring to Miami. You know, when I 'caused' that whole incident." Air quotes around the word "caused." "Even though the stewards cleared me."

"That's not what this sounds like."

"Then what does it sound like to you?" She set the bottle down with more force than necessary. "Because to me, it sounds like some fan got upset their favorite driver didn't win. It's creepy, sure, but it's not exactly a death threat."

"'Next time, you won't walk away' sounds pretty threatening to me."

"What do you want me to do, Henri?" She spun to face me fully, exasperation clear in her voice. "Go crying to the FIA? Make headlines about how poor Lily Blackwood can't handle a little hate mail? Give the media another reason to question whether I'm tough enough for this sport?"

"This isn't about being tough."

"Of course it is." She laughed, but there was no humor in it. "Everything is about being tough enough, strong enough, good enough. You think if I report this, it'll stay quiet? Someone leaks it, and suddenly I'm the fragile female driver who needs extra security or who can't handle the pressure. I saw that last year with my friend in Indy Car."

I stared at her—at the defiant tilt of her chin, the way she stood like she was ready for a fight. But I could see it now: the slight tremor in her hands, the too-quick breathing she was trying to hide.

"You're scared," I said quietly.

"I'm annoyed." She turned away. "Annoyed that you're making this into something it's not, and annoyed that you apparently think I can't handle my own problems."

"That's not—"

"Just leave it alone, Henri." She moved to the door, opening it pointedly. "It's one note. I'm not going to let some coward with a pen ruin my night."

I didn't move. "What if there's another one?"

"Then I'll throw that one away too." She gestured to the open door.

"Well, you *haven't* thrown this one away."

Without hesitation, Lily grabbed the card from me, dropping the piece of paper into the trash closest to the suite's entrance, a smug look on her face.

"Happy?"

"You should still report it," I said, softer this time.

"You know what, Henri? I'm not really taking notes right now."

I looked down at the note in the bin, almost appreciating the irony of her terrible joke.

I walked to the door, stopping just on the other end of the threshold. "Lily…"

"*Good night.*"

The door closed with a soft click that felt like a dismissal. I stood in the empty hallway, staring at her room number, pressing my palm flat against the wood for a moment before letting it drop. Then I pulled away and made myself walk.

Her kiss clung to me all the way back to my room. So did the threat.

I unlocked my door and stood there in the dark, waiting for one of them to fade. By morning, I'd stopped expecting them to.

Chapter Nine

Lily

There was nothing I loved more than visiting Georgia and Luca's Monaco flat. Their home was between a lovely bakery and one of my favorite bars in the city. Each morning, I woke to the scent of fresh croissants drifting up from the bakery below, and each night, I fell asleep to laughter.

"Don't take this the wrong way," I said, pinching the zipper at my ribs, "but your boyfriend is *exceptionally* bad at hiding a ring box."

Georgia's eyes lifted in the vanity mirror, a sly grin etched onto her face. "I've pretended all month that I haven't seen that box." She widened her eyes in mock surprise, pressing a hand to her chest. "Luca! I had no idea! What a complete and total shock!"

I snorted. "Don't quit your day job. Acting may not be your calling."

She threw a makeup sponge at me, and I caught it midair, laughing as I tossed it back.

Georgia had been there for me over the past three years. The grueling races, the endless media scrutiny, the constant pressure to prove myself in a sport dominated by men. She was the one constant in my chaotic life, and I missed her desperately as my teammate. Luca was a fine substitute, but things were always so easy with Georgia.

"So," Georgia said, turning to me with a sly grin, "Henri mentioned he saw you with Ollie the other night. How was your *date*?"

I felt my cheeks burn, and I wanted to ask if that was all he'd mentioned.

"It was really nice, actually," I said, aiming for casual. "We caught up on old times. He's clearly doing well for himself these days."

Georgia raised an eyebrow. "If I'm being honest, I've always secretly hoped you'd end up with Henri," she laughed.

How close she'd almost been to getting her wish…

"Any *sparks* after the dinner?"

I shook my head no, ignoring her shimmying shoulders and giddy smile.

"Well, maybe next time. You deserve some fun! Just because we're always traveling, doesn't mean you can't do a little dating… or other *things*. I mean, who was the last guy you even kissed?"

Henri's face flashed through my mind, and I was immediately transported back to Montreal. I reached for my drink and took a long sip, contemplating how "your brother" probably wasn't the right answer.

Georgia dabbed another layer of highlighter across her face. "Look, Ollie's cute, and he understands our world without being in it."

I nodded. "It was nice to get out. He planned everything, and it was nice to feel wanted. Even if he is a member of the press…"

Georgia laughed. "Well, Ollie sounds lovely, and he's been nothing but nice to Valkyrie in the paddock. I know

Henri was annoyed with him after the press conference in Montreal, but it's Ollie's job to ask those tough questions." Georgia shrugged. "Henri doesn't need to make enemies with the press. In fact, it's why I invited Ollie tonight. Hoping he and Henri could smooth out whatever weird tension that was in the press conference."

"You did?" My champagne sloshed dangerously close to the rim. "You think that'll work?"

Georgia glanced meaningfully at a framed photo of her and her brother on the dresser. A photo of them from her World Driver's Championship win last year in Brazil. I watched Georgia carefully. If I'd noticed the unsettling way Henri was acting in the paddock, then she *definitely* had. She toyed with a hairpin, her expression troubled.

"Something is off with Henri," she said quietly. "He's been a bit off all season. He used to be so joyful. I mean, all we'd talk about was racing. Now, it's like it's the farthest thing from his mind." Georgia worried like it was her job. It was probably what made her such a dedicated friend, and a fierce teammate at Valkyrie F1.

"He'll be fine," I said, aiming for light and breezy. "This week's Grand Prix is Monaco. He was born to win here."

"That's what scares me." She turned to look at me directly. "It's been eight years, and he's never won Monaco before. If I he doesn't this weekend, I don't know what it'll do to him. All those years of losing your home race—your *dream* race—does something to you."

I knew that feeling intimately. Three years of losing Silverstone had been gutting enough. But eight years of Monaco? That would break anyone.

I squeezed her shoulder reassuringly. "Well, maybe this weekend will be the turning point. If anyone can win Monaco, it's Henri Dubois."

Part of me couldn't believe I was saying that about my competitor. The truth was, I wanted desperately to win this weekend—a thought best kept to myself, I decided. Not that Georgia didn't see through it.

"Well, with you out there pushing him, he'll have no choice but to bring his A game."

Luca stepped fully into the room. He was dressed in tailored navy slacks and a crisp white button-down, the sleeves rolled up to reveal his tanned forearms. He really had a way of looking effortlessly stylish even in the simplest of outfits.

"Don't you two look stunning?" he said, his eyes twinkling as they landed on Georgia. "Especially you, *amore*."

"You don't look so bad yourself," she teased, pressing a kiss to his cheek. "I think we're about ready. Lil?"

I nodded, taking one last glance in the mirror before following them out to the living room. They'd transformed the flat for the party, with twinkling string lights draped along the walls and vases of vibrant flowers scattered throughout. Soft music played from the beautiful record player Georgia had gifted Luca for Christmas the year prior.

People arrived one by one, each one greeting the hosts with an unspoken eagerness. I don't think it was lost on anyone what was going to be happening tonight.

Someone shouted my name from the hallway.

"Lily!" Ollie called out, dragging me in for a hug. When he pulled back, he kept his hands on my shoulders, studying my face like I was something precious. "God, you look absolutely stunning."

"Oh, Ollie," I laughed, my cheeks warming.

Georgia just chuckled before thanking Ollie for the flowers.

"That was sweet of you to bring flowers." My eyes flicked over to the bouquet. An assortment of roses—nothing like the ones that had appeared in my room after Miami.

"I was glad to be invited. Gives me another excuse to see you! Now, I want to hear all about your Monaco prep." Ollie waved his phone in the air. "Off the record, of course." He winked.

Henri stepped through the door a moment later, looking annoyingly handsome in charcoal trousers and a tight shirt that hugged his chest perfectly. A smile broke across Henri's face, slow and genuine, and it carried a warmth that spread through his eyes and reached every corner of the room. It was almost unsettling how much gravity his smile held—how it drew me in like it was meant only for me.

Ollie said something beside me, before leaving my side, but I'd stopped listening. Henri's hair was still damp from a shower, and I could see where he'd run his fingers through it, leaving it messier on one side. I watched him touch it self-consciously before dropping his hand and shoving it in his pocket instead. The door closed behind him and carried his cologne forward: vanilla and cedar, unmistakably him. My champagne glass was suddenly slippery in my palm.

I hadn't been able to stop thinking about the kiss in the elevator all week.

The memory kept ambushing me at the worst moments. During practice laps, in team briefings, in the shower. His mouth on mine, the elevator wall cold against my back, his hand at my jaw tilting my face up. The way he'd tasted like whiskey and bad decisions. How I'd gripped his shirt and pulled him closer instead of pushing him away. The sound he'd made against my lips, somewhere between relief and surrender. I couldn't stop replaying it over again in my mind.

"Henri!" Georgia exclaimed, hurrying over to embrace her brother. "I'm so glad you made it."

"Wouldn't miss it," he replied, but there was a tightness to his voice that made me wonder how many excuses he'd gone through before deciding to show up.

He gravitated toward the back of the room, falling into conversation with Éliott about their upcoming photoshoot. But every few minutes, I felt his gaze land on me. A quick glance when he thought I wasn't looking. Our eyes would meet for a split second before one of us would look away. A game of chicken neither of us wanted to be playing.

Part of me wanted to approach him and bring up Montreal. But what would I even say? *Any idea who sent me that threat? Does that kiss also consume your every waking moment?*

Both terrible options, especially the last one.

Ollie re-appeared beside me with a fresh drink, his hand immediately finding the small of my back. "There you are. Sorry, I got distracted. I've been fielding questions about the podcast all night. Apparently, everyone wants to know who I'm interviewing next, which is a bit annoying, considering all I can think about is getting five minutes alone with you."

From across the room, I caught Henri watching us, something unreadable crossing his face before he looked away.

"The podcast's really taking off then?" I asked, turning my attention back toward him.

"It is, but that's not what matters right now." His thumb traced small circles against my back through the fabric of my dress. "What matters is that you're here, and you look absolutely stunning. I haven't had nearly enough of your attention tonight."

Before I could answer, another guest approached Ollie. I took the moment to excuse myself, mumbling something about needing the bathroom. Truthfully, I needed air, and I was happy to discover that the balcony was blissfully empty.

Grabbing a fresh champagne flute on my way out, I let the door slide shut behind me, muffling the party noise. Music from a yacht below drifted up through the warm night. I raised my glass, took a sip too quickly, and immediately regretted it. The bubbles burned down my throat. I bent over coughing, bracing one hand against the cool metal railing.

A glass of water appeared beside my champagne flute. I didn't have to look to know who it was. Henri's presence was always something I could feel—in the paddock, in press conferences, in a room full of people.

"Thanks," I managed between coughs. Our fingers brushed in the exchange. Barely a touch, but I felt it everywhere.

Henri leaned against the railing, close enough that I could see the faint scar above his eyebrow. "Try not to die." He nodded toward the drink. "It would ruin Georgia's night."

"Yours too?" My voice came out smaller than intended.

Why would you say that? I chastised myself.

But I knew why. Because despite everything—the rivalry, the tension, the careful distance we'd maintained for months—part of me still remembered when we were friends. When hearing his voice hadn't made my chest tight with frustration and anger.

Henri watched the boats floating in the harbor instead of me. "I like seeing Georgia this happy."

"You and me both." I turned to look at him. The city lights caught the exhaustion etched around his eyes, the tension he carried in his jaw, the shadows in his eyes that hadn't been there at the start of the season.

I opened my mouth, almost ready to ask about Montreal, but I closed it again. What would be the point? It was just a kiss. A kiss that had ended with me kicking him out. Nothing had changed between us.

So, instead, I opted for something safer. "How are you really?"

He glanced at me, surprise flickering across his face. Like he hadn't expected the concern. Like we didn't do that anymore—ask real questions or care about each other's answers. Like our last interaction hadn't ended with me kicking him out of my room after a mind-numbing kiss.

"Ask me Sunday night," he said quietly, almost a whisper.

"That bad?"

"That complicated." He drained his glass in one sip. "I'm just ready for this weekend to be over."

I understood that too well. It was almost impossible to describe how a driver felt about their home race. All your friends and family were there to watch you win on the streets they had raised you on. It was exhilarating and fun and magical.

Unless you lost.

"Eight years is a long time to wait for something," I said quietly.

He finally looked at me. "Three years is too."

Silverstone. He meant Silverstone.

The understanding passed between us without words. We both knew what it was to want something desperately and have it slip through your fingers year after year. To feel the weight of expectation, the fear of failure, the desperate hunger for redemption. No one quite understood it like Henri, that feeling of carrying the weight of your deferred dreams.

"Well," I said, lifting my champagne glass, "may we both be miserable together this weekend."

A tiny hint of a smile crossed his face. Our glasses clinked in the Monaco night, and for just a moment, the tension between us felt less like animosity and more like understanding, almost like we weren't enemies. The old friend I'd once longed for almost seemed recognizable, at least for a minute, and it was nice not to be at each other's throats.

His shoulder edged closer to mine on the railing, and without meaning to, I found myself leaning into it. The smallest shift of weight, just enough that our shoulders touched as we both watched the lights twinkle along the water.

Henri went very still beside me. Then, slowly, carefully, he turned his head to look at me. I could see the gold flecks scattered through his dark eyes.

"You can win this weekend, Henri."

In the moment, it felt like the right thing to say. And I believed it to be true. Henri was capable of magnificent things, and no feud between us was going to stop me from believing in him.

"Yeah?" The single word was barely more than a whisper, fragile and uncertain and achingly hopeful.

"Yeah."

For a long moment, we just looked at each other. His gaze dropped to my lips, then back up. His hand moved on the railing beside mine.

This felt like Las Vegas all over again. Like Montreal the other week. There was no denying this indescribable pull between us.

His words from Las Vegas echoed in my head even as his hand moved on the railing beside mine. I watched, heart in my throat, as his pinkie finger extended slowly toward mine. Giving me time to pull away. Time to stop this before it started.

I didn't move.

Move away, Lily, my rational brain screamed, but I couldn't make myself step back; couldn't break whatever spell had settled over us on this balcony. Even though I knew better. Even though his actions never seemed to match his words, and I was tired of trying to figure out which version of Henri was real—the one who pushed me away in Las Vegas, or the one who couldn't seem to stop pulling me close.

"Lily—" His voice came out rough, raw with something he wasn't saying. His pinkie hooked deliberately around mine, and the simple touch reverberated through my entire body.

Then Luca's voice called from inside, nervous and excited, and we both knew what was coming.

And just like that, the spell was broken. Henri recoiled back into himself, taking a step back.

"Showtime," he murmured.

"You saw the ring too? Hiding it in the guest room wasn't exactly a genius idea." I knew Henri had stayed with them while his kitchen was under renovation last month.

"Who knows? Maybe you'll be able to join them soon." Henri nodded toward Ollie, who was chatting up Éliott at the makeshift bar.

I bristled at Henri's implication. "Ollie and I are just friends," I said coolly. "And it's none of your business anyway."

Henri held up his hands in mock surrender. "My mistake. I just thought, with him being your date tonight and all…"

"He's not my date," I snapped, perhaps a bit too sharply. "Georgia invited him. That's it."

Something flickered in Henri's eyes. Relief, maybe? But he masked it quickly with a shrug. "Just be careful with that one."

I frowned, turning to face him fully. "What's that supposed to mean?"

He shook his head, setting his glass down on the coffee table with a little more force than necessary. "Nothing. Forget I said anything."

The balcony door slid open. "So sorry to interrupt," Ollie said brightly, laying easy fingers at the small of my back. "Georgia needs you both."

Henri's hand dropped from the rail. I didn't see his expression. Didn't let myself look as we walked inside.

As if on cue, Luca clinked a spoon against his glass, drawing everyone's attention. He stood in the center of the room, Georgia beaming at his side. "Thank you all for coming tonight," he began, his voice warm with affection.

His eyes shone with love and adoration as he gazed at Georgia. "I wanted to gather our closest friends and family here to celebrate something very special. Georgia, *amore mio*, you've been by my side through every triumph and challenge. Your unwavering support, your fierce determination, and your boundless compassion inspire me every single day."

Luca reached into his pocket and pulled out a small velvet box. Georgia's hand flew to her mouth, her eyes wide with surprise.

He dropped to one knee, opening the box to reveal a stunning diamond ring. "Georgia Dubois, you are the love of my life, my partner in every sense of the word. I can't imagine my life without you—without your laughter, your love, your constant support. You're my best friend, my soulmate, my everything. Will you make me the happiest man alive and marry me?"

Tears streamed down Georgia's face as she nodded. "Yes!" she exclaimed, her voice trembling with joy. "Yes, of course I'll marry you!"

The room erupted into cheers and applause as Luca slipped the ring onto Georgia's finger and swept her into a passionate kiss.

Friends and family swarmed the happy couple, offering their congratulations and excitement. Making my way over to Georgia, I pulled her into a tight hug.

"I'm so happy for you," I murmured, my voice thick with emotion.

She squeezed me back, her eyes shining. "Thank you, Lil."

I shook my head, smiling. "You two were made for each other. I'm just glad I got to be here to see it happen."

Ollie was in the kitchen, chatting with a few of the other drivers. I made my way through the hallway, only to bump my hip into Henri. In trying to move away, his arm brushed mine, and we both awkwardly tried to avoid the other's gaze.

I stepped back quickly, breaking contact. "Sorry," I muttered, ducking my head to hide the flush creeping up my neck.

Ollie and Éliott materialized behind us. "Well, I daresay everyone in the room saw that proposal coming. Too bad they've ruined this for the rest of us," Éliott laughed.

Ollie raised an eyebrow at Éliott's comment. "Ruined what for the rest of you?"

"Let's just say, some people aren't too keen on their drivers dating each other. It worked for Georgia and Luca, but I don't think the top bosses of other F1 teams want to risk their drivers sharing secrets. I've heard rumors of morality clauses starting to make their way into contract renewals."

"My Rennen contract has one. Apparently, my sponsors don't want any media circus around any potential relationships," I sighed.

"You have a morality clause in your contract?" Ollie seemed genuinely surprised.

I nodded. "My mother said a few sponsors insisted on it when they signed me. Rennen seemed to be pleased with the idea, too."

Éliott grabbed Henri, pulling him in by the shoulders. "Well, Hermes don't need to with this one."

"Ha, because his only love is racing?" I added, trying— and failing—not to sound too bitter.

Éliott leaned in, poking his friend's ribs. Henri's eyes met mine for the briefest moment, a small flash of understanding passing between us.

I held his gaze, unflinching, for a moment longer.

I need to focus on the championship next year. On winning. There can't be any distractions.

Those were his exact words right before he walked out of my hotel room, leaving me alone to process what just happened. If racing was his only love, he had no one to blame but himself.

I turned back to Ollie. The safe choice. "So, Ollie, I hear the podcast's smashing records this week."

"Yes, it's been great. Henri, have you had a chance to listen? I think you'd find it quite interesting."

Henri blinked as if coming out of a trance. "No."

"Episode four covered mental resilience in motorsport," Ollie said, his eyes lighting up with enthusiasm. "I interviewed a sports psychologist who works with several F1 drivers. Fascinating stuff about performance anxiety, the weight of expectations." His gaze shifted meaningfully to Henri. "I'd love to have you on as a guest speaker. It'd be great to get something out of a championship contender."

Henri shifted his weight, his hand going to the back of his neck. "I don't think so." His voice came out clipped. "I don't have time for that sort of thing right now."

"Of course, of course. Just thought it might be—"

"No." Henri's face went deathly still.

The rejection hung awkwardly in the air. Ollie smiled, unbothered, and turned his attention back to Éliott, but I caught the satisfied glint in his eye. He got exactly what he wanted: Henri rattled, off-balance, that careful composure cracking just enough to show.

I watched Henri retreat further into himself, his shoulders drawing in, that same haunted look settling back over his features. The one that had been there all season. The one Georgia had noticed. The one that made him look like he was carrying the weight of something far heavier than just a championship fight.

For a moment, I almost felt sorry for him.

Almost.

—

By midnight, the party had thinned to soft laughter and half-empty glasses. Outside, the harbor lights had dulled to a slow shimmer, and the noise of the bar below lulled into nothingness.

Georgia had kicked off her heels hours ago. Her hair had fallen from its elegant updo and now framed her face in happy, lazy curls. She clinked her empty flute against mine.

"You know, there's still time to change your mind," I teased.

"Wouldn't dream of it!" She nudged my knee. "I hope everyone can find their Luca. Especially you, Lily. You deserve someone special."

I snorted. "Well, until then, I'll just have to settle for my car. We have a toxic relationship, but at least it's exclusive."

That made her laugh, and it hit me how rare it was to see her this calm. No cameras, no interviews, no pressure. We rarely got these moments during the season.

Luca came in holding two cups of chamomile tea. "Now that's what I call a successful party."

Georgia reached for him, taking a mug as he set another one next to me. "It was perfect. Thank you."

He bent to kiss Georgia's forehead, the gesture so easy it ached a little to watch. "Wouldn't have been without you." He then turned to me. "Both of you."

I gestured to the empty canapé plate. "I only helped by showing up and eating most of your food."

"Exactly," Luca said, eyes crinkling. "And what an excellent job you did."

Georgia's phone lit up the dim room, buzzing harshly against the glass coffee table. She glanced at it, then away. Luca's phone followed with its own insistent hum. He sighed, shoulders dropping as he reached for it.

"Probably the team again."

My phone flashed next, screen illuminating my lap. Then again. And again. I watched the notifications stack one after another, each buzz like a tiny warning bell. My thumb hovered over the screen, not quite ready to swipe.

It was Luca who broke the silence first. "Uh… Lily?"

"What?" I asked, too slow, dread already pooling in my stomach.

He turned his screen toward me. Even upside down, I recognized it.

A grainy hotel hallway. Time stamp: 11:47 p.m. Henri, in his bright purple Hermes racing polo, his hand on a door handle. My door handle. The angle suggested security footage, or someone with a phone at the end of the corridor.

The headline screamed across every feed:

RENNEN'S LILY BLACKWOOD SPOTTED WITH RIVAL HENRI DUBOIS IN LATE-NIGHT HOTEL RENDEZVOUS.

"Shit." The word came out strangled. "You've got to be kidding me."

Georgia was already scrolling, her expression shifting from confusion to concern. "When was this?"

"Montreal. After the race." My hands had gone numb. "He followed me to my room. We were… arguing."

Among other things.

In that moment, I thanked whoever was watching above that the press had caught Henri leaving my room, and not us getting into it.

"About what?" Luca asked carefully.

I couldn't answer that. How it had evolved from a kiss in the elevator and the hallway to a fight about the note that wouldn't stop haunting me. I couldn't tell them about the note, about Henri demanding I report it, about how quickly everything spiraled.

Or the kiss. I definitely couldn't tell them about that.

Georgia kept reading, her voice quiet. "'Sources close to the situation confirm that Blackwood's late-night rendezvous with rival driver Dubois raises serious questions about her commitment to racing. The first female driver for Rennen was brought on with the understanding that she would maintain complete focus on her championship campaign, not engage in romantic entanglements compromising team dynamics and competitive integrity.'"

The words hit like physical blows.

"This is insane." I stood, my legs unsteady. "I mean… that was me kicking him out!"

"Lily." Georgia's voice was gentle but firm. "I'm sure it will resolve itself." She stood, crossing to where I'd frozen by the window. Her hand found my shoulder, warm and steady. "Lily, look at me."

Her eyes were all kind and sympathetic. The same ones that had talked me through countless bad races, terrible press conferences, every moment I'd wanted to quit.

"This will blow over," she said firmly. "You know how these things work. Tomorrow there'll be some new scandal, some other driver caught doing something worth headlines. By Thursday, this'll be buried under practice times and strategy talk."

"The team is going to be so annoyed. They basically hate Henri and Hermes. Not to mention that morality clause I told you about… Ugh, my mother is going to have a field day with this."

"You haven't done anything wrong," she cut in, her voice sharp enough to make Luca glance up. "One photo of you and Henri? That's a weak story at best. It could be anything. Like *arguing*." Her emphasis on the word told me she didn't exactly believe that was all we were doing.

"Right," I managed, though my throat felt tight.

Georgia eyed me cautiously for a moment. "So, why was my brother there so late anyway?" There was almost an edge of eagerness in her eyes.

"We were just bickering about the race." Not entirely false.

Last season, Georgia had made subtle—or not so subtle—jokes about me and Henri dating. But judging by her slightly disappointed face, Henri still hadn't told her about Las Vegas.

"Come on." She took my phone from my hands, powering it down before I could protest. "You're staying here tonight anyway. We'll deal with this in the morning."

"Georgia."

"In the morning," she repeated, gentler now. "Right now, we're going to bed. And tomorrow, when you wake up, this will already feel smaller than it does right now."

Luca appeared with a glass of water, setting it on the side table. "She's right. Rennen's PR team will handle it. That's what they're paid to do."

I took the water, more for something to do with my shaking hands than actual thirst. "Okay," I heard myself say. "Okay."

Georgia guided me toward the guest room, her arm around my waist. "Well,"—she paused at the guest-room door with a wicked grin—"with any luck, hopefully the size of this ring will distract everyone from that shitty article."

Despite everything, I choked out a snort. "You'd better flash that thing around tomorrow!"

She threw her arms in the air. "I fully intend to!"

Chapter Ten

Henri

Monaco was supposed to be *my* moment. My home race and my chance to finally win the crown jewel of motorsport. The race that had eluded me since I became a Formula 1 driver.

Instead, every "journalist" who approached me wanted to talk about Lily's hotel room. The photos of me entering her room were plastered across every tabloid, and the speculation was running wild.

And the worst part? I was to blame.

I shouldn't have followed her, but after our moment in the elevator, I'd let my heart override any common sense. All because some part of me couldn't let go. Now Monaco was consumed by speculation about a relationship that didn't exist—had never existed, because I hadn't let it.

Imagine if we'd decided to date after Las Vegas, I thought. *What a nightmare this all would be.*

Although, if I were being truthful, it felt like a nightmare anyway.

I looked out of the Hermes office and onto the harbor, where yachts crowded the water for the race weekend. Verhoeven cleared his throat as he tried to get my attention. He sat centered at the conference table in the Hermes briefing room, arms crossed. Ruth was to his right, a tablet likely full of news articles glowing in front of her. Michael took the last chair a fraction back from the table. His crossed arms did nothing to give me comfort.

Verhoeven's voice cut through the silence as he held up his phone. "Of all the drivers on the grid, Henri. Of all the teams." He shook his head, disgust clear on his face. "You were photographed leaving Lily's room? The driver currently beating you in the championship." His eyes flickered back down to his phone, clearly assessing the photo of me leaving her hotel room, before looking back up at me accusingly. "Is this why you were so unfocused in Montreal?"

I froze, pulse thudding in my ears. His words weren't so much a question as a statement he clearly believed. I stared at the conference-room table, counting each dent in front of me. When Ruth rotated the tablet toward me with manicured fingers, I had no choice but to look. The headline shone bright on the screen.

Hermes F1's Henri Dubois pictured entering hotel room with Rennen's Lily Blackwood after shocking Montreal loss.

I didn't need to read the story to know exactly what was being said about me. F1's "former" star had lost his edge because he was sneaking around with Lily Blackwood. Anger rose in my chest, but it became tangled with something worse: a humiliation that grew with every second I sat there silent.

"Nothing happened," I managed.

"Then explain to me why you were in her hotel room." Verhoeven's voice was ice.

"We just talked."

Verhoeven scoffed. "You *just* talked."

To be fair, when he said it out loud, I realized how ridiculous it sounded. In what world would anyone believe Lily and I were "just" talking at 1 a.m. after a race, and in her suite, no less?

I didn't know what was worse: Verhoeven believing I was losing control because of a woman, or because driving in the rain filled me with panic.

Fuck. It needed to be neither.

He leaned back in his chair, slowly tapping the pen between his fingers as he watched me. "Your focus *must* return before this weekend. This is not just any race. Our home hospitality is sold out. Your friends and family will be there. There will be eyes everywhere."

He leaned forward, setting the pen down with careful precision. "Monaco is where we prove Hermes belongs at the top."

Ruth shifted in her seat, her nail clicking against the tablet screen as she scrolled. "Starting tomorrow, we need you laser-focused on media appearances. We talk about the race only."

"If they ask about the photos?" I heard myself say.

"You give them nothing," Ruth said firmly. "Your sister asked you to return something to Lily, and since you were staying at the same hotel, you agreed. That's all."

I nodded, my throat tight. I didn't trust my voice to say anything that wouldn't make this worse, so I decided not to wait for dismissal. The chair scraped against the floor as I pushed back, my legs unsteady underneath me. I offered a curt nod to Verhoeven before leaving.

"Henri," Verhoeven called out just as I reached the door.

I turned back.

"We will win Monaco," he said, his voice flat with certainty. "Nothing else matters this weekend. Understood?"

"Understood."

By the time I'd reached my room, Michael caught up to me. "They're right about one thing."

I opened the door, then turned just enough to be polite. "Which is?"

"You have been off."

The words landed because they were the only ones spoken without performance. "You think I'm distracted because of *her*?"

Michael's gaze held mine. "I don't know what it is, but I'm going to find out, Henri."

He then disappeared down the hallway, his hands buried deep in his jacket pockets. I entered my room and sank onto the plush couch in the corner, pulling out my phone. The headlines were still there, waiting for me. I should've put it down, but instead, my thumb fell into doom-filled scrolling. Post after post.

Rennen's Sweetheart Corrupts Hermes' Star

Dubois Distracted. Can He Recover Before Monaco?

But it was the comments that frustrated me.

She's ruining him.

Women don't belong in F1 if they can't keep their legs shut.

She'll crash into him again next week just to stay relevant.

My jaw felt tight as I went through reach one. I closed the app before pulling up my contacts. Her smiling face stared back at me, her name in block letters above it with the jet emoji she'd demanded I add. A symbol from our first vacation together, back when our friendship was new and uncomplicated.

You okay?

I typed out the two words, staring at them until the letters blurred, then deleted them. Typed them again. Deleted them harder.

What could I possibly say to make this better?

A text popped up from my sister, but I turned off my phone altogether. There wasn't anything Georgia could say to make today any better. There was only one thing that could shut out all the noise.

Winning the Monaco Grand Prix.

My car was lightning-fast this year, but that would fade over the next few seasons when other teams caught up. And then, in three years, a new set of rules would change the makeup of the car again. In F1, when your team gave you the fastest car on track, your only option was to take advantage of that immediately.

I drove home on autopilot and felt incredibly relieved to finally pull up to my apartment. I didn't bother with lights as I walked straight to the room where my personal simulator lived.

I sat, tightened the pretend belt out of habit, and booted the system. Fans whirred awake as the screens turned on. Monaco loaded, and the first thing I saw was the white barriers that had ended my race last year. Now I hunched over the simulator, running the circuit until my fingers numbed.

"Come on," I muttered. "You can be faster in that corner."

I restarted the lap, running it over and over again, each time focusing on the turns.

And then a voice caught me by surprise.

"You didn't answer your phone," Georgia called out.

Somehow, the emergency spare key had turned into her barging in whenever she felt like it. Her shoes clicked once on the wood and then went quiet. Her reflection appeared on my screen.

"I can hear you yelling from the hallway. You know you're not actually in the car, right?"

"Feels close enough." And then I hit the wall. Virtually, but it still felt personal. The sound cut off in a hiss, and I shifted into neutral.

"Nice," she said dryly. "You planning to do that on Sunday too?"

I didn't turn around. "If you came here to lecture me, don't. I've had enough for one day."

"I came because you're trending online," she said, not unkindly, "and trending because of relationship drama is sort of my area of expertise."

I rolled my eyes at the reference to her own very public relationship drama she and Luca had experienced a few years ago. Although, in this scenario, our positions were reversed. There would be no PR relationship for me and Lily. As far as our teams were concerned, they'd rather the other person not exist.

"I'm fine." The same words I couldn't stop saying.

"So you've said." Her eyes met mine for a brief moment before I looked back at the screen.

"They had the nerve to ask me if I've been unfocused because of her."

"Well, are you? I mean, if I'm being honest, Henri, I always thought you and Lily might have ended up togeth—"

"No." The word came too fast, and I exhaled, feeling exposed. "It's this championship fight. We're only a third of the way through, and it's already brutal."

Georgia didn't look convinced. I reached for the track restart button—anything to end the conversation—but she caught my wrist midair. "Something's off. You don't have to tell the whole paddock, but you can tell me."

"I can't."

"You mean you *won't*."

I looked away, watching the monitor go idle. "It doesn't matter. It's my race. I'll fix it."

Georgia had no intention of backing down. "You've been off all season. You snap at everyone. You barely sleep. You drive like you're on a razor's edge."

"I'm preparing," I said, too quickly.

"For what? A nervous breakdown?"

"For my *home race*!" Frustration leaked into my voice.

"I think you're doing that thing you always do." Her voice softened. "You get backed into a corner, and instead of asking for help you convince yourself everyone else is the problem."

I bit down on a bitter laugh. "Did you rehearse that?"

"Only since birth." She moved closer, deliberately blocking part of the computer monitor. "You think staying silent makes you strong."

"And you think talking fixes everything."

"Not everything," she said quietly. "But it's a start."

I reached for the wheel again.

"You're burning yourself out. You keep pretending the problem is outside the car when"—she pointed to me—"it's sitting right here."

"Enough, Georgia." I jumped out of the seat, grabbing my water from the cup holder next to me.

"*D'accord*, I'll stop asking. For now. But if you crash again because of whatever this is, we're having a serious conversation about this." Then she stepped toward the kitchen, flicking on a light. "You've eaten, right?"

"I'm not hungry, and I've got laps to finish."

She turned, grabbing her bag from the counter. "You know what I think?"

I sighed. "You'll tell me anyway."

"I think you're too proud to admit when something's wrong. And too scared to figure out what'll happen if you stop pretending that you're fine." Her voice cracked a little at the end, which made me look away.

"Good night, Georgie."

"*Bonne nuit*, idiot."

She closed the door quietly. The apartment went quiet again except for the faint hum of traffic below. I could've told her everything. I almost did. But once you start naming the things that scare you, they start to become real.

So instead, I restarted the simulator. The computer hummed back to life, and the engine noise filled the apartment, loud enough to drown out everything else.

If I couldn't fix myself, I could at least fix my driving.

Chapter Eleven

Lily

My phone buzzed on the table beside my helmet, pulling me from the data analysis Mark had sent over. I glanced at the clock: still half an hour before debrief.

Unknown:

P2? This is why women don't belong in F1. Can't deliver when it matters. Tomorrow you'll learn what happens when you disappoint the wrong people.

I stared at the message, my thumb hovering over the screen. The words blurred slightly as I read them again, trying to convince myself it was just another troll, just another angry fan hiding behind anonymity.

Before I could process it, my phone buzzed again—a notification from my Instagram page. A DM from an account I didn't recognize. No profile picture, just a string of random numbers and letters for a username.

The same message.

My heart kicked against my ribs. The air in the small driver's room suddenly felt thinner, the walls closer. I quickly took screenshots of both the text and the DM before deleting them.

As if that would make it go away. As if pretending it didn't exist would keep it from being real.

I set the phone face down on the table, staring at my helmet instead. The Rennen chrome gleamed under the fluorescent lights, my number staring back at me like a reminder of everything I had to lose.

A knock on the door made me jump, my hand flying to my chest.

"Come in," I called, my voice steadier than I felt.

Ollie stepped through, a bouquet of pink roses in hand. Not the threatening kind with a note tucked inside, just flowers. Simple, elegant.

"Thought you could use these after qualifying," he said, setting them on the table beside my helmet. I gave them a quick once-over.

No note.

"Thank you." I stood, smoothing down my team shirt. "You didn't have to."

"I wanted to." He leaned against the doorframe, hands in his pockets. "P2's nothing to scoff at. And honestly, you drove brilliantly. You were so fast at the end."

Heat crept up my neck. "Henri still got pole."

Ollie crossed the room before taking a seat on the sofa next to me. "You'll get him tomorrow. I know you will."

I wanted to believe him, but P2 may as well have been P20 in my mind. There was no passing in Monaco, especially not Henri. The Monegasque driver had taken pole by two-tenths. He'd grown up on these streets, and today the racing Gods had blessed him with what he'd worked so hard for. I should've been proud, but instead, disappointment sat heavy.

Ollie watched me, a sweet smile on his face, like he really believed I could pass Henri. It warmed my heart.

"I'm sorry I've been rubbish at texting back," I said, redirecting the conversation. "Since the engagement party, it's been nonstop. Testing, media, sponsorship meetings—"

"You don't have to apologize." His grin was easy. "I get it. You're fighting for a championship. I'm just glad I get to see you at all."

The kindness in his voice made my chest tighten. He'd been nothing but patient, nothing but understanding, even when the tabloids had splashed Henri's face across headlines with mine.

"Look, about Montreal…" Ollie shifted his weight, suddenly awkward. "With Henri. I just wanted to check in…" I could see what he was fishing for. Why had Henri been there?

"We were arguing, that's all." The words came automatically. Not entirely untrue. Ollie and I weren't dating—I didn't need to justify myself, even if I felt a bit guilty.

"Right." He nodded, shifting his weight from one side to another. He had something else he wanted to say. "Good." He paused, then cleared his throat. "You know, I was thinking, if it would help take some of the pressure off, I still have that photo the server took of us at dinner in Montreal. If it's helpful, I'm happy to post it. You know, show people you're not—"

"No." The word probably came out faster than it should have, but something about that option gave me immediate pause.

Ollie blinked, surprised.

"I mean…" I softened my tone, forcing a smile. "I appreciate the offer, really. But I don't think using our dinner for PR is the right move."

Something about weaponizing a date—even a semi-arranged one—felt wrong. Like turning something real into strategy. Something my mother would do. Plus, I didn't really want people to think I was dating Ollie either.

I wasn't actually dating anyone.

"Of course." Ollie recovered quickly, that easy smile back in place. "No problem at all. Just thought I'd offer."

"Thank you, though. For thinking of me."

"Always."

My shoulders relaxed. "That was thoughtful. Really."

Ollie shrugged, but happiness softened his features. "Just trying to help however I can."

I studied him, the genuine concern in his expression, the way he just came to bring me flowers and check in. No ulterior motive written across his face, no calculation. Just kindness. Maybe I'd been too quick to dismiss his offer.

Before either of us could say any more, the door swung open without warning. My mother swept in like she owned the place, tailored blazer at attention.

"Darling, you're slouching again— Oh!" She stopped short, eyes landing on Ollie. Her expression transformed, ice melting into warmth. "Oliver. What a lovely surprise."

"Mrs. Blackwood." Ollie straightened, suddenly more formal. "Good to see you again."

"The pleasure's mine." She glanced between us, assessing. "I hope I'm not interrupting."

"Not at all," Ollie said smoothly. "I was just leaving. Big day tomorrow."

He squeezed my hand, leaving a quick peck on my cheek as he passed. "Good luck out there."

"Thanks."

My mother's gaze followed him as he left, always calculating. "Such a charming young man," she said. The dim light of my tablet turned on when I touched it, opting to turn back to my analysis.

I didn't bother looking up from my screen.

"Why do you seem so put out?" She made a show of closing the door behind her, muffling the noise outside.

"I qualified second in Monaco. Allow me a brief wallow before you start whatever lecture you've come to share."

"Do you have any idea how much work it's taken to salvage your reputation this week?" Her voice carried that familiar edge of barely contained frustration—the one that had followed me through countless junior karting championships and into Formula 1.

"I don't control the tabloids." I finally set my tablet aside, meeting her gaze. It was a weak defense—one we both knew wouldn't hold water.

"But you can control your behavior." She adjusted the cuff of her blazer. "You've embarrassed Rennen, me, and yourself. And now we're walking into a meeting where they'll decide how much of your contract survives the season."

That was perhaps a bit extreme on her part, but she'd made her point. They weren't going to throw me out for being seen with Henri, and yet it didn't look good either. I wasn't sure how much Felix cared about the morality clause itself, but I knew he'd care that I'd been seen with a Hermes driver. That was going to be a sticking point for him.

"This is exactly what I was talking about when we discussed the contract last year. Sponsors care about your image, and this is the exact opposite of what we need right now." She set down her coffee cup with a deliberate thump, as if that would further make her point. "I cannot believe you would jeopardize your contract this way, Lily."

"Jeopardize?" I rubbed my temples as I stared at the ground. "Good grief, it was five minutes."

"At one in the morning?" She took a seat on the couch before immediately standing again, pacing the room. "The male drivers might be able to get away with a playboy vibe, but under no circumstances is that going to work for you. I mean, what were you thinking?"

"Clearly, I wasn't thinking about how it would *photograph*. Next time Henri follows me to my room uninvited, I'll make sure to check the paparazzi's schedule first," I shot back, letting a wry smile tug at the corner of my mouth despite the gravity of the situation. The sarcasm rolled off my tongue easily, my default defense mechanism when cornered.

I knew I was being *flippant*, but honestly, what did she expect me to say? That I'd carefully orchestrated some master plan to destroy my reputation in the span of two days?

"This isn't a joke, Lillian. Felix called me this morning, and now we're about to be dragged in front of both him and the President of Rennen." Her finger snapped in front of my face, yanking my focus back toward her. She looked like a toddler ready to scream at any moment.

"You cannot afford this kind of mistake. You're not a man, Lily. You don't get the privilege of indiscretions like they do."

There it was, the familiar sermon. I stopped listening at "you're not a man." As if this were some shock for me. Like I hadn't spent my entire life realizing this.

For a moment, I was thrown back to my conversation with Georgia from three seasons ago, the one where I'd told her no one really cared about our sex lives or who we dated. She'd told me I was dreaming, that there would always be a double standard.

I was young and naïve then. It turned out everyone loved a bit of gossip, and what was more salacious than the top two rivals dating each other?

"You've made your point," I said finally, letting my thumb run over a patch on my racing suit that held a few different sponsor logos. My mother wasn't entirely wrong: I'd been careless. And now everyone, from my sponsors to team leadership to the tabloids, had opinions about my private life.

"Wait." The word came out quieter than I intended.

My mother paused mid-pace, eyebrow arched.

"Ollie actually offered something. Earlier."

"What kind of something?"

I picked at a loose thread on my race suit. "He has a photo of us from our dinner in Montreal. Ollie said if it would help with the situation, he'd be willing to post it. You know, show people that I'm…"

"Dating him instead of Henri Dubois?" my mother finished, her expression sharpening with interest.

"No, he didn't say that, because we *aren't* dating. It's more like… it would relieve some speculation on me and Henri, right?"

She crossed back to the couch, settling beside me with renewed energy. "What exactly did you tell him?"

"I said no. It felt wrong, using our date like that. Using *him* like that."

My mother's hand found mine, surprisingly gentle. "Darling, you aren't using him if he's offering."

"But—" I interjected.

"But nothing." Her grip tightened slightly. "Let me handle this." My mother stood, already pulling out her phone. "I'll float it by Felix and the communications team." She checked her watch, a small look of desperation crossing her face. "Come on. Felix is waiting."

I followed her out of the room and into the office hallway, my footsteps falling into a reluctant rhythm behind hers. I felt like I was being led to the guillotine.

When we approached the large conference room, my mother made a show of fixing her blazer, not sparing me a glance. "I want you to apologize before Felix has to ask."

I pressed my tongue to the roof of my mouth before whispering, "For the photo or simply existing?"

She only sighed as the doors parted slowly, revealing Rennen's largest conference room. In the center of the room was one long table, spotless except for the lineup of espresso cups and Felix's folded hands. Rennen's logo shone on the far wall, always watching me. Thomas, President of Rennen, was also there waiting, staring down at his phone with a large frown.

Felix raised his arm, gesturing for me to sit. Across from me at the table was Bertha, whose expression was unreadable. Part of me wondered if she was secretly enjoying this, seeing my downfall. I hadn't exactly made the season easy. Mark stood in the back, tirelessly working on his tablet.

Great. They'd even brought in my engineer to witness my humiliation.

Felix always looked tired, but this morning the bags under his eyes almost looked like bruises. He didn't bother with small talk, just slid his phone across the table toward me. The photo stared back.

"I'm going to ask you one question," Felix said quietly. "And I want an honest answer."

I swallowed. "Okay."

"Are you involved with Henri Dubois?"

"No." The truth.

Felix studied me for a long moment, then nodded. "Good. Because if you were, we'd be having a very different conversation." He pulled the phone back, pocketing it. "Unfortunately, what's true and what the paddock believes are two separate things."

"The paddock thinks—" I started.

"I don't care what the paddock thinks," Felix interrupted, his voice sharp. "As the team principal, I just need to make sure every part of the contract is being respected." He exhaled slowly. "But if I'm being honest, for Rennen, this is about our lead driver looking like she's in bed with her top rival. It's not a great look for you, Lily."

I nodded, struggling to find the words to say, then I remembered my mother's command from earlier. "I know," I said quietly. "I'm sorry. It won't happen again."

"Good. Let's be careful with the off-track fraternizing with Dubois, yeah?" Thomas added. "Not that Henri would… but I don't trust Hermes around our documents."

When it came to Hermes, Thomas and Felix absolutely thought the worst, which felt a bit ironic, since they didn't worry about Georgia visiting Luca. Unlike Hermes, Valkyrie actually needed the help. And definitely no more kissing.

After that, the meeting dissolved with the quiet efficiency of a well-oiled machine, which felt aptly Rennen. My mother immediately reached for her phone, her fingers already flying across the screen as she shifted back into full crisis-management mode. I watched her transform in real time. The parent side of her had melted away years ago, replaced by the calculating strategist. In the end, only Mark lingered, his hands folded loosely in his lap as he remained seated at the conference table.

"You did good today," he said quietly.

I smiled, small and tired. "Didn't get P1, though."

"We will."

I managed a nod. "Thanks. Sorry you had to waste time listening to all that."

He paused, looking contemplative. "You ever feel like this sport just devours people whole?"

"Every single day," I replied.

A slight grin tugged at the corner of his mouth. "Then give it something to choke on."

When he left, the room was completely quiet. I closed my eyes, letting the silence soak in. A single buzz of my phone caught my attention.

An unknown number.

Oh, good. Just what I needed right now.

I didn't respond. Didn't breathe for a second. I locked the screen, slipped the phone into my pocket, and told myself it was another coincidence. It was just spam. A wrong number. Anything but what it sounded like.

But I couldn't avoid the truth.

This someone knew my number.

I opened my phone back up and stared at it too long—long enough for the screen to dim. Then I quickly screenshot it before deleting it. My hand was shaking, thumb trembling over the glass.

You can't tell them. Not yet.

Today had made me a thorn in their side; now was not the time to add to that. I could get through more of this season, and then, once I was properly leading the championship, I could tell them.

Chapter Twelve

Lily

"Morning, superstar!" Mark greeted. His smile was too wide for him, and I knew he was trying to overcompensate for me coming in P2 during qualifying.

"Morning," I managed, accepting the earpiece he held out.

He handed it over with careful fingers, like I might shatter if he moved too quickly. "Car's all ready to go!" His cheerfulness was almost contagious, and I appreciated the effort.

Monaco was unlike any other circuit—narrow streets flanked by barriers, no room for error, no forgiveness for mistakes. The harbor sparkled in the morning sun, yachts bobbing gently against their moorings. Millionaires watched from balconies above the streets where our cars were threading at top speeds.

At eight years old, I'd sat cross-legged on the carpet, nose inches from the TV screen, watching the race. My fingers would grip an imaginary wheel, turning it in perfect sync with whatever F1 driver the film crew were following.

Monaco may not be my home race, but it was still one of the crown jewels of motorsport. Every driver wanted to win here. There was no street race like

Monaco. Everything about this race brought me to life, and I wanted this win. The only problem? I was sitting behind the one person who knew this track better than me. Yesterday, no one had been surprised when Henri squeaked out pole. He'd driven with cool, calm precision.

Which meant this race was going to come down to strategy—and pit stops.

Or one hell of a pass from me. Something that hadn't been done in years. Even Georgia hadn't managed to do it when she'd beaten Henri last year, and the year before—her wins had come purely from pole position or better pit stops that had allowed her to come out ahead.

Truly daring passes were so rare at Monaco, because if you were one millimeter off, your whole race was over. These streets were old and narrow, not exactly designed for high-speed racing.

I lowered myself into the cockpit. The harness straps tightened across my shoulders with familiar clicks—*one, two, three, four, five*—and my hands found the wheel. For the first time that morning, my pulse felt steady. Henri's car sat ahead on pole, almost teasingly.

Rain had started falling an hour before the race, turning Monaco's streets into a skating rink. The forecast said it would ease but never fully clear. The purple-and-gold livery of Henri's car gleamed under gray skies, water already beading on the bodywork, rain falling steadily. Twenty-three hundredths of a second had separated us in yesterday's dry qualifying. Less than the length of a car. Nothing, really.

But he'd gotten the better time.

The track cleared for the formation lap. I followed Henri through the streets, the spray from his rear tires obscuring my vision, making the already tight track feel claustrophobic. The wet setup felt good beneath me, responsive and balanced, but this was Monaco in the rain. One wrong input, and you were in the barriers. The city walls pressed in on either side, closer than any other track, painted lines barely visible through the standing water.

We settled on the grid, rain drumming against my helmet. Not hard enough to stop the race, but enough that passing now was inconceivable.

Five red lights blinked above the track, holding us in suspended animation.

Mark cut in. "Starting on wets. It's going to be raining all race."

I exhaled once, twice, then the world launched forward as soon as the lights went out.

Henri had the cleaner start, but it was chaos into Turn 1. The wet surface amplified everything. He sliced ahead of me through the first part of the track, but it was survival mode for all of us drivers in this rain, trying not to get swallowed by the chaos of twenty cars fighting for position through a corner that was barely wide enough in dry conditions.

Someone locked up behind me. I felt the spray hit my rear wing; heard Mark's sharp intake of breath over the radio.

"Just focus forward."

"Copy."

Lap after lap, we threaded the city together in the rain. Henri was perfect through most of it, impossibly fast despite the conditions. The spray from his rear tires created a gray curtain between us.

Through Casino Square, he was flawless. Past Mirabeau, committed and precise. Down to the hairpin where most drivers were lifting early, playing it safe in the standing water.

But then, right after the hairpin, threading through turns seven and eight, I saw it.

The hesitation.

His car twitched, just slightly. A correction that didn't match the Henri I knew. He lifted earlier than he needed to, even for the rain. The gap between us closed by a tenth, then another.

The radio crackled on. "He's braking early after the hairpin. Keep pressure."

"Copy."

Lap after lap, the same thing. Henri flew through the tunnel, that brief respite from the rain where the car suddenly found grip, but the moment we emerged back into the downpour, heading toward the chicane, he hesitated.

What was going on in there?

By lap twenty, the rain had eased from downpour to persistent drizzle. Not enough to switch to better rain tires yet, but the track was slowly improving. The racing line started to darken as water cleared from the most used parts of the asphalt.

"Rain's easing," Mark reported. "Give it another ten laps, and we'll look at changing tires. Most other drivers will probably pit between laps thirty and thirty-five."

"Copy."

I stayed glued to Henri's gearbox, close enough to see every correction, every moment of doubt. The rain lessened, visibility improving from terrible to merely bad. And still, every lap, Henri hesitated after the hairpin.

By lap thirty, the rain had reduced enough to switch tires.

"Box this lap," Mark said. "Window's open, and we need to be aggressive." Both teams had the same idea, and we both headed into the pit lane.

"Shit!" I yelled when I pulled out just behind Henri. Our stops had been almost the same.

"Rain's holding steady," Mark reported. "Just mist for the rest of the race."

I had to find a spot to make my move. The track conditions were perfect for my driving style: commitment rewarded, hesitation punished, and this race wasn't over yet.

Henri was still hesitating, and each lap, I closed the gap—three, two-point-five, then two.

"He's losing time through that part of the track every lap," Mark said, and I could hear the excitement building in his voice. Mark didn't have to say the quiet part out loud.

Pass him here, or accept second place.

By lap fifty-five, I was right behind Henri, close enough to see his helmet moving in the cockpit. It was now or never. I went for it at the hairpin, diving inside, my front wing practically kissing his rear tire in the spray, but he was ready for me. His car went wide enough to box me out, forcing me to lift or lose the front of my car.

I swore under my breath, biting back the urge to punch the steering wheel in frustration.

"Not yet," Mark said quietly, maddeningly calm. "Patience, Lil."

I reset my breathing and waited. The city opened into the harbor straight, water glittering through the mist beside the track, mega-yachts bobbing in their slips as attendees watched from under awnings.

I found his rear tires again through the spray. He reached the turn again, heading toward the hairpin in the mist.

And again, as he exited, he lifted.

But this time I was ready, and I went for it.

The move was pure instinct, the kind you don't think about or you'll ruin it, the kind that separates drivers from champions. I dove inside through the mist and the spray, the walls close enough that I could have reached out and scraped paint off them if my hands weren't locked on the wheel. For a second, we were side by side, two streaks of color threading through a space not meant for more than one car.

Hold. Please hold.

And then, just as I was sure we'd run out of space, he faltered. A tiny lift, a fractional backing off, that gave me the sliver of room I needed.

"Holy shit!" I'd passed Henri Dubois.

At Monaco. In the rain.

"Yes!" Mark screamed into the radio, and I'd never heard him sound like that—pure, unfiltered joy and disbelief. "Lily, you absolute mad genius!"

The last twenty laps blurred into a fever dream. Henri stayed close, but he never mounted a real challenge. Whatever demon he was fighting in that sequence, it held him back just enough.

The final lap barely felt real. The city passed in snapshots through the mist, and when the checkered flag waved through the light rain, I screamed into my helmet with everything I had, my voice going hoarse, my hands shaking on the wheel.

I'd done it. I'd won Monaco.

"P1! P1!" Mark shouted, and I could hear other voices in the background, the whole garage erupting.

Static laughter filled my radio, joy and relief and triumph all tangled together. I slumped against my belts, cold sweat coating my skin beneath the race suit, my heart hammering so hard I thought it might break through my chest. Outside, the harbor erupted with noise and color despite the rain, horns blaring from yachts, crowds screaming from the grandstands.

But for a single moment, that pure triumph had a dollop of anguish threaded through it, because in my mirrors during that pass, I'd seen something. The hesitation that didn't belong to someone second in the championship—especially not Henri Dubois.

Why had Henri done that? He'd raced this track over and over again, never flinching like that. What had happened to the driver who threw his car into gaps that didn't exist; who won previous races through sheer audacity and skill, regardless of conditions?

Something was wrong.

Marshals waved flags as I pulled into parc fermé, my car coming to a stop. I climbed out to blinding flashes, raising trembling hands to the crowd as I waved. My team waited by the barriers, their smiles wide and welcoming.

But a part of me couldn't stop staring at Henri. While his team greeted him with such excitement, his response was anything but joyous.

I wrapped my arms around Mark, and his embrace was brief but genuine, his hand clapping my back, both of us soaked. "You drove like a champion," he said into my ear, rain running down both our faces, and I had to blink hard against sudden tears that mixed with the rainwater.

He deserved this win too. He'd worked tirelessly on the wet setup, spent countless hours in the simulator with me preparing for exactly these conditions, believed in me even when the results weren't coming.

The podium came and went in a blur of champagne sprays and bright, flashing lights. Henri stood one step down, face carved in restraint. He clapped once when I lifted the trophy, his face wide with a fake smile. Afterward, I was dragged from one journalist to the next as I told them time after time how incredible it was, that I was proud of the team, that Monaco was a dream.

Through the circus of the celebration, Henri's eyes never met mine. For all his quirks, he'd never not congratulated me after a race. Not once in three years. Even when I beat him, even when we were barely speaking, there was always a handshake, a nod, a quiet "good drive" when the cameras weren't looking.

I let Bertha usher me through the crowd. Somewhere behind us, I heard Henri's voice, low, distant. I almost turned. Almost waited for him to say "good job" the way he always did.

But he didn't.

Monaco's air was thick with excitement. Yachts glittered like chandeliers, champagne popping on million-dollar decks as the crowd's noise followed me to the waiting car. I replayed the moment I'd passed him in my head, analyzing it frame by frame through the spray and the mist. The way the car seemed to shudder like it didn't trust him anymore. Or he didn't trust it anymore.

My car turned up the hill toward the hotel, the city's party fading behind me. By the time I'd reached the suite, I'd decided I was done worrying about him. I was going to take a shower, eat something that wasn't an energy gel, and get ready for some drinks tonight.

I kicked off my shoes and tossed my bag on the table. My body ached for a hot shower, but something stopped me halfway across the room.

Another fucking envelope. White, unmarked, and on the ground by the door. Someone had just slid it under. I walked closer, watching it like a bomb about to go off. The handwriting on the front was the same blocky, all-caps scrawl as before. The envelope had just my name.

"Bertha?" I called out as I opened the door, half-hoping she'd somehow followed me up, praying, for the first time ever, to hear my PR officer's voice.

The silence that came back was deafening, and the hallway was empty.

Picking it up, my fingers tore the flap before my brain caught up.

HE WAS SUPPOSED TO WIN. YOU'RE NOT GETTING THIS, ARE YOU, LILLIAN?

I read it once, then again, because the words didn't want to make sense the first time.

He was supposed to win.

I crumpled the letter in my fist, the edges biting into my palm.

Everyone *wanted* Henri to win this weekend. Everyone *expected* Henri to win. But then I came in and stole his win. I beat him on the track, fair and square, with a pass that would be replayed for years. And what did that make me?

The villain who stole Monaco from F1's golden boy.

And yet, now I had the honor of receiving this note, written by some lunatic who clearly had strong opinions about who should've won, and apparently enough money riding on the outcome that they felt entitled to threaten me about it. They had the nerve to invade my personal space, to make me feel small in a room that was supposed to be my safe haven.

More anger started to flood me. I didn't think, just moved. Jacket in one hand, crumpled note stuffed in my pocket, I stormed out. When I jabbed the elevator call button, pain shot through my thumb. The mirror inside caught my reflection. Eyes blazing, hair frizzed, I looked like a woman crazed.

My fist hit his door harder than I meant to, three sharp thumps that echoed down the hallway.

The door opened after a moment, and Henri stood there looking startled.

"Lily?" His voice was rough, confused. His eyes searched my face, taking in my disheveled appearance, the fury that must've been written all over me. "What are you—"

I shoved the note against him before I could lose my nerve. The paper crumpled between us. He just stared at me, then down at what I had shoved into his hand, then back at me.

"What is this?" He shook his head, confusion and concern warring on his face.

"Just fucking read it," I snapped.

Chapter Thirteen

Henri

He was supposed to win.

I read it once, then again, because the words refused to make sense the first time.

"Where did this come from?"

"My room," she said bitterly. "It was waiting by the door when I got back from the podium. Lucky me."

I stared at her, the noise of the city suddenly gone, the only sound her heavy breathing.

"And you called security, yes?" I already knew the answer, but the small shake of her head confirmed it.

Her frown was set in that stubborn line I'd come to recognize over the years—the one that meant she'd already made up her mind and wasn't about to be swayed by logic or reason. "I came here instead."

Of course she had, because Lily Blackwood didn't do things the sensible way. Stepping aside, I gestured her in. The wooden door clicked shut, sealing the two of us inside the quiet.

"Lily, you need to tell—"

A loud groan from her cut me off mid-sentence.

"Out of the question." She snatched the paper out of my hand, cursing under her breath as her fists clenched around it. "I didn't come here for pity, Dubois. I came because I want *answers*. I want to know what happened to you during the race, because"—she waved the paper in the air, her voice rising—"whoever this is? They're right. You were *supposed* to win."

Her boots scuffed the carpet as she took two angry steps toward me. "You don't flinch, Henri, but there you were in the hairpin, driving like…" She didn't finish that thought. "What is going on with you?" Her eyes burned into mine, daring me to look away.

"Nothing." Even as the word left my mouth, I hated the sound of it, too fast and defensive.

"Oh, right. Because everything's *fine*," she fired back. "And yet, you somehow happened to forget how to drive in Monaco? You basically let me pass in *Monaco*. That's not like you."

"I had a bad race." *An understatement.*

My hotel room suddenly felt suffocating, the walls pressing in, too small to contain both her relentless determination and my carefully guarded secrets.

"I'm not buying it, Henri." She stepped closer—close enough that I could see the faint tremor in her hands and the tiny flecks of gold in her eyes as she watched me.

I opened my mouth to argue, to say something clever or cruel, but nothing came out. Just the light whisper of my own breathing. Her voice had none of the pressroom polish she usually carried.

"You wouldn't understand."

Lily didn't flinch. Didn't back down.

"Try me." The way she said it, steady, relentless, hit harder than yelling. I wanted to shout, to throw her out like she'd done to me in Montreal. To tell her to mind her own business and go celebrate her victory and leave me alone to wallow in my defeat.

I took a seat on the couch, letting my head rest in my hands. Forget losing Monaco earlier today—*this* was what defeat felt like.

"I see it every time."

Lily joined me on the couch, her head tilting slightly, encouraging me to go on.

"That corner from Miami." The words felt jagged in my mouth, too tough to swallow. "The crash. The loud banging of the car and the smoke that rose from it. The way the barrier came at me too fast to stop." I forced myself to keep talking before I could change my mind. "It was raining that day, and so I think because of that, it feels worse whenever it rains. My body becomes possessed with fear. I've only experienced this once bef—"

I stopped, my throat closing as I let out a small sob. I wasn't ready to face that thought again.

"It doesn't go away," I continued, the confession spilling out now that I'd started, unstoppable. "Every time I hit a section like that in the rain, my mind and all reasoning abandons me. The lifting and the hesitation? It's not a choice. It just… happens."

Her arms fell to her sides, and I heard her catch her breath. "Henri… oh, I'm so sorry. This is my fault."

The pity in her voice made me want to crawl out of my own skin. I couldn't sit still anymore. I got up and started pacing, wearing a path in the carpet between the window and the bed.

"No, it's not. I mean, racing incidents *happen*. We can't be scared of them. I just… I thought it would fade." The words came out faster now. "I told myself I just needed to push harder, focus more. That's what we do, right? Drive through it. But every time I get there, it's like my body betrays me. I lift without realizing. And I can't stop it."

The memory pressed against me. The screech of tires losing grip on wet asphalt. The heat from the engine as I struggled to climb out, my hands shaking so badly I could barely work the harness release.

She didn't move for a long time. Just watched me, quiet and still.

"Have you told the team?" she asked finally.

"Told them what?" My fingers tapped against my leg. "That I can't drive in inclement weather?"

Her voice softened, the original hardness in it giving way to something gentler. "Yes, exactly that. So they can get you help." She patted the seat next to her, and I begrudgingly took a seat.

"What good is a driver who can't focus during a third of the races? They might consider benching me." The words sounded scarier once they were out in the open. "I haven't told Georgia or Éliott."

Lily grabbed my hand, stopping the nervous tapping. "But you should tell Hermes, Henri. Or Michael, at least. You've been with him since you started in F1—he'll want to help."

"No."

"Henri…"

"I'll tell Hermes when *you* tell Rennen about these notes." I gestured to the crinkled paper that was now cast aside on the coffee table.

"That's different."

"Really?" I crossed my arms, holding my ground. "You're getting threats and refusing to report them. I'm having panic attacks and refusing to tell the team. Seems pretty similar to me."

"I'm trying not to ruin my reputation here, Henri." But her voice wavered, just slightly. "But…" She looked away, focusing on something past my shoulder—anything to distract her from this conversation. "I did mention it to my mother."

Of all the things she could've said, that was the least expected. Victoria was not known for her warmth or concern, although I realized this was probably a thought I'd had as an outside observer looking in. I was glad Lily had told her mother, although I wasn't convinced the result would yield what I wanted.

"And what did she say?"

Lily's laugh was shaky. "She told me not to add any trouble for myself. Said reporting it would make me look weak, like I couldn't handle pressure. That female drivers already have enough scrutiny without inviting more. Reminded me that one of Rennen's largest sponsors is a sports betting company, and we don't want negative press coming out around that."

Now that was Victoria Blackwood to a tee. It had taken me all of five minutes to know she was a narcissist dressed in designer clothes. But was she truly calculated enough to downplay these threats?

"Lily, that's..." My blood boiled as I thought of Victoria dismissing her daughter's concerns. "That's insane. Someone left this at your door, and your mother told you to keep quiet about it?"

"But she has a point." Her voice lacked conviction, the words sounding rehearsed, like if she told herself enough times, she'd almost believe it.

"She absolutely does not." The anger in my chest shifted direction, redirecting toward someone who wasn't even in the room. "This is serious. These notes, whoever's sending them—"

"I know," she said finally. Her fingers tightened around the note she was holding. "But it's for me to deal with."

In that moment, I knew nothing was going to sway Lily, even if I could see the glint of fear growing in her eyes. Lily wasn't one to back down, but as athletes, we often got threats in our DMs or emails, or even through money-sending apps. But something this close?

This felt different.

I moved to the minibar, needing something to do with my hands. The cold light turned on when I opened it. I pulled two cans of sparkling water from the back and handed one to her before taking a seat next. Her fingers brushed mine when she took it, barely-there, the barest whisper of contact. But that fleeting touch sent something warm spreading through my chest, settling somewhere dangerous.

I wanted to touch her again.

She looked away first, breaking whatever moment that was, before opening the can. The hiss of carbonation was the only sound in the room. I waited for her to toss some retort my way, to break the tension with sarcasm the way she usually did.

"No one gets what we're going through except for the other eighteen drivers on the grid," she said finally. "The perseverance and toughness needed to perform in this sport, and the mental capacity, it feels too much at times. One inkling of self-doubt can wreck your entire season. You always looked so unshakeable, Henri."

"That Henri feels like a lifetime ago."

She leaned back, and I could almost see the guarded walls over her heart being brought down. "Then we just have to find him again."

Her words were so sure, reeking of that quintessential Lily confidence that made impossible things seem achievable.

For the first time in months, the silence between us didn't feel like punishment. It was just *silence*. Neither of us reached for our phones. Neither of us looked for an excuse to leave.

"Thanks. For telling me." Her words were quiet. "I miss talking to you. We used to actually talk about stuff that mattered. Before everything got so…"

She stopped, her mouth still parted around the next word. Her gaze dropped to where her fingers twisted the edge of her hem. The rain tapped against the glass, filling the space where her words should have been.

"Yeah." I agreed. "I miss it too."

I desperately missed these moments between us. Talking to Lily had always been so easy, so natural, in a way that nothing else in my life was. I let the moment of comfort stretch, hoping she'd find another reason to smile. But gradually, I watched the tension creep back into her shoulders. Her knee started bouncing with that restless energy she could never quite contain. She picked up the note again, unfolded it, read it, folded it twice, and set it back down.

My knee brushed hers as I shifted to get more comfortable, but her leg didn't move away, didn't flinch. The tension was different now, slower, almost aimless, curling around us with nowhere urgent to go.

I watched the side of her face, the way her jaw ticked when she wasn't thinking. How her mouth pursed slightly every time she almost said something and then swallowed the words instead.

For a woman who never stopped talking, who filled every silence with commentary and jokes and observations, she could also be impressively comfortable with quiet. Silence didn't bother Lily. I wasn't sure anything *really* bothered Lily for long. She may be knocked down today, but she would be back up tomorrow, her smile never too far from the surface.

For a moment, I let myself imagine what it would be like to just exist like that. To not carry every mistake, every fear, every failure like a stone in my chest.

She turned her head toward me, catching the way I was watching her.

"What?" she asked.

I should have looked away. Should've made a joke or changed the subject or done anything except what I was doing: leaning forward, just like I'd done in Montreal. Everything about Lily was so intoxicating and addictive, and I was too weak to back away.

The faintest wrinkle appeared between her eyebrows, confusion mixing with something else. Something that made my pulse kick up. She noticed the shift.

I closed the space a little more, half-expecting her to laugh in my face, to shove me back and tell me I'd misread everything. And I would have deserved that.

For a moment, we hovered together. There was something unexplainable about Lily that had always drawn me in, some gravitational pull I'd spent the past six months resisting. Every word I knew fled my mind. The only thing left was her soft stare. Curious, defiant, and a little reckless.

When it came to Lily Blackwood, I couldn't fight the magnetic pull between us. The person I needed to stay away from was becoming my kryptonite.

Lily shifted closer, just slightly, her knee brushing mine. It was nothing and everything, all at once. My breath hitched, and I watched her eyes flick to my mouth for a fraction of a second before returning to meet my gaze. I felt myself lean in. At this point, it wasn't a decision or even a conscious thought. Just a pull I couldn't describe, didn't want to fight.

Every instinct screamed at me to stop, to not open my heart to this impossible situation. To remember all the reasons this was a terrible idea, because if the past week had proven anything, it was that we could never be together.

Her gaze snapped to mine just as the gap between us started to vanish, and the way she looked at me— not angry, not even triumphant, but open and wanting— made me want to tell her every secret I'd ever hidden.

Maybe I should tell her, I thought to myself. *Or at least, tell her that we can't keep doing this.*

"Lily, about—"

Before I could finish and tell her why I abandoned her in Las Vegas, Lily's lips gently pressed against mine. The first contact was hesitant, like she was still deciding whether to let this happen. I waited for her to pull away; come to her senses and remember all the reasons this shouldn't happen again.

But she didn't.

Her hands found the sides of my face, fingers cold from the water, and she drew me closer. I leaned in, my hand finding the base of her jaw, as she deepened the kiss.

For a second, the world was nothing but her. The taste of her, the way she fit against me, the impossible relief from it. She shifted, climbing onto my lap in one fluid movement. The weight of her settled against me, solid and real, chasing away everything that had been haunting me.

I let my hands settle on her waist, fingers spreading across her sides, loving the way she moved against me. Her mouth moved against mine, slow and deliberate, like she was savoring every second. Like we had all the time in the world and nowhere else to be.

Which wasn't true. Not for either of us. But for this moment, I let myself pretend it was.

Her fingers tangled in my hair, tugging slightly, and I couldn't stop the sound that escaped me. She smiled against my mouth—that smug, satisfied smile that usually annoyed me but now just made me want to kiss her harder.

A loud buzz cut in between us, making us both jump.

Lily flinched, breath still uneven, eyes slightly dazed. My hands were still on her waist, hers tangled in the fabric of my shirt. For a heartbeat, neither of us moved.

Then I looked down. Her phone had lit up, vibrating against the wooden coffee table.

Ollie's name appeared.

Something inside me went cold. Reality came crashing back on top of me. His name was there, ringing, because he was the one who could be with her. Not me.

Lily hesitated, then she turned off the ringer with a flick of her thumb. She looked back at me, lips still swollen, eyes searching my face, like maybe she could pull us back to where we were a second ago. Her hands returned to my chest, fingers sliding toward the buttons of my shirt, and for a heartbeat I wanted to let her— wanted to forget about Ollie and the teams and every complication that made this a catastrophically bad idea.

But I couldn't. I'd said no to Lily last year for a reason, and those reasons very much still existed. I couldn't give her a proper relationship, and seeing Ollie's number pop up on her cell phone had reminded me of that. She'd just won Monaco, and I couldn't even be out celebrating with her without it causing a PR storm.

All I could offer was stolen moments and complications.

"You should go." The words came out as if I'd just swallowed sand, difficult and rough.

She blinked, pulling back slightly. The heat between us evaporated, replaced by something brittle. "Henri—"

"No, really." I carefully moved her off my lap, standing up and putting necessary distance between us. I couldn't think with her this close; couldn't remember all the reasons this was impossible. Our team principals, her contract, the championship battle—nothing had changed between us.

"Ollie's waiting."

The silence that followed was excruciating. She stared at me for a long moment, something unreadable crossing her face. Not anger. Worse: resignation. Like she'd expected this exact outcome and hated being right.

"Right." Her voice came out flat, empty of the fire I was used to hearing. She slid off the couch, movements careful, measured. She was trying very hard not to let me see how much this hurt. She grabbed her jacket off the chair, taking her time with it, and I wondered if she was waiting for me to take it back, to tell her to stay. But I didn't.

"This was a mistake," she said quietly, not looking at me as she shrugged into her jacket.

"Lily—"

"No, it's okay." She finally met my eye, and the careful blankness in her expression made my chest ache. She moved toward the door, pausing with her hand on the handle. "Good luck in Austria," she said, her voice professionally neutral, like we were nothing more than competitors exchanging pleasantries in the paddock.

The room felt colder once Lily had left, the echoes of our conversation—the kiss—lingering. I stared at the closed door, the empty space a stark reminder of everything I couldn't have. My heartbeat finally slowed, returning to normal, but I knew I wouldn't forget what had just happened, or how easily we'd slipped back into trouble.

Chapter Fourteen

Lily

The bulbs around the vanity were so bright I felt like I was in an interrogation cell rather than a dressing room. I squinted at my reflection, watching my makeup artist apply what had to be the third layer of foundation, and wondered if there was enough concealer in the world to hide the exhaustion carved into my face.

I'd barely slept since Monaco. My mind bounced between what had now become several threatening messages, my podium, and Henri's lips on mine before he'd unceremoniously kicked me out.

Visiting Henri's room had been a massive mistake. If I'd stayed, we probably would have ended up in bed together, and then I'd just be back where I was in Las Vegas. With the championship battle being so tense between us, neither of us had time for a relationship with the other. Even if it had felt wrong when he'd said that exact sentiment in Las Vegas, he wasn't wrong. And I couldn't fault Henri for that, even if a small piece of my heart kept forgetting when I was with him.

Starting now, I needed to stay soundly away from Henri.

Mum materialized in the mirror's reflection. Blue suit without a single wrinkle, phone clutched in her hands like a weapon, and an expression that told me everything I needed to know about her current mood.

"You're on in ten, Lily." She didn't look up from her phone, fingers flying across the screen.

I gave her a thumbs-up with my most winning smile—the one I'd been practicing since childhood. "Good morning to you too."

She ignored that, of course. My mother had perfected the art of selective hearing years ago. "The producers are very excited about this new segment. It's specifically focused on the women of Formula 1—drivers, team principals, and engineers. Really highlighting female voices in the sport through a female lens. And with Ollie as the host, no less! He's really championing women's voices in the paddock."

The irony of a man hosting a female segment was not lost on me. "Because what women in F1 really need is a man to ask us questions specifically about being women."

She finally looked up from her phone, meeting my eye in the mirror with that calculating expression I knew too well. "Having a reputable journalist focus on the women of the paddock is exactly what we need. And to start with you? What an honor!"

The door creaking caught us both off-guard. "Speak of the devil," my mother said, brightening in a way she never quite did for me. "Ollie, darling!"

Ollie stepped into the doorway, camera-ready in a crisp white shirt with a stylish checkered blazer and black jeans. It was impressive how he always managed to look like he'd walked out of a photoshoot.

"Victoria, always a pleasure." He kissed her cheek then turned that smile on me. "Lily, you look incredible."

"Five minutes, darling," my mother said, squeezing my shoulder in what might pass for affection if I didn't know better. "Make us proud."

She slipped past Ollie, phone already back at her ear before she cleared the doorway.

Ollie waited until her footsteps had faded, then he crossed the room to lean against the vanity beside me. "I was not kidding when I said you look amazing, Lil. I'm so excited to be hosting this segment. We've been working hard to bring some female-focused content to F1. It's exactly the kind of journalism I want to be known for."

"Happy to help," I lied, my smile feeling more plastic by the second.

He shook his head like he couldn't quite believe his luck. "You have no idea how much it means that you agreed to do this. With you as the first interview, the championship leader and Monaco winner, it's going to set the whole tone for the series. Now, just remember, for this format, I'm going to ask you some questions, and then you'll answer as honestly as you can. Don't worry if you make a mistake or ramble on—we're not live or anything. It'll all be edited down for mini social-media shorts."

Then he paused, raising his finger as if he had one last thought. "I should probably warn you, production had the final say on questions for this first episode, and some of them are… well, a bit cheesy. Maybe more than a bit." He made an apologetic face. "They want to play it safe, test the waters. But still, I'm so excited for this. Definitely more fun than Henri's interview later."

My spine straightened at hearing *his* name. "Henri's interview?"

"Oh, yeah. We're also doing a documentary on Hermes. We've got a couple of new projects going on this week, actually." Ollie smiled widely. "But this segment? This one truly matters. Not talking about some stuffy old F1 team."

Of course Hermes got another documentary about themselves. The most established team in F1 history, dripping in sponsorship money. They probably had more documentaries than championship wins at this point.

My shoulders dropped, tension I hadn't realized I'd been carrying easing out. "Very on brand for them."

"Right?" Ollie grinned, encouraged by my reaction. "Meanwhile, we're actually doing something meaningful here. Highlighting female voices that deserve to be heard. Your story, what you've overcome to get here, that's what people need to hear."

"All right, we're ready for you both!" The coordinator popped his head in.

Ollie pushed off the vanity, straightening his blazer. "Ready to make history?"

"Always."

He offered his hand, helping me up from the chair with a gentlemanly flourish that would probably look great on camera. Which, I suspected, was entirely the point.

The studio was smaller than I expected, set up in a corner of the media center with soft lighting and that generic gray loveseat that appeared in every F1 behind-the-scenes video. A small crew bustled around—camera operators, sound techs, producers with clipboards and headsets. I sat down on the sofa, careful to maintain my posture, and watched Ollie settle across from me. A producer appeared to clip a microphone to my collar.

"Ready?"

I nodded, trying to find some confidence.

The camera operator counted down silently—*five, four, three, two*—and then the red light was blinking, and Ollie's entire demeanor shifted into presenter mode.

"Welcome to Racing in Heels," he began.

I nearly choked. *Racing in Heels?* Had my mother mentioned this name to me?

"We're excited for our new segment celebrating the women who make Formula 1 incredible. Today I have the absolute pleasure of sitting down with championship leader and female powerhouse, Lily Blackwood."

I smiled into the camera, trying to recover from nearly choking on the name.

"Lily, thanks so much for joining me." Ollie's smile was warm and genuine. "Let's start with something fun. You're always so put-together in the paddock. What's your secret? Do you have a pre-race beauty routine?"

Was this the question Ollie had mentioned?

I forced my smile wider, channeling every media training session Bertha had ever subjected me to. When you're one of a handful of women in the paddock, you try to avoid answering questions that typically wouldn't be asked of the men. Still, I'd told Ollie I'd keep an open mind.

"You know, I just try to stay hydrated and get enough sleep when I can. Racing takes a lot out of you physically, so recovery is key."

A solid answer.

Ollie nodded enthusiastically, like I'd just revealed the secrets of the universe instead of basic athlete maintenance.

"Absolutely." He leaned in, giving me a thumbs-up. "All right, Lil, here's the next one. F1 is such a male-dominated sport, as we know. Tell us, how do you cope with being a woman in this environment?"

Let's hope they're not all like this.

My smile felt plastered on. "I try not to think about it that way. Each year, more and more women are on the grid. We're drivers, engineers, part of leadership teams. So, you know, I'm just focused on driving the car as fast as possible, same as anyone else on the grid."

"Of course, of course." He leaned forward, all earnest concern. "But you must face unique challenges as a woman." He motioned, and I could tell he was trying to get more out of me. "Like, how do you handle the physical demands? F1 cars require significant upper-body strength. Do you have to train differently than the male drivers?"

"Like all the drivers, I have a personalized training plan put out by my team. No driver's training plan matches," I said, keeping my voice even. "It's all very individualized across the entire sport. I don't think you'll find any driver has an exact routine that matches another, so it's less about me being a woman, and more about me being an individual."

Something flickered across Ollie's face—confusion, maybe, or the first hint that this wasn't going as smoothly as he'd hoped. But I wasn't sure what he expected me to say. Admit that as a woman I wasn't as physically capable? Because that almost felt like what the question was implying.

"Now, tell me, how do you deal with the emotional side of racing? Women are naturally more in touch with their emotions. Does that help or hurt you in high-pressure situations?"

Women are naturally more in touch with their emotions? Ollie, to his credit, did give me a quick apologetic side-eye. Even he knew this one was purely for clickbait.

But I could do this. I'd been trained my entire life to answer sexist questions. "Everyone experiences pressure differently, regardless of gender. What matters is how you channel it."

"And speaking of pressure,"—Ollie flipped to another page on his notes—"do you feel pressure to dress up all the time? To represent women in motorsport in a certain way?"

"I wear what the team or sponsors give me, just like everyone else." For that one, I couldn't smile. "Truthfully, I'm probably one of the least fashionable drivers on the grid. Luca definitely has better style than me."

"Right, but you must *think* about it more, surely? I mean, you're always so stylish—"

"Ollie, the only thing I'm focused on during race weekends is lap times." The words came out frustrated, but I couldn't stop the burning inside me. "Fashion isn't really on my mind when I'm preparing for a race weekend. Getting the car set up properly, analyzing data, working with my engineers—that's where my focus is."

Movement in my peripheral vision caught my attention. Someone entering the studio, probably another driver waiting for their slot with whatever unfortunate segment they'd been assigned to.

Then I saw who it was.

Henri.

He stood just inside the doorway, freshly emerged from makeup but still in his Hermes team shirt, hair artfully disheveled in that way that had probably taken someone twenty minutes to perfect. His expression was carefully neutral, but his dark eyes were locked on the interview with an intensity that made my skin prickle.

Great. Just what I need, an audience for these terrible questions.

"Let's talk about balance," Ollie continued, mercifully unaware of Henri's presence. "How do you balance the demands of racing with your personal life? Dating, friendships, self-care?"

"I don't really think about it in terms of balance," I said, aware of Henri watching this train wreck unfold. "During the season, racing is my life. Everything else has to fit around it in terms of priorities."

"But surely you must have hobbies? Interests outside of motorsport?" Ollie's smile was encouraging, like he was trying to coax a shy child into speaking. "What do you like to do to relax? Spa days? Shopping?"

I could see Henri's eyebrow raise slightly. That subtle lift that I'd learned to recognize over three years of competing against him. He was absolutely judging this entire situation, and by extension, probably judging me for participating in it.

As if I have a choice. I couldn't just walk out of a scheduled interview because the questions were patronizing and misogynistic.

"I sim-race on my computer," I said, an edge creeping into my voice despite my best efforts. "When I can, I race on a few different virtual teams."

Henri shifted in the doorway, arms crossed over his chest. Even from across the room, I could see the arch of his eyebrow.

I stared at the card in Ollie's hand—the one he'd just pulled from the stack the producer had handed him before the start. His apologetic wince told me everything before the words left his mouth. This one would be good.

"Walk us through your race-day makeup look. Do you go full glam or keep it natural under the helmet?"

The camera's red light blinked as the crew watched. My mother stood behind the monitors with her arms folded, nodding encouragingly, probably hoping I'd drop a sponsor's name.

I opened my mouth. Closed it. Opened it again.

"Under the helmet," I repeated slowly, "where no one can see my face. Where I'm pulling five lateral G's and sweating through a fireproof balaclava."

Ollie nodded.

"I wash my face in the morning. Then I put on my balaclava, which covers literally my entire face. And then I drive the car."

Back in the corner, I could see Henri almost laugh at that one.

The studio had gone quiet except for the soft hum of equipment. Even the crew seemed to sense my frustration. My eyes met Henri's, and I could see his finger lift slowly, pointing to the door. His face almost looked sympathetic to my plight.

But I couldn't leave. Not now, with the cameras rolling and my mother watching. Rennen's sponsors expected me to be gracious and media-friendly, and all the other things that apparently mattered more than actual racing ability. Plus, Ollie had warned me about this. I couldn't walk out on his opportunity to host this segment.

Ollie cleared his throat, glancing at the producer, who made a subtle gesture. "We're almost out of time, but I want to ask one more question." His tone shifted, becoming slightly more serious. "Now, there's been a lot of conversation about mental health in motorsport this season—the pressure, the scrutiny, the constant travel. What does taking care of yourself look like for you?"

Finally. A real question.

I took a breath, feeling some of the tension drain from my shoulders. "I think it's easy for people to forget that we're human. The helmets make us look bulletproof, invincible, but none of us are."

Out of the corner of my eye, I saw Henri straighten up, his finger no longer pointing to the door.

"Everyone talks about physical fitness," I continued, warming to the topic. "The diet, the simulator hours, the training regimen. But mental health is just as important. Your head is what drives the rest of you. If that falls apart, everything else follows."

Ollie nodded encouragingly, and for once, his interest seemed genuine rather than performative.

"Honestly?" My mind raced back to what Henri had said in Monaco. About his fears and his unwillingness to tell the team. Or do something about it. "It's important to have people around you who keep you grounded. And more than anything," I added, my voice firm now, confident, "it's important to know when to ask for help. To admit when you're struggling instead of trying to power through alone."

The words hung in the air, and I couldn't help it—my eyes flickered toward Henri. He looked away quickly, lips tight, and I wondered if my words had landed the way I'd meant them to.

If you won't tell anyone what you're going through, maybe this will at least make you think about it.

"During the season, I work with a sports psychologist," I said, returning my attention to Ollie and the camera.

"They help me stay focused when the noise gets too loud. After Miami, I made sure to book extra sessions, because I knew I needed support."

Although, I strategically left out the part about the note—a thought that made me feel like a hypocrite.

"That's really brave to admit," Ollie said quietly, and this time there was no patronizing edge. Just genuine respect.

"I don't think it should be something we hide," I said firmly. "You can train your body endlessly, perfect every technical skill, but if you ignore your mind and pretend you don't need help, you're just running on borrowed time until everything collapses."

The silence that followed felt different from the awkward tension earlier. More contemplative. More real.

"Well said, Lil," Ollie said finally. "Really well said."

After a few more questions, the director called, "And cut! Perfect, Lily. Beautiful."

Applause rippled through the crew, and I managed to smile and nod, even though I felt wrung-out and exposed and angry about the whole situation.

Ollie pulled me into a quick hug. "That last bit was gold. Really powerful stuff."

"Thanks," I said awkwardly, pulling away from the hug, keeping my voice low. "Those questions, Ollie. They were—"

"I know." He grimaced with a shrug. "Production really pushed for the beauty routine angle, the femininity stuff. I told them it was too much, but—"

"It was degrading at some points."

His face fell. "Lily, I'm sorry. Really. I fought for better material, but for the pilot episode they wanted to play it safe, appeal to a broader audience, or whatever corporate nonsense they fed me." He shook his head. "I hated every second of it."

I studied his expression, the genuine regret there. He'd warned me the questions would be cheesy. And he did look uncomfortable asking some of them.

"Look," he said, reaching for my hand, "let me make it up to you. Dinner tonight? Just us, no cameras, no producers telling me what to say. I'll even let you pick the place."

"Sure," I heard myself say. "That sounds nice."

Ollie took my hand, giving it a squeeze. "You handled that with so much grace. I mean it, you were incredible."

Before I could respond, he leaned in and pressed a kiss to my cheek. "Can't wait to see you later."

Warmth flooded my cheeks. I withdrew slightly, striving for what I hoped resembled an authentic smile instead of the awkwardness that I felt. "Yeah, same here."

He released my hand, still beaming, and I resisted the urge to touch where his lips had been. Not because it felt particularly meaningful, but because the gesture had caught me off-guard.

"Such a gentleman," I said, aiming for light and teasing but landing somewhere closer to strained.

Ollie's smile widened, clearly taking it as a compliment rather than the observation it was. "My mother raised me right."

He squeezed my shoulder once more before heading toward the producer, already launching into conversation about the next interview slot.

I stood there, suddenly aware of the studio chaos around me again. The crew packing up equipment. The bright lights that had made me sweat through my makeup.

And Henri, still watching from the doorway.

Ollie's smile returned, bright and relieved. "Perfect. I'll text you?"

"Yeah. Sounds good."

Chapter Fifteen

Henri

I watched Ollie kiss her cheek, his hand lingering on hers a beat too long. The easy affection between them, the way she smiled up at him—uncomplicated in a way we'd never been. I hadn't asked Lily about her relationship with Ollie. Probably because I didn't want to know. But as I watched them together, I knew there was something forming between them. Something we couldn't have.

Lily gathered her things, said something to the makeup artist, and headed for the exit. She passed within feet of me but didn't look my way.

I wanted to stop her. Ask if she was okay after that ridiculous interview. Tell her she'd handled it better than most would have.

But the words never appeared, and then she was gone.

The production assistant finished clipping the microphone to my collar and stepped back, giving Ollie a thumbs-up.

"We're all set," she said, then she disappeared behind the camera setup.

I'd done dozens of these interviews before. Promotional content, documentary pieces, behind-the-scenes footage—it was all part of the job. Usually, they were harmless. A few questions about racing philosophy, team dynamics, what I ate for breakfast. Easy content that made the sport feel accessible to fans.

But something about the way Ollie watched me made my shoulders tense. Or maybe it was just him in general.

I hated that the team had decided to use him in the upcoming Hermes documentary, but there was no getting out of this one. Hermes was turning seventy-five this year, and F1 had agreed to air a special documentary on their streaming app about the team. This interview would be one of those soundbite ones they'd spread in throughout the series as they talked about different races. Of course, this segment was on the pressures of racing and how Hermes helped their drivers compete at a high level.

The irony wasn't lost on me.

The room they'd set up for the interview was smaller than I expected. A conference room in the hospitality suite, chairs positioned at an angle to each other, a single camera on a tripod with a boom mic hanging overhead. Intimate. That was what they always called these setups. Like we were just two people having a conversation.

And not old teammates with a bitter past.

"Comfortable?" Ollie asked, settling into his chair across from me.

"Fine."

"Great. This shouldn't take too long." He glanced at his notes then back at me. "Just want to get your perspective on a few things. The real Henri Dubois, you know?"

I nodded, keeping my expression neutral. "Sure."

The camera operator—a young guy with a beard and a vest over his button-down—counted down from three with his fingers. The production assistant stood behind him, tablet in hand, watching a monitor I couldn't see.

The camera light blinked red, and Ollie flipped his notepad open. "Let's start small. Australia, the first race of the season. That late safety car—what went through your head?"

"The tire temp." I kept my hands folded in my lap, knuckles pale. Ollie perhaps didn't appreciate my short answers, but he continued to roll through the past nine races.

"You've looked incredibly sharp this season." His eyes stayed on my face, not the paper. "As an F1 veteran in their eighth season, how would you describe your growth as a driver since joining the team?"

"It's been a good learning experience," I said. "The team has given me strong machinery and great support. I'm focused on maximizing every opportunity."

Ollie nodded, making a show of checking his notes. "So far, this season has had its ups and downs for you—some brilliant performances, some more challenging races. How do you maintain consistency at this level?"

"You learn from every race." I shrugged. "Analyze what went right, what went wrong, and apply those lessons moving forward."

"Interesting." Ollie tapped his pen against his notepad. "Because looking at the data, your qualifying sessions have been particularly strong this year. You've had great qualifying, but the race results haven't always matched that pace. What do you think accounts for that gap?"

I shifted in my seat slightly. "Racing is unpredictable. Strategy, tire degradation, pit stops—there are a lot of variables that affect the outcome."

"Of course. But some might argue that there's also a mental component." He paused. "Would you say you're better at the sprint—the single fast lap—than the marathon of a sixty-lap race?"

"I wouldn't characterize it that way."

"How would you characterize it then?"

"I'd say I'm working on being complete in all aspects of race craft."

"Hm, that must add a lot of pressure," Ollie nodded, leaning forward slightly. "Formula 1 is one of the most mentally demanding sports in the world. We've seen drivers over the years struggle with anxiety, burnout, the weight of expectations. How are you coping with that pressure this season?"

"I'm managing it well," I said. "Every driver faces pressure. It's part of the job."

"Of course. But some might argue that there's also a mental component to racing consistency." Ollie glanced at his notes. "The ability to perform under pressure for two hours straight, lap after lap, managing the car and the competition simultaneously. That's a different challenge than a single qualifying lap, isn't it?"

"It is," I agreed. "But that's true for every driver on the grid."

"Fair point." He nodded thoughtfully. "But again, looking at your results during this season specifically, there does seem to be a gap between your one-lap pace and your race-day execution. Five front-row starts, but only two podiums. What do you attribute that to?"

"Like I said—strategy, tire management, race circumstances. There are a lot of factors."

"Right, of course." Ollie made a note on his pad. "Continuing on the mental side of that, though. How do you personally handle the pressure of a full race distance?

The decision-making, the focus required over those two hours?"

"The same way every professional does," I said. "You train for it, you prepare, you execute."

"Do you work with anyone on that side of things? A sports psychologist? Mental performance coach?"

"I work with the team's performance staff," I said carefully.

The conversation Lily and I had in Monaco replayed in my head uninvited. She'd told me to get help. Practically begged me to talk to someone, anyone. And like the coward I was, I'd shut her down. I stared at the camera operator, searching his impassive face for some kind of answer, some script to follow.

"But," I added, "it's… good that people talk about it." The words came out thin, rehearsed.

"And you?" Ollie pressed. "How do you personally deal with the burnout, the mental fatigue, the constant pressure to perform?"

My throat felt tight. The lights seemed to pulse, too bright, exposing every lie I was about to tell.

"I focus on racing," I heard myself say. "That's my job, and I love it. You don't burn out on something you love. It's not a problem for me."

The moment the words left my mouth, I wanted to take them back. Wanted to swallow them down and say something—*anything*—else instead.

I could hear Lily's voice now: "*Of course you burn out on things you love, Henri.*" She was right, of course. I'd learned that lesson before. Hell, even Georgia had to learn that lesson when she first joined F1. Racing couldn't be the only thing I did—not if I wanted to stay sane.

Ollie looked genuinely incredulous. "You never struggle? Never feel the fatigue, the pressure, getting to you?"

"Like I said, I'm fine."

He paused as if he was almost surprised by my flat-out lie. "What about Barcelona in F2? I remember there was some kind of incident—"

"No," I said firmly. Now that wasn't something I was willing to revisit. The microphone caught the edge in my voice, a snap I couldn't quite hide.

Perfect. Now I sound defensive and dishonest.

Ollie tapped his foot in a slow rhythm, studying me like I was a particularly interesting specimen under glass. After a few more questions, he nodded towards the Director. "Right," he said after a pause that lasted too long. "I think we have what we need."

Ollie closed his notebook and gave the camera a subtle nod. The red light blinked off.

"Thanks for your time," Ollie said, already gathering his things.

The quiet of the room that followed wasn't relief. It was the hollow, uncomfortable silence of a disaster barely contained. I sat there for a moment, frozen, the weight of the microphone still clipped to my shirt. Finally, I reached up and unclipped it with shaking fingers, setting it down on the chair with more force than necessary.

Back in the dressing room, the door opened without a knock. I didn't turn around; kept shoving things into my bag with more force than necessary.

"Dubois." Ollie's voice startled me. "Wasn't sure you'd bother showing up after Monaco."

I turned slowly. He was leaning against the counter, arms crossed, blocking my exit with infuriating casualness.

"You're not that lucky." I focused on zipping my bag, fingers fumbling with the zipper.

Also, I was contractually obligated to show.

His laugh echoed off the cream walls, too loud for the small space. He picked up a makeup brush, twirled it between his fingers, then dropped it with a deliberate thump.

"You look tired, mate. Monaco take that much out of you?"

Everything takes that much out of me these days.

"Something like that." I slung my bag over my shoulder, moving toward the door, toward him.

He didn't budge, just stood there, that easy smile fixed in place, picking at his fingernails with studied nonchalance.

"Must've stung," he continued, voice dripping false sympathy. "Pole position, home race, wet conditions that should've played to your strengths. And still…" He made a sympathetic clicking sound. "You couldn't do it. I mean, if you keep driving like that, you'll have to get used to finishing behind her."

"You finished behind me for three seasons straight, Ollie. Didn't see you getting used to it."

His expression barely flickered. He pushed off the door, closing the distance between us, ignoring my last comment. "So, you and Lily in that hallway back in Montreal."

I went still. "What about it?"

"Come on, Henri." His tone was almost friendly. "You visited her late at night? The way you looked at her…" He gave me a disbelieving scoff. "What, did you tell your team you were just talking?"

Ollie's smile was knowing. "Look, I get it. Lily is brilliant. She's beautiful and a catch."

I said nothing.

"Which is why we've been hanging out," he continued, examining his nails casually. "Last night, we were at her hotel until past midnight, chatting away about old times. Tonight, I'm taking her out to dinner."

My hands clenched at my sides, but I kept my face neutral.

"Something you can't do." His voice was light, conversational, even if the intent was anything but. "But me? I'm not a driver anymore. Lily and I can do whatever we want. So maybe step back. Let her be happy with someone who won't tank her career."

Ollie took advantage of my inability to speak, patting me on the back with mock sympathy. "Good luck this weekend, mate. Weather forecast says rain for qualifying. Hope you can keep it together out there."

The blood drained from my face. He knew. Somehow, he knew about the fear, the hesitation, the way my hands shook every time the track got wet.

But I shouldn't have been surprised; he'd watched me have an accident before.

"Get out."

"Touchy." He raised his hands in mock surrender, backing toward the door. "Just trying to be supportive."

"Get. Out."

He left whistling, the door clicking shut behind him with infuriating softness.

I stood there in the silence, gripping my bag so tight the strap cut into my palm, before pulling out my phone, checking the weather app.

Rain for qualifying. My hands were already shaking.

I grabbed my jacket and left before anyone else could find me.

Chapter Sixteen

Lily

The restaurant Ollie chose was tucked away in a quiet street, far enough from the circuit to feel like an escape. Warm amber light spilled from tall windows, and inside, white tablecloths and flickering candles created an intimate atmosphere that felt worlds away from the harsh glare of the studio.

A hostess led us to a corner table, menus already waiting. The low murmur of conversation mixed with soft classical music playing from hidden speakers.

Ollie pulled out my chair. "I figured we both needed something a bit nicer than the paddock cafeteria."

"You're not wrong," I said, settling into the seat and accepting the menu from the hostess.

Once we'd ordered, Ollie leaned back, candlelight playing across his features.

"Thanks for coming," he said. "I know today was rough."

"That's putting it mildly." I took a sip of water, trying to wash away the bitter taste the interview had left. "Those questions were patronizing at best."

"I know. Production really pushed for that angle. I fought them on it, but for the pilot episode—"

"It's fine," I said, picking at my salad. "At least it's over."

Ollie nodded.

"So, how did the interview with Henri go?" I asked, trying to shift the conversation to something a little easier. "For the Hermes documentary?"

He was quiet for a moment, swirling the wine in his glass. "It was... difficult. Or, at least, he was difficult."

"Really?" That surprised me, considering it was essentially a press piece on how Hermes was F1's most beloved team. Felix had done nothing but rant about it in the office since it'd been announced.

He let out a scoff. "We talked about pressure and mental health in the sport. Hermes wants clips for when they're discussing the work they're doing for mental health in racing. The usual documentary fodder." He shook his head. "And Henri flat out said he doesn't burn out on things he loves. That it's not a problem for him."

I went still, my fork frozen halfway to my mouth.

"Can you believe that?" Ollie continued, oblivious to my reaction. "Like burnout is just something that happens to other people. As if loving what you do makes you immune to the pressure, the exhaustion, the constant scrutiny."

My mind flashed back to Monaco. To Henri sitting on that couch, his voice raw and vulnerable as he described seeing the crash every time he approached certain corners. The way his hands trembled slightly when he talked about lifting without meaning to, his body betraying him. That wasn't someone who couldn't burn out. That was someone already burning.

"That's..." I said quietly. "That's quite a statement."

"It's typical Henri," Ollie said, taking a sip of his wine. "Always has to be the strongest, the most dedicated, the one who never cracks." He paused, studying me. "We have history, you know. Not good history."

I leaned forward slightly. "Oh?" Georgia had mentioned they'd raced together, but nothing about anything necessarily negative.

He hesitated, as if choosing his words carefully. "Henri and I go way back to F3 and F2. We were teammates. Shared data, spent long nights at the track, had dinners that turned into arguments about strategy, but still, we were friends." A faint nostalgic smile crossed his face. "He was brilliant. Everyone knew he was going to be a champion."

I took a sip of wine, saying nothing.

"But he was also intense," Ollie continued. "Like if he relaxed for even a second, the whole world would fall apart. He never switched off. Never let anyone in. The pressure was eating him alive, and everyone could see it except him."

I thought of Henri's behavior this season, the way he seemed to carry the weight of the world on his shoulders. The way he'd looked at me in Monaco, like he was drowning and didn't know how to ask for help.

"What happened?"

"He was burning out." Ollie's voice dropped lower, more intimate. "Skipping meals, sleeping in the simulator, pushing himself past any reasonable limit. And then, one day, he had this crash. He just… wasn't the same, and as his teammate, I was worried. We were supposed to be friends, you know? I tried to help."

I leaned forward, desperate to hear more. "How?"

"I went to our team principal," he said quietly, almost reluctantly. "Told them I was worried about Henri. Didn't give specifics, just said maybe he needed support, like from a sports psychologist, or to even take a break. Just something before he hurt himself or someone else on track."

He took a sip of his wine, eyes fixed on the candle flame between us. "He found out and thought I'd betrayed him. That I'd gone behind his back to sabotage his career and make him look weak to the team." Ollie took a moment to bite his lower lip as he seemed to debate what he was about to say next. "But the truth is, he saw me as a threat. There was only one open F1 seat with Hermes, and we were both fighting for it, even though it was pretty obvious Henri was going to get it. But that didn't stop him from making me the enemy, just to make sure he'd get it."

"What did he do?" I asked quietly.

Ollie scoffed. "He made up some story and told the team I'd gone to the press. That I was going to leak something. Well, they believed him, and they released me from the team. Just like that. And the following season, Henri got his seat."

The silence stretched for what felt like days. I stared down at my plate, processing what he'd just told me. It didn't fit with the Henri I knew—but then again, maybe I didn't know Henri as well as I thought.

Or maybe Ollie's version wasn't the whole truth.

"That's…" I struggled to find the right words. "I'm sorry that happened." It sounded hollow even to my own ears, but what else could I say? I didn't know what had really happened between them. I only had Ollie's side of the story.

If this were true, why had Georgia been so inviting of Ollie into her home back in Monaco? Unless Henri hadn't told her the truth about how his friendship with Ollie had ended.

Now, that did sound like Henri.

"Classic him, though," Ollie said, leaning back in his chair, cutting off my racing thoughts. "When it comes to winning, to getting what he wants, he'll do anything. Step on anyone in his way." He paused, meeting my eye. "Even people who care about him. Even people trying to help. He needs this championship, Lily. And when Henri needs something, everyone else becomes expendable."

I thought about Monaco again, about the kiss, about how he'd pushed me away immediately afterward. In Las Vegas he'd said he needed to focus on winning, that it was all that mattered to him.

That part I did believe.

My eyes watched Ollie and the way he absently ran his thumb around the rim of his wineglass as he talked, how the candlelight shimmered on his face, highlighting the shadow under his jaw. He kept glancing at me, as if checking to see if I'd react, or maybe to see if I already knew all this and was just politely waiting for him to finish.

"You talk like you're warning me," I said quietly.

Ollie reached across the table, taking my hand in his. His grip was warm, reassuring. "I just wanted you to know," he said quietly. "It felt important to tell you. I believe in being open and honest, especially with people I care about."

Something in my chest softened at that. Vulnerability. Actual, genuine vulnerability, the kind Henri had never once showed me—at least not willingly. Even in Monaco, when he finally opened up about the crash, it'd been like pulling teeth. He fought every word, guarded every admission like it was a state secret.

But here was Ollie, laying his past out in front of me without prompting. Trusting me with something painful.

"I appreciate that," I said, and I meant it. "Really. Thank you for telling me."

He squeezed my hand once before letting go, that easy smile returning to his face. "What do you say we get out of here? Early day tomorrow."

The walk back to the hotel was quieter, more comfortable than the tension of dinner. Ollie kept the conversation light—stories from his early journalism days, a funny anecdote about a botched interview with a former world champion. I found myself laughing, the heaviness of the earlier conversation lifting slightly.

We reached the hotel entrance, the warm glow of the lobby spilling out onto the street. Ollie turned to face me, hands in his pockets.

"Thanks for tonight," he said. "I know it wasn't all easy conversation."

"No, I'm glad we talked." I managed a smile. "Get some rest, yeah?"

"You too." He leaned in quickly, pressing a brief kiss to my cheek before stepping back. "Good night, Lily."

"Night, Ollie."

I watched him walk away down the street, then I turned and headed into the hotel lobby. The elevator doors opened, and I stepped inside, watching the numbers tick upward as I rose toward my floor, thinking back to Ollie's story.

Something about that story didn't sit right with me.

I had to ask Henri. Not tomorrow, maybe not even this week, but eventually. I needed to hear his side of what had happened in F2. This whole thing had to be a massive misunderstanding blown out of proportion by two competitive drivers fighting for the same seat. Even with everything going on, I couldn't believe Henri to be so cruel—but I also didn't think Ollie to be a liar.

The elevator doors slid open on my floor. I stepped out into the empty corridor, the soft carpet muffling my footsteps as I made my way to my room.

Whatever the truth was, it had to wait until after Austria.

Chapter Seventeen

Henri

I looked out the window of my driver's room, thanking the universe that the rain had cleared up. Qualifying for the Austrian Grand Prix had been today, and once again I'd managed to squeak out a much-needed pole position. This race had to go well, or I'd be even further behind Lily in points. I was starting to feel the desperation of being behind her in the championship. Two race wins separated us, and a third would feel almost damning.

My sister was curled on the gray sofa, legs tucked under her, scrolling through her phone while demolishing a protein bar. Her eyes looked tired, and I knew she hadn't been sleeping well. This season the Valkyrie car hadn't been performing, and based on their data, Georgia wasn't expecting this weekend's Grand Prix to go well. I knew she'd started to accept that for the first time in three years, she wasn't going to win this year's World Driver's Championship. Still, she never took her frustration out on me.

Georgia's phone screen dimmed as she set it face down. Her face hardened into that look she gave me when she was disappointed. "So, now that you're P1 again after this afternoon's qualifying, are we going to talk about what the hell happened out there in this morning's free practice, Henri?"

I turned. "*Quoi?*"

"You know exactly what I mean. You drove erratically. It's *free practice*, and you nearly took Lily out in Turn 6. Then you came within inches of the barriers during your next lap. I watched the whole thing."

My collar suddenly felt too tight. I tugged at it, the fabric rough against my fingertips. "I was pushing the car. That's what free practice is *for*."

"Pushing the car?" Her voice rose slightly, disbelief coloring every word. "There's a difference between testing limits and being reckless."

"I needed to get data for the team," I said through gritted teeth. "They need to know where the car is, what adjustments to make for qualifying. That's my *job*."

Georgia took a step closer, her eyes searching my face. "Henri, what's going on with you? This isn't normal. This morning you looked desperate."

I flinched at the accusation. "I'm not desperate."

But that wasn't true, not that Georgia understood how I was feeling. This season might have been tough for her, but that didn't take away the fact she'd achieved her dream of a win in Monaco and three championships.

I didn't have either. "I need to win this race, Georgia. I *need* to."

"Why?" Her voice softened slightly, but the concern in it only made my frustration worse. "We're not even halfway through the season, Henri! One race doesn't—"

"I'm already behind!" The words burst out of me, louder than I intended. "Lily's ahead of me in the standings. Every point matters. One more mistake, one DNF, and the gap gets bigger. I can't afford to give her any more ground. Not here. Not anywhere."

Georgia stared at me, her expression still soft even though my voice was rising. "So, you're going to kill yourself trying to prove a point in free practice? That's your strategy?"

"I'm not trying to prove anything," I said, forcing my voice to stay level even as anger simmered beneath the surface. "I'm trying to *win*. That's what we're here for, isn't it? Or have you forgotten?"

The moment the words left my mouth, I regretted them. Georgia's face went carefully blank, the way it always did when I'd crossed a line.

"That was low," she said quietly, and the apology sat on the tip of my tongue, but nothing came out. Georgia sighed, and I could hear a small hint of desperation in my sister's voice. "Henri, listen to me. I know you're under pressure. I know what it's like to feel like you're carrying the weight of everything on your shoulders. But you can't drive like this. You're going to hurt yourself, or someone else. I need to know you're okay out there."

"We needed the data. I'm—"

"—fine. Yes. So, you've said." She sat back down, taking a sip of her coffee, trying to find the right words. "You know, Éliott told me you haven't answered any of his texts or calls since Monaco."

I winced, guilt settling heavy in my chest. Éliott didn't deserve that. He'd been my best friend since we were kids, and I'd been ignoring him like he was just another person trying to get something from me. "I know. I've been a terrible friend." I rubbed my hand over my face. "I just haven't felt like myself lately. Everything feels… off."

"That's not an excuse," Georgia said, though her voice had lost some of its edge.

"I know it's not." I sighed. "I'll catch up with him after this weekend. Properly, not just some five-minute check-in."

Georgia nodded, seeming satisfied with that answer at least. The tension in the room eased slightly as she settled back on the sofa, picking up her phone again. We sat in silence for a few minutes, and after a refill of Georgia's favorite coffee, I could feel us both start to relax.

Suddenly, a smile crossed her face. "Oh, look! Ollie posted a photo of him and Lily from Montreal, from their dinner. They look cute together, actually."

I thought back to our conversation after my interview. *Wonder if he posted that as a reminder to me?*

Peering over Georgia's shoulder, I glanced at the photo. "She'd better watch out with that one. He's a snake."

Georgia's phone slipped slightly in her hand, her eyes widening. "What?"

"You heard me." I turned back to the window, unable to look at her. "Ollie's using her. For his career, his profile."

"Henri…" Her voice had changed—gone softer, more probing. "Why do you say that? I know you're annoyed that he asked you some tense questions in Montreal's press conference, but that doesn't mean he's a snake."

"He's just… not right for Lily."

She scoffed. "If you ask me, you're acting jealous."

"I'm not."

"Sometimes I wish you'd just admit you like Lily." Georgia said it with the certainty of someone who'd finally solved a puzzle she'd been working on for months.

Suddenly, I felt incredibly warm. "Georgia—"

"I just… I really thought you guys had something, that's all. And now you make comments about Ollie when I mention him with Lily." Her eyes searched my face, possibly seeing something she shouldn't have. "Henri, is there something you're not telling me? Did something happen between you two?"

"Nothing happened." The words came out too quickly, too defensive.

"But you wanted something to happen," Georgia said quietly. "Or… maybe something almost did?"

I pushed away from the window, grabbing my water bottle from the table with more force than necessary. "I'm done talking about this."

"Henri—"

"I said I'm done, Georgia." My voice came out harder than I intended, echoing off the bland walls. "*Arête*."

She stared at me for a long moment, her expression caught between sympathy and frustration. "Fine," she said finally. "But you acting like this isn't helping anyone. Especially not yourself."

I didn't respond, just stood there gripping my water bottle like it was the only thing keeping me grounded, trying not to think about Ollie's photo. About his arm casually draped near Lily's shoulder. About the way he'd captioned it with some charming quip that had hundreds of comments speculating about them as a couple.

She'd better watch out.

The thought circled in my mind like a warning I couldn't voice, a truth Georgia wouldn't understand, because she didn't know what I knew. Didn't know what Ollie was capable of when he wanted something.

The door swung open hard enough to rattle the glass. Ruth swept in, her Hermes lanyard bouncing against a white silk blouse. Her gaze landed on Georgia with veiled disapproval.

"I see you're still here."

The team didn't love having my sister in the Hermes driver's suite, even if she was family. Georgia had learned to keep her distance over the years, to fade into the background when the cameras came out. But Ruth never missed a chance to make a point.

"Hello to you too," Georgia said dryly, crossing her legs with the kind of calm that only irritated Ruth more.

Ruth didn't bite—didn't even spare her another look. "Do you have any idea what you've done?" She pointed her eyes squarely at me.

She slammed the tablet onto the coffee table hard enough to make both of us flinch. My own face stared back at me from the screen, frozen mid-blink in a still from the Ollie interview. I looked like someone I barely recognized, jaw tight, eyes cold, every muscle in my face betraying barely controlled anger.

Ruth jabbed the play button. My voice filled the room, flat and cold.

You don't burn out on something you love.

Georgia's eyebrows shot up. "Henri…"

"Compelling television," Ruth said, tapping the screen again to stop it, "if the goal was to tank an interview about mental health."

I exhaled slowly through my nose, trying to keep my expression neutral. The moment I walked out of that interview, I knew it would come back to haunt me. It hadn't felt right in the moment, and hearing it back now? It felt even worse.

"I didn't mean it like that." *Except I did.*

She turned her gaze back to me. "Then what did you mean?"

"Just that I love racing, and I'm lucky to be here in the Hermes seat. That this has been my dream since I was a child."

"Then why didn't you say that!" she groaned. "And don't get me started on the rest of the interview. The short answers? The monotone voice? You couldn't look less pleased to be there." Ruth spun toward Georgia as if searching for an ally, only to find her least favorite person in the room. "This seems like something out of your playbook. Have you been teaching him this?"

A not-so-subtle dig at the fact my sister was famous for her one-word press-conference answers.

Georgia's mouth twitched with amusement. "Besides the burnout answer, he didn't sound that bad, Ruth. Being your authentic self is what people like these days."

Ruth gave a humorless laugh. "Authenticity is a luxury reserved for people without seven-figure contracts. I need Henri to be someone else in this interview."

"Come on, it's not that bad."

"Oh, please." She waved Georgia off. "Look, Henri, I get that you're a genius in a car, but out here?" She gestured around the lounge. "Out here, none of that matters. You can't be a PR liability."

I scratched my nails against my leg. "You done?"

Ruth took a measured breath, visibly reining in her frustration. "Fortunately, they're going to let you redo the interview. As the documentary won't air until after summer break, we have some time. I will prep some questions and get that redone. Understood?" Her tone left no room for negotiation.

I raised both hands in mock surrender. "I'll do my best."

"Lately, your best has left much to be desired." Ruth closed her eyes as if reciting a prayer for patience. "Now, we have your post-qualifying press conference. Henri, please, try not to dig your press hole any deeper between now and tomorrow. Your conference is in twenty minutes. Don't make me chase you."

She straightened her lanyard, spared Georgia one last icy glance, and marched out without waiting for a response. The door shut behind her with a loud click.

Georgia let out a low whistle. "Remind me never to get on her shit list."

"Too late for both of us," I muttered.

"That interview with Ollie, though. What was that about?"

I rubbed my face with both hands. "What do you mean?"

"The burnout question. You told him you don't burn out on things you love—that mental fatigue isn't a problem for you." She tilted her head, studying me. "Why would you say that?"

"I didn't know what they wanted me to say."

"Henri." Her voice softened. "It's not true. Nobody goes through what we go through and doesn't struggle sometimes. You know that."

I shrugged, picking at a loose thread on my sleeve. "I thought it was what they wanted to hear."

"Who? Ollie? The team?" She leaned forward. "Or are you trying to convince yourself?"

When I didn't answer, she pressed on. "You've been off all season. Snapping at people, isolating yourself, and now you're lying in interviews about how you're handling the pressure. Are you sure there's nothing I can do?"

"It was just a bad interview," I said finally. "I'll do better next time."

Georgia studied me for another long moment, clearly unconvinced. Then she sighed and leaned back, arms crossed over her chest. "You know what's going to happen, right? You keep acting like this, shutting people out, snapping at everyone, making scenes, and eventually, you'll run out of people willing to put up with it."

She stood, brushing off her jeans with deliberate casualness. "You've got twenty minutes to pull yourself together and not piss off Ruth any further." She headed for the door, pausing with her hand on the handle. "Good luck with that press conference. Try not to make any more headlines."

—

On Saturday, the post-qualifying press room was already hot. Rows of reporters leaned forward in their seats, phones raised, recorders blinking. The low hum of voices quieted the moment the moderator stepped up to the mic.

"Post-qualifying conference for the Austrian Grand Prix," he announced, his voice the same neutral drone used for every circuit. "We have Henri Dubois for Hermes, Lily Blackwood for Rennen, and Luca Rossi for Rennen. Congratulations to our top three."

I gave a half-smile. Next to me, Lily's posture was perfect, hands folded neatly on the table. She didn't bother to look at me, not even a glance. We hadn't spoken since Monaco.

"Henri," the moderator began, "another pole position. How are you feeling heading into tomorrow?"

After a long and arduous qualifying, I'd managed to secure P1. Thankfully, sunshine had finally arrived. Not five minutes after Q3 ended, the rain had started coming down.

"Confident," I said. "The car's been solid all weekend. The team executed perfectly."

"And Lily, P2, your thoughts?"

"Rennen has really strong pace. The car's been improving every week, and we're in a great place for the race tomorrow." She plastered her usual deflection-ready grin onto her face. The same one Luca often wore.

Wonder if they practiced it in the garage, I thought sarcastically.

The moderator adjusted his mic. "Next question, please."

A hand shot up in the third row. "Question for Henri and Lily. In FP3 this morning, there was that close call in Turn 6. No penalties were given, but it looked tense. Care to comment?"

My stomach felt sick. Lily and I had another close call during qualifying, and while no one received a penalty, both teams had been screaming that we'd tried to block the other.

Before I could answer, Lily reached for her microphone.

"Closer than I would've liked." Her knee bounced ever so slightly—that sign she was feeling uncomfortable. "But it's a tight track. I know Henri was probably frustrated, but I left as much room as I could."

As soon as she said that, the scripted answer Ruth had provided me immediately fled my brain. Lily had blocked me, plain and simple.

"I was on a flying lap. She was just starting hers. I had the right of way."

Lily turned toward me, finally looking at me for the first time since we'd sat down. Her brows lifted slightly, like she couldn't quite believe I'd decided to go there. "And I respected that and stayed off the racing line."

"You nearly forced me off the track," I said bluntly.

"I was six car lengths back." That diplomatic tone was starting to thin, cracks showing beneath her polished tone. "You had room, Henri."

"You know, Lily, there's a difference between racing hard and creating unnecessary risk."

Lily lightly scoffed. "Unnecessary risk? I just said that I was *six car lengths back*." Her voice was restrained, but I could see I was poking the metaphorical bear.

I knew I should stop, just leave it as it was, but I couldn't get myself to stop. The frustration from last weekend's race loss, the interview with Ollie, and this morning's practice had led me to this place. A place that I hated to be but could not escape.

"That's plenty of distance, and you know it. Maybe—" She stopped herself, but frustration danced in her eyes.

"Maybe what?"

She shook her head. "Nothing."

"No—say it." I leaned forward, my pulse quickening. "*Maybe what*, Lily?"

The air all of a sudden felt thinner, and my throat began to swell. Breathing felt nearly impossible. Reporters leaned forward, phones and records in hand. The constant clicking of camera shutters intensified, a rapid-fire percussion that seemed to come from all directions at once.

Luca shot me a look from beside Lily, his brown eyes almost pleading with me: *Stop, before this gets worse.*

But I couldn't seem to stop. Couldn't pull back from whatever precipice I was standing on.

So much for not digging a deeper hole.

Lily grabbed the mic, her knuckles going white. "Maybe the problem isn't where I was, Henri. Maybe it's that you apparently seem to see a ghost whenever there's even a hint of rain."

The words hit like a gut punch. My vision tunneled slightly, the edges of the room going fuzzy and indistinct. My mouth hung open as I stared at her, desperately searching for words that would make this okay; that would deflect and smooth over and return us to the safe, professional territory we were supposed to occupy.

"What's that supposed to mean?"

"Nothing. Henri, I shouldn't have—" Lily's voice dropped to just above a whisper.

The room felt unnaturally still, and even the moderator seemed frozen. His hand hovered uselessly near his microphone, like even he didn't know what to say. With one hand pressed to her temple like she was physically holding back a migraine, Ruth's face did nothing to control her evident fury.

Expectant faces and recording devices watched me like a hawk. The perfectly crafted answers that Ruth and I had rehearsed repeatedly disappeared entirely.

"Fuck this."

My hands moved on autopilot, and I set the mic down on the floor. I stood abruptly, my chair scraping against the stage floor with a harsh screech. The moderator's hand reached out to me, but then he set it down, like he too could see I was done.

My feet dragged me out of the seat and away from the sea of journalists. On my way out I could hear their whispers, and I did everything to shut them out.

I'm sure Ruth will fill me in on what they said later.

As soon as I was outside the room and into the hallway, I felt a tear slide down my cheek, hot and unwelcome, like a physical betrayal of my carefully constructed façade. I swiped at it roughly with the back of my hand.

"Henri!" Ruth's voice echoed through the quiet. She caught up beside me, breathless, her phone already buzzing with notifications. "What happened to not making a scene?"

"I answered their questions," I said, my voice rough and unsteady.

"You *detonated* on live television!" She waved her arms in the air, her phone still clutched in one hand, the screen lighting up with what I could only assume were increasingly frantic messages from team management. "Do you even care how that looked?"

More footsteps joined us.

Georgia.

"Henri." Her voice was gentle, concerned in a way that made my throat tighten. She was already reaching for my arm, that familiar protective instinct I'd known my entire life written across her face.

"Don't," I said sharply. "Please. Just… don't."

"Hey." Her tone was careful. "You're shaking."

"I'm fine." My voice came out clipped and hollow, but my body told a completely different story. My hands trembled at my sides, fingers tapping my side. The slight tremor ran up my arms, into my shoulders. I could feel my heart racing against my ribs, like it might crack through the bone.

Ruth exhaled through her nose, the sound dripping with barely restrained frustration. "Just brilliant, Henri."

"Enough," Georgia said, stepping between us.

My PR officer threw both hands into the air with theatrical exasperation, her phone nearly flying from her grip. "Fine. You deal with him then." She spun on her heel, storming off down the corridor without a backward glance. Within three steps, she already had the phone pressed to her ear, her voice rising as she began barking rapid-fire instructions into it.

The hallway grew quiet again.

"Henri, talk to me." Georgia's voice was stripped of any judgment, but I couldn't even look at her. Every breath felt shallow and too close together. The walls felt larger, like they were starting to crowd me.

"I need—" I started, but the words wouldn't finish.

"What?" Georgia's hand hovered near my shoulder, not touching, but close.

"Air. I need air. I can't—" I couldn't finish. Couldn't explain that the walls felt like they were pressing in; that my lungs wouldn't fill properly; that every sound seemed too loud and too far away at the same time.

"Let's go outside."

The moment the door to the hallway opened, the humid Austrian air hit my face, thick and warm, but at least it was *different*.

And then I ran.

Not a jog or a quick walk, but a full sprint, footsteps pounding against pavement, my chest heaving, until I reached the entrance to the driver facilities.

My hand closed around a familiar door handle, and I slammed the door shut as soon as I was inside, letting myself fall against the door, head on my knees. Everything

I'd tried to bury clawed its way back up. The flash of the crash, the interview with Ollie, the press conference.

Losing Monaco.

My chest hurt. My throat burned. I tried to slow my breathing, but it only made it worse, the inhale catching, the exhale coming too soon. I pressed my palms to my eyes until I saw stars. Lily had been right. I'd pushed her too far, and she'd said what everyone else was thinking.

For a few long seconds, I didn't feel like a driver, or a brother, or anyone worth interviewing. Just a man sitting in a silent room, trying not to fall apart.

Chapter Eighteen

Lily

The compact gym tucked into the Rennen garage carried the subtle odor of rubber flooring and deodorant. Andy knelt next to me, murmuring numbers as I worked through my shoulder stretches.

"Five… six…" His thumb dug deeper, and I bit back a hiss. "You're tighter than usual, Lil."

"Long week." I winced.

"Oh, I *know*." He passed me the resistance band—the red latex one we used for shoulder mobility—settling back on his heels. "I watched yesterday's press conference."

This time, the wince had nothing to do with the knot in my back. Each time I replayed it in my head, guilt crawled a little bit deeper into my heart.

"*Maybe it's that you still see a ghost whenever there's a hint of rain.*" I shouldn't have said it. Not like that. Not in front of everyone. I had so much regret that I'd felt physically sick all day.

That wasn't me. I didn't want to fight fire with fire, especially not with Henri.

"It's all anyone in the paddock could talk about this morning," Andy continued, watching me with those sharp eyes that missed absolutely nothing. "Well, that and speculation about whether you and Henri are going to actually come to blows during today's Grand Prix."

Andy grabbed the band from me, setting it down on the table. "Lil, what is going on here? That press conference yesterday, that wasn't you. I know you and Henri have your differences—"

I stared at the floor. "I didn't mean to say it."

"Then why did you?"

I pulled my right knee to my chest, feeling the familiar overstretched burn at the front of my hip. Physical discomfort, I could handle. This conversation? Less so.

"In the moment, all I could think about was Henri's driving. He was so erratic during free practice, nearly crashing into me. He got lucky, but it was so out of character, even for this season." I pressed my forehead against my knee, taking a breath. "It was like something snapped in him, and I was worried. So, I just… blurted it out. Thought maybe if I called him on it, he'd stop spiraling."

"And instead?" Andy prompted gently.

"Instead I made it worse." The admission tasted bitter. "I hurt him in front of everyone."

Andy stayed quiet, watching me with those patient eyes that'd seen me through countless bad days. Finally, he said, "Lil, what's really going on between you two? Because this feels like more than just competition."

I sighed. "I haven't told anyone this. I guess mostly because… I'm embarrassed? Or it makes me sad? I don't know. But last year, in Las Vegas, Henri and I…" I stopped, sucking in a breath. "We slept together. It was like three years of dancing around the temptation was finally over, and afterward, I thought we'd be something."

I picked at the loose thread on my leggings, not looking up.

"And then, the next morning, he said he didn't want a relationship. That we should just forget it happened." The memory still stung. "And so, I tried to move on."

Andy stayed quiet, his hands gently resting on mine as his soft eyes stared at me with sympathy.

The words came faster now. "Then, in Monaco last week, I went to his room…" I paused, thinking about why I'd gone to his room in the first place. I hadn't told Andy about the notes yet, because I knew he'd tell the team immediately. So, I opted for the safer version. "I went to ask him about why he slowed down so much during the curves… and we kissed again. Well, again after *Montreal*."

Andy looked incredibly surprised, which was usually hard to do.

"Wow. Lily. I had no idea. I wish you'd told me. You know, you don't have to carry all this alone."

I flashed him an appreciative smile.

"So, where does this leave you and Ollie? You've been hanging out; not sure how serious it all is."

"Ah, now that's had an interesting development."

Andy's face was a mixture of curiosity and wariness. "Oh?"

Ollie's voice popped into my head. His story about F2, about Henri, delivered with that perfect blend of concern and reluctance that made it sound so goddamn believable.

"Back in F2, Ollie said Henri was burning out. Pushing too hard, not sleeping, the whole spiral. He'd apparently had an accident, and it was causing him to struggle. So, Ollie went to their team principal to try to help, suggested Henri might need support, like a sports psychologist or something."

I paused, the next part sticking in my throat.

"Henri found out and turned it around on him. Told their team principal that Ollie was lying, and he was unstable and jealous. That Ollie was going to leak his private life to the press, make them think he couldn't be trusted. The F2 team let him go, ending any hope of him having an F1 career."

Andy turned to face me fully, the towel draped over his shoulder slipping slightly. His expression was carefully blank. "That's quite a story."

I nodded. "I know. It just… doesn't feel like Henri."

"You know," Andy said, "I partly wonder if the truth is somewhere in the middle. Either way, you should ask Henri about it."

"I know. I will. Probably should be after I apologize for yesterday…"

Andy's expression softened. "Look, Lil, when you put the helmet on today,"—Andy gestured vaguely toward the garage door, toward the paddock beyond—"leave all this drama outside the car. It just needs to be you in there. Nothing else gets to come along for the ride."

I nodded, and the door to the gym swung open. Andy motioned toward the exit. As he walked behind me, he called out, "You ready to go win something?"

"Always," I said, stepping into the corridor, which was full of mechanics.

Andy squeezed my shoulder once before heading toward the garage. I watched him disappear into the chaos of race-day prep, then I turned toward my driver's room.

My phone buzzed in my pocket, and I pulled it out.

Unknown number. Again, with another thinly veiled threat.

The only thing that could make this day any worse.

"Last lap," Mark said in my ear, voice calm. "Gap is under a second to Henri."

This win in Austria was so close I could almost taste it.

For most of the race, Henri and I had traded places. But a perfectly timed pit stop from his team, and a few small mistakes from me, had handed him the lead. Now, with one lap left, he was still there. Right in front of me.

Untouchable.

I pressed the brake a little too late into Turn 3. The rear end shivered in protest, a warning tremor vibrating up through the seat. A message from the car that I was pushing too hard and asking too much.

Henri stayed where he always was. Just out of reach.

Don't think about him. Just drive.

The track blurred by, then the grandstands became a large blur of color and noise. I was supposed to love this part. But my thoughts were too loud. I clipped the next apex tighter than I intended.

My radio crackled. "Careful, Lily. Keep it clean," Mark said, a trace of warning now.

"Copy."

Henri was a three-second lead ahead of me, and there was no way I could pass now. My car wobbled through the next corner, the balance just slightly off. Every movement felt sharper now, more desperate.

"Can you give us more?"

No, was the actual answer. The car just didn't have the pace underneath. The steering wheel felt slick under my gloves despite the moisture-wicking material, sweat pooling in my palms from effort and frustration in equal measure.

Henri's car flicked through the final corner, absolutely flawless. A machine in perfect harmony with its driver. Mine followed half a heartbeat later, desperately trying to catch up. The checkered flag waved from the marshal's post.

Henri crossed the line first.

The silence on the radio said a lot about how we were all feeling, but then Mark's voice burst through again, surprisingly cheerful. "P2! Great job, Lily! Fantastic drive!"

I didn't answer right away. The words were stuck, refusing to come out as anything coherent or media-friendly. I exhaled slowly, counting the beats like I would during a qualifying lap, trying to ground myself in something familiar and controlled. When I finally spoke, I hoped to God my voice would sound normal, calm, professional, like this was just another Sunday afternoon.

"Copy." My voice sounded flat, emotionless, like it belonged to someone else entirely. "Nice job, everyone. Good strategy today."

I told myself second place was fine. The rational part of my brain, the part that remembered we had more than half the races to go this season, knew that P2 was excellent. The championship was by no means over—not that it was any consolation.

I watched his car slow ahead of me on the cooldown lap, the faint crimson flash of his brake lights visible through the tarmac's reflection. He raised one hand in acknowledgment as he passed the marshal posts, that polite little wave of sportsmanship the cameras always loved.

I parked on my mark, killed the engine, and stepped out into a tidal wave of noise.

"Lily, over here!" the post-race interviewer called out. "Wow, what an incredible race! Walk us through Turn 1. Any regrets on the strategy? What did you make of Henri's pace in sector two?"

I said all the right things. That the fans were incredible and the car was coming alive, that our upgrades were working, that Hermes had nailed it today, but we'd be ready to fight next race. The words tasted like artificial sweetener, but I kept that fake smile fixed in place.

Henri did the same, keeping his answers safe. After yesterday, we'd both been scolded to no end by our press teams, and we were under strict instructions to ignore each other. Even the journalists this morning avoided asking us any questions about the other.

We went up for the podium, and Henri held up his trophy—that massive, ornate thing that weighed more than it looked. He didn't bother to look at me when he lifted the trophy, but I clapped anyway. Because cameras were recording every moment, analyzing every micro-expression for signs of drama.

And because maybe, despite everything, he'd earned it today.

As soon as I stepped off, a familiar voice called out to me. "Well, well, well, if it isn't my favorite driver!"

"Ollie!" I said, managing a smile.

He swept me into a hug, planting a kiss on my cheek for good measure. "You were incredible!" he said. "Second place looks good on you, though, personally, I think you deserved better."

"Do you?" I said lightly, stepping back. Because I didn't.

"Absolutely," he said, flashing his charming grin at a nearby camera before lowering his voice. "You had him on the ropes. Another lap, and you'd have taken him."

"Yeah, well." I shrugged, suddenly exhausted by the whole conversation. "Didn't happen."

"Next time," he said easily. "There's always next time." He meant it as encouragement, and I flashed him a thankful smile.

"Lily!" Georgia's voice cut through the crowd, and I turned to see her jogging over, still in her Valkyrie team gear, sunglasses pushed up into her messy ponytail. "You were amazing," she said, pulling me into a hug.

"Tell that to my engineer," I said, unscrewing the cap of my water bottle and taking a long drink.

"I will," she said, laughing, knowing full well that Mark would never say otherwise. "Actually." Her expression shifted to something more hopeful. "I'm throwing a little thing tonight. Nothing fancy, just a few of us. You know, the usual post-race decompression situation. Drinks, food, very low-key. You should come!"

I blinked, caught off-guard. "For Henri?"

Georgia looked around, taking in the surroundings before leaning closer. "He's been wound so tight lately. I thought it might help to have people around after a win, you know? Remind him that this"—she gestured vaguely at the podium, the champagne-soaked celebration, the cheering crowd—"is supposed to feel good. That he's allowed to enjoy it instead of just… existing through it."

I hesitated. "I'm not sure he'd want me there, Georgia." *Not after yesterday.*

"Nah," she said with a dismissive wave, although she did seem to be contemplating what I'd said. "He'll be all right. You should be there. Besides, it's not just him.

Éliott's coming too. You'll like the place. Quiet corner, good fries."

Ollie stepped forward before I could answer, slipping his sunglasses back on. "That sounds perfect," he said smoothly. "Count us in."

Us.

I gave him a look. "I don't remember RSVPing."

"You were about to," he said, tone teasing, but his hand brushed lightly against my arm.

Georgia looked between us, watching Ollie's arm around me, but she didn't say no. "Um, okay. Sounds great," she said. "Eight o'clock. I'll text you the address, Lil. It's nothing formal."

"Got it."

Ollie and I started walking back to the Rennen garage. "You don't have to come." Truthfully, it didn't feel like a great idea after what he'd told me.

"What? I want to." Ollie pinched my arm playfully. "It'll be nice to do something outside the paddock. Something *together*."

I nodded. "Well, thanks for the support today," I said, reaching up to touch his arm. "I'll see you later, yeah?"

"Count on it," Ollie said, that easy grin still in place.

I slipped away before he could say anything else, weaving through the lingering crowd and ducking into the paddock's quieter corridors. The noise faded behind me, replaced by the hum of generators and distant conversations. My legs felt heavy, the adrenaline finally draining away and leaving nothing but exhaustion in its wake.

The Rennen hospitality building loomed ahead. I nodded at a couple of mechanics on my way through, their congratulations bouncing off me without sticking.

My driver's room waited at the end of the hall, door half-open like someone had just left.

I pushed inside and froze.

The bouquet sat on the narrow table beside my helmet, arranged in a glass vase. Roses this time, deep red and beautifully wrapped.

The irony wasn't lost on me. Someone who'd apparently lost money betting on me, spending a small fortune on flowers to remind me of exactly how much I disappointed them.

I crossed the room slowly, and my hands reached for the small white card tucked between the stems almost against my will, fingers trembling slightly as I pulled it free.

SECOND PLACE SUITS YOU. DON'T GET COCKY. STAY THERE.

I take that back, I thought sarcastically, *maybe they made money on Henri.*

My fingers curled around it, crumpling the expensive cardstock into a tight ball. Squeezing it felt good, even if it accomplished nothing.

"Lily?"

I spun around so fast I nearly lost my balance, my heart jumping into my throat. My mother stood in the doorway, her gaze landing first on the flowers, then me.

"Oh, I see you finally got some flowers better than those grocery-store ones." She moved closer to the arrangement, one perfectly manicured finger reaching out to touch a petal with the kind of delicate care she usually reserved for expensive things.

I opened my mouth then closed it, looking down at the crumpled note still clenched in my hand.

"Who are they from?"

The words stuck in my throat. I'd kept quiet for weeks, convinced it would go away, that it was just noise. But now I couldn't deny that this wasn't going away.

I held out the wrinkled note.

She crossed the room in three strides, plucking it from my fingers and smoothing it out against her palm. Her expression didn't change as she read it.

"How many?" she asked.

"Three letters," I said quietly, my own voice sounding small and uncertain even to my ears. "Maybe four. There was a text too. I'm not sure if that counts or if it's someone different—"

She looked up, eyes hard. "Have you mentioned this to anyone else?"

"No." A lie, but I didn't think telling her that Henri knew would help anything.

"Just leave it with me." She exhaled slowly, folding the note with precise, deliberate movements. "I'll bring it up when the time is right. We don't want to look hysterical over a few notes. Keep smiling," she said, sliding the note into her purse like it was a receipt. "You've had a good day. Second place, solid points. Don't let this ruin it."

"Okay…"

"You know that better than anyone, darling. We must be twice as composed, twice as professional, twice as unflappable as the men. That's just the reality of our position." She reached for the crystal vase, lifting it with both hands, flowers and all, and walked toward the door with the kind of graceful efficiency that made it clear the conversation was over.

"Mother…" I started, not quite sure of what I was going to say.

She smoothed her jacket. "Go fix your makeup. You have media obligations in twenty minutes, and I won't have you looking rattled."

I stared at her, waiting for something more. For concern to crack through that composed exterior, or anger on my behalf, or even just some acknowledgment, but she just looked at me for one more long moment, her expression carefully neutral, before stepping through the doorway.

Chapter Nineteen

Henri

The bar Georgia had picked was the opposite of the paddock chaos I'd been drowning in all weekend. Low ceilings, warm amber light pooling in corners, wood beams overhead. A track played softly through hidden speakers, the kind of classics that belonged in piano bars, not the aggressive club music that usually followed race weekends.

I stood at the far end of the polished mahogany counter nursing a whiskey I couldn't really taste. Today had been perfect and everything I'd worked for.

So why does it all feel so fucking hollow?

Éliott planted himself beside me like a loyal guard dog. After the race, I'd finally called him and apologized for being so cold, and in typical Éliott fashion, he was incredibly forgiving and understanding. He always had been. Éliott was talking with his hands, gesturing wildly, expressions cycling thought at least six different emotions per sentence.

I nodded at what I hoped were the appropriate beats, making the right sounds of acknowledgment, but my mind was somewhere else entirely. My eyes felt heavy, gritty, like I'd been awake for days instead of just one long, exhausting weekend.

The door opened with a soft chime.

I felt her before I saw her. That inexplicable awareness I'd developed over years of racing alongside Lily Blackwood, of knowing exactly where she was on track without even looking in my mirrors. Some sixth sense that existed independent of logic or reason.

Lily stepped through the doorway first, hesitating just inside the threshold like she was already regretting coming. She wore dark jeans and a simple top, her hair down around her shoulders instead of pulled back like it usually was for racing. She looked softer somehow, less armored than she did in team gear.

Beautiful. She looked absolutely beautiful.

The light caught the gold in her hair, turning it warm honey. Without makeup, freckles dusted across her nose— the same ones I counted that night in Las Vegas.

Her eyes found mine almost immediately, like she'd been looking for me. For a suspended moment, we just stared at each other across the crowded bar. Then a small smile tugged at the corners of her mouth. She lifted her hand in a small wave, almost shy, and my chest tightened so hard I forgot how to breathe.

I managed a nod, unable to trust my voice—unable to do anything but hold her gaze, an unspoken congratulations floating between us. Was she thinking about our kiss in Montreal? Or Monaco?

Then Ollie stepped in behind her, his hand settling possessively on her lower back, guiding her forward like she needed his direction to navigate a simple doorway.

The smile disappeared from her face as if it never existed. She looked away first, breaking whatever fragile connection we'd forged, and let Ollie guide her deeper into the bar.

Georgia's head snapped up mid-laugh, her eyes clocking them before they fully entered. She excused herself from the cluster of Hermes engineers she'd been entertaining, her smile widening in that genuine way that meant she was happy to see Lily, not just being polite.

"You made it!" Georgia's voice carried across the bar as she wrapped Lily in a hug.

I turned back to my whiskey, staring into the amber liquid like it held answers.

"Henri." Éliott's voice pulled me back. "You even listening to me?"

"Sorry." I took a sip, the whiskey burning pleasantly down my throat. "What were you saying?"

He gave me a long look—the kind that said he knew exactly where my attention had gone. "I was saying that you drove brilliantly today. Best I've seen you all season. Whatever was in your head this weekend, you channeled it perfectly into the car."

If only he knew what was actually in my head.

"Thanks," I managed.

"But." Éliott's tone shifted, becoming more serious. "You also look like shit. When's the last time you slept?"

"I sleep fine."

"Bullshit." He flagged down the bartender, ordering another round without asking if I wanted one. "You've got that look. The one you get when you're running on fumes."

I didn't argue, because he wasn't wrong.

My gaze found them again, almost involuntarily. Lily and Ollie made their way to the bar, Ollie already signaling the bartender with that easy confidence. His hand returned to her back, casual and possessive in a way that made my head hurt.

Or my heart.

Then Lily stepped sideways, creating space between them. His hand fell away.

Ollie seemed to notice me at the same moment I was staring. His eyes met mine across the crowded bar, blue and calculating, a smirk playing at the corners of his mouth like he'd won something.

Then Lily's gaze followed his.

Her expression when she saw me was complicated, layered with things I couldn't quite parse in the dim light. Not quite a glare, but definitely not happiness either. After Saturday's press-conference disaster, I couldn't blame her. We'd both said things we shouldn't have. Her press-conference insult still stung like an open wound.

I looked away first, focusing on my drink with more intensity than it deserved.

"You want to leave?" Éliott asked quietly. "We can go somewhere else. Grab Luca, head back to the hotel, and drink just the three of us."

"No." I set my glass down. "Georgia organized this. I should stay."

"Being here out of obligation isn't the same as actually being present, my friend."

When did Éliott become so wise?

The bar filled up gradually, more team members, a few other drivers, the usual post-race crowd seeking refuge from the intensity of the paddock. The noise level rose, conversations bleeding together into an indistinct hum punctuated by occasional laughter.

"You won today. You're supposed to look at least moderately happy about it." He studied my face with a scrutiny I could never quite escape. "What's going on?"

"Nothing. Just tired."

His gaze flicked toward where Lily had disappeared into a booth in the back with Georgia. "Does this have anything to do with—"

"Don't." I cut him off before he could finish. "Please. Not tonight."

He squeezed my shoulder before collecting his drink from the bartender.

I nursed my whiskey and tried not to track Lily's movements across the room, failing spectacularly. The booth in the back corner had become a small gathering: Lily, Georgia, Ollie, and a few other drivers.

"I need some air," I told Éliott, setting down my glass with more force than necessary.

"Want company?"

"No. Just give me a minute."

I stepped outside through the side door that led to a narrow alley behind the bar. The night air was damp and cool, carrying the faint smell of rain. Cigarette smoke drifted from somewhere nearby, mixing with the scent of garbage bins and old cooking oil.

I leaned against the brick wall, letting my head fall back, eyes closing against the dull throb building behind them. The muffled bass from inside the bar pulsed through the wall, a steady rhythm that did nothing to settle my nerves.

You won today. You executed perfectly. This should feel good.

So why did everything feel like it was falling apart?

I went to head back inside but stopped just inside the doorway, something cold settling in my chest that had nothing to do with the windy weather outside.

Ollie had his arm stretched along the back of the booth behind Lily, not quite touching her, but close enough to stake a claim. She laughed at something Georgia said, her face more relaxed than I'd seen it in weeks. Luca was gesturing wildly with both hands, probably telling some ridiculous story, and Éliott was shaking his head with that fond exasperation he reserved for Luca's antics.

The rational part of my brain knew I was being unfair. Knew that Georgia had invited them, that there was nothing wrong with Lily being here, that I had no claim on who my friends spent time with.

But the irrational part—the exhausted, emotionally raw part that had barely held it together all weekend—couldn't stand there and watch this. Couldn't pretend to be happy while Ollie smiled that easy smile and Lily laughed with my sister and everything I wanted sat right there, impossible and out of reach.

I turned and walked back out before anyone noticed me standing there.

The street was quiet, rain-slicked pavement reflecting the amber glow of streetlights. A few tourists hurried past, hunched under umbrellas, oblivious to the man who'd just won a Formula 1 race and felt more alone than he had in years.

I pulled out my phone and sent a quick text to Georgia: *Sorry. Had to leave. Thanks for organizing tonight.* No explanation, because I didn't want to admit what I was doing.

Running away.

—

As soon as I walked into my hotel lobby, I couldn't bring myself to head up to the room, so I opted for the hotel bar instead. A tired bartender polished glasses with the detached focus of someone working on pure muscle memory. A few scattered patrons occupied various corners, nursing late-night drinks in that particular solitude that hotel bars specialized in.

I claimed a table in the back, half-hidden by the darkness of the restaurant, jacket discarded over the chair beside me. I rolled up my sleeves at some point, undid the top buttons of my shirt, shed the layers of presentation I maintained for cameras and sponsors.

The whiskey in front of me was my second. Or third. I'd lost count and didn't particularly care. The party had started to feel like too much, and I was pleased to escape into something quieter.

The ambient music shifted to something slower, lonelier, the piano barely audible over the quiet murmur of conversation and the clink of glassware. I was halfway through a thought about whether I should just go to bed when I saw her.

Lily stood at the bar, her back to me, talking to the bartender. Her posture was tense, shoulders drawn up slightly, one hand fidgeting with something I couldn't see. It looked like she'd ordered a Manhattan, her favorite drink. She accepted it with a nod of thanks then turned to survey the mostly empty bar. Her eyes found me almost immediately, like she'd known exactly where I was sitting the whole time.

For a beat, we just looked at each other across the space. Her expression was complicated. I waited for her to look away first. To pretend she hadn't seen me, to take her drink and claim a seat on the opposite side of the bar, to maintain the awkwardness we'd established over the past few days.

Instead she picked up her glass and walked over, sitting down at the table across from me.

"I, um, missed you at the bar," she said when she reached my table. "I just wanted to say congratulations on a good race. I mean it—you drove amazing today."

I looked up slowly, taking her in properly now. The fatigue around her eyes mirrored my own. Today had been exhausting for both of us. For a second, maybe less, surprise filled me. I genuinely hadn't expected her to approach, to willingly step into this conversation, after that press conference yesterday. She had every right to be upset with how I'd acted.

"Thanks." The word came out flat, emotionally stripped.

She gestured vaguely toward me with her glass, the maraschino cherry bobbing against the rim. There was something expectant in her face, and she kept swirling her Manhattan around as if it might release a magic genie who could give her the words she was clearly missing. Finally, she looked up at me.

"Can I ask you something?"

I nodded, not sure where this was going.

"Why did you kiss me in Monaco? And Montreal?"

Nothing could have prepared me for that question. It wasn't that I didn't have an answer, it was just that I didn't have a good one.

I stared into my glass, giving it a little swirl. Now it was my turn to beg the genie to appear. The silence felt heavy with things unsaid. Because what was the point? We'd already established the boundaries. I drew the line in Vegas, told her we should just be friends, and nothing had changed since then.

Our teams still hated each other. Her contract did forbid us dating.

"Henri?" Her voice was softer now, almost hesitant.

She seemed to take my silence as answer enough. I could hear her tap against the hardwood table—not with impatience, but like someone who was willing to wait a lifetime for an answer. When I didn't provide one, because I couldn't let the words form on my lips, she tried again.

"Can you tell me this then—what happened between you and Ollie? In F2?" She wasn't accusatory, just searching, like a detective on a new case. "He told me a story a few days ago, but I wanted to hear your side of it."

I set my glass down slowly, buying myself a moment to think. "What did he tell you?"

"That you were struggling, and he tried to help. That you… got him fired for it." She met my eye. "But it doesn't sound like you, Henri. So, I'm asking."

The fact that she was asking, that she hadn't just accepted Ollie's version as the truth, made something loosen in my chest. A tension I hadn't realized I'd been carrying.

I leaned back in my chair, studying her face in the dim light. Then I laughed—short, bitter, utterly disbelieving. The sound scraped out of my throat like fingers on a chalkboard.

"That's the story he's going with." Not a question.

She nodded, waiting.

My gaze met hers, unblinking. The corner of my mouth twitched upward in a smile that didn't quite reach my eyes. A defense mechanism, maybe. Or just the absurdity of it all finally breaking through.

"The truth? He was right. I was struggling in F2," I said quietly. "After a huge crash in the rain, I had panic attacks before any qualifying where it was even remotely wet. I couldn't sleep more than a few hours without nightmares.

There was this constant noise in my head telling me I wasn't good enough, that I was going to crash, that I was going to fail whenever there was bad weather, which seemed to be all the time that season."

I paused, my eyes flicking to the glass between my hands, watching the amber liquid catch and refract the low light.

"I told Ollie because I thought I could trust him. Because we were friends, and he was the only other person in that program who seemed to understand what the pressure felt like." My laugh was hollow. "Stupid, right?"

Lily had gone very still, and I wanted more than anything to be able to jump inside her head and know what she was thinking.

"A week later," I continued, my voice growing harder with each word, "I found a blog draft open on his laptop when I was at his flat. I'd borrowed his computer to check emails because my phone had died. And there it was, everything I'd told him, in an email to a media outlet. He called me reckless, unstable, and dangerous behind the wheel. He didn't use my name, but anyone who read it would've known exactly who he was writing about."

"So, he did write about you?" Her voice was barely above a whisper.

"He was *planning* to," I corrected. "Said it would start an important conversation about mental health in motorsport. Called it advocacy, like he was doing some noble public service, instead of—" I broke off, shaking my head. "Exploiting someone's private pain for clicks and credibility."

I took a slow breath, trying to steady myself, to push past the anger threatening to crack through my carefully maintained composure.

"I showed the draft to our F2 team principal, Charles. Explained what had happened, what Ollie was planning to do." The memory still burned. "Ollie was released from the academy within forty-eight hours for severe breach of confidentiality and trust. End of story."

Lily fidgeted in her seat. "Henri… I'm so sorry."

"Well, unfortunately, firing Ollie didn't fix all my problems," I sighed. "The damage was already done. Once I admitted to struggling, to being mentally weak, that was how the team saw me from then on." I ran my thumb along the rim of my glass, focusing on the simple sensation rather than meeting her eye. "Mental health wasn't a priority back then."

"What did the team say?"

I swirled my drink, watching the remaining brown drops slosh in the crystal glass. "After firing Ollie, Charles pulled me aside and told me to get my head sorted. Said champions don't break under pressure, and that if I couldn't handle the stress of F2, I had no business dreaming about F1."

My mouth was suddenly dry. It had been so long since I'd said any of this aloud, and even then, I'd only told one person. Éliott had convinced me to go to the team and tell them everything that happened.

"I was told to man up, that Hermes only had room for *real men*, and that I needed to stop being weak. Drivers all over the world would kill for my seat. He told me—" I paused, taking a long, final sigh. "He told me that he'd do me this one favor, that he would make sure the article never saw the light of day. But that I should learn from my mistakes." I finally looked up at her, finding her watching me with an expression I couldn't quite read. "So that's what I did. I buried it. Pretended it never happened.

Somehow won the F2 championship six months later and never mentioned it again."

Until Miami broke me all over again.

I could see Lily putting the pieces together in her head. "Is that... is that why you won't tell them now, about the driving?"

I nodded. "I've been trying to figure out why I'm so bothered. It's not like *I* crashed on my own this time." I looked sheepishly at her, and she seemed to get the subtext. She'd crashed into me, after all.

"But that's not how our brains work, is it?" Lily said softly. A statement we all knew to be true—that how our brains brought back memories remained a mystery to even the best psychologists.

"That crash from Miami, it stirred up something in me again, that fear I'd experienced after the crash in F2. It was so similar, and every time I go through the corners in the rain, I realize it's not Miami I'm necessarily seeing all over again... it's the crash in Barcelona."

"I'm so sorry I said what I said in the press conference, Henri." Lily was quiet for a long moment, her eyes searching my face, then she added, "Do you think Ollie has made this connection?"

I shrugged, even if I knew the answer. "He's figured out enough. I'm guessing he told you all this because he wants to seem like the hero. Or keep me away from you..." I picked up my glass, staring into it. "In his version, he's the hero trying to help a reckless teammate. In mine, he's the friend who betrayed my trust for a byline. He'd love for you to believe I deliberately destroyed him out of spite than to face the possibility that I was just... broken." My voice dropped even lower. "Or that I'm *still* broken."

I took a final sip of whiskey, the burn going down my throat. But it was nothing compared to the look on her face. Setting the glass down with quiet finality, I got up to start walking away.

I made it three steps before I stopped, back still to her, hand gripping the jacket draped over my shoulder. "You want to know why I kissed you?"

Her eyes snapped to mine.

"Because I wanted to." The words tumbled out of me, raw and stripped of any pretense or defense. "Because I missed you. *Miss* you, every day, and that night in Monaco and Montreal, for just a moment, I let myself forget all the reasons why I shouldn't kiss you."

Her lips parted slightly, but no sound came out.

I shook my head, frustrated with myself—with this whole mess. "The truth is, this all got away from me after I decided to push you away in Vegas."

Now, this caught her attention.

"I heard the doubt in your voice when you said that you weren't sure about the contract. I didn't want you to jeopardize the Rennen offer, especially not for me, so I removed myself from the equation." I looked down at my hands, picking at my fingernail as I debated what I should say next. "I thought it would be easier for you if I was just… not an option anymore. You deserve a boyfriend who can be public with you. Someone who can kiss you after a race or take you to dinner. With that clause, I can't be those things for you."

Lily's eyes widened. Her arms crossed, quick and defensive. She stared at me like she was trying to reconcile the man in front of her with what I'd just admitted.

"But that doesn't change how I feel about you." My confession hung between us, vulnerable and raw. "The feelings I had for you in Las Vegas, the ones I never said… those haven't gone away. Nothing has changed how I feel about *you*. Not all the arguments between us this season or the coldness we've been hiding behind." I had to force myself to hold her gaze, to not shy away and hide from this conversation. "I'm sorry I didn't say this back in Las Vegas. You weren't entirely wrong when you said I was scared. I was… scared for *you*."

I took a step back, creating distance before I could change my mind about what I was about to say.

"I'll stay out of your way for good, Lil. You won't have to worry about mixed signals or complicated feelings or any of this mess anymore. It's wrong of me to do that to you."

Her mouth opened like she might say something, might stop me, but I couldn't let her. I didn't want to hear whatever she was about to say, whether it was rejection or something worse: pity.

Chapter Twenty

Lily

It was a week before Silverstone, and my head was in absolute shambles after the Austrian Grand Prix. When Georgia texted asking if I'd be interested in joining a charity event featuring rescue dogs with Valkyrie, I jumped at the idea. Anything to take my thoughts off Henri and that conversation in the hotel bar.

I was shocked by his story about Ollie. It was obvious there was tension between them, but I hadn't expected that sort of betrayal from Ollie.

But what I expected the least was Henri's final admission.

"Because I missed you. Miss you, every day, and that night, for just a moment, I let myself forget all the reasons why I shouldn't kiss you."

Those words haunted me, but him finally admitting the reason why he'd walked out in Las Vegas haunted me more. Would I have fought back on my contract?

When I arrived at the event, the park was already buzzing. Dogs were everywhere: big dogs, small dogs, and dogs so shaggy they struggled to see—my particular favorite. Georgia was in the center of it, headset on, clipboard tucked beneath her elbow, like a general marching into war. She spotted me, and her whole body relaxed.

"You made it!" she said, threading through a tangle of leashes to reach me.

"You look terrifyingly competent," I said, dodging a corgi who was fully committed to tripping me.

Georgia laughed. "It's nice to get out and do something other than racing for a bit, yeah?"

"Georgia Dubois, how the times have changed," I laughed. "There was a time when all you thought about was racing."

She waved me off. "What can I say? New me." Then she shrugged. "I just wish Henri felt the same. He was so down after his Austrian win."

My chest tightened at the mention of his name. "Did you invite him to this?"

"I did, but I doubt he'll come. Probably slaving away on his home simulator, preparing for Silverstone." She paused, looking around. "You didn't want to invite Ollie?"

Well, now I knew Henri hadn't told her about his past with Ollie. "Nah, not today."

She didn't press me on it, which I appreciated.

I was going to have to confront Ollie, ask him why he'd told me that story. After talking to Henri, I'd called Éliott to confirm, which he'd done. With all this knowledge, I knew even if I couldn't have Henri, I didn't want Ollie anymore. Not after what I'd learned.

The idea that this had been a misunderstanding between them was no longer an acceptable excuse.

Still, that felt like an after Silverstone conversation.

A volunteer dropped off a bag of toys, and Georgia looked down at them.

"We need to get these distributed. You mind dropping these off over at the blue pen? They need some more toys." She handed me a grocery bag brimming with squeaky ducks, plush bones, and something that looked suspiciously like a rubber Formula 1 car in Valkyrie livery. The absurdity made me smile.

I took the bag and navigated toward the blue pen, careful not to trip over the canine obstacle course underfoot.

The blue pen was a cordoned area with a wet tarp and about a dozen puppies climbing all over each other. They were incredibly adorable. Most of the volunteers, busy in Valkyrie jackets, were trying to rally puppies for the cluster of parents and sponsor representatives who crowded the pen, begging for photos. I set the bag down and was immediately mugged by three wriggling bodies. A golden-brown mutt reared up against my shoe, delicately untying it, before running away.

"Um, sir," I told him with mock sternness, scooping up the brown bundle of mischief before he could leave with my shoelace entirely. "That's hardly appropriate behavior for a first meeting."

He responded by attempting to lick my face.

I was in the process of liberating my shoelace when I caught a flicker of movement at the edge of the pen, and then a loud squeal of excitement. For one surreal second, I thought I was hallucinating him. But there he was.

Henri, wrapped up in an embrace by his sister.

He looked good—too good for someone who'd probably spent the past week drowning in data and simulator runs in a dark room. His dark hair fell across his forehead like an invitation for someone to push it back. Late-morning sunlight spilled across his face, gilding the rough scrape of stubble he clearly couldn't be bothered to shave. But shadows pooled beneath his eyes, deeper than they should've been, and there was a tightness around his mouth that wasn't so noticeable before Austria.

He stepped back from Georgia, and his gaze swept the crowd.

Then it landed on me, causing my heart to race against my chest. The puppy I was holding squirmed in my arms, but I couldn't look away.

Henri's jaw worked like he was chewing on words he couldn't let loose. The air between us crackled with everything unsaid—everything we'd left bleeding in that hotel bar.

"*Because I missed you.*"

Georgia grabbed his arm, oblivious to the moment that hung between us.

"Come meet these little guys. They're absolute lunatics—you'll love them," I heard her call out to Henri.

She dragged him toward a fenced area, where a chaos of small dogs yapped and tumbled over each other. Henri let himself be pulled along, but his eyes stayed on me until the last possible second. When he finally turned away, I released a breath I hadn't known I was holding.

My fingers tangled in soft puppy fur as I watched Georgia shove a squeaky toy into Henri's hands. He crouched down, and immediately, three terriers launched themselves at him, but he sat very still, as if sudden movement would spook them. Slowly, his hand came up and found a head. He scratched, and the puppy's eyes rolled back in bliss. Something unspooled in his face, tiny changes, like a knot loosened by patient fingers. The harsh lines of his mouth softened, and the space between his eyebrows let go.

For a moment I looked away, feeling almost guilty for watching what seemed like a private moment of peace.

A voice from behind me made me jump. "Thanks for the toys," Mina, another volunteer, called over to me. "Do you want to meet one of our stars? He's not in the puppy pen, because he's technically a grown-up."

I nodded enthusiastically, and she cast a look at the dog lying with crossed paws like a gentleman near the volunteer tent, golden-tan and calm as ever. His tail thumped lazily when he saw her.

"That's Archie," Mina said, and the affection in her voice was unmistakable. "Although, I call him Professor Archie, in honor of his dignified demeanor. Looks like he should be teaching literature at a university, doesn't he?"

I laughed, already charmed. "He does have that distinguished gentleman energy."

"He washed out of seeing-eye school because he loves people, and food, too much. Couldn't not say hello."

"Relatable," I laughed.

"Right? Now he's retired therapy dog. He used to visit hospitals, schools, and libraries, but then his owner unfortunately had to let him go. Really a shame, but something we see often, even for dogs as amazing as Archie."

"Can I…?" I asked, nodding toward the pen, but Mina was already motioning me forward.

Archie sniffed the air, tail waving in approval. When we reached the fence, Mina unhooked the leash, and he sat, polite as a diplomat.

"Want to say hi?" she asked Archie.

But Archie had other ideas. He eyed me for a bit, then he looked past me, toward another pen, and just like that, he started to stroll away.

"Archie!" Mina yelled.

Henri looked up as the retriever approached. Archie stopped a foot away and gave him a long, considerate sniff.

Henri extended his palm slowly, cautiously, the way you'd approach something wild that might bolt. His fingers uncurled to reveal an empty hand. Archie considered for exactly three heartbeats. Then he leaned his entire golden head into Henri's palm with a sigh that sounded like coming home. Henri's brownish-green eyes softened to something warmer—something that looked almost like wonder mixed with relaxation.

His fingers moved behind Archie's ears with deliberate slowness, finding that sweet spot with the instinct of someone who understood exactly what it meant to crave comfort without knowing how to ask for it. He scratched the place all dogs have universally agreed is perfect.

Archie responded by settling down completely, lowering himself to the ground beside Henri's feet with the satisfied grunt of a creature who'd found exactly where he was meant to be. His golden face tilted upward, basking in the cool mist drifting down from the gray sky, eyes half-closed in that expression of pure, uncomplicated contentment that only dogs seem capable of achieving. Rain-dampened and peaceful, he looked like he'd been Henri's dog for years.

"Who's this?" Henri asked, voice low.

"Archie," Mina said as we approached. "Failed seeing-eye dog. Too social, and a bit too much of a foodie."

Henri's mouth twitched. "Unforgivable."

"He did some work as a therapy dog. He's exceptionally good at it. Has this uncanny ability to know exactly who needs him."

"What does he do?" he asked carefully.

"Whatever's needed. Hospitals, schools. Sometimes people just need a warm head to hold. The world keeps being the world," she continued quietly, "and sometimes you just need something steady and warm and unconditionally present to hold onto until you can breathe again. He's good at being that."

Archie bumped his nose against Henri's knuckles once, twice, then settled his chin there with a sigh.

"Does he…"—Henri swallowed, the movement visible in his throat—"have a home?"

"Not yet," Mina said gently. "We're looking for the right fit."

He nodded, almost to himself. His fingers resumed their slow work at the base of Archie's skull, and the dog leaned in with his full heart. For a few minutes, the rain was only background, the crowds only texture, and everything else felt distant.

Georgia came back over a few moments later, asking me to help with some towels they'd laid out for the dogs, and I excused myself quietly to assist her. But even as I moved between the pens, distributing the soft fabric and making small talk with the other volunteers, I kept looking over my shoulder, the way you do when you've spotted a rare thing in the wild and you're afraid if you glance away too long it will vanish like morning mist. I saw Henri still there, still kneeling in the damp grass with Archie pressed against him, the dog's tail creating lazy arcs in the air.

Georgia noticed it too from her position across the lawn, where she paused mid-conversation with another volunteer to track her brother's position. She stood there holding an armful of donated blankets, her gaze locked on Henri with an intensity that made my chest tighten uncomfortably.

She met my eye across the muddy distance, and something like relief bloomed in her expression. Like she'd been waiting a very long time to witness this particular moment and was terrified it might dissolve if she acknowledged it too directly.

I felt my throat go tight with emotion I had no right to be feeling, because I understood exactly what she was seeing: Henri, unguarded. Henri, breathing without visible effort. Henri, finding something like peace in the simple act of holding onto something that asked nothing from him except to be present, to be real, to exist in this moment without performance or pretense.

"Tea?" Georgia asked me a few minutes later, appearing with steaming paper cups.

"He looks so… relaxed," I said, like it was a secret.

"I know," she said softly. "He used to volunteer at an animal shelter all the time."

"You told me he wanted a dog," I said.

"Years ago," she said. "Before Hermes, before the championship battles. He said it wouldn't be fair, with the travel, the grind. Said he'd wait until everything calmed down." She huffed a small laugh. "As if that will happen. But I don't know. More and more drivers bring their dogs everywhere. Look at Éliott—he's barely separated from Brownie, and Brownie loves traveling with him. He's basically a mini star of the paddock!"

I watched Archie plant himself like royalty and press his full weight against Henri's legs. Watched Henri's hand settle against the dog's chest, palm flat, finding the calm rhythm beneath it. Georgia gestured me over, and we drifted toward the pen where Henri sat.

Mini was talking to Henri. "Don't let me pressure you," she was saying, "but we can bring him for a trial weekend if you want to see how it feels."

Henri shrugged. "I don't know where I'll be."

"That's okay," she said. "He does. He's very good at finding people."

His gaze flicked up to me before sliding away. Almost as if he was asking what I thought. "I'll think about it," he said at last.

Henri stood, brushed damp grass off his knees, and gave Archie one last scratch. Then he handed the leash back, stepped out of the pen, and reassembled himself as his public self. But the echo of the smile stayed around the edges of his face.

I gave him my best smile. He didn't take it, exactly, but he didn't reject it either. He just moved on, and I let him.

The event thinned with the rain. Mina tucked Archie into a van with a blanket and a kiss to the nose. I carried a stack of bowls to the supply table and set them down before picking up the adoption papers.

Georgia came to stand beside me.

"You look like someone who has a mischievous idea," she said.

"I hate that about my face," I laughed. "Always gives me away."

She scoffed in response.

"Georgia?"

"Yes…?" she asked, though I could tell from her expression that she already knew.

"You think Henri would say yes?"

Then a small smile began to curve at the edges of her lips, knowing and slightly conspiratorial and touched with something that might have been hope.

"Well," she said slowly, her eyes returning to meet mine with that glint that suggested she was fully on board with whatever chaos I was about to unleash, "judging by the expression on your face, he very well may not have a choice in the matter."

Chapter Twenty-One

Henri

Today had a certain ease about it. After yesterday's charity event with my sister, I felt considerably lighter and more relaxed. Georgia had texted me three times about the charity event, each message more insistent than the last. The last one had been accompanied by a photo of a golden retriever with soulful eyes that she'd clearly found on the internet.

But it wasn't her texts that had got me there. It was my new therapist and sports psychologist, who'd finally convinced me isolation wasn't the same as healing, that wallowing away in my apartment replaying my fears wasn't productive to my recovery.

After that session, she'd told me to set aside an entire day for myself to do nothing but relax with some "self-care."

I wasn't used to taking care of myself.

And I *definitely* wasn't used to relaxing.

The apartment felt too quiet. I'd already cleaned the kitchen twice, answered several sponsor emails, and memorized the talking points Ruth wanted me to learn for my upcoming interview. A nice re-do of the last one I'd done with Ollie. My coffee had gone cold twenty minutes ago, but I still held the mug anyway, out of habit.

The mug was chipped—Georgia had given it to me years ago: *World's Okayest Driver*. At the time, it had been a joke. Now it felt a bit too on the nose.

I moved to the couch, kicked my feet up on the coffee table, and opened my book. I could do this. I could *relax*.

That was when the knock came. Three sharp taps, and a scuffling of something unfamiliar.

I ignored it. Probably Georgia. She'd been hovering lately, popping by with excuses like "forgot my charger" or "can I borrow your blender?" All of them terrible.

The knock came again, louder.

I sighed, pressing the heels of my hands to my eyes. "For fuck's sake."

When I opened the door, I forgot how to speak. Lily stood there, auburn curls clinging to her cheeks in soft spirals. She looked out of breath, like she'd run up the steps.

My heart launched into a rhythm that had nothing to do with training, and everything to do with the woman standing in my hallway looking at me with those eyes that had haunted every waking moment this season.

In Austria, I'd finally told her how I felt. She'd just stared back at me, wide-eyed, not saying anything. Which was fine—I didn't need her to say anything. I just needed her to *know*.

Before I could say something, a panting caught my attention, and I looked down.

There, next to Lily, was Archie. The same Lab who'd spent half of Valkyrie's charity event draped across my lap. The same dog who'd leaned into my hand like he'd known me for years. The same dog whose easy warmth had cracked something open in me I'd been trying desperately to keep sealed.

He recognized me instantly. His tail began sweeping the floor in increasingly enthusiastic arcs, and his whole body wiggled with such unfiltered delight.

She brought him here. She remembered.

The thought hit before I could stop it—before I could protect myself from the hope that came with it.

I stared at her, dumbfounded, acutely aware that I was still holding the door like an idiot, that I probably looked as shocked as I felt, that I had no idea what expression was on my face. "What the hell is this?"

"A dog," Lily said, with a brightness that bordered on dangerous.

"I'm aware it's a dog," I retorted. "But why is he *here*?"

"Because," she said, as if this were obvious, "you're his foster parent now."

I must've blinked, because she held up a plastic packet covered in Paddock Paws logos, as though visual evidence might help.

"Don't worry—it's a foster situation. For now," she said breezily. "Paperwork's all sorted. Congratulations."

My brain was struggling to process everything in front of me. She was here, with a foster a dog she'd arranged on my behalf, acting like I hadn't laid my heart bare while she said nothing.

"You—" I looked from her to the paperwork to Archie, who'd decided the conversation wasn't interesting enough and begun sniffing my doorway with focused enthusiasm. "This is crazy, even for you."

"Meh." She shrugged. Her curls bounced as she waltzed into my hallway, leaving me standing at the door, still holding a leash I didn't remember taking from her.

"Lily, you have to take this dog back!"

A smile curved her mouth, slow, warm, and infuriatingly gentle, in a way that made my chest tighten.

"Why?" She tilted her head, meeting my eye with that steady, knowing look that always felt like she could see straight through every defense I'd carefully constructed. "Well, you won't go to therapy, will you? So this is… therapy-adjacent. The next best thing." She reached down to scratch behind Archie's ear, her fingers moving with ease through his fur. "As much as a therapy dog can be anyway."

I shifted my weight, suddenly hyperaware of how close she was; how small my hallway felt with both of us in it.

"I'm actually going to therapy now, thank you." The words came out more defensive than I intended, but I needed something to break this tension, to stop thinking about how she'd looked at me in Austria when I'd walked away from the bar, to stop wondering what it meant that she was here now.

Lily's head popped up, her eyes going wide. An incredibly pleased grin spread across her face, genuine and unguarded in a way that made my heart do something complicated.

"Henri, that's—" She stopped herself, like she was trying to find the right words and was coming up short. "That's really good. I'm proud of you."

I began tap against my thigh—a nervous gesture I immediately regretted, because it probably made me look as off-balance as I felt. "After Austria," I said, focusing on the dog, because that was safer than focusing on her. "After everything with the press conference and Ollie's interview, I realized I was barely keeping it together. That everyone could tell I was struggling even when I thought I was hiding it well."

There was a tender silence between us, with neither of us saying anything.

Finally, I turned back to find Archie, but he simply trotted past my leg and jumped onto my sofa in the living room.

I gestured toward the couch, which Lily was now perched on next to Archie. Her shoes were kicked off by the edge of the seat, and she looked so relaxed, like she *belonged* on my couch.

I remained standing, watching her settle into my space like she'd done it a thousand times before, in previous years when hanging out had felt effortless. Rain-dampened curls fell across her shoulder as she leaned forward to stroke Archie's head, and my chest twisted at the sight.

She looked different here—softer somehow. The sharp edges she wore on track had melted away, replaced by this easy warmth that made my apartment feel less like a tomb and more like somewhere worth being. Her sweater— oversized, cream-colored—had slipped off one shoulder, and she didn't bother fixing it, just sat there, cross-legged on my couch, completely at home.

Beautiful.

Archie nuzzled into her hand, and she laughed this quiet, genuine sound that wrapped around my ribs and squeezed. She'd bought me a dog. Sorted the paper- work, coordinated with the charity, probably dealt with a mountain of logistics I couldn't even begin to imagine, all because she'd noticed something about me at an event we'd attended together. All because she *cared*.

That was Lily, though. Beneath all the competitive fire, the relentless drive, and the walls she'd built just as high as mine—she saw people. Really saw them. She'd noticed I was drowning when everyone else was too busy asking if

I'd keep my seat. She'd shown up, and kept showing up, even when I pushed her away.

This is why I love her.

The realization settled over me—inevitable, soaking through every defense I had left. Not because she was brilliant behind the wheel or fearless under pressure. Not even because she challenged me in ways no one else dared.

But because she was kind. Because she cared enough to do things like this—absurd, wonderful things that cracked open the parts of me I'd spent months trying to seal shut.

She glanced up, catching me staring. A smile played at the corner of her mouth.

"You all right?"

Archie looked over at me again, this time making an effort to crawl into my lap. It was disarming and unfair. Dogs had this way of melting your heart, and Archie had done a mighty job in such a short period of time.

Lily's gaze dropped to her shirt's hem, and she began peeling at a loose thread on her sleeve. "Are you sure you don't mind?" she asked, her voice almost a whisper. "Keeping him, I mean. If you want me to take him, I will. The rescue asked. He took to you, and I thought maybe…"

"That depends. Can I keep him if I also have a therapist?"

She laughed, nodding. "He seems to really like you," she said softly.

"He likes anyone with fingers."

"That's not true," she grumbled. "He didn't crawl into my lap once."

"Maybe he has taste," I muttered.

She snorted, the sound bubbling out of her unchecked, and damn it, I felt my own mouth twitch in response—

but there was no tension between us, just a casual, light air. Like it used to be.

"You know, I miss hanging out with you." Lily tucked one leg beneath her, twisting slightly to face me.

I blinked. "Me too."

"I miss how we were. Before all this. We used to be such close friends."

I stared at her, at the earnest tilt of her chin, at the vulnerability she wasn't trying to hide. Something about that, her honesty, her willingness to meet me where I was rather than where she wished I'd be, felt good. It felt right.

"You want to be friends again?" I asked.

"If you'll let me," she said quietly. "If that's still something you want."

I looked down, rubbing the back of Archie's neck.

Friends. The word felt too small. But maybe it was the only one we could fit into right now. The morality clause wasn't changing, but maybe we didn't have to do anything about that at the moment. Nothing banned our *friendship*.

We didn't need to participate in this war between our teams.

"You know, I have an idea of what we can do to solidify this friendship."

Her eyes widened a fraction. "Oh?"

"Every year, my friends host this little… competition… where we race Volkswagen Beetles."

Her mouth fell open, then it curved into something between delight and hysteria. "Beetles? Like Herbie?"

"Yes," I said. "Much like that delightful racing movie that made every F1 kid fall in love with racing."

Lily's grin bloomed. "You know, I've always wanted to drive one of those." She laughed—a warm, cascading sound that felt like it rewired the entire room.

"I wasn't planning to go initially," I admitted. "Didn't see the point. But my therapist"—the word still felt foreign, heavy—"thought it could be good for me. To remember what driving felt like before it became... whatever it is I'm feeling now."

Lily's expression softened, warm and aching. "Henri... that sounds perfect."

I paused, then added, "I'll need a partner."

Her breath caught. Just slightly, but I felt it.

"A partner?" she echoed.

"Co-driver, technically," I said. "Someone to yell at me when I'm being dramatic. And laugh when I stall out."

She grinned. "Do you stall out?"

"Look, they're hard cars to drive," I said immediately, my hands in the air. "So..." I gave her a small smile. "What do you say?"

Lily's lips curved upward, her shoulders relaxing as she leaned forward. The smile reached her eyes this time, crinkling the corners. Not the fake one I'd seen in a hundred press conferences, but something rarer that made my heart thump.

"Fuck it. Let's do it."

Chapter Twenty-Two

Henri

The fog hung thick over the countryside track, moisture condensing on every surface in heavy droplets. Handmade signs pointed toward the "paddock" in crooked letters that looked like they'd been painted by enthusiastic children or possibly drunk adults. It was nothing like the pristine Formula 1 circuits I'd spent my life navigating, and somehow that made it perfect.

My body relaxed the farther we got from London. My shoulders sat lower. My hands didn't grip the car's steering wheel with desperation.

When I pulled into the makeshift parking area, I took a moment before cutting the engine. Just sat there, breathing in the smell of old gasoline and something nostalgic that transported me back to being seventeen and stupid and fearless. We used to race these all the time, but with all my F1 obligations, it was hard to schedule a weekend. I emerged from my car looking around at the ramshackle paddock with genuine fondness.

"I can't believe you race here!" Lily laughed, climbing out into the damp air with clear amusement. "Hope you're prepared to be humbled by my racing today."

My mouth twitched toward a smile. "Don't get any ideas. Humility isn't exactly my strong suit."

"Shocking." She kicked at loose gravel, grinning. "And here I thought you'd turned a new leaf—"

"Henri!"

The shout came from across the paddock, followed by a chaotic stampede of men in racing overalls.

Before I could brace myself, they'd engulfed me in a completely mortifying group hug.

"Guys," I muttered, trying to extract myself. "This is really not—"

"Missed you too, mate!" Éliott's voice came from somewhere to my left, followed by a slap to my back that nearly knocked the air from my lungs. My friend, Max, managed to disentangle himself first, his attention immediately shifting to Lily with an obvious interest that made something territorial flare in my chest.

"Well, hello," Max said with an exaggerated wink that made me want to hit him. "Henri, you didn't tell us you were bringing *her*. You're even prettier in person than on the telly."

I'm going to murder all of them.

Lily handled it with characteristic grace, holding out her hand. "Hi. That's not true, but thank you anyway."

"Ignore them," I said flatly. "They have no social skills."

But Éliott was already leaning forward conspiratorially, his voice dropping to what he probably thought was a whisper, but which was absolutely audible to everyone.

"Personally, I'm just glad you guys finally got over all that weird, angry foreplay you've been doing all season. I mean, all Henri talked about last season was yo—"

I smacked him, hard, right on the back of his head.

"Ow! What was that for?"

Lily's eyebrows shot up, delight dancing in her eyes. "Oh, did he now?"

I made a strangled noise, heat flooding my face. "Don't you have somewhere to be?"

Éliott nodded vigorously, completely ignoring my desperate plea. "Wouldn't shut up about you, honestly. 'Lily did this in qualifying, Lily's racing strategy is brilliant, Lily passed me here.' It was exhausting."

I could feel my face burning now. "That's not… That's taken completely out of context."

Lily grinned, clearly enjoying my suffering. "Well, that's tremendously flattering, Henri."

Max elbowed me with enough force to make me stumble. "You know, mate, you really did her description an injustice."

"She's literally on TV every weekend. Now, where's our chariot of certain death?"

Éliott led us through rows of magnificently ridiculous Beetles in every conceivable state of decay.

And then I saw ours.

An orange Beetle with paint so faded it was nearly pink in places. A racing stripe that didn't really look like a stripe. The rear spoiler wobbled visibly in the breeze. And there was a crack running through the passenger-side windshield.

But what really made it special was the bumper sticker plastered across the back window: "Passenger Princess" in glittery pink letters.

Of course that's our car.

"This is perfect," Lily declared, walking around it like she was examining art. "This is absolutely perfect."

I stood motionless, staring at the orange monstrosity with carefully controlled horror. "Lily, this thing is held together with duct tape and a prayer."

"That's the best kind of racecar!" She popped the hood—which took three tries—and peered at the engine. "Look at this beautiful disaster. When's the last time you drove something that actually required skill?"

Henri snickered. "You mean, excluding our F1 cars?"

"Right then," Lily announced, rubbing her hands together with determination. "I'm absolutely testing this first."

I didn't argue. Partly because she was clearly excited. But mostly because the thought of getting behind the wheel and being responsible for controlling something with zero modern safety features in deteriorating conditions made my body weak with anxiety.

To use Lily's words, the car was alive. I watched from the passenger seat as she took the first corner and immediately discovered that this vehicle's grip was casual at best. The rear end stepped out cheerfully, and she caught it with skill and instinct. Her laugh of pure delight filled the cabin, infectious and genuine.

"Lily!" I heard myself say, my voice between panic and amusement as I braced against the door. "*Mon dieu*, slow down! This thing is older than my grandfather!"

She tackled the next corner with more confidence, letting the car slide and dance. No electronic aids, no computer control, no safety net. Just her and the car and complete disregard for mortality.

Despite my protests and my white-knuckle grip on the dashboard, I found myself laughing too. Really laughing, with my head thrown back. The kind of laughing I'd almost forgotten how to do. By the time Lily brought us back, we were both grinning like idiots. The car shuddered to a stop with what sounded like mechanical relief.

"That was the most fun I've had in a car since… Actually, I'm not sure I've ever had that much fun," she announced, pulling off the helmet.

I removed my own helmet with noticeably shaking hands, and for a moment I tried to convince myself it was just adrenaline.

But I knew better.

My breathing had gone shallow, ribs tight with an anxiety I recognized too well. The realization that I'd be expected to drive next, and in the rain, no less, made panic pulse more insistently.

Lily's hand settled gently over mine where I was gripping the dashboard. Her fingers were warm, anchoring me to something real instead of the spiraling thoughts.

"Hey," she said softly. "You okay?"

My breath stuttered despite my best efforts. "I— Yes. I'm fine."

Her fingers shifted beneath mine, our palms meeting briefly, before I pulled away. The softness of her touch lingered, warm and steadying.

Get it together. You're fine. It's just driving.

"I'm just excited to show you how it's really done," I shot back, defaulting to competition, because that was safe ground.

Lily's eyebrow arched. "My driving was perfect, thank you."

Éliott gathered everyone for the rules briefing. "Right, it's basically a sprint format. Forty laps, and whoever's fastest wins. No contact, though these things bounce pretty well."

Max pointed at me. "And no crying when your F1 skills mean nothing."

I scoffed, trying to project a confidence I wasn't feeling. "Good thing I brought the championship leader with me."

I pointed at Lily, then leaned toward her. "You want to take the first session?"

"Obviously." She was already reaching for the helmet again. "Someone needs to set a proper benchmark."

"Confident. I like it."

The rain started in earnest, transforming from drizzle to actual precipitation. Proper drops that turned the track surface into something approaching a lake in places.

My chest tightened further, watching the water pool.

It's fine. This is nothing like Miami. Except it was. Rain and an unfamiliar car, with me barely holding it together.

"Remember," I said as Lily climbed into the driver's seat, my voice steadier than I felt, "this isn't F1. You can't just point it where you want and trust electronics."

"Thanks for the revolutionary pep talk, coach. Any other groundbreaking insights?"

"Don't get us killed," I said, and there was more genuine concern than I'd intended. "Seriously, Lily. Just be careful."

"I will," she promised, touching my hand briefly. I knew she wouldn't. Lily would drive this car like she drove everything: with complete commitment.

After twenty laps, Lily pulled over for the swap. We awkwardly maneuvered in the confined space, elbows bumping, her knee catching mine as she slid to the passenger seat. The brief contact sent electricity through me that had nothing to do with anxiety.

"She's running beautifully," Lily said as I settled behind the wheel. "Just trust the slide and don't fight the steering."

"Right," I managed, but tension was creeping into my shoulders as I looked at the wet track.

"Henri." Her hand settled on my arm. "You've got this. Slow hands, quick feet. And if it gets ugly, just bring her home. We don't have to win."

I nodded, pulling back onto the track even though everything in me was screaming to stay put.

It's fine. Just drive.

For the first few laps, I maintained control. My inputs were smooth, precise. Exactly what you'd expect from someone second in the championship. But something was building with each corner. Each time the car stepped out, each moment where grip became negotiation, I could feel panic rising like floodwater. Austria had been a dry race, so I had a break from this fear, but driving now, it was starting to come back. A reminder of my F2 race in Barcelona.

The steering felt wrong, too big, too imprecise. Every input seemed delayed and disconnected.

Remember, this isn't F1. Stop trying to drive like it is.

"Henri, relax your grip." Lily's voice came gently.

But I couldn't. My knuckles were tight, arms rigid, and my breathing was becoming rapid and shallow. Then the rear stepped out unexpectedly. Instead of the smooth correction that should have been muscle memory, I yanked the wheel too hard.

We slid sideways, the world tilting at an angle that sent my stomach plummeting. For a heartbeat I was back in Miami, watching barriers approach with horrible inevitability. I got us straight again, but my hands were shaking violently now, vision tunneling, chest so tight I couldn't breathe.

"Pull over," Lily said immediately.

"I'm fine," I forced out unconvincingly.

"Henri, pull over. Now."

I jerked the car off the racing line onto grass and stopped abruptly, my whole body shaking with panic and shame so acute it burned. My head dropped against the steering wheel, trying desperately to ground myself.

Failure. Everyone can see you failing.

I tried to open the door, needing air, needing escape.

But Lily's hand caught my arm.

"Henri, look at me."

I couldn't. My eyes were wide and unfocused, seeing rain and barriers and Miami.

"I can't—" I started. "I can't do this. I thought I could, but I can't. I'm failing."

"No." Her voice came out fierce. "You're not failing. You're scared, and that's okay."

Her hand stayed on my arm. I could feel my pulse hammering beneath the surface.

"Look at me," she repeated, softer. "Not the track. Not the rain. Just me."

With enormous effort, I forced my eyes to focus on her face. On the genuine concern there, the complete absence of judgment.

"I'm sorry," I whispered. "I don't know what's… I used to be able to do this."

"Stop. There's nothing to apologize for. But I need you to breathe with me. In for four, hold for four, out for four." We breathed together, her voice counting steadily. My eyes locked on hers like she was the only thing keeping me tethered.

Gradually, my breathing evened out. The shaking subsided to something manageable.

"Remember, focus on the rhythm of the corners," she said quietly. "Trust the car. Trust yourself." A faint laugh escaped me, the weight lifting slightly.

"You don't have to finish this," Lily said, hand still on my arm. "We can walk away right now. I won't think any differently of you."

I started to chew the inside of my mouth, and for a moment I considered taking the easy out.

Instead I let out a shaky breath. "I want to finish."

"Wanting to and being ready to are different things."

"I know." I looked at her properly. "But I need to try. I just need a minute."

The rain continued its assault, creating strange intimacy in our tiny car.

"It just feels so much like Miami," I started, voice rough, "and Barcelona." My thumb traced an absent pattern on the wheel.

"I'm going to finish," I said finally, voice steadier. "Not for them, or for pride. But for me. I need to know I still can."

"You're sure?"

"No." The laugh was short and sharp. "But I'm doing it anyway."

"Okay. Then we're doing this together. Talk to me through every corner. Out loud."

My eyebrows lifted. "You want commentary?"

"I want your brain engaged instead of spiraling. So, yes, talk."

I reached for the gearshift, paused, then looked at her. Really looked at her, dropping defenses enough to let her see the vulnerability.

"Thank you," I said quietly. "For walking me through that."

"Just remember, you're not broken, Henri." She squeezed my arm. "I believe you can do this."

The smile that earned was small but genuine.

"Ready?" she asked.

No. Not even close.

I pulled back onto the track and immediately started narrating.

"Approaching Turn 3, braking late, letting it rotate." My voice wavered but held. "Rear's stepping out, catching it, powering through."

"Perfect. Keep going."

We carved through the remaining laps, my voice growing stronger with each corner completed. The panic hadn't vanished, but talking helped. Lily's presence helped. When we finally crossed the line in second place, my laugh was equal parts relief and disbelief.

"We did it," I breathed.

"You did it," Lily corrected.

I didn't think, just reached over and pulled her into a hug, her forehead pressing against my shoulder.

"Thank you," I whispered against her hair.

We both hopped out of the car, and my friends descended with whoops and a ridiculous plastic trophy that read "Second Place Loser" in glittery letters.

"About time you two stopped making out and finished the race!" Éliott shouted.

Heat flooded my face. "We were not—"

But they'd already moved on.

Eventually, as the sun descended and the celebrations wound down, the rain reduced to drizzle. I found my jacket and draped it over Lily's shoulders without thinking.

She smiled at me, soft and dangerously close to something more than friendly, and we walked slowly back to our car, alone now in the gathering dusk.

"I know we didn't win, but that felt like winning," I said, stopping beside the Beetle.

"Second place is still a podium. Though maybe 'winning' isn't the right word."

"Well, you would know," I said with deliberate lightness.

She smacked my shoulder, laughing.

"*Non*," I clarified, my accent thickening. "I don't mean the race. I mean being able to drive this car in the rain…" I paused. "That felt like winning something that matters more than any trophy."

We stood in comfortable silence, rain droplets on my eyelashes, distant laughter fading.

"Henri," Lily started, then she stopped.

I looked down at her, and something in her expression made my heart skip. Something warm and open and utterly honest.

"Lily, I—"

But I didn't get to finish.

She stepped closer, until she was in my space in a way that made my breath catch. Made the world narrow to just the two of us and the rain-soft air between us.

Her eyes met mine, searching for something. Permission, maybe? Proof that I wanted this too? I didn't move away. Couldn't have, even if I'd wanted to.

Then she kissed me.

Soft and certain and everything I hadn't let myself imagine. Her hand came up to my jaw, and I forgot how to breathe; forgot everything except the warmth of her mouth and the rain on our skin and the way she fit perfectly against me.

And every coherent thought I had dissolved completely. My promise from Austria of leaving her alone had now all but vanished from sight.

Chapter Twenty-Three

Lily

The moment our lips touched, the world felt right again. Henri kissed me back instantly, desperately, his hands coming up to frame my face like he was afraid I might stop. For this one perfect moment, nothing else existed except Henri's hands in my hair and the taste of rain on his lips and the feeling that I'd been holding my breath for months and could finally breathe again.

When we broke apart, we were both breathing hard, foreheads pressed together in the mist.

"Lily," he whispered, and my name sounded different in his voice.

His eyes were dark with something that made heat pool low in my stomach. I could see the exact moment he made his decision. His throat worked, like he was swallowing down one last objection. Then he moved.

Henri opened the door of the Beetle, and after some squeezing in, we collapsed into the back seat.

His eyes held mine with every bit of intensity from the kiss. The rain continued its gentle patter, creating a cocoon around us. I didn't think beyond the next few heartbeats. Not with him looking at me like this. Not when he was giving me the space to pull away if I wanted to.

The morality contract, the championship, the hatred between our teams—none of that was on my mind.

Just him.

I closed the distance first, kissing him again, slower this time, like I was testing the ground beneath my feet. He responded immediately, a quiet sound slipping from him as his hands came up to my hair, threading through it, pulling me closer, until there was no room left between us.

"Fuck," he murmured against my mouth, breath warm and unsteady. "Is this a terrible idea?"

"Just shut up and kiss me."

I kissed him again, cutting off anything else he might've said, and this time there was nothing gentle about it. The kiss turned hungry, desperate, all the tension that had been wound tight between us finally snapping. His shirt was gone before I fully registered it, tossed aside carelessly as our hands roamed everywhere at once, learning, claiming.

His bare chest glistened with a mix of sweat and rain, and I made sure to leave kisses up and down it. His muscles tensed while I explored with my fingers, tracing each defined line. He grabbed my face, pulling me back to him. The cold of his fingertips on my bare skin shocked a gasp out of me. He was smiling when I pulled back, his lips shiny and his pupils blown wide.

Henri's hands moved urgently as he pulled my shirt over my head, discarding it carelessly. His eyes darkened as he made sure to pay attention to each breast, before moving back up to my jaw, then down my throat, biting just shy of painful.

And God, I loved every moment of it.

"Fuck, *mon cœur*, you're so beautiful."

When I finally got my hands down to his waistband, Henri let out a hiss, and I knew that sound was something I would never get tired of. His hips rose off the seat, pressing into my palm, his eyes never leaving mine even as he kicked one leg free from the denim twisted around his ankle.

We stripped off the rest of our clothes—fumbling, laughing a little when my foot got stuck in my underwear. Henri's hands were everywhere, warm and sure. He kissed down to my collarbone, teeth dragging just enough to pull a whimper out of me. I bit his shoulder, and he grinned against my neck, breathing hard.

Then he stopped. Just for a second. His eyes locked on mine, and I could see everything in them: heat and desire and want and need. All tied up in a beautiful little bundle.

I could've asked him anything right then. *Has anything actually changed? What happens tomorrow?*

But I didn't.

He kissed me again, slower this time. Careful, like he was memorizing me. His palm cupped my face, thumb brushing my cheekbone, and God—every worry I had just melted. All that was left was how badly I wanted him.

Henri pulled back just enough to reach for his jeans, fishing a condom from his wallet. He held it up, eyes on mine, waiting.

"Fuck yes," I said.

As he put on the condom, I watched him, hard and ready. He throbbed with anticipation, pressing one hand to my hip, the other guiding himself, and our eyes met as he pushed inside.

I gasped. *Good God he felt just as amazing as I remembered.*

He went slow, holding me close, our foreheads pressed together. Every inch made my head spin. I grabbed at the headrest to steady myself, and Henri's fingers dug into my waist. We found our rhythm together, hips moving in sync with the rain drumming on the roof and our ragged breathing. Each thrust felt different, better than the last. His arm stayed locked around me while his other hand slid up my back, fingers tracing patterns across my shoulder that made me shiver.

I started rolling my hips, slow and deliberate. Henri's rhythm faltered—just for a second—and I grinned down at him. He laughed, breathless, gripping me tighter.

"*Tu vas finir par me tuer.*" His eyes were dark, desperate, wanting. "You're going to be the death of me."

I liked seeing him like this—all his walls down, face flushed, looking at me like I was the only thing that mattered. I liked that I could do this to him. We kept mumbling half-words against each other's mouths, things that didn't quite make sense but didn't need to.

I braced one hand on the ceiling as he thrust up into me, harder now, more desperate. When his thumb pressed against me in just the right way, circling, I couldn't hold back anymore. I came hard, gripping his shoulder, my whole body tightening around him. It rolled through me in waves that left me gasping.

He wasn't far behind. I watched his face as his rhythm broke apart. His whole body went tense under me, fingers digging into my hips, and he groaned, low and rough, saying my name like a prayer as he held me tight, moving me up and down in his lap.

I collapsed onto his chest, boneless, face buried in his neck. I could feel his pulse racing against my lips. His skin was warm and damp, and he smelled like sweat and rain and us. He wrapped his arms around my shoulders and kissed my hair, lips staying there for a long moment while we both caught our breath.

"I'm glad you got me into this car," I said quietly.

His eyes found mine, soft now, a little dazed. "Me too."

His fingers traced slow, lazy patterns on my lower back. The rain kept falling outside, softer now, almost gentle. I wanted to ask what he was thinking, but it felt too good right now—too easy. And honestly? Part of me was scared of the answer. Scared it might break whatever this was between us.

So, I didn't ask the burning question, and instead it sat between us. I shifted slightly, and Henri's grip tightened, keeping me close. Neither of us spoke. The rain had softened to barely a whisper against the roof.

Eventually, reality crept back in.

"We should probably…" I started, but I didn't finish.

"Yeah." Henri's voice was rough. He helped me ease off him, and we moved carefully in the confined space, reaching for our clothes.

Getting dressed in the back seat of a Beetle proved significantly less sexy than getting undressed had been. Elbows knocked into windows, my bra strap caught on the door handle, and Henri's jeans proved difficult.

We finally emerged into the damp evening air, looking thoroughly disheveled despite our best efforts. Henri's hair stood up at wild angles where I'd run my fingers through it. My lips felt swollen.

His friends were going to take one look at us and know exactly what had happened.

Henri caught my hand as I moved toward the front seat, spinning me back to face him.

"Lily—"

"Tomorrow," I said quickly. "Let's just… Tomorrow."

He nodded slowly, but his eyes held questions I wasn't ready to answer.

One day at a time.

My phone buzzed in my pocket, and at first, I tried to ignore it. But then it buzzed again.

Ollie:
Racing in Heels just dropped. You look amazing. Don't read the comments.

Don't read the comments was never a good way to start a press video.

"Fuck."

Henri glanced over. "What?"

I was pulling up social media, my thumb flying across the screen. The *Racing in Heels* segment had been posted an hour ago, and the comments section was a disaster.

Are you kidding me with this? Why is she talking about her looks instead of her pole position?

This is exactly why people don't take women in motorsport seriously. Embarrassing.

Lily Blackwood is better than this. Who approved these questions?

"Do you feel pressure to look good?" Jesus Christ. What year is this?

I scrolled further, my chest tightening with each new comment.

She should've walked out. Lost all respect for her.

Bet the male drivers aren't getting asked about their beauty routines.

"Lily?"

I looked up at Henri, and the concern in his eyes made something crack open inside me. I handed him my phone without a word.

He scanned the screen, his jaw tightening. Then he scrolled. And scrolled.

"*Merde.*"

"Oh God," I groaned. "Maybe I should've walked out. My gut told me in the moment that I was setting women in racing back fifty years."

Henri handed my phone back. "You didn't have a choice, Lily. We're contracted to these interview segments."

"I should have just paid the fine." I shoved my phone in my pocket, resisting the urge to throw it into the nearest body of water. "I should've refused. Should've made them ask me real questions."

"Your team arranged this, didn't they?"

I nodded, throat tight. "It's an F1 sponsored segment— or was. Not sure it'll continue after this mess…"

Henri grabbed my chin, forcing me to look at him. "Oh, Lily. This isn't on you."

"Tell that to everyone calling me an embarrassment." I ran my hands through my hair, which was still damp from the rain and thoroughly mussed from what we'd just done in the Beetle. "God, what if this follows me? What if every interview from now on, they bring this up? 'Remember when Lily Blackwood talked about moisturizer instead of racing?'"

"They won't."

"You don't know that."

"I know you," Henri said quietly. "You'll make them forget. One brilliant race, one perfect interview, and this becomes nothing."

"You really believe that?"

"You're Lily Blackwood." His mouth curved into something almost like a smile. "*Racing in Heels* will be a footnote. We'll think of something," he added. "Don't worry."

The rain had stopped completely now. Water dripped from the Beetle's roof, each drop catching the sun.

"Okay."

"Okay?"

"Okay."

Chapter Twenty-Four

The morning sun filtered through the floor-to-ceiling windows of my hotel suite. Silverstone had finally arrived. My home race. My dream. The race I'd been dying to win since I was a little girl karting in the Merseyside circuit.

I wanted this badly.

My phone buzzed on the nightstand with another message from my mother. I ignored it. The memory of last week crashed over me. Henri's hands panic-gripping the wheel. The rain streaming down the windshield. His body against mine in that ridiculous orange Beetle.

We'd promised to talk after the Beetle racing, but that conversation had never come, probably because we were both too scared. Not to mention, I'd been so busy dealing with the *Racing in Heels* fallout. Instead we'd spent the entire week exchanging texts and memes and talking about all the TV shows we needed to catch up on. Anything but discussing the big, fat elephant in the room.

The circumstances hadn't changed, and Henri Dubois was still off-limits.

My phone lit up with a text from Henri. *Archie misses you.* Three words that made my chest tight. They'd been together a little over a week now, and Georgia had said she'd noticed something in Henri.

I stared at the text, remembering Georgia's call yesterday. She was practically giddy, going on about how Henri had actually belly-laughed during their dinner Tuesday night.

Georgia had sent photos of Henri sprawled on his couch with Archie draped across his chest, both fast asleep. And then another of them at Monaco's harbor, Henri throwing a tennis ball while Archie bounded after it. The tension that usually lived in Henri's shoulders had melted away in those pictures.

When I walked out of the shower, a knock rattled my door.

"Room service." My mother's voice cut through the wooden door.

I snorted. After a lifetime of knowing each other, she still thought she could fool me.

Upon opening the door, Victoria Blackwood made a beeline to the cream sofa, her designer suit impeccable despite the early hour, tablet in hand.

"You're not dressed." More of a statement than a question. My mother's eyes swept over my towel-wrapped form with the kind of disapproval she had mastered over the course of my childhood. "Media day starts in two hours."

"Hello. Good morning." I grabbed clothes from my suitcase, waving them at her.

"Oh, Lillian, wear the chrome tennis dress."

Always an opinion.

I quickly got changed in the bathroom before coming back out. My mother had settled on the couch, and she was holding her tablet out like a weapon.

"Do you want to explain this?"

On the screen sat my social-media post from yesterday. A blurry shot of the orange Beetle mid-slide through mud, Henri's laughter visible even through the dirty windscreen. I'd captioned it simply:

Got buggy with it.

"It's a photo of a car."

"With Henri Dubois in the background." Each syllable dripped venom. "Do you know what this looks like?"

"Like we're friends." I yanked on my team polo with more force than necessary. "There's nothing that says I can't *socialize* with other drivers."

"Socialize?" She scrolled furiously through her tablet. "This isn't socializing, Lily. This is… What even is this? Racing Beetles in some field like teenagers?"

"It was a track day. With multiple people present." I kept my voice level, professional. The same tone I used with race stewards. "Lots of people were there, and I figured it would make for some fun social-media content. Plus, it was *fun*!"

"Don't be ridiculous." She stood, her heels clicking against the marble floor as she paced. "Do you think I'm stupid? That I don't see what's happening here?"

I focused on rummaging through my makeup bag, ignoring her glare. "It's good PR. Shows personality, relatability."

"It shows poor judgment." She thrust the tablet at me again. "47,000 likes. Every single comment speculating about you two. This is exactly what Rennen and your sponsors don't want."

I checked my reflection in the mirror. "I'm allowed to have a life outside of what Rennen wants."

"Not when that life threatens everything I've worked for." She gathered her things, her disappointment filling the room like exhaust fumes.

"*We've* worked for," I corrected.

"*We?*" My mother's laugh was nothing short of amused. "Did you negotiate your first sponsorship at fourteen? Did you convince Valkyrie to give an unknown British girl a chance?"

I didn't bother looking at her, just continued to apply my makeup. This was an argument we'd had over and over again, and there was no winning it.

"Speaking of putting in work," she continued. "Ollie's live taping for the *Home Stretch* podcast is tonight. Eight o'clock at the studio."

My stomach felt sick. I'd managed to forget about that commitment; pushed it so far back in my mind it had almost disappeared entirely. But there was no getting out of this one. *Home Stretch* had become a staple in the paddock, and the fans loved it.

"Hopefully he doesn't ask me about my beauty routine this time," I said sarcastically, capping my mascara with more force than necessary. "The *Racing in Heels* segment was a disaster."

"You're being overly dramatic." My mother waved her hand dismissively. "Tons of people loved that segment."

"Have you actually read the comments?" I turned from the mirror to face her. "Because they're calling it sexist. There's a petition with thousands of signatures demanding the segment be canceled."

"Those are just people looking for something to be offended about."

"Those are *racing fans* who wanted to hear about my driving, not my makeup choices." I grabbed my paddock pass and bag, slinging it over my shoulder. "Ollie made me look like I care more about fashion than Formula 1. I'm tired of being treated like a novelty act instead of a championship contender."

My mother crossed her arms, letting her fingers tap in slow progression. "Then maybe you should start acting like one instead of joyriding with Henri Dubois."

That one hit hard, and my mother took advantage of the silence.

"I'll send a car at seven fifteen." She scrolled through her tablet, all business now. "Please wear the black Rennen polo dress I packed in your suitcase. It photographs well under studio lights. And for God's sake, do something with your hair. That ponytail makes you look twelve."

The closed softly behind her, leaving me alone with the weight of tonight's podcast. Usually I was excited for the *Home Stretch* live taping, as it signified the start of Silverstone, but this time I was dreading it. I picked up my phone, Henri's text still glowing on the screen.

Henri:
Archie misses you.

Lily:
Tell him I miss him too.

Henri:
Can't wait to see you tonight. Got the whole crew coming, you're going to kill it.

I smiled at that.

A knock interrupted my thoughts. Andy entered with two protein shakes and his usual easy grin, his presence immediately making the room feel warmer.

"Saw your mother in the hallway," he snorted. "Always a pleasure."

I rolled my eyes, taking the protein shake from his hand.

"Just visiting to remind me about my duties."

He let out a short huff. "Wish she remembered her duty as a mother."

I gave him a look that said, "Don't start," and he put his hands up.

"Just saying, we can always find you another manager."

He took a seat on the edge of the bed, sipping his protein shake. "All right, I saw the Instagram post. I'm going to need you to fill me in here. How did we go from Austria to racing Beetles in the English countryside with Henri?" He crossed his legs, but I could tell from his face that he was enjoying this as he eagerly waited for the gossip.

"I don't know…"

Andy raised an eyebrow, that knowing look he got when he could see through my bullshit. "You don't know how you ended up in that orange Beetle with him." He leaned forward, a playful grin on his face. "Kidnapping?"

I scoffed out a laugh. "After Austria, back at the hotel bar, Henri and I talked. He—" I stopped, not sure where to go, but Andy leaned forward.

"He…?"

"He told me he *missed* me. In Austria. At the hotel bar, after the race."

"And you said…?"

"Nothing." I busied myself with my makeup, avoiding his stare in the mirror. "I just sat there like an idiot and said absolutely nothing."

"Lily."

"I know." I slammed down the mascara a tad too hard, causing my other items to shake. "But what was I supposed to say, Andy? 'Thanks, that's lovely, but my contract explicitly forbids me from dating you—you know, the whole reason you didn't want to date me in the first place?'"

Andy stood, crossing to lean against the bathroom doorframe. "I mean… you could've just said you missed him too."

"That would've made it worse." I turned to face him properly. "Henri isn't wrong—I'm not supposed to want him. I can't want him."

His expression softened. Andy always had a way of getting the truth out of me. "But you went to the Beetle racing anyway."

"Well, we're friends… or something like that." Even saying it felt like swallowing glass.

"Friends who have sex in the back seat of vintage race cars?"

"How did you—"

"Please." He rolled his eyes. "You came back looking thoroughly debauched and couldn't stop smiling during our training session." He paused, studying my face. "Does your mum know?"

"God, no." I grabbed my team jacket from the chair. "And she's not going to. Neither is Felix or anyone else at Rennen."

Andy's jaw tightened. "And what about Ollie? You know, the journalist who's been actively pursuing you *and* who's interviewing you tonight?"

Ollie. He'd definitely seen the photo—there was no way around that. His texts had been colder the past few days, and I was going to have to talk to him. It was the right thing to do.

"He's probably not loving that post," Andy said, straightening from the doorframe.

"I know." I zipped my jacket, avoiding his eye.

"You need to be careful tonight. A pissed-off, scorned journalist isn't good for anyone, especially one who's already proven he's willing to stoop low for a story."

"He's not scorned," I said, though the words rang hollow even to my own ears. "We've only been to dinner a few times, that's all."

"Well, I'm not sure he'll see it that way. Don't get me wrong, Lil. You don't owe him, or any man for that matter, your time. Especially not a liar. But still, it behooves us to be cautious." He rubbed the back of his neck, the way he always did when something worried him.

"I know, I know," I groaned. "I've got to say something, but after Silverstone."

"Well," Andy said with a sigh, "I just hope he sticks to his usual script during the podcast tonight."

I laughed bitterly. "I don't think even Ollie is that stupid. Plus, it's all fan questions tonight. He doesn't really get to ask anything."

Andy caught my arm, stopping me. "Let's hope tonight doesn't turn into payback."

I pulled free, straightening my shoulders as I tsked. "Even Ollie has some professional standards."

"Does he?" Andy's voice followed me to the door.

Chapter Twenty-Five

Henri

I settled into the seat beside Georgia, scanning the podcast studio with mild interest rather than the anxiety I might have felt months ago. The set looked upgraded since I was last here: better lighting, a sleeker couch, and bookshelves.

"Glad you decided to come," Georgia said quietly, adjusting the bag in her lap. "I know you probably have better things to do the day before a race weekend."

"Supporting Lily is exactly where I need to be." I meant it entirely.

Ever since that muddy afternoon in the Beetle, we'd been texting constantly. Photos of Archie doing something ridiculous at three in the morning. Her sending screenshots of terrible reality TV moments with commentary that made me laugh until my ribs hurt. Me sharing terrible French memes that somehow translated perfectly into her sense of humor.

We snuck in calls between training sessions, during the quiet moments most people spent alone. It felt just as natural and easy as breathing. We both skirted around the conversation we should actually have, but I was fine with that. During summer break, we could revisit the conversation, but Lily's focus needed to be on Silverstone now. Nothing else mattered. If I couldn't have my home race, then I at least wanted to make sure she had an opportunity to win hers.

I glanced toward where Lily would be sitting, reassuring myself with the knowledge that this was just fan questions. Nothing Ollie could weaponize. Nothing that would put her in a position to defend herself or me or whatever this thing between us was becoming.

The stage door opened, and Ollie emerged with his usual energy, clipboard in hand. He was halfway through saying something to a production assistant when he spotted me.

He stopped mid-sentence, genuine surprise flickering across his features before he caught himself. "Henri." My name came out slightly strangled. "I didn't… I wasn't expecting you."

"The studio invited several of the F1 drivers. Figured I'd pop along with Georgia and support Lily." I kept my tone pleasant, neutral.

"Of course, of course." He recovered quickly, but I could see the wheels turning behind his eyes, recalculating whatever plan he'd had. He started to move toward us, probably to engage in some awkward small talk, but the studio door opened again.

Éliott walked in first, then Sebastian and Luca, all in casual clothes. Within minutes, eight more F1 drivers had filled the front-row seats I'd reserved.

"Mate!" Éliott waved, exchanging quick greetings with Ollie, whose smile had gone tight.

"Quite the turnout," Ollie managed.

The energy in the room shifted noticeably. What had probably been intended as his controlled environment now felt decidedly less controlled.

Georgia murmured beside me, "What is everyone doing here?"

Éliott chuckled next to Georgia. "Just thought we'd come and support, Lil, that's all."

"Henri." Sebastian leaned over. "How're you feeling about Silverstone?"

"Good. Ready." I glanced toward the stage door, where Lily would emerge from shortly. "Should be interesting."

"That's one word for it." Luca grinned. "You should've seen Lil on the simulator this week. She was lightning at the office."

The overhead lights dimmed slightly, and a production assistant called for everyone to take their seats. The casual energy condensed into focused attention as we waited for Lily to appear.

Ollie recovered his composure, settling into his chair across from the empty couch with his notecards arranged just so. But I caught him glancing toward our group with wariness.

Good. Let him be off-balance for once.

The stage door swung open, and Lily emerged wearing dark jeans and a woven Rennen sweater. She spotted our group immediately, surprise and relief flickering across her face. Ollie guided her to the couch with his hand on her lower back, the touch lingering just long enough to be noticed.

"Ready?" he asked, throwing her a wink.

She nodded, crossing one leg over the other with perfect composure. The red recording light blinked on.

"Welcome to *Home Stretch*," Ollie began, his voice dropping into that smooth cadence he used for his podcast intro. "Today we have someone very special, our very own Silverstone star, Lily Blackwood!"

Lily's laugh was flawless. "That's very generous, Ollie. Although, easy to be the star when you're the only Brit on the grid this year."

"Oh, come on now—you're being far too modest, Lily!" Ollie laughed. "You've been a star every year."

A nice little suck-up before the sucker punching begins, I thought.

Georgia audibly groaned next to me, clearly also feeling the bullshit onstage.

"Now, we have some fan questions for you this evening." He leaned forward. "And after we get through those, we'll open it up to some Q&A from our audience here." He gestured toward us with a smile that didn't quite reach his eyes.

Lily nodded, her expression attentive but guarded.

"Let's start with Miami," Ollie said, all sympathetic concern. "Erin from Austin, Texas, says, 'Was that crash in Miami on purpose so you could ensure Henri didn't score more points than you?'"

Lily's eyes widened fractionally, a subtle twitch—barely noticeable unless you knew her tells.

"That's absurd. The data showed clear mechanical failure. I mean, in what world would I purposely risk wrecking my car so that Henri might not get some points? Who's to say I wouldn't have won that weekend in Miami?" Lily's voice stayed level, professional, but I caught the slight rise in pitch.

Her chest lifted and fell, and I could tell she was debating with herself on how angry to get. These were supposed to be fan questions, after all.

"Well, it's good to see you guys can still be *friends*." His forehead creased as he squinted at Lily, like he was trying to peer deeply for a different answer. He'd certainly seen that photo of us racing the Beetles.

"There's only twenty of us on the grid," Lily said, her voice clipped. "I consider us all friends off the track."

"Speaking of 'off the track'..." Ollie glanced down at his notecards with theatrical casualness. "Rachel from Germany asks, 'You and Henri were spotted at a Valkyrie event together and then racing Beetles. Are you two dating?'"

Ollie looked expectantly at her, but Lily didn't avoid his gaze. She'd mentioned they hadn't spoken since *Racing in Heels* dropped. She'd expertly avoided him, and I guessed this question had been selected as a way for him to pry.

"Well, unfortunately, Rachel, this isn't a *Love Island* podcast. There is no story or tea to share. We're friends." She winked out into the audience, who spared her a few laughs.

He flipped to a card at the back. "All right, this is from the UK. John from Manchester asks, 'You've had some bad luck at Silverstone in the past. The Silverstone curse, as some of us fans call it. Does that leave you a bit hesitant for this year?'"

"I don't believe in curses," Lily said evenly, her posture straightening slightly in the chair. "Just like I don't believe in luck. What I do believe in is preparation and execution. Everything else is just noise."

There were a few claps from the audience, which Ollie allowed with a small smile before continuing.

"But you have to admit, you haven't had the best performances on this track. Is there something about this pressure that makes it different compared to other races? Your face is practically all over the crowd on fans' posters."

Georgia leaned over, whispering, "Think anyone actually believes these are fan questions?"

I snorted in response. "If they are, he definitely hand-selected his favorites."

Georgia lightly snickered at the air quotes around "favorites."

"I'll let my driving speak for itself this weekend," Lily said coolly.

"Let's hope so." Ollie's smile turned sympathetic. "All right, next one, and this is a good one. Came up several times in our survey. Your move from Valkyrie to Rennen raised some eyebrows. Some people say Rennen hired you as a symbol for inclusivity. What are your thoughts on that?"

"I was hired because I'm fast, and because I earned my seat through years of results in junior categories." Lily's voice was sharp, even, not a smile on her face.

"But did sponsors push for your seat? I've heard rumors that sponsors at Rennen wanted a woman on the grid for marketing purposes."

Lily leaned forward, her green eyes blazing as she looked Ollie directly in the eye. "Ollie, are you asking if I'm a diversity hire? Because that's what it sounds like."

"I'm just asking what people are wondering." He waved the cards at her.

"Then let me be clear. I earned my seat the same way every other driver on the grid earned theirs. Through talent, hard work, and results. If sponsors like the fact that I'm a woman, then great. But it's not why I'm here, and my results this season speak for themselves."

The audience applauded again, more claps this time, but Ollie wasn't done.

"Of course, of course. You're incredibly talented—there's no doubting that. Though it must be hard sometimes, being compared to Georgia constantly. She's had such an incredible career, such a presence in the sport. Do you ever feel overshadowed by her?"

My sister sank a little more into her seat, trying to hide her face.

"Georgia is an exceptional driver and an even better person. I don't feel overshadowed. I feel *inspired*."

"But was it hard to live in her shadow while you were at Valkyrie?" Ollie was quick with that one.

"Georgia and I support each other. We're not competing for some imaginary title of 'token woman in F1.' We're both competing for race wins and championships." She put up her hand, adding, "And above all else, we're proud to support each other. Women supporting women is important."

Ollie's friendly mask flickered, just for a second, before he recovered with a practiced smile. "Women supporting women. I love it! Okay, this is our last question. This is from James of Paris, France. 'There's been some interesting chatter online about betting patterns this season.'" Ollie looked up, as if he was immediately trying to gauge her reaction, but Lily just kept staring at him, a face of perfect stoicism. "'Specifically, people who bet against you and lost significant amounts of money. How does that make you feel?'"

"I don't follow betting markets, Ollie. I focus on racing."

"But surely you're aware that some people have lost quite a bit of money betting against you?"

Lily sat up straighter, repositioning herself in the chair. "What people choose to do with their money isn't my concern."

"Even when those people might feel resentful? When they blame you for their losses?"

Lily's smile turned brittle. "Racing outcomes aren't guaranteed. This is why I think people should be careful about all this."

"Of course." Ollie shuffled his cards. "You don't sound like a fan of this all?"

"It's not that I'm not a fan of it. Every team has sports betting sponsors. Some teams probably need the funding just to survive. But…"

I could see the uneasiness in her face.

"But we, as a sport, still have to be careful with how far we let it go, that's all. Limits probably need to be put in place."

Georgia leaned close to my ear. "I suspect we're going to hear that soundbite later."

"And how far do we let it go?" Ollie had picked up on that one.

"Some fans can take it too far, that's all."

"Too far?" Ollie tilted his head, feigning confusion. "Can you elaborate on that? Have you experienced something negative from betting fans?"

Lily's fingers curled against her thigh. "Let's just move on."

"No, no, this is fascinating." He leaned forward, all false concern. "Have you received threats? Messages from people who lost money on you?"

The silence stretched thin and dangerous. Lily's face had gone pale, her composure cracking at the edges. She shifted forward as if she might stand; might end this whole charade right here.

Our eyes met across the studio.

I shook my head once, small and deliberate.

Don't give him what he wants.

Lily settled back into the couch, that mask of perfect professionalism sliding back into place even as her eyes blazed. This felt a bit more like an interrogation than a podcast about her home race.

"The fans who support me do so because they believe in my talent," she said, voice as steady as steel. "I'm thankful for them every day. Now, speaking of my fans, let's get to those audience questions, hm?"

I could see Ollie's eyes searching, looking for a hopeful way to bring that conversation back. But before he could, I stood up.

Ollie's head snapped toward me, surprise flickering across his face. "Henri? Did you have a—"

I turned to face Lily fully, letting a beat of silence settle. Her eyes met mine, confusion and relief warring in her expression. I could see the question there: *What are you doing?*

Trust me.

"Lily, you've shown exceptional racing this season, particularly your overtake on me in Monaco. That corner entry required precision and commitment." I paused, letting the serious tone settle. "But I'm curious, when you're making those split-second decisions at 200 miles per hour, do you ever worry about chipping your nail polish?"

For a split second, the studio was silent, say for some uncomfortable snickering from people sat behind me.

After another brief pause, Lily's hand flew to her mouth, her eyes crinkling at the corners as she dissolved into genuine laughter—the first real, unguarded expression I'd seen from her all night.

There she is. There's my Lily.

She gave me a shocked, questioning laugh before answering. "Constantly, Henri. It's my biggest fear out there." She wiped at her eyes. "That's why I only use gel. Regular polish can't handle the g-forces."

Éliott was already on his feet, catching on immediately. "I've got one. Lily, serious question about Silverstone's high-speed corners. When you're pushing through the corners at full speed, do you worry that the g-forces might cause some… premature aging? And if so, what's your skincare routine to combat that?"

"Éliott, the only thing causing me premature aging is racing you." Lily's face lit up with genuine amusement.

"Follow-up question then. Do you use different products for qualifying versus race day? You know, for optimal aerodynamics?"

Lily promptly spat out the sip of water she'd just taken, laughing. "Race day requires SPF 50, minimum. Can't have sun damage affecting my downforce."

Éliott nodded. "Excellent, I also use SPF on my skin to protect it from the sun. Turns out, that stuff is for men too."

Lily just snorted at that.

Luca stood next, not bothering to wait for permission. "My turn. Lily, you mentioned earlier about preparation and execution. Can you walk us through your mental preparation process before a qualifying session? And more importantly, does *racing in heels* affect your brake pedal pressure, or do you switch to flats for that?"

The entire front row of drivers erupted into laughter. Georgia buried her face in her hands, shoulders shaking. Ollie's face had almost gone white. At least I knew he'd got the point, as had the audience members in the room.

"I find stilettos give me better feel through the pedals, actually," Lily deadpanned. "The extra three inches helps me see over the halo."

"Brilliant strategy." Luca nodded sagely. "I should try that."

"I think you'd look excellent in heels, Luca. I believe your fiancée can loan you a pair."

"Fat chance!" Georgia snickered.

After that, Ollie reeled the questions back in, making sure to pick out fans sitting way in the back.

Once the final question was answered, Ollie thanked everyone for coming and then promptly left the stage, not pausing to bid farewell to Lily or anyone else in the room. The door swung shut behind him with a loud thud, leaving an awkward silence.

Lily glanced over, a playful smirk in her eyes. "Well, that went differently than planned. Thanks for the assist."

I chuckled. "Anytime. Maybe next time they'll think before cramming a bunch of silly questions into an interview with another female driver."

After another ten minutes with the group, I noticed Lily yawning. "Hey, you want an escort back to your hotel?"

Lily nodded, and we stepped out into the cool evening. The streets were quieter than I expected, most people already home for dinner. We walked in comfortable silence for a block, our shoulders occasionally brushing.

"You know, Max hasn't shut up about you. Says you drive like someone stole your lunch money."

"High praise from someone who took out three hay bales."

"Four, actually. He went back and counted."

I paused like I was waiting for an opportune moment to ask my real question. "Those betting questions tonight bothered you," I said finally. Not a question.

She wrapped her arms around herself despite the jacket. "I shouldn't have given Ollie that last quote. My sponsor is going to be pissed—I just know it."

"I wish you'd tell someone—"

"We've been over this, Henri. I can't stir the pot, be the one driver who complains about some of our biggest sponsors."

"I'm not asking you to hold a press conference. Just tell Georgia. Or your team principal. Someone who can actually help."

Lily stopped walking. The streetlight caught the shadows under her eyes, the fatigue she'd been hiding all evening behind that polished mask. "Not yet."

"Lily—"

"After summer break." She held up a hand. "Let me get through Silverstone and the next few races without this hanging over everything. Then I'll figure out the right way to handle it."

I studied her face, searching for any sign she was stalling indefinitely. Her jaw was set, her eyes clear. This wasn't avoidance. It was strategy.

"Fine." I stepped closer, holding her gaze. "But I need you to promise me. By summer break, you'll tell someone. Not just me. Someone with actual power to do something about it."

She chewed the inside of her cheek for a long moment. "I promise."

"I'll keep your secret until then." I extended my hand between us. "Deal?"

She looked at my outstretched hand and laughed softly, shaking it with a firm grip. "Deal."

Her fingers lingered in mine a beat longer than necessary before she let go.

We reached the hotel entrance, the glass doors spilling warm light onto the sidewalk. Lily turned to face me, her bag sliding off her shoulder.

"Thanks for walking me back. And for the silly questions. That was—"

"Do you want to do something crazy?" I blurted out.

She blinked. Her mouth opened, closed, then opened again. A laugh escaped her, half-nervous, half-curious, the kind that came out when someone wasn't sure if they were being pranked.

"Maybe?" The word pitched up at the end, a question wrapped inside an answer.

"Follow me."

I turned and walked toward the parking garage across the street without waiting for a response. My car sat on the second level—a silver Audi, nothing flashy, just functional. I heard her footsteps behind me, quick and uncertain on the concrete, her bag bouncing against her hip.

"Henri, I have free practice tomorrow morning."

I pulled open the driver's door. "So do I."

She stood on the passenger side, fingers resting on the handle, still unsure if this was a good idea.

"If this ends with me in a ditch somewhere—"

"Get in the car, Lily."

Chapter Twenty-Six

Lily

The headlights of Henri's Audi cut through the darkness as we turned off the highway and onto the service road that led to the back of Silverstone. I sat in the passenger seat, my feet tucked under me.

"I don't think we should be here this late," I said. "We'll get caught."

Henri glanced at me, the corner of his mouth twitching. "Ye of little faith."

"I'm serious. There'll still be mechanics working on the cars. And engineers. Night security. Someone will see us."

"No one is going to see us."

"You don't know that."

Henri slowed the car as we approached a gate I didn't recognize—some kind of service entrance on the far side of the circuit, well away from the main paddock. He pulled up and lowered his window. A moment later, a stocky man in a high-vis jacket appeared from a small booth, torch in hand. He leaned down to the window and broke into a grin.

"Mr. Dubois, good to see you!"

"Dave." Henri reached across and shook the man's hand. "Good to see you, mate."

I stared at him. "You're joking."

Henri ignored me. Dave was already waving us through, the gate sliding open with a mechanical groan. Henri eased the car forward, and I turned in my seat to watch the gate close behind us.

"Who was that?"

"Dave. Head of track security."

"And he's just… letting us in?"

"I signed some stuff for his kid. Caps, a race suit, a couple of model cars. His daughter's a massive fan, apparently."

"Of yours?"

Henri shot me a look. "And yours, actually. I nicked a signed hat you left at Georgia's when you stayed with her in Monaco."

I shook my head, a disbelieving laugh escaping me. "And there's no one else here? No mechanics? No engineers doing late checks?"

"Not on the track. Plus, there's no changes to the track anyway. Nothing we won't see in tomorrow's official track walk with the teams." He pulled the car into a dark corner behind one of the hospitality buildings and killed the engine. "Come on—we don't have to do it all, but let's take a walk!"

I looked out at the circuit. The floodlights were off, but the moon was bright enough to paint the grandstands in silver. The place felt enormous in the silence. Enormous and somehow intimate at the same time.

"Fine," I said. "Let's do it."

We climbed out of the car. The night air was warm, carrying the faint smell of cut grass and rubber that I'd associated with this place since I was a child. Henri came around to my side and stood beside me, hands in his pockets, looking out across the circuit.

"Ready?"

"Born ready."

We slipped through a gap in the barriers and stepped onto the track. The tarmac was still warm under my trainers, holding the heat of the day. I looked down at the surface—the faded tire marks, the rubber buildup on the racing line—and felt something loosen in my chest.

This was Silverstone. My track. The place where my dream had started.

We walked in comfortable silence for a while, following the racing line through the first few corners. Our footsteps were the only sound, soft and rhythmic against the asphalt.

"It's strange being here when it's this quiet," I said. "I've only ever known it loud."

"I prefer it like this."

"You would. You're French. You probably think Silverstone's too noisy and the food's terrible."

"The food *is* terrible. Last year, they served me a jacket potato with beans in the media center and acted like it was fine dining."

"It *is* fine dining. That's a national treasure you're disrespecting."

Henri's shoulders shook, his head tipping back. The sound bounced off the empty grandstands.

We walked on. I pointed out the spot along the old fence line where my dad used to bring me as a girl. Where I'd press my face against the chain link, imagining the day it would my turn to race here. Henri listened the way he always did—quietly, completely, like he was filing every word away somewhere safe.

The silence settled back over us after that, but it was different now. Heavier. Like we'd both arrived at the edge of something and were waiting to see who would step forward first.

It was Henri.

"We should talk about this," he said. His voice was quieter than before. Careful. "About us."

I kept walking for a few steps then slowed. "I know."

Henri stopped. I stopped too, turning to face him. We were standing in the middle of the track with nothing but moonlight and empty asphalt in every direction.

"I've had since Las Vegas to think about this," he said. "About what this could be." He paused, and I could see the war brewing inside of him as he fought to choose his words carefully. "I worry that I can't give you what you want. The way things are—the teams, the contracts, the press. We'd have to hide. For a long time. Maybe longer than either of us wants."

The moonlight caught the uneasy mask of his face, the furrow between his brows. Henri was worried. Genuinely worried. Not about being caught or about what the press would say, but about me. About whether this could be enough.

"I want to try," I said.

Henri blinked. "Lily—"

"I know it's complicated. I know we'd have to be careful. But I think we owe it to each other to at least try to work it out. Don't you?"

He didn't answer right away. He looked at me for a long moment, searchingly, like he was waiting for the qualifier. The "but." The escape clause.

It didn't come.

"At the end of the year," I continued, "I'm going to ask Rennen to renegotiate my contract. With a new manager."

That landed differently than the rest, surprise breaking through the careful composure.

"A new manager?"

"It's time."

"Your mother—"

"Has been my manager since I was fourteen. And she's good at it. She got me to where I am. But I need someone who sees me as a human first, driver second."

His eyes softened at the corners, crinkling in that way they did when he really meant something. He reached for my hand, his thumb brushing over my knuckles. "I'm proud of you," he said simply. His fingers tightened around mine, warm and steady. "*Mon cœur*," he whispered, bringing my hand to his chest, where I could feel his heartbeat through his thin shirt. He held it there for a moment, his gaze never leaving mine. "You've outgrown her, and it's okay to accept that you need something different. It's a big change in your life. It's okay to be scared, but I know you're doing the right thing here."

I stepped closer, closing the gap between us until my forehead rested against his collarbone. His free arm came around me, pulling me in. I stood there, breathing him in, letting myself be held. Henri cupped my face, his thumb catching the single tear that had escaped despite my best efforts. He didn't say anything. He didn't need to. He just held my face and looked at me like I was the only thing in this enormous, empty circuit that mattered.

I kissed him first. Rose up on my toes and pressed my mouth to his, and for a second he went completely still—

surprised, maybe, or savoring it—before his hand slid from my cheek to the back of my neck and he pulled me in.

The kiss was slow and unhurried. Nothing like the desperate, stolen moments we'd had before. This was two people standing in the open, choosing each other.

When we finally broke apart, his forehead rested against mine. His breath came uneven against my lips. He tucked a strand of hair behind my ear, his fingers lingering against my cheek.

"We should head back," he murmured. "Early start tomorrow. Just need to grab something from my room."

"Yeah, alright."

He sighed and stepped away, and the night air rushed into the space between us like it had been waiting. We turned and started walking back toward the paddock, shoulders almost touching, not quite holding hands.

As we neared the pit lane, Henri slowed.

We ducked through a side entrance near the Hermes hospitality unit. Henri punched a code into the keypad, and the door opened. The corridor inside was dark, lit only by the green glow of emergency-exit signs. Our footsteps echoed against the polished concrete.

Henri found his driver's room by memory, guiding me with a hand on the small of my back. The room was small and sparse. A massage table, a mini fridge, a screen mounted to the wall. He closed the door behind us and turned the lock.

"Welcome to my office."

I leaned against the doorframe and watched him. "What are you looking for?"

"Need to grab that hat for Dave's daughter. I promised her a visor."

"You're like Father Christmas."

"I'd like to think of myself as more handsome than that."

He found what he was looking for—a tinted race visor, still in its packaging—and tucked it under his arm. Then he turned and looked at me leaning against his doorframe in his driver's room.

"What?" I said.

"Nothing. Just… this. You, here."

"Don't get used to it. If anyone from Rennen catches me in the Hermes garage, I'll be explaining it to Felix until I'm forty."

Henri crossed the room toward me. "Then we should probably stop standing here."

"Probably."

Neither of us moved toward the hallway.

Henri set the visor down on the massage table without looking at it. His eyes stayed on me—dark, intent, the careful composure from the track walk dissolving.

"We should go," I whispered.

"Say it like you mean it."

I couldn't. Not with him standing this close—not with the lock turned and the corridor silent and his hand finding my hip like it belonged there. I grabbed the front of his shirt and pulled him against me, my back pressing flat against the doorframe.

His mouth found mine—harder this time, nothing slow about it. His fingers dug into my waist, and I gasped, arching into him. I bit his lower lip and felt the groan travel through his chest into mine.

He picked me up like I weighed nothing, my legs wrapping around him as he carried me to the massage table. My back hit the padded surface, and he leaned over me, one hand braced beside my head, the other sliding under the hem of my shirt, his palm hot against bare skin.

"Door's locked?" I breathed.

"Door's locked."

His mouth traced down my jaw, my neck, my collarbone. I pulled at his shirt, and he helped me get it over his head, tossing it somewhere behind him. My fingers mapped the landscape of him—the hard ridges of muscle, the scar on his shoulder from a childhood karting crash, the rapid drumbeat of his heart under my palm.

He tugged at the hem of my top, and I sat up enough to let him pull it free. The air was cool against my skin for half a second before his body covered mine again, warm and solid and everywhere.

His hand slid up my ribs, thumb brushing the underside of my bra, and I sucked in a breath that sounded embarrassingly desperate. He paused. Looked up at me.

"Lily."

"Don't you dare ask me if I'm sure again—"

He kissed me before I could finish. His fingers found the clasp at my back and made quick work of it, and then there was nothing between us but skin and the faint green glow of the exit sign bleeding under the door.

I pulled at his belt. He helped, kicking his jeans off the edge of the table. My shorts followed, his hands hooking under the waistband and dragging them down my legs with a slow deliberateness that made me want him even more.

When he came back up, he pressed his forehead to mine. Both of us breathing hard. Both of us still.

"Hi," he whispered.

I laughed, shaky and breathless. "Hi."

His hand cupped my face, thumb stroking my cheekbone. When I got up, I motioned for Henri to sit on his driver's-room sofa, which he did eagerly. I pressed a finger to his lips. Then I replaced it with my mouth with a single kiss before turning my attention elsewhere.

"Oh, *mon cœur*—" he started as I began kissing down his body.

I took my time, savoring every hitch in his breathing, every muttered curse in French. His hand knotted in my hair, gripping tight and trembling, caught between wanting me to stop and never wanting me to stop. After everything in the world that had tried to control me, there was a fierce, electric joy in knowing I could take him apart with just my hands and my mouth, knowing exactly what he needed.

I hollowed my cheeks and took him deep. Henri's gasp rolled through me like thunder. He was clinging to control, to some last scrap of composure, but I wanted him to lose it so I picked up my taunting. Getting him close, then backing off right before he came.

"Keep fucking teasing me, *mon amour*—"

But he couldn't finish that sentiment. His breathing grew more ragged with each pass of my tongue, his grip on my hair tightening almost painfully. I could feel him unraveling beneath me, all that careful control Henri maintained in every other aspect of his life now dissolving under my touch.

"Lily," he gasped, the word half-strangled. "Please…"

God, I loved it when he begged in that thick, French accent.

"Please what?" I asked, my voice husky even to my own ears.

Instead of answering, Henri pulled me up his body and onto his lap with surprising strength. His arms locked around me, hands pressing hard into my back.

"No more teasing," he growled against my neck.

Henri reached into his wallet, rolled on a condom, and pulled me back on top of him, watching my face, as gentle as always, but I didn't want gentle. I planted my knees on either side of his hips, the sofa cushions dipping beneath us, and sank down slowly. The stretch stole my breath, but I wanted it—the ache, the fullness, the way he filled every empty space in me.

I braced one hand on the armrest behind his head and found my rhythm, rolling my hips until his head fell back against the cushion and his mouth dropped open. His hands gripped my thighs and slid up to my waist, pulling me down harder. I dug my nails into his shoulders, and he groaned, louder this time, sitting up just enough to press his mouth to my neck, teeth grazing. Heat coiled low in my belly, building and building, until I was grinding against him, desperate, whimpering, right on the edge.

"Fuck, Lily, fuck," he moaned over and over.

I picked up the pace, chasing my high. His hips bucked up to meet mine, and I let go. I shattered fast and blinding, biting down on his shoulder to keep from screaming, too aware of the thin walls and the paddock just outside. He followed seconds later, hands bruising my hips, shuddering beneath me, cursing, whispering my name like it was the only word he had left.

We stayed like that for a long time. Tangled together on the narrow sofa, skin cooling, hearts settling back into their normal rhythms. His fingers traced lazy circles on my hip. My cheek pressed against his collarbone, right over that old scar.

"We need to go," I murmured into his skin.

"Five more minutes."

I closed my eyes. Five more minutes in this locked room where nothing existed but us. No teams, no contracts, no cameras.

I enjoyed every second of it.

Chapter Twenty-Seven

Lily

I'd just finished tucking my hair into the fireproof balaclava when the door to my driver's room opened behind me.

"Lily."

I didn't need to turn around to recognize my mother's voice, that particular blend of disappointment.

"Not now, Mum." I reached for my gloves, focusing on the familiar texture.

"Just popping by to wish you luck." Her heels clicked against the floor as she approached. "Although, starting from pole, you shouldn't need much of that. Though hopefully we don't have a repeat of last year's Silverstone."

"How is that helpful, Mum?" Did she really think reminding me of last year's failure was going to improve this year's performance?

Her perfect mask slipped for a moment, eyebrows lifting as if I'd suddenly started speaking a language she didn't recognize.

"No." I put my hand up before she could say something. "You're trying to make me doubt myself. I'm not hearing it today. Not at Silverstone."

"Lily—"

"I can do this." My hands were steady as I pulled on my gloves. "I am on pole today. I have the fastest car on track. And I'm going to go out there and win this race—not because you think I can or because you think I can't, but because I'm bloody good enough to do it."

This was why she needed to go as my manager. Every pre-race conversation got twisted into some excavation of my failures, every pep talk laced with poison. And the pattern became impossible to ignore: she'd hollow me out then build me back up on her terms, until I couldn't tell whether my confidence belonged to me or was something she loaned me to repossess at will.

My mother's perfectly composed face cracked just slightly, revealing something I couldn't quite name. I'd never seen Victoria Blackwood look stunned. But just like today, there was a first time for everything. A first time for Victoria, and a first time for me, when I would stand on Silverstone's podium in first place.

"I need you to leave," I said, quieter now but firm. "I need to focus, and I can't do that with you here."

For a moment, I thought she might argue. But she didn't. For once in her life, my mother saw sense.

"Good luck, then." The room felt considerably calmer the moment the door clicked shut behind her.

I exhaled slowly, letting every piece of tension I felt when she walked into a room with me disappear. On the TV, I could see the Silverstone crowds already gathering, a sea of British flags and team colors. My home race. My pole position. My chance to prove to myself exactly what I was capable of.

Mark appeared in my doorway, his headset already settled over his neck.

"Ready?" he asked simply.

I grabbed my helmet, running my thumb over the smooth surface, as I looked down at the design on it. Lillies had been painted all over it, along with photos of my early karting days. A specially designed helmet for a special race. A little piece of me, to remind me I could do this.

"Ready."

The formation lap felt different from pole position at Silverstone: a position I'd never held here. It felt like I owned the place—which, considering half the fans were wearing my shirt, it looked like I did.

"Radio check, Lily." Mark's voice crackled through my earpiece.

"Loud and clear."

"Weather's holding, and the track temperature's optimal. Remember, it's a long race. Manage those tires, especially through those turns."

The formation lap brought us around to the grid slots. I rolled the Rennen car into position at the front, the tarmac still bearing faint rubber marks from earlier sessions. Through my mirrors, I watched the field settle into place, all behind me.

This was it. Everything I'd worked for was ahead of me.

The red lights illuminated one by one. Five lights.

And then none.

I nailed the start, wheels gripping perfectly as the Rennen car launched forward. Behind me, the field surged, but I was already pulling away, claiming the racing line into Turn 1. The crowd's roar was so loud I could almost hear it over the engine.

"Good start, Lily. P1. Henri's close behind, two-tenths back."

Good, I thought. *I like a fight. Will make this win even more satisfying.*

The first few laps settled into a rhythm. Every time I glanced at my mirrors, there was his distinctive Hermes livery, never quite close enough to attack, but never far enough away to ignore. He was studying me, learning my movements, waiting for the moment when I'd make a mistake. Like I had done in Monaco.

Lap twenty-seven, I pulled off the track so my crew could change my tires. They had me back out in under three seconds, and I rejoined the race still ahead of Henri.

But only just. He closed the gap somehow.

The next several laps became a chess match at two hundred miles an hour. Henri tried everything to get past—darting to one side, then the other, trying to bait me into a mistake. But I knew him. I'd studied the way he raced, the way he threw himself into every corner like he had something to prove.

More importantly, I trusted myself enough to hold my ground.

By lap thirty-five, he was right on me. I could feel him there even before I saw him—that prickle of awareness that came from knowing someone was inches away at speeds that could kill you both.

We emerged onto the straight, side by side.

He pulled alongside again at the next corner. It was a proper battle, the kind of racing that reminded me why I'd sacrificed everything for this sport.

But then he had the better position, and I could either back off or risk us colliding. For a heartbeat, Miami flashed through my mind. The sickening crunch, the terror of watching Henri's car flip, the weight of knowing I'd caused it.

But this wasn't Miami. This was clean, hard racing between two drivers who respected each other. Who wanted to win, but not at any cost.

I gave him the corner but stayed close. Then I used the speed I'd saved to swing back past him at the next turn. He tried to block me, but it was too late. I had the better position.

Now or never.

I held my line, leaving him no choice but to fall back. We roared through the next stretch side by side, so close I could hear his engine alongside mine. But I had more speed coming out of the corner.

One more straight, and I was clear.

"Seventeen laps to go. Bring it home."

Behind me, Henri was fading. That was the thing about him—he drove with so much fire that he wore his car out before the race was over. He had the speed, but I had the patience.

The final laps blurred. *Stay smooth. Stay focused. No mistakes.* Henri pushed for a few more laps, but gradually he shrank in my mirrors until I could barely see him.

"Final lap, Lily. You're going to win Silverstone."

The words hit differently than I expected. Not triumphant or overwhelming, but steady and sure. I'd dreamed of this moment since I was eight years old watching races with my family. Since my first go-kart race. Since every sacrifice and setback and small victory that had led here.

One last time through the famous first corner, the crowd's roar building like thunder. Then another turn. Then another. Then—

The checkered flag.

"Yes!" I shouted into the radio, the word ripping out of me with all the emotion I'd been holding back. "Hell yes! We did it! We actually bloody did it!"

"Lily Blackwood wins the British Grand Prix!" Mark's voice cracked with emotion, and I could almost hear a sob in his voice. "P1, you beautiful, brilliant driver!"

Tears blurred my vision as I pumped my fist, the Rennen car carrying me on a cool-down lap past grandstands full of fans waving British flags and checkered banners. My radio filled with congratulations from the team, voices overlapping in a chaos of joy that matched the chaos in my chest.

I'd won at Silverstone. In my home race.

But that feeling, that insurmountable joy, lasted for exactly forty-seven minutes.

I was back in the Rennen garage, still in my champagne-soaked race suit, surrounded by celebrating mechanics, when Mark's expression changed. He saw Felix in the back, coming toward us, a determined, angry look on his face.

"Lily." Felix's voice cut through the celebration. "We need to talk. My office. Now."

The garage fell deeply quiet, and no one said a word as I followed Felix, with Mark in tow.

"What's wrong?"

He motioned for me to take a seat.

"I've just come from the FIA offices." He stared at me, watching my face start to grow with horror.

No, I thought to myself. *Don't say what I think you're about to say.*

"They did their usual inspection on the car, Lily. I'm sorry to say, but we've been disqualified. The ride height was too low by one millimeter."

"No." The word came out hollow. "No, that's not—We can't—" I stuttered.

"The car was too low to the ground," he said again, quieter this time. "We pushed the setup too aggressively, and the plank wore down below legal limits. It's a clear technical violation."

I couldn't even describe the feeling that hit my chest, almost like a million bricks had been dumped on top of me. All those congratulations, the champagne, the anthem, the podium.

None of it counted.

My dream?

It was still just a dream.

"Can we appeal?"

"Lily." Felix's voice held defeat. "The measurement is objective. There's no gray area here. There's nothing to appeal."

"So, Henri gets the win then?" The trophy always went to whoever was P2. "I guess Silverstone will always just be a dream."

Felix didn't say anything else as he stared at me, heartbreak all over his face. I'd barely seen any emotion from my team principal, but now, when I finally did, it was the exact emotion I'd never wanted to see.

"I need…" I couldn't finish the sentence. I needed to get out; needed to be anywhere but here, watching the team's joy curdle into devastation. "I'm leaving."

"Lily—"

I was already moving, stripping off my gloves, unzipping the race suit. Someone—I didn't even know who—handed me my street clothes, and I changed in the back of the motorhome, muscle memory taking over when my brain couldn't process anything beyond the crushing weight of loss.

Security ushered me quickly to my car, and I kept my head down and walked faster, ignoring the cameras, ignoring the journalists calling my name, ignoring everything except the need to be alone.

As soon as I got into the hotel, I dropped my bag on the floor.

I made it three steps before I saw it. A white envelope on the bed, attached to some chocolates, identical to all the others.

My hands shook as I picked it up, already knowing what I'd find inside but unable to stop myself from looking. The same block letters that haunted me each time I saw a small piece of cardstock.

YOU REALLY FUCKED UP THIS TIME, LILY. SO MUCH FOR BEING A SURE BET, EH? DON'T LET ME FIND YOU AT THE NEXT GRAND PRIX.

I crumpled the note in my fist and sank onto the bed. The hotel room was silent except for my ragged breathing.

Someone had been in this room.

Someone who knew I'd be here, in this hotel, in this specific room. I dropped the note like it burned and pulled out my phone. I couldn't wait until summer break to tell someone. That plan was crazy. My fingers hovered over Henri's name in my contacts. Then over Mark's. Then over the number for hotel security.

Instead I called no one. I sat there alone, letting the silence eat me alive.

Chapter Twenty-Eight

Henri

The rain hadn't stopped since we arrived in Belgium two days ago. It drummed against my hotel window in an endless, maddening rhythm that matched the anxiety churning in my chest. I'd been standing aimlessly for twenty minutes, phone in hand, thumb hovering over Felix's contact information.

This is insane. I shouldn't be doing this.

But the image of Lily's text to me last week, the one with a photo of the threat she'd received in Silverstone, had left me feeling sick. Silverstone was devastating for her. She'd gone from winning twenty-five points and her dream race, to nothing. And then to get this?

I was nothing short of worried.

She'd barely spoken to anyone all week. Lily had refused to let me into her hotel room afterward and had basically ignored all my calls and Georgia's ever since. In the drivers' briefing yesterday, she'd sat alone, hood pulled up, avoiding eye contact.

But I knew that look in her eyes. I'd worn it myself, that desperate attempt to hold everything together while falling apart inside. Silverstone had stolen more than points from her. It had stolen that spark, that fire that made her Lily. And now, with these threats piling up on top of everything else, I was terrified of what might be left when the dust settled.

How much could one person take before they shattered completely?

My thumb pressed the call button before I could talk myself out of it.

"Hello?" Felix's confident voice came through. "Who's speaking?"

"Felix, this is Henri. I need to talk to you. In person. Are you at your hotel?"

A pause. "Yes, but—"

"Which room? I'm coming over."

Another pause, longer this time. "1247. Henri, what's this about?"

"I'll explain when I get there."

I hung up before he could ask more questions—before I could second-guess this decision again. The walk to his hotel took less than ten minutes through the rain. Each step felt heavier than the last.

Felix opened the door on the first knock. His expression was wary, guarded, in a way that reminded me he'd spent years managing difficult personalities and navigating team politics.

"This is unexpected," he said, stepping aside to let me in.

The hotel room was immaculate, as I'd expected from Felix. His laptop sat open on the desk, displaying some racing data from last week. A half-eaten room-service meal rested on the table by the window. The man never stopped working.

"You want to sit?" Felix gestured to the chairs.

I shook my head. Sitting felt too casual for this conversation. "I need to tell you something. About Lily."

His expression changed, concern replacing wariness. "If this is about your attachment—"

I stopped him, putting my hand up. He thought I'd come to tell him about my feelings for Lily—a gesture that would have been dramatic, although not warranting a hotel conversation like this.

That was a conversation hopefully for another time.

He studied me for a long moment. "What is it, Henri? I have work—"

"She's been receiving threats." The worlds fell out of my mouth.

The color drained from Felix's face. For several seconds, he simply stared at me, processing. When he finally spoke, his voice was dangerously quiet. "Excuse me?"

"She received the first one in Miami. Then another in Monaco. There's been a few, almost one per race." The words were tumbling out faster now. "I told her to tell you, but she refused. And now they seem to be escalating."

"And she told you this?" Felix's tone carried an edge I'd never heard before. "She confided in you?" He seemed almost not to believe me.

"I found one." I almost added "in her hotel room" but thought better of it. No need to get Lily in more trouble.

Felix turned away, moving to the window. His reflection in the glass looked older somehow, the weight of responsibility visible in the set of his shoulders. "How specific were these threats?"

"I don't know all the details. You'll have to ask her."

"Oh, I intend to." He spun back around, and I was struck by the fury in his eyes—not directed at me, but at the situation. At himself. "Why wouldn't she tell me?

I'm her team principal. Her…" He stopped, composing himself.

"She's proud and stubborn. She didn't want to make a big deal of it." I paused, running a hand through my damp hair. "But I think it's more than that. Silverstone destroyed her confidence. She's been spiraling all week. I can see it, even if she won't admit it. And these threats?" I shook my head. "She doesn't have the bandwidth to deal with them. Not right now."

"I wish she'd come to me." Felix scratched his head, his face turning slightly pink. "I just don't understand why."

"Because of the sponsor."

Felix's hand froze mid-scratch. His eyes locked onto mine.

"BetHere," I said. "She knows how much that deal means to Rennen. She was terrified that if she raised the alarm, it would spook them. The threats mention losses from sports betting."

Felix closed his eyes. A vein pulsed at his temple. When he opened them again, his expression changed—the anger was still there, but underneath it, guilt clawed its way onto his face. That was a look I recognized all too well.

"You did the right thing, telling me," he said finally. "Even if it was difficult."

The words should've have brought relief. Instead they settled like lead.

"She's going to hate me for this."

"Probably." He didn't sugarcoat it. "But it doesn't change that it was the right thing to do."

I nodded, though the guilt didn't ease.

Felix opened his phone, already shifting into crisis-management mode. "I'll contact security immediately," he said, more to himself than to me. "And the FIA. They need to be aware. We'll need to review all her mail, increase security presence around her." He looked up. "How is she right now? Beyond the obvious."

I thought of Lily in the paddock this morning, hood up, shoulders hunched. The dark circles under her eyes that makeup couldn't quite hide.

"Barely holding it together. Silverstone was rough."

"Rough" didn't capture the hollow look in her eyes or the way her hands shook when she thought no one was watching.

He nodded, walking me to the door. "Henri?"

I turned back.

"Thank you. I know this wasn't easy." He paused. "She's lucky to have someone who cares enough about her."

The words should've comforted me, but they didn't.

The walk back to my hotel felt longer than the journey over. The rain had intensified, coming down in sheets that soaked through my jacket within minutes. I didn't bother running. The cold water felt appropriate somehow, like penance.

What have I done?

Lily had trusted me. Not completely, not with everything, but she'd let her guard down enough to admit vulnerability. And I'd taken that trust and thrown it back in her face by going to Felix.

Except that wasn't fair. She'd told me about the threats, yes, but she wasn't dealing with them.

By the time I reached my hotel, I was thoroughly drenched and no closer to resolving the war in my head. The elevator ride to my floor felt dreadful. I wanted to text Lily, to warn her, to apologize, but there was nothing I could say that would make this better.

I'd made the right choice. I had to believe that.

Even if it had cost me whatever we were building between us.

Even if she never forgave me.

I did this for you, I thought, as if she could hear me. *I hope someday you'll understand.*

But understanding and forgiveness were different things. I knew that better than anyone.

Chapter Twenty-Nine

Lily

The knock came as I was pulling my hair into a loose braid, still trying to get ready for my media day in Belgium. I padded across the hotel room in bare feet, expecting room service to deliver the latte I'd ordered twenty minutes ago.

Instead, Ollie stood in the hallway, shoulders slightly hunched. He was dressed ready for the paddock, already in his nice jeans and a blazer.

"Hey," he said.

I didn't say anything for a moment, just stood there, one hand on the door, the other gripping the frame as I tried to work out why he was here and what it was going to cost me emotionally.

"Hey," I said eventually.

"I wanted to check on you. After Silverstone." He paused. "Can I come in?"

Every instinct screamed no. I was tired of speaking to people, and I didn't have the energy to navigate whatever this was going to be. I didn't have the reserves for careful words and managed expectations. I barely had the reserves to stand upright.

But he'd come all this way. And he was looking at me like he genuinely just needed to see that I was in one piece.

"Sure," I said, and I stepped aside, though everything in me wanted to close the door and crawl back into bed.

He walked in and looked around the room the way people do when they don't actually care about the décor but need somewhere to put their eyes. I closed the door and leaned against it, arms folded, keeping the distance between us. The room felt too small with him in it. Everything felt too small lately.

"How are you feeling?" he asked, turning back to me.

"Tired." I shrugged, the gesture empty.

He nodded slowly, then he sat down on the edge of the armchair near the window, elbows on his knees. I stayed where I was, by the door, like I might need the exit.

The silence between us was full of a mountain of things unsaid.

"Ollie—"

"Lily—"

We both stopped. He huffed out a small laugh and gestured for me to go first.

I made myself cross the room and sit on the edge of the bed, though I kept my arms wrapped around myself.

"I think you know what I'm going to say," I said quietly. The talk I needed to have with Ollie. I wanted to ask him about Henri and the story, but most of all, I needed to tell him I wasn't interested anymore.

"Yeah. I think I do."

I pulled at a loose thread on the comforter, winding it around my finger until the tip went white.

"I really appreciate all the dinners and chats, Ollie. But we need to stay friends."

The words came out plain. No softening, no preamble. I owed him that much—the clean version, not some dressed-up speech designed to make me feel better about delivering it.

Ollie's entire body seemed to go rigid for a second before relaxing back into his usual comfortable ease. He studied the carpet between his shoes.

"I'm sorry if I led you on. That wasn't fair, and I know it. I genuinely enjoyed hanging out with you. The dinners, the paddock stuff. You made me laugh when I really needed it."

"You don't have to do that." He looked up. His eyes were dry and clear, no trace of surprise in them. "The whole letting-me-down-easy thing. You've chosen Henri, I can see it."

I nodded uncomfortably.

"After your photos from the Beetle racing in London, I knew I'd lost." A light smile tugged at his lips. "I am a journalist, after all." He sat forward, rubbing the back of his neck. "I owe you an apology too, actually."

"For what?"

"The fan questions. During the podcast taping." He wouldn't meet my eye now. "I picked the meaner ones on purpose, to rattle you."

I'd suspected this, somewhere in the back of my mind, but hearing him confirm it was different. The ground shifted under something I thought was solid.

"That's—"

"Spiteful. It was spiteful. I was jealous after seeing those photos of you and Henri, and I took it out on you in the pettiest way I could find." He finally looked at me again. "I'm not proud of it. I've been carrying it around since Silverstone, and it's been eating me alive."

I sat with that for a moment, letting it settle into place alongside everything else.

"It's also why I told you that story about Henri. The story about F2—I shouldn't have told you that." He pressed his palms together between his knees. "I was young and stupid, and what I did to Henri back then was wrong, period. I should apologize to him, too." Our eyes finally met. "I only told you that because I wanted to drive a wedge between you two. I could see what was happening, and I thought if I made you doubt him, you'd pull away and pick me."

"I appreciate you saying that." I chewed my lower lip, tasting the remnants of my lip balm. "And Henri… He'd appreciate an apology." I wasn't so sure about the last bit, but it felt right in the moment. Deep down, I believed that leaving negative energy in the universe would come back to haunt us. If there could be some peace between Ollie and Henri, that would be a win.

"Yeah, well." He gave a half-smile. "It's long overdue."

His gaze drifted past me, toward the desk by the window where I'd spread out the notes earlier that morning. I'd been photographing them for safekeeping, arranging them in order, and hadn't bothered to put them away.

"What's all that?"

I followed his eyes to the desk. My first instinct was to wave it off—nothing, just work stuff—but I'd just asked him for honesty, and he'd given it. The least I could do was return the favor.

"Someone's been leaving me notes."

His eyebrows lifted. "Notes?"

"Well, threats. In written and virtual form, all anonymous."

Ollie stood and crossed to the desk, not touching anything, just looking. His head tilted as he scanned the handwriting.

"Do you know who it is?"

The question lingered, and I watched his face carefully—the set of his mouth, the way his fingers curled at his sides as he read the notes.

"No. I have no idea."

His shoulders relaxed, just barely. The change was subtle, barely perceptible, but I caught it—a release of tension he'd been holding since he walked over to the desk. His chest dropped half an inch with a breath he'd been keeping shallow.

"That's creepy, Lily. Someone in the paddock following you around, leaving anonymous… Have you told anyone? Security, the FIA, your team?"

"No."

He turned from the desk, disbelief plain on his face. "No? Lily, this is— Some of these are genuinely threatening."

"I know what they say. I've read them enough times."

"Then why haven't you—"

"Because I don't want to make a scene." I pulled my knees up onto the bed and wrapped my arms around them. "I mean, you're part of the media. They'll make a circus out of this one. And then my sponsors… I don't think BetHere Gaming will love this very much. No one wants to talk about how sports betting is affecting athletes. There's no money in that."

Ollie's mouth opened then closed. He looked back at the desk, at the careful rows I'd arranged.

He ran his hand along his jaw and neck the way people do when they're sorting through too many responses and none of them feel right. Then he stepped away from the desk and faced me.

"Look, I get it. I do. But if you change your mind—if you need someone to dig into this, or just someone to talk to about it—I'm here. Journalist hat off. Just as a friend." He paused. "If you'll still have me as one."

I rested my chin on my knees and studied him. He wasn't angling for anything, or so it seemed. No agenda behind his eyes, no calculation. Just a guy who'd screwed up and was standing in the wreckage of it, offering what he had left. He had a long way to go before I genuinely believed that, but forgiveness had to start somewhere, right?

"Thanks, Ollie."

He nodded once, shoved his hands into his blazer pockets, and headed for the door. He paused with his hand on the handle.

"For what it's worth, he's lucky. Henri."

Then he was gone, and the room felt enormous again, and I sat there on the bed with my arms around my knees, staring at the desk full of poison someone had written just for me.

Chapter Thirty

Lily

That night, I'd barely slept, tossing and turning while dreading the day ahead. When I finally woke, my phone buzzed incessantly. I picked it up, dread pooling in my stomach as I saw the notifications from my friends and family. My heart raced as I opened a link to an article Andy had sent me. The headline glared back at me.

The Dark Side of Racing: Female F1 Driver Faces Harassment Campaign

Each word painted a picture of vulnerability I didn't want to see. I recognized quotes, details, and anonymous notes that had never left my lips. Specific phrases from the notes—ones I'd only ever shown to a handful of people. Details about which races they'd appeared at, about the flowers they'd left, about the escalation. Things I didn't remember telling Ollie yesterday.

How much had I spilled to him?

My hands trembled as I scrolled further. He'd positioned himself as some kind of crusading journalist, exposing the "disturbing pattern of targeted harassment" faced by women in Formula 1. He'd painted me as a brave victim standing strong against anonymous threats and invasive attention—a narrative I'd never consented to, built from information I'd never given him.

Except I had given him the information he needed, hadn't I? I'd let him into my room, let him see the notes arranged in their careful rows, and he'd stood there studying them with that furrowed brow and those earnest eyes, offering friendship and discretion while memorizing every detail he could use.

My phone buzzed again. The world was waking up to Ollie's article, and with it, to every private terror I'd been carrying alone.

A text from Felix arrived.

Felix's hotel room was three floors above mine, in the section reserved for leadership and other important people. I knocked once, heard the President of Rennen's voice call, "Come in," and pushed through the door.

They were both standing. That was my first clue this wasn't going to be a pleasant strategy meeting. Thomas leaned against the hotel desk, arms crossed, his expression carefully neutral. Felix stood by the window, backlit by the morning sun, and when he turned to face me, I saw something in his eyes I'd never seen before.

Uncertainty.

"Sit down, Lily," he said.

"I'm fine standing."

"Sit. Down."

I sat. The chair was too soft, too low. It made me feel like I was a child who'd been called to the principal's office. Felix studied me with an intensity that made my skin prickle. "I've heard something concerning. About threats you've been receiving."

"I know. The article." Then I paused. "But I thought my mother might have told you about them?"

Felix's eyebrows lifted. "Your mother? No." He exchanged a glance with Thomas. "Henri told me."

The words hit like a physical blow.

"Henri," I repeated, my voice flat.

"He showed me photographs of the notes. Said you'd been receiving them since Miami and refused to report them." Felix's disappointment carved lines deeper into his face. "Your mother knew about this?"

"She—" I stopped. Processed. "She took the last one. Said she'd handle it."

"She didn't."

"I'm handling it," I said, although my voice lacked confidence.

"Handling it?" Thomas's voice cut through my defensive haze. "How? These aren't random hate messages, Lily. Someone's been accessing your hotel rooms."

The room tilted slightly. My mother had dismissed my concerns, pocketed the evidence, and done nothing. And Henri… Henri had gone behind my back after I explicitly told him to stay out of it.

"Henri had no right—"

"Henri did exactly what he should've done." Felix stepped closer. "What you should've done weeks ago."

My hands clenched the chair's armrests. Betrayal burned hot in my chest, mixing with embarrassment. It was stupid to keep this from the team for so long. Deep down, I knew my mother wasn't going to deal with the notes. It's probably why I'd told her in the first place.

I couldn't meet Felix's eye. My gaze fixed on a small star on the carpet, tracing the pattern while my mind raced through possible responses.

"I need to know how many," he demanded.

"A lot…" My head ached. "Between the texts and the DMs, I stopped counting."

"Why didn't you tell me?" The hurt in Felix's voice was worse than anger would have been.

"Because I didn't want to be a problem. I mean this kind of story isn't exactly what sponsors want to see, is it? And I figured why make a big fuss when it's just some asshole trying to get in my head."

"Trying to get in your head?" Felix's voice rose. "They're threatening you. They know where you're staying. They have access to you." He stopped, visibly forcing himself to calm down. "This is serious. This is incredibly serious. We're going to team security with this," Felix said finally. "The FIA too. And you're getting protection."

"I don't need—"

"Not negotiable." His tone left no room for argument. "Someone is threatening my driver. That makes it team business. You should've made it team business the moment the first note arrived."

Shame burned hot in my chest, and I knew my face was red. Felix was right.

"I'm sorry," I said quietly.

"Don't be sorry. Just don't hide things like this, Lily." Felix stood. "It's not your job to worry about what sponsors might think. We, Rennen F1, selected you to be our driver; their opinion only matters so much. And sure, this article might not be ideal for BetHere Gaming, but I'd be remiss if I didn't point out that if you'd come to us earlier, we may have avoided this article in its entirety."

That irony wasn't lost on me, although I'd sort of hoped it had maybe been lost on Felix.

"Look," he added. "We're going to take care of this, but I need you to promise me that if anything else happens, anything at all, you tell us immediately. I'm mostly annoyed it took Henri coming to tell us about it."

"Which he shouldn't have done—" I started.

Felix looked at me for a long moment, and something finally shifted, the team principal falling away, replaced by something more personal, more paternal.

"Lily, I want you to think about something." His voice was measured now, careful in a way that told me he'd been turning this over in his head. "I know you and Ollie have been… hanging out, but I want you to consider this. Two people found out about these threats. Two people acted on that information this week."

He held up one finger. "Henri came to me privately because he was worried about your safety. He didn't call a press conference. He didn't tip off a journalist or tell his team so he could use it to his advantage. He came to your team principal and said, 'Someone is threatening her, and she won't ask for help, so I'm asking for her.'"

He held up a second finger.

"And then there's the person who wrote that article. Who took your pain—your private, personal terror—and published it for the world to consume over breakfast. Who used your vulnerability to build their own platform." Felix shook his head with disbelief. "One of those people exposed these notes out of care, Lily. The other did it for personal gain. I need you to be very clear about which is which."

The words landed like stones dropped into still water, the ripples spreading outward through everything I'd been feeling since I woke up. I thought about Henri's face in the drivers' briefing yesterday, the way he'd watched me from across the room when he thought I wasn't looking. The quiet worry in his eyes that I'd mistaken for pity. The calls I'd ignored all week. The texts I'd left unread.

He hadn't gone behind my back to hurt me. He'd gone behind my back because I'd left him no other choice.

"He promised he'd stay out of it," I whispered. It was the only defense I had left, and even I could hear how thin it was.

"And if he had?" Felix's voice was soft. "If he kept that promise and something had happened to you, how do you think he'd have lived with that?"

I didn't have an answer. Or maybe I did, and it was sitting right there in the center of my chest, aching.

Felix crossed the room and pulled me into a hug. Brief, firm, the kind that said more than words could. When he stepped back, his eyes were bright.

"We're going to take care of this," he said. "But I need you to promise me, if anything else happens—anything at all—you tell us immediately."

I nodded, not trusting my voice.

"I promise."

Thomas walked me to the door. "We'll figure this out," he said quietly.

I nodded, not saying anything in return. What was there to say?

Back in my own room, I sat on the edge of the bed, Felix's words still reverberating through me. "*One of those people exposed these notes out of care, Lily. The other did it for personal gain."*

But before I addressed this with either of them, I had another person I needed to talk to, and it was a conversation I should've had much earlier this season. After free practice, I was going to finally talk with my mother.

Chapter Thirty-One

Henri

The article sat at the top of the feed, authored by Oliver Johnson, published just three hours ago, when most of Europe was still asleep.

"How did he get this information?" I wondered aloud as I continued to read, each word worse than the last.

Ollie had taken Lily's private struggle and turned it into his breakout piece. Over a thousand words of her vulnerability, packaged for clicks and career advancement. He'd included details about deliveries to locked hotel rooms, about the escalation pattern from Miami onward, about specific phrases from notes that Lily had kept hidden from almost everyone.

Details that a journalist covering the sport wouldn't have access to. Details that someone *sending* the notes would. That felt too wretched, even for Ollie.

My phone was in my hand before I'd made the conscious decision to pick it up. I called Lily. Straight to voicemail. Called again. Same result. A third time— nothing. She hadn't read any of my texts either. Her phone was either off, or she was somewhere without signal, and neither possibility did anything for the dread climbing out of me.

I pulled on yesterday's jeans and a crumpled T-shirt and went down to her floor. Knocked once, then harder. Still nothing. I tried the lobby, the hotel restaurant, the gym. She was nowhere.

Back in my room, I tried her again, again getting her voicemail.

Why was she ignoring me?

I scrolled through my contacts and landed on a name I hadn't called in months.

Alex Muncy. Sports journalist and friend from my early karting days who was now a senior correspondent for one of the largest sports media networks in Europe. He'd been asking me for an exclusive for two years, but I'd always said no.

The call connected on the second ring.

"Dubois?" A laugh, warm and surprised. "It's not even eight in the morning. You in trouble?"

"Remember when I did that photoshoot for you, and you said you owed me one? I'm calling in that favor."

A pause. "All right. What do you need?"

"I'll explain later." I made it to my room, desperately shoving items into my bag. "Meet me at the track. Driver's room. In an hour?"

"Henri, what's this about?"

"Just meet me. Please."

The drive to the circuit passed quickly. I tried Lily again, but still nothing. The paddock was quiet, except for a few mechanics.

The knock came shortly after I'd settled in my room. Alex looked like he'd dressed in a hurry: jeans, wrinkled button-down, press credentials hanging crooked around his neck.

"This had better be good, Dubois."

I closed the door. And for a moment, I just stood there, because I knew that once I started, there was no going back.

"Have you seen the article?" I asked. "Oliver Johnson's piece, published this morning."

"The harassment story about the Rennen driver?" Alex nodded. "It's a small sports magazine that published it, but I hear it's getting a little traction."

"He didn't have permission to run that." My voice was steady, but my hands weren't.

Alex's expression didn't change, but something shifted behind his eyes, the journalist in him waking up. "That's a serious accusation."

"I want you to bury his story," I said, and the words came out harder than I intended.

"I mean, in order to do that, we'd have to run something bigger, Henri."

"I know. And I have something that might do the trick."

Alex leaned back, studying me with that careful, assessing gaze I'd seen him turn on interview subjects a hundred times. "And what exactly would that something be?"

This was the part I'd been dreading. Not because I didn't want to do it, but because I'd spent so long building walls around exactly this. Years of deflection, of "I'm fine," of toughing it out.

"Me," I said. "You run my story."

Alex blinked. "Your story?"

I sat down across from him and made myself hold his gaze.

"After Miami, that crash with Lily, I started having anxiety attacks in the car." Alex perched on my desk, his phone already recording. I could see the small red dot on the screen, but he didn't draw attention to it. He just let me talk about Miami. About F2. About what my old racing director had told me.

About the panic that filled me every time I drove in the rain.

"Henri…" Alex's voice was careful. "Did you tell your team?"

"No, and I know I should have." The certainty in my own voice surprised me. "I've hidden this from everyone. My team, my family, my physio. I convinced myself that if I just pushed through it, it would go away. That admitting it would make me weak, like I was told in F2." I laughed, and it sounded hollow even to me. "Back in those days, I also had a big crash, but we didn't treat mental health the same then. I was worried about their reaction."

"What changed?"

And there she was. Right at the center of everything, exactly where she always seemed to end up.

"Lily." Her name felt different when I said it out loud to someone else. Heavier. More real. "After she banged on my hotel door one night, she demanded I tell her what was going on with me. I told her everything, and afterward, she didn't look at me with pity. She didn't treat me like I was broken or fragile. She sat with me and said, 'You need to talk to someone.'"

Alex was very still.

I could feel my throat tightening, but I kept going.

"She's the only person in the entire paddock who knew. For weeks, she carried that secret for me and never once used it. Never told her team, never leveraged it for a competitive advantage. She just listened."

It felt good to say that out loud.

"And I've watched her carry her own weight this entire season—the pressure, the harassment, a mother who treats her like a brand instead of a daughter—and she never once asked anyone to carry it for her."

"I need you to include that," I said. "What she did for me. How she helped me when nobody else could, because she understood what it was like to be struggling and too proud to say it out loud. I mean, hell, she even got me a dog, Max."

"Henri—"

"I'm serious. This isn't just about me. The woman Ollie tried to reduce to a victim in his article is the reason I'm still racing at all." My voice cracked on the last word, and I didn't bother trying to hide it. "I need the world to know that, before they decide who she is based on what he wrote."

"Sounds like you're not just talking about a colleague," Alex said quietly.

I stared at the wall behind him. There was a hairline crack in the paint, thin and jagged, running from the ceiling down to the corner. I traced it with my eyes while the silence stretched between us.

"I'm not."

The admission sat in the room, simple and enormous.

"She's the bravest person I know," I said. "And I know how that sounds—like hyperbole, or some rehearsed line—but I mean it literally. She walked into a sport that was designed to exclude her, and she didn't just survive it. She's winning. She's beating people who've had every advantage she never had, and she's doing it while someone terrorizes her in private and the whole world scrutinizes her in public. She never complains. Never uses any of it as an excuse." I paused. "She just drives."

Alex looked at me for a long time—long enough that I felt every wall I'd ever built sitting in rubble at my feet. Then he nodded once, slowly. "There's going to be a lot of questions from your team about this. You sure?"

"I know."

He paused. "And look, I'm not saying what Ollie did was right, but I want mention that Lily's story is one that should be told as well."

"But on her terms," I agreed. "And not by the person I suspect might be sending her the notes…"

Alex exhaled slowly. Shook his head. Then he pulled his laptop from his bag and set it on the table between us. "All right, Dubois. Let's write this." He cracked his knuckles over the keyboard. "When do you want it live?"

"Today, if we can. Before Ollie's article gains another hour of traction."

"That's an outrageous deadline! I need to write it, get editorial approval, fact-check—"

"Then you'd better start now."

Alex studied me for another moment. Then he turned back to the screen. "You know, I've been asking you for an exclusive for two years. I always figured it'd be about lap times and championship battles."

"Sorry to disappoint."

"Disappoint?" He smiled. "Championship leader admits to mental health struggle, finally decides to talk about his therapy journey? This is the best human-interest piece I've ever been given… and who knows, maybe you'll pass me that other piece from Lily."

I scoffed. "Typical journalist," I muttered. "One story at a time."

Chapter Thirty-Two

Lily

I hated how everyone looked at me when I arrived at the garage this morning for free practice. Pity was written all over their faces. I didn't want to be pitied.

I didn't want anything but to crawl back up to my hotel room and cry. I climbed out of the car, pulling off my helmet. At least the Friday free practice sessions were done, and soon I'd be back at my hotel.

My phone buzzed in my pocket as I walked back toward the garage. Georgia's name lit up the screen.

Georgia:
Have you seen this?

A link followed. I almost didn't tap it—I'd had enough of articles about myself for one lifetime. But the preview thumbnail showed Henri's face, not mine, and the headline beneath it stopped me mid-stride.

Formula 1 Champion Opens Up: "She's the Reason I'm Still Racing"

I leaned against the concrete wall outside the garage and opened it. A major sports outlet. Not the small magazine

Ollie had used—this was one of the biggest platforms in European sports media. Published forty minutes ago.

My eyes caught fragments before my brain could process them. *Anxiety attacks. Hidden struggle. After Miami.* Then my own name, threaded through his words like a pulse.

"She's the bravest person I know."

My thumb hovered over the screen. The concrete pressed cold through my race suit.

"She walked into a sport that was designed to exclude her, and she didn't just survive the sport. She's winning in it."

I read that line three times. My vision blurred on the fourth.

Georgia:
Lily? Are you reading it?

"Lily!" Felix's voice cut through the garage noise, and I turned to see him beckoning me toward his office, a smile on his face that seemed oddly genuine given the circumstances. I followed him, grateful to have a proper reason to escape the chaos of the garage. Felix closed the door behind us, and the sudden quiet was almost jarring.

"Well, here's some good news." He picked up his phone, scrolling through something. "Look what I just got sent!" Felix began reading, his face lightening up as he reached a particular passage he must have liked.

"'Henri Dubois has long been considered the golden boy of Formula 1. Talented, the kind of good-looking face sponsors love, and with a successful career to back it up. But behind the carefully crafted image lies a struggle that Dubois himself has only recently begun to acknowledge:

the debilitating anxiety following his near-fatal crash in Miami earlier this season.'"

My breath caught in my chest.

"'In an exclusive interview, Dubois spoke candidly about his battle with anxiety, the intrusive thoughts that plagued him since the accident, and his determination to face these demons rather than run from them. "I could've hidden it," Dubois told Alex Muncy. "I could've pretended everything was fine, like I'd been doing. But I realized that hiding it was making me weaker, not stronger. If I want to be the driver I know I can be, I have to be honest about what I'm fighting."'"

Felix paused, glancing up at me.

My hands were gripping the armrests of my chair as my brain tried to catch up. I couldn't speak. The words had stolen my voice, replacing it with something hot in my throat that might have been tears if I had any more to cry.

Felix set his phone down, his expression softening. "I haven't seen an article spread this fast in years. Who knew Henri was going through all of this?"

"He…" I swallowed hard, trying to organize the chaos of emotions swirling through me. Pride. So much pride it felt like it might burst out of my chest. "He did that for me, so the Ollie article on the threats would be buried."

"I suspect he did it for both of you," Felix said. "But yeah, the timing probably wasn't coincidental. Obviously, we don't want these threats circling around the media until we've been able to investigate ourselves, so this article couldn't have been timed better."

I pressed my palms against my eyes, trying to process all the words I'd just heard. Henri had exposed his deepest vulnerability and made himself the story to protect me.

The same Henri who guarded his privacy like Smaug the dragon hoarding gold. The same Henri who'd been so terrified to even tell his engineer.

Or his sister.

"Felix, I—"

"I know," Felix sighed. "I'm proud of him, too, Lily. And honestly? I'm proud he came forward about the threats too. That took guts."

I nodded, not trusting myself to speak yet.

"Felix, I need to ask you something."

"Go on."

"The morality clause in my contract." I steadied my voice, forcing it into something resembling calm. "I want it removed."

"Lily—"

"Luca doesn't have one. You never insisted on it. My mother was the one who negotiated it in because she thought it would make me look professional, make the sponsors feel safe. But it's been hanging over my head all season, and it's not fair." I was speaking faster now, the words spilling out with a conviction I hadn't felt in weeks. "Your two drivers are dating other drivers, and so far? We're winning the Constructors' Championship. It's not hurting the team. It's not hurting the sponsors. The only thing it's hurting is me."

Another pause. Then Felix laughed—a warm, genuine sound that loosened something heavy in my chest.

"You know, I was going to bring this up with you after the race. Thomas and I discussed it yesterday." I could hear him smiling through the phone. "Consider it done."

"Really?"

"It's unfair. It always was, and I should've have pushed back on it sooner." His voice softened. "I think we can manage this with Hermes. I already do with Valkyrie."

I leaned my head back against the garage wall, blinking up at the strip lighting. "Felix, thank you. I'll have my… new manager… reach out."

"New manager, huh?" Felix leaned back in his office chair. "Good for you. Feels like its time."

I laughed, the sound cracking through the emotional dam I'd been holding back all day. "Yeah. Yeah, it does."

—

I walked straight to my hotel suite after leaving Felix's office, my mind still buzzing with everything—Henri's article, the morality clause, Ollie's article. But underneath the warmth of those revelations, there was something harder. Something that had been festering since the beginning of the season.

I needed to talk to my mother.

I swiped my key card and pushed open the door, already rehearsing what I wanted to say. But the words died in my throat.

My mother was sitting on the sofa in my suite, with her legs crossed and a glass of sparkling water in her hand, like she owned the place. And sitting across from her, leaning back in the armchair like he belonged there, was Ollie.

They both looked up when I walked in. My mother smiled. Ollie at least had the decency to look uncomfortable.

"Lily, darling," my mother said, rising to her feet. "I was just telling Oliver how well things are going. Have you seen the engagement numbers since—"

"Get out."

The words came out quieter than I intended, but they landed like a grenade. My mother blinked back surprise. Ollie shifted in his seat.

"Lillian—" my mother started.

"No. I want to know why *he's* in my room." I pointed at Ollie without looking at him. "Why is he here, Mum?"

"He came to see me, and I thought we could all have a civilized conversation about—"

"About what? About how he published my private life for clicks?" My voice cracked, and I hated it. I hated that I couldn't even be angry without sounding like I was about to cry. "About how he took things I told him in confidence and turned them into a headline?"

My mother set down her glass with a delicate clink. "Lily, I think you're overreacting. The article wasn't ideal, I'll grant you that, but all PR is good PR. Your name is everywhere right now. This is exactly the kind of visibility we've been—"

"We?" I stared at her. "There is no *we*. And my name is everywhere because of *Henri*. Not him."

Something flickered across my mother's face—hurt, maybe, or the performance of it. It was always hard to tell with her.

"I'm trying to help you, Lily. That's all I've ever done."

"Then stop." The word came out raw. "Just stop."

Ollie cleared his throat, and I finally forced myself to look at him. He looked smaller than I remembered. Less polished. The confident media personality who'd sat across from me in restaurants and smiled like we shared secrets—he looked like a man who'd been caught.

"Lily, I know you're upset—"

"Upset doesn't even begin to cover it."

"I understand that. And I want to explain—"

A knock at the door cut him off. I almost ignored it, but something—instinct, maybe—made me cross the room and open it.

Henri stood in the hallway, still in his team gear. He looked like he'd come straight from the circuit. His expression was tense, guarded, but when his eyes found mine, something in them softened.

"Lily, I—" He stopped. Looked past me into the room. Saw Ollie. Saw my mother. He reflexively stepped back.

"Oh," he said, his voice cooling by several degrees.

"They were just leaving," I said, stepping aside to let him in.

Henri walked into the suite with the kind of quiet authority that I'd recognized from last season. He didn't acknowledge Ollie, and he barely glanced at my mother. Instead, Henri just stood near the window with his arms crossed, radiating a calm that I knew—from years of knowing him—was barely held together.

"Lily," Ollie said again, standing now, his hands raised slightly like he was approaching a spooked animal. "Just let me explain. Please. Five minutes."

"You don't deserve five minutes," I said.

"You're right. I don't." He avoided my gaze. "But I want you to hear it from me before you hear it from someone else."

I folded my arms. Said nothing. Let the silence do the work.

Ollie scratched the back of his neck. "The podcast was killing me. You have no idea what it's like. The producers wanted gossip, they wanted drama, they wanted me to turn every conversation into content. I hated it. I hated what I was becoming." He paused, and for a half-second, something genuine passed over his face. "I want to be a real journalist. An actual writer, not just some guy with a microphone making hot takes for downloads. And when your mum started pushing us together—"

"Excuse me?" My mother's voice was sharp.

"—I saw an opportunity," Ollie finished, ignoring her. "You were the story of the season, Lily. A female driver in Formula 1, fighting for points, dealing with threats. It was everything I needed to prove I could write something that mattered."

The room was very still.

"So, I was your audition piece," I said flatly.

Ollie's mouth opened and then closed. He looked at the floor. "That's not—I didn't plan it like that. Not at first." His voice dripped with apology, but I didn't believe him. Not this time.

"In the article, you mentioned things I knew I hadn't told you, Ollie."

He didn't respond to my unspoken accusation. The thoughts that I'd spent the last several hours piecing together. The article contained details that went beyond what he could have gleaned from my desk. References to notes I hadn't laid out that morning. Descriptions of deliveries he shouldn't have known about, unless—

Unless he'd known about them before he ever walked into my room.

"You used me for a story! And even worse, a story that you created!"

"Lily—" The panic on his face was confirmation enough. And perhaps I should have been relieved. Of all the options about who it could have been, this was a better one. I stared at him for a long moment. The anger was still there, burning steady in my chest, but underneath it was something worse. Disappointment. Not because I'd trusted Ollie, but because I'd wanted to. Because for a brief, stupid moment, I'd thought maybe he was actually someone safe. A mistake I wouldn't make so easily next time.

"Get out."

Ollie looked at Henri, maybe hoping for some kind of intervention, but there would be no sympathy to be found.

"You might want to hurry, Ollie," Henri said, his voice low and even. "I spoke with Alex Muncy this afternoon. I don't think you'd like to be the focus of his next article." He paused, letting that sink in.

Ollie stood frozen for a moment, looking between us like he was searching for a crack in the wall. He didn't find one. He grabbed his jacket from the back of the chair and walked to the door. He paused with his hand on the handle, like he was going to say something else—some final appeal, some last attempt to rewrite the narrative.

But wisely, he thought better of it, not caring to look back as he left the room. The silence that followed was enormous.

My mother smoothed down her skirt, her composure slowly rebuilding. "Well. That was rather dramatic."

"Mum." I turned to face her. "You're fired."

Chapter Thirty-Three

Lily

I'd finally said it, and damn, it felt liberating.

"I beg your pardon?"

"You heard me." I kept my voice level, though my heart hammered against my ribs. "You're fired as my manager… and if we're being honest, you're probation as my mother."

"Lily, you're upset. I understand. But let's not say things we can't take back—"

"I'm not taking it back." I stepped closer to her—close enough to see the micro-calculations happening behind her eyes, the pivot she was already planning, the angle she was about to work. I'd watched her do it my whole life.

"You let Ollie into my room after you knew what he'd done. He published my private life, Mum. He took the worst thing happening to me and turned it into content, and your reaction was to check the engagement numbers."

She drew herself up, her chin lifting the way it always did when she felt cornered. The posture of a woman who had never once admitted fault in her life.

"Everything I've done has been for your career."

"No." The word choked out of me. "Everything you've done has been for *yours*. You negotiated a morality clause into my contract so sponsors would feel comfortable—not so I would. You took that threatening note I gave you and buried it, because dealing with it might've been inconvenient for the brand. You pushed Ollie at me because a media boyfriend looked good in a press packet. Everything you've done has been about controlling me, not helping me."

Her mouth thinned to a pale line. Henri shifted by the window but said nothing. He was letting me do this on my own, and I loved him for it.

"You don't mean this," my mother said, quieter now, the dismissal dressed up as concern.

"I've never meant anything more." My heart ached, but I didn't look away. "I needed a mother this season, but instead, I got a publicist."

She picked up her handbag from the sofa with a deliberate slowness, every movement a performance of dignity. At the door, she turned back. Her eyes were bright, and for one terrible second, I thought she might actually cry.

"You'll regret this," she said.

The door closed behind her, and the room went still. I stood in the middle of it, breathing hard, my hands shaking at my sides. Something enormous had just shifted—a load I'd been carrying for so long my spine had curved around it, suddenly gone, leaving me standing straighter than I had in years.

When I turned around, Henri was still standing there, watching me with awe.

"You just fired your mother."

"I just fired my mother," I confirmed, and suddenly, I was laughing.

Henri crossed the room in two strides, pulling me into his arms. I buried my face against his chest, feeling the solid warmth of him anchoring me as the laughter dissolved into something that might have been tears.

"You're shaking," he murmured into my hair.

"I know." My voice came out muffled against his team polo. "I can't believe I just did that."

His arms tightened around me. "I can."

I pulled back enough to look at him, and the expression on his face made my breath catch.

"She's your mum," he said softly, brushing a strand of hair from my face. "That couldn't have been easy."

"It should've been harder." I leaned into his touch. "But after everything… the lies, treating me like property, the control, it was the easiest thing I've done all season. Well, until I tell Felix about my suspicions on Ollie, at least."

Henri's thumb traced along my jaw, gentle and deliberate. "I almost can't believe it."

"I know…" I reached up, covering his hand with mine. "And to be honest, I don't know if they're all him, but it doesn't matter right now. I told Felix I'd leave this with the team, and that's what I'm going to do."

He leaned down, resting his forehead against mine. "I don't know if I've said it enough but I'm proud of you, Blackwood."

I took a moment to look at Henri. He looked bashful, of all things. Henri Dubois, who could stare down journalists and rivals with equal intimidation, was standing in my hotel room looking almost nervous. His hair was more disheveled than usual, his hazel eyes uncertain in a way I rarely saw them.

"I should have told you about my visit with Felix—" he started.

I didn't let him finish. Instead I crashed my mouth to his, pouring everything I couldn't say into the kiss. All the pride, all the gratitude, all the anger I'd been holding onto, all the fear I'd been carrying. It all translated into this—into the way my hands fisted in his shirt, the way his arms wrapped around me like he'd been waiting for permission to hold me this close.

The kiss was passionate and messy and perfect, Henri stumbling backward slightly before catching his balance and pulling me tighter against him. His hand came up to cup the back of my head, fingers tangling in my hair, and I made a sound against his mouth that might have been his name.

When we finally broke apart, both breathing hard, Henri's eyes had gone from uncertain to smoldering.

"I read the article," I managed, my voice rough.

"Lily, I—"

"You beautiful, brave, absolutely reckless idiot," I said, cutting him off again, but this time with a smile.

A slow grin spread across his face. "Is that your way of saying thank-you?"

"Thank you," I said, more seriously now. "For what you did. For being honest. For…" I swallowed. "For caring enough to do that."

"Always," he said simply, his thumb tracing the line of my jaw. "And Lily, I'm so sorry. I just… After Silverstone, I had to tell Felix."

"I know," I agreed. "God, I should have said something when you told me to. I was such an idiot."

Henri leaned in closer, his lips grazing mine ever so softly.

"We're going to remove this stupid fucking relationship clause," I said, watching his eyes widen. "We don't have to hide anymore, Henri."

"What do you mean?"

"Felix is going to get rid of it. Luca doesn't have one, and Rennen doesn't care." I leaned up to kiss him again, softer this time. "So, this—*us*—we can actually do this… if you still want."

Henri's laugh was quiet, almost disbelieving. "That might be the best thing I've heard all week."

"Better than your article going viral?"

"Infinitely better." He rested his forehead against mine, his hands settling on my waist. "Though, I have to admit, the response has been overwhelming."

"You knew it would be," I said. "Now it's my turn to be proud of you, Henri."

"You know, I thought I'd feel more shame about all of this, but instead? I feel relief. Like I'm Atlas, but I've finally been able to put the weight of the world down. And the team? God, they were so kind and thoughtful. And just happy to hear I'd gotten help."

"We're going to be okay," I said, and I wasn't sure if I was telling him or myself.

Henri kissed my forehead, gentle and reassuring. "Yeah," he agreed. "We really are."

He kissed me again, slower now, all that restraint from earlier evaporating. He didn't try to take control—not at first. His hands were everywhere they were supposed to be, but he waited for me to make every next move. I pushed him back toward the bed, letting him fall onto the plush duvet. His eyes were hungry as he watched me, and I loved every moment of it. Loved how his eyes darkened.

Loved him.

It was as if he knew what I was thinking. Henri pulled me down on top of him, kissing me again. Hungrier this time. When we parted, he looked at me, his hazel eyes boring into mine.

"*Je t'aime*, Blackwood," he whispered softly.

"I love you too, Dubois."

There was nothing gentle about the way I eagerly undid his belt. My hands shook a little, but Henri's didn't. He let them fall to his sides, palms up, as if to say, *Go on, surprise me. I'm all yours.*

Kneeling between his thighs, I looked up at him, daring him to look away first. He didn't—not even when I yanked the zipper open and tugged his trousers down. The way he watched me, eyes wide but glassy, mouth barely open, was better than getting pole position. I wanted him to know what I meant; that what we'd just said to each other meant something to me.

He meant something to me.

I dragged my tongue along his hip bone, barely grazing, slow enough to torture. Henri shuddered but didn't make a sound. He was stubborn—almost as stubborn as me. I could have made a bet that he'd try not to break first.

Finally, I reached his hard, throbbing cock.

I didn't take him in my mouth at first, instead licking the tip, long and slow. Looking up, I caught him watching, his pupils now completely blown with desire. My tongue drew a lazy circle around him as my ears enjoyed every moan and grunt he let out.

His breathing began to quicken, and I pressed my lips harder around the tip, sucking and letting him slide free, slow enough to make him twitch. After a few more teases, I swallowed him. He gasped, one knee jerking, and I let my hands brace his thighs so he couldn't thrust, which only made his groans louder.

"Fuck, Lil, I can't," he panted.

He grabbed my shoulders, pulling me off him, and before I knew it, I was being thrown onto the bed, my pants and shirt now discarded.

He was faster than I'd ever seen him, rolling me onto my back and pinning my wrists above my head with one hand, the other tracing my ribs, my hip, the hem of my underwear. I almost laughed. He was the desperate one now, trembling as he hooked his fingers into the fabric and yanked them down my legs. He kissed everywhere but where I wanted, teasing me, the slide of his mouth up my thigh, across my hipbone, lingering just a breath away from where I was wet and aching.

"Oh, Henri, fuck, more," I gasped, squirming.

He smiled against my skin, and then, finally, his tongue was on me, slow and confident, unhurried, as if we had all night. As if we didn't have a race weekend to get back to.

His fingers left my wrists to cup my thighs, spreading me wider, holding me steady as he devoured me. And that was the only word for it. Henri Dubois, F1's golden boy, was tongue-deep in me with every moan and curse I gave him lapped up one by one.

My head thudded back against the pillow, body arching to meet him. And then he stopped, and I heard a crinkling noise form. He pulled out a condom, sliding it on, his face desperate for me.

"I need you, please."

I nodded, as hungry as he was, and pulled him back down on top of me.

He didn't hesitate. Not even for a second. He lined himself up with a single, hungry thrust, and I yelped out of shock at the intensity of it, at how good it felt, how much I needed this—needed him. Henri groaned, the sound vibrating into my neck where his lips had found my skin again. He started slow, like he needed to get used to the way we fit, but it wasn't long before he was thrusting hard enough to rattle the headboard.

"Fuck, Lily." His voice was ragged, each word digging right into me. "God, you feel so good."

I could barely answer, too busy rocking up to meet him, sucking in gulps of air, feeling that pressure build too fast in my core. He was so deep, every inch of him making me feel owned, and I loved every moment of it.

I bit his shoulder, hard, and he only groaned louder, thrusting harder and faster. The headboard banged against the thin hotel wall. Henri's hand found my jaw, the pad of his thumb stroking my cheek with a reverence that didn't match his movements.

"I love you, Lily," he said again, and I believed it with every ounce of my heart.

"I love you, too," I managed, and then his hand was on my nub, working it in tight, rapid circles while he thrust into me.

When I came, I bit his shoulder again to stifle the scream, clenching around him so hard his rhythm stuttered, and for a moment I thought he'd come right then—but after another few thrusts, he was joining me in absolute ecstasy.

He collapsed on top of me, body heaving for air. We lay tangled for a while, catching our breath. His hands roamed lazily over my body, tracing my wrists, my hip, the curve of my thigh. For the first time in weeks, my brain was silent, and I just soaked in the warmth of him.

Henri rolled to his side, pulling me with him. He found my hand and laced our fingers together, kissing my knuckles. "You're incredible," he whispered, his smile lazy and soft. "I've never wanted anything more in my life than this."

I pinched his shoulder, grinning. "Well, now that we've broken every team rule in the book…"

"Technically, no more rules," Henri reminded me, smug.

I snorted. "Just don't get too cocky. I still plan to beat you tomorrow."

He leaned in closer, giving me a small peck on the cheek. "I expect nothing less, Lillian Blackwood. Not from you." His smile turned wicked, familiar and new all at once. "See you at the finish line."

Epilogue

Lily

The roar of the Silverstone crowd was so loud it almost drowned out my engine. I settled deeper into the seat, my fingers grabbing the steering wheel for dear life, as the mechanics made their final adjustments. Through my visor, I could see the Union Jack flags rippling in the July wind, a sea of red, white, and blue stretching as far as the eye could see.

One full year since my gutting loss at Silverstone, and we were back with another pole position.

"Radio check, Lily." My race engineer's voice crackled in my ear.

"Loud and clear," I replied, running through my mental pre-race checklist.

The championship standings flashed on the Jumbotron across from the large grandstand at the start of the race. After twelve races, I led Henri by eighteen points—a comfortable margin, but not insurmountable. Not with another fourteen races still to go. Last year, he'd edged me out by two points in the final race in Abu Dhabi, his Hermes car crossing the line just ahead of my Rennen. The trophy presentation had been bittersweet: pride at watching my boyfriend claim what he'd fought so hard for, mixed with the burning desire to be standing in his place.

This year, the script had flipped.

"One minute to formation lap," Mark announced.

I glanced at the timing screen, finding Henri's name in P3. He'd qualified brilliantly yesterday, but a mistake during Q3 had cost him the front row.

Just as well. After he won Monaco this year, I told him Silverstone was mine.

The formation lap began, and I fell into the familiar rhythm, weaving to heat the tires, testing the brakes, feeling for any inconsistencies in the car's behavior. Silverstone stretched out before me, every turn and apex etched into my muscle memory from countless laps over the years. This circuit haunted my dreams, a victory here always just out of reach.

But not today.

The lights began their sequence, and time seemed to slow. Five red lights, each one illuminating with mechanical precision. Then lights out.

My car launched forward, the acceleration pressing me back into the seat. Turn 1 approached fast, the pack bunching as we all fought for position. I held my line, defending the inside, as the driver in P2 tried to dive up my left side through the turn, the high-speed complex that separated the truly brave from the merely fast.

Or, at least, that was what the commentators liked to say.

By lap ten, I'd pulled out a three-second gap to Georgia in P2, the car singing beneath me. Every input felt telepathic, the car responding to the slightest touch of the wheel. This was what I lived for, that perfect harmony between me and the car.

"Henri's fastest lap," my engineer informed me on lap twenty-three. "Purple in sectors one and two."

I smiled inside my helmet. Of course he was pushing. That was Henri—never giving up, always finding another tenth of a second somewhere. Even now, after everything we'd been through, we were still racing each other with everything we had.

The pit stops came and went, a perfectly executed 2.3-second stop that maintained my lead. Henri had gone long on his first stint, trying an alternate strategy, but it wasn't enough to overcome the pace advantage. By lap forty-five, with seven laps remaining, I had a twelve-second cushion.

"Manage the tires," my engineer said. "We don't need to push anymore."

But I did push. Not because I needed to, but because this was Silverstone, and I was leading my home race with a handful of laps to go, and I wanted to savor every single second of it.

Three laps to go.

Two laps to go.

Final lap.

The crowd was on their feet now. I could see them in my peripheral vision, a blur of motion and color as I powered past the grandstands. My throat felt tight, tears threatening behind my visor through each curve. The checkered flag waved in the distance, and I crossed the line with my fist pumping the air.

"P1, Lily! P1! Silverstone winner! Brilliant drive!"

The radio erupted with cheers from the entire team, but I could barely hear them over the pounding of my heart. I did my cool-down lap in a daze, waving to the grandstands, letting the magnitude of it wash over me.

Silverstone. Winner. The two words I'd been chasing my entire career.

And this time, no ride height was going to take this from me. Felix had checked the margins himself.

I parked in the P1 spot, the number-one board waiting for me like a promise finally fulfilled. My hands shook as I disconnected my radio headphones from the steering wheel and hauled myself out of the cockpit. The moment my feet touched the ground, my knees nearly buckled.

The team swarmed me, hands slapping my helmet and my shoulders, voices shouting congratulations. I pulled off my helmet, gulping in the sweet English air, tasting victory on my tongue.

Then I saw him.

Henri was pushing through the crowd, still in his race suit, having apparently abandoned his own post-race obligations to get to me. With his helmet off, his hazel eyes were bright, that devastating smile breaking across his face as he closed the distance between us.

"You absolute maniac," he said, breathless. "That defense through during lap thirty-two—"

"—was perfectly legal," I shot back, grinning.

"Was brilliant," he corrected.

Then his hands were cupping my face, and he was kissing me right there in front of everyone—the cameras, the team, the hundred thousand fans in the grandstands, the millions watching around the world. I melted into him, wrapping my arms around his neck, the rest of the world fading to background noise.

When we finally broke apart, his forehead rested against mine. "Your home win," he murmured. "You finally got it."

"Our home," I corrected softly. "We both live here now, remember?"

His smile widened, and there was no trace of the haunted look that had plagued him a year ago. Therapy had helped. Time had helped. Racing together, supporting each other through the highs and lows, had helped most of all.

"I don't care how cute you look winning this race, I'm coming for you in Hungary."

"I'm counting on it," I replied.

Because that was the beauty of it, wasn't it? We could love each other fiercely and still race each other harder. Could celebrate each other's victories and mourn each other's defeats. Be partners off the track and rivals on it, and somehow, impossibly, that made both parts stronger.

My media officer was frantically waving me toward the cool-down room, where the podium ceremony awaited. I kissed Henri once more, quick and fierce, then pulled away.

"See you up there." I grinned.

As I jogged toward the cool-down room, my Silverstone win finally secured, the Championship lead building ever so slightly, I couldn't stop smiling. But the World Driver's Championship was far from over. The battles with Henri, on track and off, would continue.

And I wouldn't have it any other way.

Acknowledgement

They say racing is a team sport disguised as an individual one. Writing, it turns out, is exactly the same.

To my agent, Megan: my race engineer. You kept me on strategy when I wanted to go rogue, talked me through the corners I couldn't see, and never once told me to box when I still had laps to give. This book wouldn't exist without you.

To my editor, Dan: my safety car. You slowed me down when I was spinning out of control, brought order to the chaos, and gave me the space to reset before pushing again. Thank you for your vision and for letting me tell my story!

To my dear friends: my pit crew. You held me together when this book was taking me apart. You brought wine, honesty, laughter, and the kind of unconditional support that no acknowledgment page could ever repay. I wrote about chosen family because I already had one.

To my husband, Jon: my home race. Thank you for learning to recognize the difference between "I'm writing" and "I'm staring at a blank page in despair." For the endless cups of coffee, the dinners you made when I forgot to eat, and the nights you went to bed alone because I was somewhere between Miami and Silverstone arguing with fictional people. You are my podium. I love you.

To the real women of motorsport: the drivers, engineers, team principals, mechanics, and journalists who show up every day in a world that still questions whether they belong. You do. You always did. Lily carries a piece of each of you in her words.

To anyone who has ever said *I'm fine* when they weren't—Henri's story is yours. Remember, reaching out for help isn't slowing down; it's finding the fastest path forward.

And to you, dear reader: thank you for climbing into the cockpit with Lily and Henri. Your willingness to listen, feel, and engage is what makes stories come alive. May their tale inspire you to chase your own path with courage and a racing heart.